Gods and ANDROIDS

ANDRE NORTON

GODS AND ANDROIDS

Copyright © 2004 by Andre Norton. *Wraiths of Time* © 1976 Andre Norton. *Android at Arms* © 1971 by Andre Norton.

A Baen Book

Baen Publishing Enterprises
P.O. Box 1403
Riverdale, NY 10471
www.baen.com

ISBN: 0-7434-9911-5

Cover art by Bob Eggleton

First paperback printing, June 2005

Library of Congress Cataloging-in-Publication Number 2004000543

Distributed by Simon & Schuster
1230 Avenue of the Americas
New York, NY 10020

Production & design by Windhaven Press (www.windhaven.com)
Printed in the United States of America

CONTENTS

In Memoriam

Andre Norton
1912–2005

TALLAHASSEE LASSIE

It was like being caught in an explosion. There followed light, heat, pain, and such a noise as deafened Tallahassee. The girl had a terrifying sensation of being swung out over a vast void of nothingness. Then the nothingness closed about her in a vast and horrible wrapping of utter blackness and she lost consciousness.

She opened her eyes. It was hot, and she was lying under the sun—where? Immediately before her was an outcrop of rock. She crawled to that rock, using its support to gain her feet. Then she turned, giddy and sick, feeling as if each labored movement might send her sailing out again into that dark void.

More rocks beyond. But at their foot. . . .

Tallahassee stifled the scream in her throat, made herself blink, and blink again, to be sure she really saw that body stretched out on rock and sand.

The stranger lay face down, arms flung out above the head. There was a thin, almost gossamer cotton robe on the body. The stranger's shoulder-length hair had been woven into many tiny braids, each tipped with a bead of gold, and there was a headband of the same precious metal.

Tallahassee dropped carefully to her knees. With an effort she rolled the stranger over, the body limply slack. She was sure somehow that this was death. But, as the other's face came into view, she screamed and flinched away.

Save for the slight difference in the color of their skins, she was looking down at the same features she saw every time she stood before a mirror! The headband rose in front to the likeness of a striking serpent.

"Egypt—" Tallahassee whispered. "This is Egypt, and she is royal . . ." For that serpent diadem could be worn only by a woman of the Blood and one placed very close to the throne itself.

—from *Wraiths of Time*

BAEN BOOKS by ANDRE NORTON

-1-

It was a sere wasteland, riven by stark gashes, as if some intolerant and sadistic god had lashed it with a flail of lightning. There was no vegetation, whether gray, green, purple, or blue, nothing but the broken rock that sometimes reflected the heat of sun blaze, sometimes lay grimly dark under a thick massing of clouds—which was true now.

The building clinging to the rock tenaciously was so squat that it might be crouched awaiting some annihilating blow. It was uglier than the wasteland, for it had been built, not wrought by pitiless wind and weather.

Not that the prisoner, huddled by the narrow window slit that gave him so small a view of the world, could see the building. That he was a prisoner in a prison he understood. Why he had come here—who he was—

Sometimes he dreamed, and in those dreams he thought he knew. But though he tried to hold on to

3

even a scrap of such a dream, he never succeeded. Upon waking, all he carried into the next stultifying day was a discontent, a dim belief that there was a different life he had once known.

There was food for his body and clothing, and now and then that discontent set him to force his sluggish mind to work—not to uncover lost memories, but to look through the slit, to wonder a little at the bare and blasted landscape. Yet never in all the time he had so watched had he seen any movement or life there.

Cloud shadows reached out, spread, dwindled— nothing else, save when the storms came in their wild fury and torrents of rain ran in the gullies cut by earlier floods and hail fell in great chunks to lie melting in the hollows.

One thing he could remember—why he did not know. He had a name—Andas Kastor. Was it really his name? He frowned now as his lips shaped that name, which was all he had.

There must be a different life out there somewhere, but what had he done to be exiled from it? How long had he been here? Once he had tried to count the days by scratching on the wall, but he had been sick and lost count. After that it had not mattered. There were the robots that brought food at intervals, that had tended him when he was sick—faceless things that he hated with what emotion had not been wrung out of him, but that were impervious to any attack or rebellion on his part. Twice he had tried that, only to have sleep gas flood his cell.

It was going to storm again. A faint flicker of interest stirred him. That was out of the normal pattern, and anything that broke the pattern was to be treasured. They had had one of the bad storms only two days ago. The pools it had filled out there among the rocks had not yet entirely drained. To have a second so soon was most unusual.

The clouds were gathering so fast that it was as dark as night. The lights in the corners of his cell came on, though they usually did not in storm time.

He stayed by the window slit, though the aspect outside was threatening. Somehow the fear it caused sharpened his mind. There had been many storms. Wind, hail, pouring rain had done no harm to the building. Why should he feel apprehensive this time?

Night darkness and the howling of the wind—he could hear it even through these sound-deadening walls. He put his hands flat against the windowpane and felt a vibration of force. Solid and secure as the building was, the storm was striking at it with no ordinary power.

Now the lightning began, and the flashes were such that he was driven from his viewpoint, his hands over his eyes. He stumbled to his bed, crouched there, his head down on his upthrust knees, his hands over his ears. He was afraid as he could not remember having been before. This storm was such fury unleashed that he could only cower.

There was a great burst of light—then nothing.

Imperial Prince Andas sat up to stare about him dazedly. His head spun. He felt more than a little sick. But he steadied himself with one hand against the wall and looked about in desperate disbelief. He could not be seeing this! A dream—surely a dream!

Where was his own bed? There should have been four posts of Caldroden golden marble, each carven into a losketh with wings outstretched, and over his head the Imperial demi-crown of precious darmerian wood inter-set with the five gems. The walls—these gray walls? Where were the proper hangings of painted Iamn skin, bronze-green, with here and there a tinge of faded red? There were no rugs—no—

Where was he?

Andas shut his eyes firmly to this nightmare and tried to think, to fight panic, which was a sour, foul taste in his mouth, a shaking throughout his body.

Anakue! This was Anakue's doing! But how—how had that half-crazed rebel—whom none took seriously—done this?

Andas kept his eyes closed. The how—that was something he could discover later. The now was more important. Grisly events from past history crowded into his mind, a montage of all the horror tapes one could imagine. Palace intrigues—he had heard of those—but only in the past. Such things did not happen nowadays—they could not! Why, no one with any sense listened to Anakue's ravings. His right to the throne was nonexistent, coming as he did from the illegitimate lines both long discounted.

Cautiously Andas opened his eyes again and forced himself to study what lay about him. This was not his bedroom, this gray box with its very simple furniture, lacking all the color and beauty he had always known. Now he looked down at himself, running his hands along his body to assure himself by touch that his eyes reported the truth.

No silken nightrobe—no, a coarse one-piece coverall

such as laborers wore, gray as the walls. His hands—
their natural brownness had a yellow tinge, as if they
had not felt sun for a long time. He missed the rings
he had always worn as his status insignia, just as his
two wristbands were gone when he hurriedly pushed
up his sleeves to make sure.

Now he began to explore his face, his head, by
touch. His thick hair was not as long as it should be.
It was clipped closer to his skull.

Shakily Andas got to his feet. Out—he had to get
out, to discover where he was. But, this must be a
prison—only, when he looked to the far wall, he saw a
half-open door, though that part of the room was very
dim, for the only light came from a slit of window.

Wary yet of the door, Andas went to the window and looked out on a scene that was a new and
sharp shock. This was not Inyanga. Nor Benin, nor
Darfur—he had visited both of those sister worlds
in the Dinganian system. He braced himself by one
hand on either side of the window and stared out at
the forbidding wilderness of twisted and broken rock
now running with streams of water. This was nowhere
in the world he knew! Which meant—how could it
be Anakue's doing?

Swaying, Andas edged along the wall, steadying
himself with one hand. He had to find somebody, to
learn—He had to know!

But when he came to that half-open door, Andas
hesitated. It was even darker beyond, and what might
lie in wait? His hand went to a belt he no longer
wore. He had not even that ceremonial long knife
which was seldom drawn from its elaborate sheath.
He had nothing but his two hands. But the need for

knowing drove him on, to sidle around the door and stand in a dark corridor.

There were one or two faint beams of half-light, as if they issued from other rooms. He slipped on, keeping to the wall, heading toward the nearest of those.

This was like combat training at Pav. He was suddenly fiercely glad that he had argued his grandfather into letting him have that experience. Of course, he had been then only third in line for the seat of the Lion, and it did not matter that he wanted to see life beyond the Triple Towers.

He reached the doorway and froze. The faint scrape of sound was from within. The room was not empty. Andas flexed his hands. He had learned a lot in combat training, and now he felt, rising above his bewilderment and fear, that cold and deadly anger that was the heritage of his house. Someone had done this to him, and he was ready to make the first comer among the enemy account in return.

"Please—is there anyone—anyone at all?"

A woman. But this was not too strange. Many times in the past a throne had toppled from intrigue begun in the Flower Courts of the Women, though he knew none favoring Anakue.

"Anyone—" The voice was a low wail.

Andas read fear in it, and that brought him into action. He rounded another half-open door to confront the occupant of a cell exactly like his own. She stared at him, and her mouth worked. In another moment she would scream. He did not know how he guessed that, but it was true. He moved with trained speed to catch her, holding his hand over her mouth.

But she was no palace woman, nor even of the Dinganian system—he would take knife oath on that. Her skin was very light against his own, and it was covered with tiny pearly scales, which felt rough to his touch. Her hair was green, and she had odd lumpy growths on either side of her slender neck.

"Be quiet!" he whispered.

After her first instinctive recoil when he had caught her, she ceased to struggle. Now she nodded, and somehow he trusted her enough to take away his hand. It was plain as he looked about that cell that she, too, must have been a prisoner, though her race and home planet he could not guess.

"Who are you?" Her voice was steadier than it had been earlier when she had cried for help. It was as if by seeing him she had gained assurance.

"Andas of Inyanga, Imperial prince of the Dinganian Empire," he told her, wondering if she would believe him. "And you?"

"Elys of Posedonia." There was that in her tone which made that name as proud a title as the one he had voiced. "What is this place?"

Andas shook his head. "You may guess that as quickly as I. I awoke and found myself here. By rights I should be in the Triple Towers at Ictio."

"And I in Islewaith. This—this is a prison, is it not? But—why—?"

He nodded again. "There are a number of 'whys' for us, lady. And the sooner we get some answers, the better."

She spoke Basic as well as he, Andas noted, which meant that she was from some planet within the general sphere of influence of the Terran outflow in the past.

But since no man recently had attempted to number those worlds, there was no reason why she should know his home system, any more than he hers.

"Do not leave me!" She caught his sleeve as he turned back to the door.

"Come quietly then," he ordered.

But an instant later they heard a footfall in the dark corridor that made them both tense. A shadowy form appeared in the doorway. Andas half crouched, his hands ready to deliver the blows he had been drilled in.

"Peace!" The newcomer held up a hand, palm out in a gesture of good will as old as time in the galaxy. He was a little taller than Andas, but this time his race was known to the prince.

Salariki! From his point-tipped ears to his sandaled feet, their claws retracted now, he was unmistakably of that feline ancestry. The fur on his head and outer arms and down his shoulders and spine was blue-gray, his skin a shade or so darker. And the slanted eyes in his broad face were a brilliant blue-green. He did not wear a coverall like the other two, but a kilt of the same coarse material. Now he stood with his hands on his hips, surveying the two of them.

"Two more fish in the net," he commented, his Basic slightly slurred with the hissing inflection of his species.

"And you?" Andas demanded. He found the Salariki's stare irritating.

"And I," agreed the other readily enough. "Though how I got here from Framware—"

"Framware?" Somewhere Andas had heard that

name. Then he put memory to good use. "Framware, the trading station of the Growanian Six Worlds!"

The Salariki showed his fangs in a grin, which Andas thought did not denote much humor.

"Just so. In fact, I was the head of our trade mission—I am Lord Yolyos."

Andas introduced himself, as did his companion. The Salariki rubbed a forefinger across his chest, the long, dangerous-looking claw at its tip extended to the fullest.

"It would seem," he remarked, "that someone has been collecting notables. You are an Imperial prince of somewhere—which doubtless has a weighty meaning in the right time and place. And you, lady"—he turned to the girl—"are you perhaps a ruler, or ruler to be?"

"I am the rightful Demizonda, yes." There was pride in her swift reply.

"We have other companions in misfortune," Lord Yolyos continued. "There is one, Hison Grasty, who assures us, and continues to do so regularly, that he is Chief Councilor of some place called Thrisk. And an Iylas Tsiwon, Arch Chief of Naul, and also one called Turpyn, who so far has not seen fit to supply us with more than his name. Now, what do you remember?" He shot that at Andas in an entirely different tone of voice, a sharp demand for information that the prince found himself supplying before he had a chance to resent such inquisition.

"Nothing. To the best of my memory, I went to bed in my own chamber—and woke up here. And you?"

"The same. Where here may be none of us seems able to supply. You, lady?"

The girl shook her head. "No more. A familiar room—then this!"

"There are indications," Lord Yolyos continued, "that there has been a power failure in this building."

"Power failure—" Andas repeated. "Inhibitor! They may have had an inhibitor on us!"

"Inhibitor?" Apparently Elys did not understand.

"A mental block—to keep us from remembering. If none of us can, that must have been it!"

"Possible, yes. There is another point," the Salariki said. "We seem to be alone here. To all purposes, this prison was run by robots only."

"But that is impossible!" Andas protested.

"I shall be most happy to have the opposite proved true." Lord Yolyos held up his hand, extending all his finger claws, armament that Andas eyed with respect. He would not like to meet the Salariki in unarmed combat, not even with his own training. "I would like," the other continued, "to have an interview with the lord of this place. I do not think he would deny me any answers I desired."

Search the place they did, thoroughly. But when the band of prisoners gathered once more in the central space, they pushed among robots halted statue-like, sure that there were no other humans but themselves under this roof.

Of their company Iylas Tsiwon was clearly the eldest, though with all the rejuvenating methods now generally in use, plus the fact that there were great differences in the aging speed of various races, they could not be sure of that. But he was clearly the least strong, a small man, close to the Terran norm physically. His hair was thin and white, his face a pallid wedge with deeply graven lines on either side of his beak of a nose. His coverall seemed too large for his shrunken frame, and he pressed his hands tightly together to still the tremor in them.

Hison Grasty loomed over Tsiwon as if to make two of the frail Arch Chief. But it was mostly blubber that made up his bulk, Andas decided with inner aversion. His round face was rendered doubly unattractive by a dull red flush about his nose and mottled dewlaps. His obese body strained the seams of his clothing with every ponderous movement.

Turpyn, who had impressed Andas with his skill at seeking out every possible hiding place in the prison, was in great contrast to the other two. He, also, was probably Terran, but there were certain subtle modifications of the original that hinted at planetary mutation.

His hair was cut very short and looked almost as thick and plushy as that on the Salariki, but it was white, though not with age. In addition, he had a thick tuft of it jutting from the point of his chin. And his eyes were very curious indeed, showing no whites at all, only a wide disc expanse of silver. He spoke seldom and then only in monosyllables, nor had he made any other statement concerning his past than his name.

But he was the first to speak now. "No one here— robot controlled."

"We must get away," broke in Elys eagerly. "Get away before someone comes to start the machines again."

Turpyn turned those cold discs of eyes upon her. "How? We are in desert country. There are no transports here. And we don't even eat unless we can activate the food section again."

"And if an attempt to activate that starts everything— even the guards?" Andas demanded.

Turpyn shrugged. "I don't know if you can live without food. I know I can't."

Andas realized that he himself was hungry. So Turpyn was right—they had to have food.

Yolyos spoke first. "What chance have we of getting at the food supplies? I freely admit my people seldom deal with robotic equipment, and I am totally ignorant of the field. Have we an expert among us?"

Tsiwon shook his head, and a moment later Grasty's jowls wobbled in the same gesture. Elys spoke aloud.

"My people are of the sea. We do not use such off-world machines."

Andas was angry that he must also deny any useful knowledge. But when the Salariki looked to Turpyn, there was a faintly different expression on his face.

"But you, I believe, do know. Is that not true?"

Andas wondered if the Salariki was purposely extending his finger claws as he asked that question, or if it was an unconscious reaction brought out by that hostility Andas, too, was sure lay beneath the surface of Turpyn's attitude.

"Enough—maybe—" The man turned and went to the far side of the room, being closely trailed by the rest. There was a control board there, and he walked along it slowly, now and then extending a hand as if to push some button or lever, but never quite completing that movement

Was he a tech, Andas wondered, an engineer of such standing as would make him equal in rank to the rest of their prisoner band? Yet he did not have the manner of the techs Andas knew. He had, rather, the self-confidence of a man well used to giving orders. But unless he was playing a part now, he was not very familiar with these controls.

At length he appeared to make up his mind and returned along the wall installation, pausing only a second now and then to flip up a switch. When he reached the opposite end, he stopped and glanced over his shoulder at them.

"This is the test," he said. "I will switch on to an alternate power source. That may or may not work. I hope I have turned off the guard robots—perhaps I haven't. It's stars across the board, risking all comets." He reduced their chances to that of the galaxy-wide gambling game.

Tsiwon put out one trembling hand as if in protest, but if that was what he had in mind, he thought better of it and said nothing. Grasty backed to one side, into a position from which he could better see both the board and the robots. The Salariki did not move. Andas felt Elys's light touch on his arm, as if she thus sought some reassurance.

Turpyn pulled a last switch. Lights went on. They blinked against the brightness. Andas thought that those lights were a concrete argument that this room must sometime be used by humans—robots did not need them.

He was watching those robots with the same apprehension that held the others tense. Only one moved, and as it trundled doorward, he saw that it was a servo. It passed them at a steady pace and came to the wall at the end of the room, where it flashed a beam code against what seemed solid surface. A panel opened.

"So far, so good." Even Turpyn appeared to relax visibly. "But if we are going to eat, I would suggest that we get back to our rooms. That thing is programed to deliver the food there." And he started for the ramp leading to the cell corridor.

A little hesitantly the others followed. Tsiwon and Grasty first, the other three behind. As they started up, Yolyos made a small signal for caution.

"He knows more than he admits." There was no need for the Salariki to indicate who "he" was. Suddenly Andas had an idea. What if their jailer now posed as one of them? What better way to conceal himself than to claim to be another prisoner?

"He might be one of them you think?"

Yolyos again displayed his fangs. "An idea clever enough to be born from the mind of Yared himself! But not to be overlooked. I will not say that he is our enemy, but I would not hail him as cup-brother with any speed. We must discover the purpose for our being here, because only then can we bring our true enemies into the open. Think about that while you eat—"

"Need we eat apart?" Elys cut in quickly. "I confess freely to you, my lords, I have little liking for entering that room again, less for sitting there on my own. Can we not take the food when it comes and bring it to some common place?"

"Of course!" Though he would not have mentioned it, Andas knew the same uneasiness. To enter that cell and wait gave him the feeling that once more the doors might lock.

"Your room is between mine and the prince's." Yolyos fell in with her suggestion at once. "Let us collect our food and come to you."

Andas did not even go in his cell, but waited outside until the robot came rumbling down the corridor, pushed into the empty room, slid two covered containers and a lidded mug on the table, and went out. Then he collected all quickly and went to Elys's cell, from the doorway of which the robot was just emerging.

When he entered, she stood away from the wall. Andas pulled the upper covering from her bed and rolled it into a tight ball, which he pushed down to keep the door from closing automatically.

"Well thought on." As the prince got to his feet, the Salariki arrived with his own dishes.

It was when they opened all the containers that they had a new surprise.

"This," announced Yolyos, "cannot be prison food. Smalk legs stewed in sauce, roast guan—" He now flipped up the lid of the mug to sniff its contents. "Vormilk well aged, if I can believe my nose."

Since the Salariki sense of smell was famous, Andas thought he could. But he was bemused at his own supplies. This was food such as might reasonably have come from the first table at the Triple Towers, except it was not ceremoniously served on gold platters and he was not wearing a dining robe of state.

"They put us in cells, dress us so"—disdainfully Elys flicked the stuff of her coverall—"and then feed us richly. Why?"

"Food of our own worlds, too." Andas looked at the girl's main platter. He did not recognize the round white balls resting on a mat of green resembling boiled leaves.

"Yes." The Salariki raised a spoon to suck noisily at its contents. And the prince remembered that the aliens made a practice of eating with sound effects, so that the host might be sure of the enjoyment of his guests.

Just another question to have answered, he thought. Then he fell to eating with full appetite.

-2-

Whether their fellow prisoners had been moved to dine together, Andas did not know or care. But once his hunger was satisfied, he realized that their party seemed to have divided in two. He, Yolyos, and Elys—the other three (unless Turpyn walked alone) in the other group. He commented on this.

The Salariki replaced the lid on his mug, having drained the last drop of its contents with relish.

"Of Naul I know something," he said. "It is close to the Nebula, a collection of three systems, ten planets. We have trading stations on three. One exports the Tear Drops of Lur—"

He must have noticed Elys's baffled expression, for he explained.

"Perfume, my lady, and a very rare one. It is distilled from an exudation that gathers on certain stones set like pillars among native vegetation—but it is not traders' information you seek now. It remains that I have heard of Naul, and if this Tsiwon is who he says he is, then in him you see one of equal power perhaps with your emperor, Prince. Incidentally, where lies this empire?"

"From here—who knows? We of Inyanga hold the five planets of the system of Dingange—Terran rooted. Our First Ships came with the Afro outspread," he said proudly, and then knew that this history meant nothing to these aliens and hurriedly added, "That was a very first outspread."

But since that appeared to mean nothing either, he elaborated no further. Instead, he waited for Elys to add her bit to their pooled information.

"I am Demizonda of Islewaith. We have spread to no other planet, since our sun has but three, and two are near waterless. But I have heard of Thrisk where this Grasty must rule. They control the Metallic Weed Combine."

"Naul, Inyanga, Thrisk, Posedonia, Sargol—" Andas began when the Salariki corrected him.

"Not Sargol—if you mean from where I was snatched. As I have said, I was on Framware then. I wonder how the trade treaty advanced after my disappearance." He flexed his claws, eying that display absently.

"Time!" Andas got swiftly to his feet, for the first time sharply aware of what might have been for him a disastrous passage of planet days—even weeks. "What day—month can it be now? How long have we been here?"

Elys gave a little cry. Her hands, with the delicate webbing halfway up the fingers, flew to her mouth. "Time!" she repeated. "The full tide of Qinguam! If that is past—"

"So." That word in Basic became the hiss of a

feline in Yolyos's mouth. "May I guess that each of you also were faced with a situation in which time had importance?"

Andas caught the significance of that at once. "You think that is why we are here?" And he followed that question quickly with an answer to Yolyos. "Yes, time has importance for me. I am not in direct line to the throne. Among my people it is not as on some worlds; the crown does not pass from father to son. Rather, since my ancestors had a number of wives—officially one from each of certain noble families—the Emperor designates his choice from among those of the royal clan houses who are of suitable age. Though such multiple marriages are no longer common, yet the choice still lies among all the males of the royal line.

"It is my grandfather who rules the Triple Towers now, and he had three possible heirs of my generation—four if one counts Anakue. But when he summoned me to his presence, it was thought he had chosen. Only to make it final, I must appear on the day of Chaka and be crowned by his own hands in the presence of all the houses of a Hundred Names. If I am not there—"

"You lose the throne?" Yolyos prompted as Andas's voice trailed away. For the first time he realized just how deeply disaster might have struck.

"Yes." He sat down on the edge of Elys's bed.

"Now I have a treaty instead of a throne to protect. But if I am not at Framware to argue it through, then it is not only that I shall have my name and clan blackened, but also Sargol loses." Once more the Salariki flexed his claws, and his voice dropped to a low throated growl.

"I must sing the full tide in, I must!" Elys clenched her hands into fists. "If I do not, the charm passes from the blood of Elden to Ewauna. And that must not be so!"

"Three of us, and perhaps them also." Andas nodded to the door to signify the others. "But why? Those who might wish us elsewhere are widely scattered and have nothing in common. Who would collect us here?"

"Well asked, young man." The voice might have had the tremor of age, but the words came forcibly. They looked up to see Tsiwon within the door. "I, too, can add to your list of people who have reason to want to know the present date. If I have not been present to speak against the proposed alliance with the Upshars—" He shook his head. "I fear for Naul. Now"—he rounded on Andas—"on what day do you remember being last in your proper place?"

"It was the fifth day past the feast of Itubi. Oh, you mean in galactic reckoning—wait." Andas did a sum in his head—planet time was for planet life only, and from world to world the length of days and years varied. "As far as I can make it—but it would be the year only—2230 A.F."

"You are wrong!" Elys shook her head emphatically. She had been tapping fingers on the table top as if counting off some numbers. "It was 2195. I know that's true," she continued triumphantly, "because I had reason to consult the overdating just the day before—the day—"

"You say 2230, this young lady 2195," Tsiwon repeated. "Now I have good reason, very good reason, to know the proper date, since I had contact with the

Central Control commissioner and thumb-signed two documents. And the date on those was 2246."

"I shall add the final confusion." Yolyos broke across the assurance of that statement. "My last date was 2200."

Andas glanced from one to another. There was indignation plain to read on Tsiwon's age-seamed face and Elys's youthful countenance. Only the Salariki appeared unruffled by what must certainly be the most inaccurate working out of galactic dating he had ever heard.

In his head the prince did some adding and subtracting. Between his date and Elys's lay thirty-five galactic years, between Yolyos's and his thirty years, while he differed sixteen years from Tsiwon.

"Do you now begin to wonder"—Yolyos broke the silence of their dissent—"just how long we have severally been here and whether it is possible we did not all come at the same time?"

But Andas did not want to consider that. If Tsiwon's reckoning was correct—why, then, long since had his chance slipped from him! Who ruled now—Jassar, Yuor, even Anakue? How long had he been here? He looked at his smooth brown arms and what he could see of his body. He did not seem any older. He could not be so—he would not!

"First, how do we get away?" Elys demanded. "What matters speaking of time until we do? We have been under a mind lock here—we must have been, or we would remember how we came to these holes!" She glanced about with disdain. "So perhaps we do not remember clearly even now. But get away—I must!"

Andas had gone to the window slit. The scene outside was almost exactly what he saw from his own cell, save that the water which had been there earlier was drying, leaving pools and threads of streams where there had been small lakes and rivers. But the bleakness promised nothing in the way of escape.

"I think we should ask Turpyn," Yolyos said.

Andas looked back. "Do you think then that he might be a guard, pretending to be one of us?" He repeated his earlier thought.

"Ingenious and possible. Though I believe on our first meeting I detected in him some of the same reactions to awakening here in the unknown. But he either knows this place better than we do, or else he is aware of its purpose and that of our being here, for his first reaction was outrage."

"As if some trap of his own had sprung on him?" Tsiwon interrupted. "You are right, Lord Yolyos. I had a similar impression when we first gathered. So, let us ask questions of Turpyn and this time receive straight answers." The old man's face had not looked benign before, and now his straight-lipped mouth and the expression in his eyes made Andas shift from one foot to the other.

The history of Inyanga was bloody enough. There had been rebellion, the rise and fall of dynasties accompanied by blood spilling, much his people had to feel shame for. But that they did today feel shame for such acts was hailed as a definite step toward another civilization. In Tsiwon's face he read recourse to older and darker ways.

But there was nothing to say until they found their man and he either refused to talk or otherwise opposed them. He followed the Arch Chief of Naul and the Salariki out the room, Elys behind him.

Neither Turpyn nor Grasty was in his cell, and once more the others descended the ramp. The standing robots made it difficult to see the whole of this room. It was a perfect place for an ambush. Andas motioned the girl behind him. He wished he had even a knife of ceremony. One man with a stunner or blaster could master them all.

"Over there—" The prince started at that hiss from his left. The Salariki was pointing to the far right where a door stood half open.

They took the long way around, not weaving among the stalled robots, but keeping to open spaces along the walls, a precaution Andas heartily endorsed. He had not trusted Turpyn from the first, and whether there might be others here they had not located in their search was a question that continued to plague him. Somehow the idea of a prison run only by robots did not seem possible.

"—no better than the rest. So don't try it! My offer is the only one worth taking."

Grasty's voice, thick and throaty, reached them. There was a muttered answer they were too far away to hear. Once more Grasty spoke, his tone one of exasperation and rising anger.

"You will do it because you are no better situated than we are, Veep!"

Veep! That title was one which almost every civilized planet in the galaxy knew to its sorrow. Thieves' Guild boss! It fitted this situation exactly! Kidnaping on the scale their presence here represented could only have been carried out by the Guild. In that case, they were being held for ransom, and Turpyn was the one left in charge—

Andas caught the Salariki's eye. The alien made a quick gesture of assent. Tsiwon and the girl—Andas motioned them to stay where they were. Shoulder to shoulder with Yolyos, he moved toward the door, aiming a kick that sent it flying fully open. The alien entered with an effortless leap, and Andas followed. Grasty was standing over Turpyn, the Veep, who was sitting before a small control board.

Both swung around at the entrance of the other two. Grasty fell back a step or so, which in that narrow space brought him against a cabinet for tapes. Andas crowded him, hands coming up to deliver the blows that would render this man helpless before he could move his flabby bulk. The Salariki had gone for Turpyn, hooking his claws in the other's coverall at the shoulders, dragging him up and out of his seat.

"What—" began Grasty.

"Close your mouth!" Andas scowled at him. "Or I'll close it for you. What deal were you making with this Veep?"

"Ask at the source," Yolyos said. He gave his captive a deceptively gentle shake, and the man's pallid face twisted, though whether in pain or apprehension of what might happen to him, Andas could not guess.

"Now, little man," Yolyos continued, "tell us what you know that we should be aware of." With apparently little or no effort, he held his captive so that Turpyn's feet no longer touched the floor. Though the man writhed and fought, he could not break free. His face smoothed, then, as if he had come to some decision, and he stopped his useless struggles.

"I will tell you what I know," he agreed in a flat tone. "It is little enough, though there may be that here which will inform us." He pointed with his chin to the wall facing him.

Andas saw then that the cabinet against which Grasty leaned was not the only record depository. Three of the four walls were so furnished, and behind the control desk where Turpyn had been seated, there was a visa-screen, now blank.

"Speak." Yolyos lowered him into the chair, but he did not release his hold. He stood behind Turpyn, those claw points visibly piercing the fabric, at some places marked with small red stains.

"I don't know much." Turpyn's face was now expressionless. "And a lot is guessing—from things I once heard—"

"Spare us time waste," ordered Yolyos. "Begin with what you do know and let us judge whether it be small or large."

"Mind you—I have only bits and pieces," he still insisted. "But what I have heard is this—that there is a place where, for a price, one could exchange a man for his android double. And that double could be programed to do what the buyer desired, while the real man was kept in storage, to be disposed of later if wished."

"A likely story!" Andas burst out.

"Be not so quick, young man." That was Tsiwon now inside the door. "Never say anything is impossible. And this service"—he advanced to the other side of the desk and leaned across to better meet Turpyn eye to eye—"was run by whom? The Guild?"

Turpyn shook his head. "None of ours. Would I be here if it was?"

Grasty snickered. "You might, if there was a power struggle on. Promotion in the Guild changes often by force."

Turpyn's mouth drew tight, but he neither looked at the councilor nor answered that taunt. "The Mengians were responsible—according to what I heard."

Andas was bewildered. That name was new to him. But he saw the change on three other faces. Grasty speedily lost that malicious grin, and both Tsiwon and Elys looked startled. There was a shadow of what could only have been fear on all three.

"Enlighten us," Yolyos ordered. "Do not complicate matters. Who—or what—are the Mengians?"

"The heirs of the Psychocrats." Tsiwon spoke before Turpyn. "It is not generally known, but those were not totally wiped out when their oligarchy fell. There have always been tales that a handful escaped, withdrew to some hidden place to carry on their experiment, the code name for their headquarters being Mengia. Now and then legends have a remarkable core of reality."

Andas shivered. Psychocrats had not meddled in Dingane's system. But they had heard tales. If their sort still existed, it would be dark knowledge to set at least a quarter of the galaxy having nightmares.

"This—this could be so." Grasty had lost his arrogance. "It is the sort of plan they would make, this introducing rulers of their own. And, by all accounts, their techs had the skills to make undetectable androids. Why, they could reconquer all they had lost, without discovery until too late! Back—I must get back to Thrisk—warn—"

"It may already be far too late," Tsiwon said slowly. "We do not know how long we have been here. Our replicas could well have turned our rulerships into holdings for the Mengians."

That first chill Andas had felt was nothing to the cold encasing him now. If they had been prisoners of some remnant of the Psychocrats, why, then even the weird difference in time they had worked out earlier could also be true! They could have been kept here in some state resembling stass-freeze. And that had been known to last for centuries of planet time!

It was Yolyos who spoke. "You mentioned earlier, Turpyn, that this service was run for sale. Then you speak of it being a Mengian plot to regain their control. Which was it—transactions with those who had good reason to wish us personally out of the way, or a plot aimed at us simply because we held the positions that we did?"

Turpyn shook his head. "That is one of the things I can't answer, and it is 'can't' and not 'won't,' I assure you. I heard of this setup as a straight transaction. On payment, anyone selected would be taken, his android double substituted. Then there was a second rumor that the buyer himself was double-crossed. How true I can't tell."

"But to fashion such an android, implant it with the proper memories—how could they do it?" Elys wondered. "They would have to be almost flawless to deceive those who know us well. Such a process would take time. And if we did not lend ourselves to memory taping, how could they do it?"

"If the Mengians are the Psychocrats and they are responsible," Andas said, though he shrank from what seemed the truth, "then they could do it, somehow. They did stranger things with men's bodies and minds when they ruled."

"All the more reason"—Grasty pushed forward—"for us to get back as quickly as possible and see what has happened, repair the damage—"

He must not have considered time lapse, Andas decided. But to get away from here, yes, that was their first concern. Only how? Yolyos was already on that track.

"You know something of such installations as this." He addressed Turpyn. "How do they get supplies? I do not believe that the food we have just eaten was grown from proto cells."

"Behind you is a ship call, but the setting suggests a robot autocontrol," the Veep answered. "If any supply ship comes, it must also be robot, locked on a single course. In order to use it for escape, we shall have to substitute tapes, and where will you get another? Unless the ship has a collection—which is not always the equipment of a locked course transport."

"What is this room? There are records of some sort stored here." Andas tried to fit his thumb into the release on the nearest cabinet and found it impossible.

"Locked—on some personna lock."

"Since when has such a thing as a personna lock," inquired Grasty, "kept a barrier intact when faced by a Guild tech? You can open these."

"Given time and tools, yes," Turpyn admitted.

"You'll have both," the Salariki promised. "Suppose we start looking for tools now."

Though Turpyn grumbled and swore that he probably could not find the delicate instruments he needed, he went to the smaller section of the outer room where one of the robots, halted like the rest in mid-section, had been engaged in repairing one of its fellows whose outer casing sat to one side. The main parts of its inner works were spread out on a bench.

There the Veep picked and chose until he had a handful of small tools Andas could not identify. They had all trailed along to watch him, as if their united wills could spur him to greater efforts.

With his possible pick-locks he went to the record room and set to work. That he was an artist in his field was clearly to be seen. Andas wondered at his dexterity. If he were a Veep, surely he would not be one of the general workmen of the Guild—unless there were criminal actions that fell to the upper class alone. At any rate, he knew what he was doing.

It took a long time. Tsiwon pleaded fatigue and went back to his cell. Sometime later a drooping Elys followed him, seeming to have lost her fear of being alone.

Grasty had taken the chair before the visa-screen, fitting his flabby bulk into it with difficulty. Andas watched for a while, but was too restless to stay on in that narrow room, choosing to prowl about the larger chamber, moving less warily now among the stalled robots.

Beside the repair alcove was the room into which the food robot had gone, but he could not open that door. However, there was another, which yielded.

A burning hot wind blew into his face. His eyes squinted against a glare as he took one step into the outer world, his hand keeping the door ready for retreat from this heat, light, and smell, for the air had an acrid odor that set him coughing. He feared to remain outside long. He had had time enough to sight the burn-scarred, slag-frosted surface of a landing field. How long had it been since the last ship set down there?

Coughing, he retreated, sealing out that atmosphere. One thing was plain. Without some form of body protection, probably also breathing masks and eye goggles, none of them could last long planet-side here.

There were no other openings. He made the circuit of the walls, returning to the room where Turpyn still worked. And he arrived just in time to see the Veep stand back and give a jerk with a tool he had set point-deep in one of those depressed locks. There was a splintering sound, and the drawer opened.

His guess was right. Orderly rows of taped records faced them. Grasty was still trying to pry himself out of the chair, but Yolyos elbowed Turpyn aside and raked out the nearest tape case.

Where there should have been a title there was only a code—as they might have expected.

"A reader—where is a reader?" Grasty hammered on the desk top with the puffy palm of his hand as if that would make the necessary device rise out of its surface.

But it seemed that Turpyn knew something more of the room. He snatched the tape from the Salariki, shook it from its case, and snapped it into a slot topping a small bank of controls that took up more than half of the desk surface.

"Out of the way, you tub of sogweed!" He pushed at Grasty, sending the big man away from the desk.

Turpyn paid him no more attention, turning instead to thumb a lever. The visa-screen rippled alive, and a clear picture showed there in tri-dee detail. It was the body of an alien, totally naked.

"Zacathan." Andas did not know he had made that identification aloud until he heard his own voice. But that was speedily drowned out by a precise voice, human in timbre, reciting a series of code sounds that had no meaning. The picture changed from the whole body to sections, each enlarged, and always accompanied by the code.

They watched to the end of the tape, learning nothing more than the exact details of the unknown Zacathan's body. Then both the pictures and the voice were gone.

"I think," Yolyos remarked, "that that was a pattern for the making of an android. Some other unfortunate who was meant to join our company, but he did not. Suppose we try another."

The second tape was poised in his hand to be inserted in the reader when the visa-screen flashed a new image. But now the code symbols running across it meant something to Turpyn.

"Ship planeting," he announced.

At the same time there was a clanking noise from the outer room, and Andas, nearest to the door, moved to look out.

Three of the largest robots, which had been in one line against the far wall, were moving forward as if the arrival of the ship activated them when it was still off-world. They were cargo carriers, and they were rumbling on toward that door through which Andas had looked out into the waste.

-3-

"That is the present situation." Yolyos had their full attention as he stood with one hand resting on the broad back of a carrier robot. "We have managed—or rather Turpyn has—to halt the unloading. And until the ship is emptied, it will remain finned down out there. It is not a passenger ship, but there is a life-unit section in it for emergencies, though we shall find those quarters very crowded if we can retape the ship and take off."

Andas considered all the ifs, ands, and buts that now faced them. It would be easy enough to stow aboard in that life section and allow the ship to transport them back. Only that would land them in the hands of the enemy. They must reset the ship with another trip tape. But so far all the cabinets had offered them were broadcasts of code and series of pictures in detail of men and aliens.

Watching those as they tested tape after tape, Andas wondered if they would turn up those pertaining to any

35

member of their own small company. So far that had not
happened. And Turpyn was raiding more compartments
than the first he had opened, now choosing samples in
a random fashion.

They ate again and, driven by fatigue, slept. And
they continued to split into two parties, though Tsiwon
at present stayed closer to Andas and his companions.
While they kept together, neither Grasty nor the Veep
appeared very friendly.

It was on the second day that Turpyn admitted
defeat. He stood surrounded by gaping drawers, a
full tide of discarded tapes rising almost ankle-deep
on the floor.

"Nothing." He announced failure in a flat voice.
"Nothing we can use."

Andas spoke up. "We have not tried the ship."

"Getting into her will be the problem," but there
was a trace of animation in Turpyn's tone. "I have
some tech knowledge, but I am no spacer. What
of you?" He swung his head slowly, giving each a
searching stare.

Andas's own experience went no farther than that of
a passenger. And he believed no one here could say
more, unless Turpyn, in spite of his denial, was holding
out on them. To their surprise, Elys spoke first.

"I know that the entrance ramps are controlled
from within. But certainly this is a problem that must
have arisen somewhere, sometime before. Are there
no emergency ways to enter a ship?"

It was as if her words turned a key deep in Andas's
memory. He had a fleeting picture of a ship finned
down on a landing strip, a figure climbing by handholds on the outer edge of the fin itself, something

he had seen in passing. He had asked an idle question at the time.

"The service hatch!"

He was not even aware they were all watching him. Surely all ships were general in some points of construction. If so, this one should have the same hatch.

"Above the fins." He cut his explanation. "A repair hatch for techs. There's a chance that might open."

"Any chance is worth taking now." Tsiwon's usual quaver disappeared in an excitement that strengthened his voice.

"At night or at twilight anyway," Yolyos said. When Andas, eager to try to prove his memory right, would have objected, the Salariki pointed out the obvious.

"We have no protective clothing. To go out in the glare of that sun and perhaps have to remain in the open working—"

He was right. To none of them, different in race and species as they were, did this world hold welcome beyond the door of their prison.

And Andas, impatient as he was, was aware of another problem. Once within the repair hatch, if they could find and open that, was there access to the rest of the interior of the ship or only to a confined section for techs? If he, if any one of them, only knew more! The education of an Imperial prince was certainly lacking in survival training. Not that they would speedily die here if they could not find a way out, but perhaps quick death would be better than lingering stagnation.

The party attempting to invade the ship narrowed to three—Andas, Yolyos, and Turpyn, whose tech knowledge was indispensable. After the harsh sun that blistered this unknown world set and its glare was gone, they headed for the field.

Whatever remote controls triggered the landing of the cargo had not functioned. It was as hatch-sealed as if in space. But they wasted no time in heading directly for the fins. Luckily the winds, with their torturing dryness, had died away, though it still hurt to breathe too deeply, and Andas wondered what long exposure to this atmosphere might do to their bodies.

The hand and foot holds were there. Though they did not want to, they must let Turpyn make the first climb, since if the hatch was to be forced, only he could deal with it. Andas swung up close on his heels. He had no trust in the Veep.

Clinging to the holds below Turpyn, whom he heard now and then spitting an oath in a tongue not Basic, Andas tried not to breathe too deeply and to ignore the stinging of his nose and the way his eyes teared.

Turpyn gave a louder grunt and humped up, Andas quick to follow, with Yolyos behind him. As he pulled within the shell of the ship, he found himself in a narrow passage, so narrow that it was difficult to squeeze through. There was a second hatch Turpyn's torch showed, but the Veep had started to climb again, using more handholds to ascend to the upper levels.

So they won through the narrow ways meant only for techs, on major repairs, into the living quarters. After a quick inspection Turpyn gave a sigh of relief.

"This has been in use and not too long ago—perhaps on the last trip of the ship. It can be activated with some work. But we shall have to see about the controls. It will do us no good otherwise."

They followed him up to the control cabin. There were signs that at times this drone did carry a crew, for webbing seats were slung for both pilot and astrogator before the proper controls.

Turpyn pushed past those to stand before the pilot's board, studying the array of buttons and levers. Then he pressed one, and there was an audible click as a trip tape arose from a slot.

"If there is a file of these—" He weighed the useless one in his hand. Andas had already started searching by the astrogator's seat. And his prying and pulling at a snug thumbhole paid off. A compartment opened to show in its well-cushioned interior four more tape casings. He clawed the first out to look at the symbol on its side. But he did not recognize it. In fact, they might be entirely off any galactic map he was familiar with. He dropped it to the web seat and picked a second.

Again disappointment. No longer did he expect any luck, but perhaps some other of their company would know more. Only—the third! At first he could not believe the report of his eyes, running his finger back and forth to feel the slight roughness of that raised design, assuring himself that it was there.

"Inyanga—it is Inyanga!"

Yolyos had scooped up the two discarded ones. "And that one—" He pointed to the last in the compartment.

"It does not matter!" The prince treasured his find in his two hands lest someone snatch it from him. He had his key to home. "Don't you understand? This will take us to Inyanga—and from there you can reach your own worlds."

"Still I am interested." Yolyos secured the last one.

"Naul—"

Andas held to his tape with a jealous grip. All right, so there was one for Naul. But they would go first to Inyanga.

"I think"—the Salariki might have been reading his mind—"that you will find some slight opposition to such a plan, Prince. And we do not know where we are, so that Naul may well be the best and safest choice after all."

Yolyos shoved the two unknowns back into the compartment. He kept the one for Naul. But Andas had no intention of surrendering the one he held until he himself dropped it into the right slot and knew the ship was heading for home.

Oddly enough, Turpyn paid little attention to their exchange. He was moving around the control cabin testing this lever, pressing that button, as if to assure himself that the ship could be switched from drone to active status. Finally he spoke.

"It will do. Cramped quarters for all, and no knowing how long a flight. There ought to be E-rations on board. But we had better see to supplies."

They went down into the living space again. As the Veep had pointed out, that section was never meant to house more than four at a time. But to get away from their prison was worth any amount of crowding.

There were stored rations, and the air plant was in action, though if their voyage was too long—Was Naul nearer? Perhaps their best chance lay with one of the strange tapes. Yet why would Naul or Inyanga be stored at all unless they were both within easy cruising distance? Only a First-In Scout or a Patrol cruiser carried tapes on long voyages.

So reassured, Andas was ready to do battle for his choice as they returned to the prison, this time down the ramp they could lower from within. They found the others waiting eagerly.

"Naul, of course," Tsiwon said as if there could be no possible question. "We have excellent transshipping from our ports, and you will have no difficulty in reaching your homes. Also we have a Patrol Sector office. This offence must be reported at once. To discover how deeply this conspiracy has taken root needs expert investigation."

"Inyanga's ports are also Sector centers," Andas stuck in, determined to hold his ground. "I see no reason for choosing Naul."

"The two of you," Elys said wearily, "can doubtless continue to argue for days. I, for one, have no wish to waste time sitting here listening to you. To my mind, Naul has no advantage over this Inyanga as far as I am concerned, and perhaps that is also true for Chief Councilor Grasty and Lord Yolyos, as well as Veep Turpyn. After all, on my own world I had never heard of either, which means I may have half the galaxy to cover before I reach home. Since we cannot guess where we are at present or in what relation we lie to either of your two worlds, it will be largely a matter of chance as it is."

"Naul!"

"Inyanga!"

Almost in one voice Andas and Tsiwon answered.

Yolyos made a sound not far from a growl. "The lady is right. We have two tapes and six of us who may be bound in directly opposite directions. Neither of the ports you urge upon us has any great appeal as far as we are concerned. Therefore, let us let chance decide. Here—" He picked up one of the lidded basins in which their last meal had been delivered. Taking up the cloth that had served as a napkin, he wiped the basin out thoroughly.

"Now"—he offered it to Tsiwon, who held to the Naul tape as tightly as Andas did his—"drop it in, Arch Chief. You, too, Prince. We shall have a drawing—"

"And who shall do the drawing?" Tsiwon demanded before Andas could. "The lady has been with you, and you—you have been his constant companion." He stabbed a finger at the Salariki and then at Andas.

"True enough." Yolyos put the lid back on the basin. "Turpyn, can that robot doing the repairs be activated enough to pick up one of these? We cannot accuse it of any favoritism."

"Yes, it can." The Veep sounded almost eager, as if he had despaired of their ever coming to a decision. "Come—"

With all of them watching, Yolyos placed the basin, uncovered once more, where the robot stood. Andas and Tsiwon dropped in the tapes. One of the tentacle arms that had been so long raised in the air dropped the small tool it held and descended to the basin after Turpyn had made the adjustments he thought necessary. It raised jerkily again, one of the tapes gripped fast. The Veep hastened to kill the power, and Yolyos pried the selection loose.

"Inyanga," he informed them.

Tsiwon could not say that the choice had not been fair. But his expression was sour, and he took the rejected tape, holding it as if with it in his possession he might still have a chance to use it.

They had no luggage, but they raided the food room, bringing with them all that was container-stored. The harsh dawn was breaking when they finally climbed the ramp into the ship and somehow fitted themselves into the life section. There was some relief from the crowding when Turpyn, Yolyos, and Andas went to the control cabin. Though he was no astrogator, the tall Salariki settled in that seat, while Andas took the stand-by officer's seat just behind. Turpyn was in the pilot's place. The prince watched the Veep slip in the tape and set the auto-pilot to take off.

The warning sounded, and they strapped in, ready for the force of the blast. When that came, Andas found the strain to be far worse than he expected. There was less cushioning that eased the passengers through this ordeal than on the usual flight.

He aroused groggily only to discover another difference between this and the transportation he had been used to. There was no artificial gravity in the drone, and he had to adjust to weightlessness. The ensuing period of time was a new form of torment.

Among the others, Yolyos, though he admitted he had not met this before, was the first to learn to handle himself in space. Tsiwon, Grasty, and Elys felt it the most. They had no drugs such as were normally issued, nor voyage-sleep, which was the final refuge of those who could not stand the physical discomfort.

The monotony itself was hard. Elys and Tsiwon stayed

mostly in their bunks. The other four, though Grasty
grunted and groaned and was as uncooperative as he
dared be, took turns sharing the other two sleeping
places. Time had no meaning. There was no ship's timer
to cut the crawling period into night and day. There
was sleep, but one could only do so much of that, and
Andas found it harder and harder.

Grasty's eternal grumbling was so much a source of
tension that at times Andas found himself having to
use all his control not to turn on the man with a blow
across his whining mouth. Turpyn, once he had taken
them into space, said little or nothing. If he had the
use of a bunk, he slept; if not, he slouched in one of
the webbed seats of the control cabin, his eyes still
closed for most of the time. Andas suspected that the
Veep was engaged in thoughts he had no intentions
of sharing with his ill-assorted companions.

There remained Yolyos, though the Salariki had his
periods of deep silence also, and Andas respected them.
But when he was willing to talk, he described a new
way of life with barbed humor. Andas found himself
babbling away on the state of an Imperial prince, with
a tongue loose enough to shame him now and then.
He had never believed that talkativeness was one of
his faults, but now it seemed a major one.

"Have you thought"—the Salariki advanced a thorny
question—"of what might have occurred during your
absence, always supposing that our time differences
are true?"

Andas had, though he did not want to. Suppose he
had just vanished? Then they would have selected one of
the other princes as heir. But what if there had been an
android in his place—then he must prove substitution.

There was a way. He glanced around, for they were in the control cabin. Neither Turpyn nor Grasty was present. He could not conceive of the Chief Councilor ever successfully playing eavesdropper. His wheezing at the slightest movement in free fall heralded his presence in a way that could not be concealed. Turpyn was another matter, but by swinging his web seat around a little, Andas could be sure that the Veep could not come swimming into the cabin without his knowledge.

As for Yolyos, somehow, with the alien Andas had not the least fear of being frank. The Salariki had no ties with the empire, and the more Andas saw of him, the more he found him the most congenial of this company. Also there was some pressure in Andas himself driving him to talk, as if by discussing a few concrete plans aloud, he could ensure their success.

"There is more to the Triple Towers than most of those who live within their walls know. Building has spread far beyond the original towers—like throwing a stone in a pool and watching the ripples run out. Only those ripples are walls, pavilions, gardens, halls, audience chambers beyond number. No one, I am certain, knows them in entirety. There would be surprises even for the Emperor. Parts have been closed from use for generations. There have been ill doings in the past, and portions have been shunned because of the tales of slayings and worse, for the royal clans have warred among themselves for generations. Some parts of our history have been deliberately suppressed or altered, so the truth is lost.

"But fragments are rediscovered. We do not inherit from father to son as in some monarchies, which is the simpler and more direct fashion. The son of an emperor's sister, always providing that her marriage has been within a defined circle of the royal clans, may have first consideration. However, the sister of the present emperor has no sons, so the choice has reverted to the second line of sons. But it is the Emperor's duty to select his heir in good time and see him crowned as throne-son before the families of the Hundred Names. Once that is done, to dispute his right is treason.

"I am one of three—four if you count Anakue, even though his line is illegitimate. It was a surprise to all when Akrama the Light-Holder summoned me. The Emperor waited a long time before he announced he would name his heir. There have been many urging a need on him—especially with Anakue leading what is close to rebel forces. Three years ago there was an uprising in Anakue's name on Benin. It took four regiments of the Inner Guard to put that down. But he denied all knowledge of it, and there was no one, even among the Eyes and the Ears, to tie him to it.

"If I just disappeared, then it may be that Jassar or Yuor is now the Imperial Prince. That I must discover before I make myself known. Which means I shall make use of the secret ways to learn what has happened."

"Secret ways? You know such?"

"By luck I do. It is almost as if I have been prepared by fortune for what has happened. My father was a recluse. Shortly after my birth, within two years of his marriage to his cousin, the Princess Anneta, the daughter of a former emperor, he was injured in an explosion of his private flitter. He was one of the unfortunate few who cannot tolerate plasta-flesh transplants, and his face was terribly scarred without hope of recovery. My mother was very young and of such a nature that she had accepted her marriage as a duty that she took no joy in. Also she found disfigurement in others made her ill. Realizing this, my father forswore her with honor and withdrew to one of the remote and half-forgotten portions of the palace, such as I mentioned.

"His one pleasure in life became history, first of the empire, and then of the Triple Towers and the intrigues and secrets of the royal clans. Since he was second son to the Emperor, his position was secure, and he lived undisturbed.

"In fact, he was largely forgotten as the years passed, keeping his own small court apart from the general life of the Triple Towers. And I lived in that solitude, with nurses and then with tutors he selected, until I was of an age to be sent to Pav for warrior training. I never saw my father without a mask fashioned by one of the great artists of the court, which gave him a semblance of the handsome face he had once had. But I learned to know him as well as he would allow anyone to penetrate to his private world.

"Part of his training for me was the rediscovery of palace secrets. There were hidden ways within the walls, spy holes through which one might watch, even chambers with secret doors in which were stacked weapons of another time, or treasure. And he made me memorize each new one he discovered. I do not know how his passion for the strange research developed, but he was certain that such knowledge would be of benefit to him who knew it. And it finally brought about his own death."

Andas no longer saw the Salariki's face, the searching brilliant eyes. His attention was for a mind picture that had mercifully begun to dull a little now, but that he would never forget.

"How?" Yolyos asked. "Or is that something you do not wish to speak of?"

"For a time I could not. I know it, and one other—Hamnaki, who was my father's personal servant. We—I had come back on leave from Pav—missed him all through one day. So at last we took torches and started hunting the ways. We found him in a newly discovered section, but it had been designed by some builder who was more suspicious of mind or had a greater and darker secret to hide, for there was a man trap set within. There was only the belief that he died instantly to comfort us. We got him out and said that he had died of a fever. Since no one any longer cared or remembered him much, there was no question. They gave him a funeral of state as was his right and a lesser name-carving in the temple. Do you know, until I saw that in place, I had not even known my father had the right to wear the two plumes. He had won that during the pirate invasion of Darfur—but no one had ever told me.

"What he gave me—and he was right that it may be of the greatest importance now—was his knowledge of the ways. Let me get to Inyanga, to even the outermost wall of the Triple Towers, and I shall be able to discover what has happened."

"And if Turpyn's suspicions are true and an android is acting out your role?"

"Then I will learn enough to be able to present the Emperor with the truth."

"Let us hope so."

There sounded a sharp signal they could not mistake. The ship was about to pass out of hyper. They were that near to their journey's end. Andas's hands shook a little as he made fast his safety belt. Inyanga—they were home!

-4-

They landed. Andas aroused from the effects of a hard
fin-in to see the visa-screen providing a view of what
lay beyond the ship walls. But—

Not Inyanga!

At first he could not believe what he saw pictured
there. They had not set down in any port. As the
screen slowly changed to give them bit by bit a view
of the surrounding land, he saw that there were the
scars of deter rockets, yes, but old—no recent burns
to show a recent visit.

The vegetation, which appeared a massively thick
wall beyond the edge of the open land, differed in
shade from that he knew. It was a lighter green,
broken here and there with splotches of a pallid
yellow.

Not Inyanga! Then the tape—why had the tape
been listed wrongly? Andas had the same disoriented
feeling he had had when he first came to his senses
in that unknown prison.

"I can guess that this is not what you expected."
Yolyos's voice broke through his bemusement.

"Yes. I—I never saw this before."

"Instructive," was the Salariki's comment.

Instructive of what, wondered Andas. He could not
have been mistaken—it had been the tape marked
with the symbol of his home world that had landed
them here. Perhaps—perhaps those had been purposely mislabeled to prevent the possibility of just
such an escape as the storm had made possible for
them! Perhaps it had landed them in an unknown
port where they could be easily recaptured.

"Bait in a trap—" Either Yolyos had read his
thoughts from some change in his expression, or the
Salariki's suspicions matched his. "If so, the one for
Naul might also have delivered us here. But it would
be of some value to know where 'here' is."

He worked an arm out of the protective belting of
his pilot's seat and thumbed a button on the control
board. Moments later the unaccented reply of the
vocalizer reported atmosphere and gravity near to
normal for at least two of them.

"We can survive. And we aren't going to take off
again until we know more about where our choices
will land us."

"They could all be for here—those tapes." Andas
voiced his suspicion.

"Ingenious." Yolyos unlatched the protect-straps.
"Worthy of a master of trade." There was honest admi-
ration in his voice. "If that is true, we can look forward
to being collected—by someone—sometime. I would
suggest we make that collection as difficult as possible.
Have you noticed one thing—"

"That there are no recent ship-burns? No one has been here—for years maybe."

"But at one time this field had been steadily visited. Yet"—Yolyos's extended claw indicated the visascreen—"if this was a regular port, where are the buildings? Beyond the burns, that looks like deep vegetation which has never been penetrated."

"Fast growing, maybe." But even fast-growing vegetation would have taken some years to swallow up all port buildings. In the first place, even at a small way station, the buildings were generally made of resistant-to-vegetation materials. Such a precaution was standard when they had to have buildings that could be erected with a minimum of effort on worlds differing greatly. Either the time since this port had been in use was so far in the past that the vegetation had finally conquered or there had never been any standard equipment here to begin with.

A semi-secret landing place—only one type of ship would use that. Jacks!

He said that and heard an answering rumble from Yolyos.

"And"—the Salariki put the finishing touch on danger—"the Guild has been known to make common cause with the Jacks."

Normally the Jacks were the "peasants" of the crime confederation. They raided frontier worlds, selling the best of their loot to Guild fences. Now and then they were used by some Veep of the Guild for a project in which he needed easily discarded help.

"A Veep of the Guild!" Again Yolyos's thoughts matched his. "Turpyn" growled the Salariki.

"Then he knew—about the tapes!"

They could handle Turpyn among them. Why, Andas could take him alone probably. Somehow they must choke some information out of him. Andas got to his feet, ready to seek out the Veep and begin the job at once. His furious disappointment was chilling to that cold rage notorious in the House of Kastor.

"The tapes—" As if unconsciously, the Salariki moved between Andas and the ladder that would lead to his prey. "I am wondering about those tapes, Prince. A Veep of the Guild is a master at his craft. And I have seen Guild men who could lift a jeweled ring from a man's thumb without his knowing it. It could be that your Inyanga tape landed somewhere else than in the autopilot—that Turpyn was able to substitute another."

"He couldn't have! I was watching while he did it."

"As was I," Yolyos agreed, "but I do not say that I can better any master in his own trade. And how many encounters with Guild experts have you had in the past, Prince?"

"None. But if he could do that—" Andas drew a deep breath. If Turpyn could so cheat while they watched him!

All those tales about the legendary exploits of the Guild! It was said that they bought up, or took by darker means, new inventions that even the Patrol could not counter. But Turpyn had been a prisoner, possessing nothing but his garments. He could not have worked any hallucinatory tricks on them—or could he? At that moment Andas's belief in his own sense of sight, his own ability to outthink an opponent, was badly shaken.

"So we have two answers," Yolyos continued. "Either those tapes were left as bait, perhaps all of them, in spite of their markings, set to deliver us here. Or else Turpyn, for reasons of his own, made the switch. He took no part in our debate over Naul and Inyanga. Perhaps he did not need to, seeing that he could have his own choice after all."

There was a sharp ping of warning. Above the visa-screen flashed a signal.

"The ramp!" Andas jumped for the ladder. Someone was leaving the ship, had been ready to depart almost as soon as they completed fin-down. And he had no trouble in guessing who that was. They must prevent Turpyn from reaching whomever he had come to meet, get him first and learn what danger lay ahead.

Andas swung down at top speed, Yolyos so close behind that once or twice the Salariki's heels almost bruised his fingers.

"What is it—where are we?" Elys asked. Behind her stood Tsiwon.

Andas, unwilling to lose a minute, did not take time to answer, pushing past the girl, heading for the ramp hatch.

They had made good time. As their sandals flapped upon that bridge over the ground, still hot from their rockets, they saw Turpyn out in the middle of the landing area. Andas had expected to see him running, heading for the protection of the growth. Once in there, the prince feared, they would have little chance of finding him.

But the Veep had slowed to a halt and was looking about him like a completely bewildered man. If he had left the ship with a goal in mind, it would seem he had lost his guides. He turned first this way and then that, shading his eyes against the strong sunlight, searching the vegetation wall for some break not there.

Andas pounded down the ramp, Yolyos still behind him. He expected Turpyn to hear, to turn and see them, to run. But the Veep continued to look about as if nothing mattered save to find what he sought.

He did not turn to look at them, even when they came pounding up. Andas caught at his shoulder and jerked him half around, ready to demand answers. But he never asked them, for he had not seen such an expression on the Veep's face before. Blank astonishment was as easy to read as if Turpyn had spent a life time cultivating the mobile features of a tri-dee actor.

"It's—it's gone!" He spoke as if to himself, trying to impress the fact of a loss on his own mind.

"What did you expect to find?" Andas kept his hold and now gave the other a quick shake to break through the maze of bewilderment that held him.

"But it can't be gone!" Apparently Turpyn was shattered. It was as if, up to this point, he had been armored by some certainty that he need fear nothing. Now that certainty had been reft from him.

"What is gone?" Andas began to wonder if the man had been shocked out of his full senses. He spoke slowly, spacing his words, in an effort to get through.

"The—the port. Wenditkover—the port!" Turpyn sounded impatient, as if he expected Andas to know already.

The name meant nothing to the prince. He glanced

at the Salariki who made a gesture signifying like puzzlement.

"What is Wenditkover?" Andas asked again.

But then came a call from the ramp. Grasty was plunging down it at a pace that might be fatal for his footing unless he slowed.

The councilor's voice shrilled higher and higher as he ran, but Andas could not understand the words he sputtered. He had apparently in his excitement abandoned Basic for the tongue of Thrisk. His face was red under the muddy, greasy surface skin, and he pounded one fat fist against another as he spat forth what could only be abuse—aimed at Turpyn.

The Veep stood very still. That cloud of shocked amazement lifted from his face. He was once more the disciplined, enigmatic man of the prison. Andas could have cursed Grasty. If the councilor had not arrived at just that moment, they might have been able to learn something from Turpyn. Seeing the man now, he was sure it would take more than any art he possessed to force the Veep to talk.

Still half screaming, Grasty reached them. He paid no attention to Andas, but aimed a wild blow at the Veep, who avoided it easily. Then, not quite sure what or how it had happened, Andas found himself spinning away. He would have hit the ground had not Yolyos's arm, sturdy as a city wall, steadied him.

Grasty, though, had hit the ground with force enough to expel the air from his lungs in an explosive grunt. Turpyn stood over him, rubbing the knuckles of one hand. He was as impassive as one who had watched Grasty take a tumble from a clumsy stumble.

The councilor wheezed, clutching his protuberant

belly with both hands, his mouth working, but sound-
lessly as if he had run out of words as well as breath
in that short encounter. Turpyn stepped away. He
looked at Andas, at Yolyos, and then at that wall of
green. Then he turned toward the ship.

It was then that the Salariki took a hand. Though
the Veep had handled both Andas (who had prided
himself on his skill in unarmed combat) and the clumsy
Grasty with contemptuous ease, he learned that the
warrior from Sargol was different. Yolyos's move was
made so swiftly that his body, big as it was, seemed to
be a blur. There followed an instant of struggle, and
Turpyn again stood still as Yolyos loomed over him,
his extended claws digging into the Veep's shoulder
muscles.

So holding him, Yolyos shook him gently, or what
seemed gently. Yet Turpyn's mouth twitched, and
Andas did not miss the two telltale red spots beneath
a couple of claws.

"So this place is Wenditkover. You must excuse our
ignorance, Turpyn. Not having had your advantages, we
do not know the name. I think that you will explain a
few matters. First, where is Wenditkover—not in relation
to us at the moment, of course, but rather in relation
to where we thought we were going? Second, what
is—or was—Wenditkover? At present you must admit
it is very little. Third, who—or what—did you expect
to find here? We have a great deal of time, since there
is no use trying to lift ship until we know why we came
here in the first place."

"And in that time, Turpyn"—the Salariki's voice
was a rasping purr of promise that made Andas glad
he did not stand in the Veep's place—"there can be

more than one way of asking questions. Politely in this fashion, or more roughly. That you have tried to betray us in some manner is very evident. So there is no reason why we should treat you gently."

Andas believed that Yolyos would do exactly as he hinted. The Salariki's voice carried complete conviction. And it must have impressed the Veep, because talk he did, in short, toneless sentences. Nothing he said had any reason to make them happier.

"Wenditkover is a Jack port—or it was. I don't know what has happened. Or"—emotion touched his voice fleetingly—"how everything could have gone this way—" He shook his head. "It doesn't make sense. You'd think no one had finned down here for years. And it is a regular refit and unload station."

"With a Guild fence in residence?" suggested the Salariki. "Like that pirate's hold of Waystar?"

"Smaller, but like, yes.

"I tell you," the Veep continued then, "I don't understand this at all! There should be buildings here—maybe a ship refitting. It couldn't all just disappear!"

"Suppose"—Yolyos did not loose his hold on the Veep, rather propelled the man ahead of him toward the green walls—"we just go over and see what is behind this growth."

Andas matched them stride for stride. But Grasty remained where he was on the ground, breathing easier now, but watching the Veep with a murderous glare, a glare that perhaps included the rest of them, too. Had the councilor been armed, Andas would never have turned his back on him. But the prince did not believe the fellow was dangerous now, not at least for a while.

It was when they approached the green wall more closely that they saw buildings were still there, at least in part. But they had been taken over by a jungle of growth so that only small vestiges were visible.

"It might be fast-growing vegetation," Andas suggested. But that shadow in the back of his mind was darker. No matter how fast growing that vegetation was, it could not have taken such a stranglehold in less than years. Yet Turpyn had been confident that this was a well-known Jack port, important enough for Guild connections.

"Not that fast." It was Turpyn who answered. "And this isn't that kind of growth either."

"You have been here before then?" Yolyos asked.

"I was taken from here—at least my last memory—"

That struck home like a blow. Andas had only one question: "What year—galactic?"

For a long moment Turpyn did not reply. Was he trying to reckon the time or change some planet accounting into galactic? Or had the question of time startled him into that silence? But at last he spoke.

"The year 2265."

Thirty-five years after Andas's reckoning, forty-five after Yolyos's—and differing widely again from that of Elys and Tsiwon! Time—Andas's shadow fear was gathering substance—how much time lay behind him in that prison?

"You say 2265," Yolyos commented. "And how long would you say that this port of yours has been abandoned?"

"I do not guess." But Andas thought that sounded

rather as if the Veep did not choose to. Also he knew that once implanted in Turpyn's mind, that fear would be as hard a companion for him as it was for the rest of them.

"Since we know now what Wenditkover once was and what you expected to find here, may we also believe that you fed its tape into the ship's pilot?" If the date bothered the Salariki, he did not show it, but had returned to the business of getting straight answers from Turpyn.

"I recognized the symbol on one of the other tapes. It was easy to palm and exchange." He was impatient, as if they should have guessed the truth at once.

"But you still have the Inyanga tape?"

"Yes."

"And I think that we can believe that Inyanga will not have disappeared into some waste of time as thoroughly as this has," Yolyos continued. "So—"

He staggered back, the coverall on Turpyn's shoulders ripped, there were red furrows on the skin beneath, but the Veep had broken that hold. He burst from them, heading into the mass of growth where the ruins of the buildings offered so small a defense against the jungle.

Andas started after him when Yolyos's voice, having the snap of an order, brought him up short.

"Let him go. You cannot find him in that tangle. And once he sees that there is nothing there for him, he will come back."

"Liar—cheat!" The rasping cry came from behind. Grasty, bent over, his hands clasping his belly, his face gray, tottered toward them, this time crying his abuse in Basic. Then he sputtered again in his own tongue. But he did not follow the Veep. Perhaps the folly of such a chase struck him as quickly as it had the Salariki.

"Liar—cheat?" repeated Yolyos. "You seem even more heated over this matter than the prince here, yet he had good reason to believe he was on the way home. Or, Councilor, did you have reason to think that you were headed in some other direction? I remember you were talking confidentially once to our late guide. Had you made a separate deal with him? Did you think we were coming to Thrisk?"

"But there were no tapes marked Thrisk." However, Andas thought Yolyos had hit upon something. When the Salariki growled that question, Grasty had actually flinched. The attack on him must have shaken him as badly as the first sight of this deserted port had Turpyn. And while he was in this state, they had better get to the bottom of any private deal he had thought he had made.

"I am Chief Councilor of Thrisk." Grasty might have been trying for dignity, but he could not stand straight. And he groaned and clutched at the belly so cruelly outlined by his clothing. "I have resources—"

"And you made an offer to Turpyn," Yolyos supplied when the man seemed unable to continue. "Where did you think we were going?"

"He said Kuan-Ti. They have a strong tie with Thrisk."

"And you believed him?" Yolyos was plainly amused.

"He was to get a million credits." Grasty choked out the words as if each hurt.

A million—what kind of personal fortune did Grasty

have to draw on? Or did he intend for that to come
from the safekeeping of Thrisk? Or had he intended
not to pay at all, having once achieved his purpose?
Andas suspected the last as the truth. Two of them
making a bargain neither intended to keep—well
might Grasty curse.

"It would seem that your trust was not mutual,"
commented Yolyos. "I do not think you are going to
see Kuan-Ti, nor Thrisk for a while—"

"Help!"

The cry came from the ship, not the woods into
which Turpyn had plunged. Tsiwon stood at the foot
of the ramp beckoning wildly. And crumpled at his
feet lay Elys. Andas reached them first and went down
on his knees beside her.

She lay with her eyes closed, and those odd growths
on her neck had an unhealthy look, shriveled, pucker-
ing up in scaled patches.

"She said," Tsiwon cried out breathily in his thin
voice, "that she must have water, that she smelled it
and must reach it or she would die. She started to
run—in that direction—" He pointed.

"Aquatic race." Yolyos had gone down on one knee,
too. "I wonder how she has managed so long. But she
will have to have her water or die. There is undoubtedly a limit on the time she can remain dry."

"But her prison cell seemed no different from
mine—"

"We don't know what type of mind-lock we were
in back there. The point is—she needs it now and
in a hurry." The Salariki scrambled to his feet. "Can
you carry her? If so, I'll break trail."

Andas got to his feet, glad she was so light of

frame—unusually so. He had not been aware on the ship that she was so thin. Her bones seemed almost starting through her pale skin. Maybe that was caused by dehydration.

They headed to the spot Tsiwon had pointed out. There Yolyos went into action, beating down, breaking off branches and vines, clearing a rough path through which Andas could steer a way with Elys resting across his shoulder. She had not moved or made a sound since he had picked her up.

"She's right—water—" Yolyos was sniffing, as though water might have a scent—though at that it might, for the Salariki. For a race whose sense of smell was so acute that they habitually wore scent bags about their persons, the smelling of water might not be too great a feat.

What had Yolyos endured without his scents? It was customary that off-worlders coming to Sargol had to steep themselves in aromatic odors before having any dealings with the natives. What had Yolyos endured without his scents—pent in the ship? It must have been very hard on him, yet never once had he complained.

They broke through a last screen of brush and came out at the side of a pool.

"What do we do?" Andas was at a loss.

"No telling how deep this is. Do you swim?"

"Yes." Andas laid the girl down and unsealed his coverall. The air was humid, warm enough so that he felt no chill. He lowered himself cautiously and found that the waters curled only slightly above his waist. Good enough—he could manage.

"Let me have her."

Yolyos lowered the limp body into his grasp. The
coverall dragged as he dipped her below the surface,
save for her face. Her hair floated out, hardly differing in shade from the water weeds. Andas steadied
her as best he could and hoped that the pool had
no dwellers interested in meat meals. There were
always unpleasant surprises on new worlds, and only
a great emergency would drive a man to take such
a chance as this.

Elys sighed and her eyes opened. Already those
scaled patches on her throat were less shrunken,
more the normal color of her skin. She wriggled in
his hold.

"Let me go!" There was such force in her order
that he did that. She pushed away, disappearing under
the surface of the water before he could prevent it.
He started to splash after her when she bobbed to
the surface some distance away.

"This is my world. Let me be!"

Already she seemed to have regained her vigor. If
that was the way she wanted it—but she had already
gone under the water again. Andas climbed out of the
pool and found the Salariki waiting with handfuls of
dried grass. The prince toweled himself as dry as he
could with those and dressed again, wishing he had
fresh clothing to wear.

Yolyos had gone a little way along the pool side.
From a bush there hung festoons of creamy flowers,
and the Salariki buried his face deep among them,
his wide chest rising and falling in deep breaths as he
drew in all of their scent his lungs would hold.

-5-

It was a new Elys who finally emerged from the pool in answer to Andas's calls, though it was apparent that she came reluctantly. As a starving man might have reacted to some weeks of careful feeding, her too-thin body was normally rounded once again.

"I feel"—she flung her arms wide as she still stood with her feet awash—"like a priestess of Lo-Ange who has flung her name tablet into the sea and so is reborn again!"

Andas was impatiently pacing up and down. A thought pricked at him. What if Turpyn had made his way back to the ship? Neither Grasty nor Tsiwon would be prepared, or perhaps wish, to prevent the Veep's taking off to locate some other Guild lair. By lingering here they were offering him a chance to do just that. And to be marooned here—no!

He looked to the Salariki, but Yolyos had wandered on, like a man drunk with Formian wine, or else bemused with happy smoke, to sniff at some purple veined leaves, which, after smelling, he crushed between his hands, rubbing the resultant mass up and down his wide chest. Their aromatic scent was strong enough to reach even Andas's nostrils.

"We have to get back to the ship!" The prince said to Elys. "If Turpyn tries to take off—"

But she was too fascinated by her own form of refreshment, stooping to catch up palmfuls of water, splashing about like a child. He was thoroughly exasperated by both of them.

"Ahhhhhh—" A rumble of sound from Yolyos, who had now wandered out of sight, was startling enough to bring Andas on the run.

The screen of flowering and scented growth that had been planted about the pool was a thin one. And the prince pushed through it to see the alien facing a small glade.

For a moment of surprise and awe, Andas was misled enough to think he might indeed be fronting the owners of this overgrown garden. Then he saw the truth. Tree trunks had been rough-hewn into those figures, gathered in a half circle about a spring bubbling from a stand of rocks. Bleached, perhaps by some rotting process of the jungle from which they had been hacked, they had an aura of life. Their bodies were humanoid, if gross and clumsy, but their faces were pitiless and alien. Some jungle vines had rooted on their bulbous heads, perhaps by accident, perhaps by long ago design, presenting them with tendrils of hair. And these vines produced purple blooms around which buzzed a multitude of insects. But there was also a sickly scent that made Andas give an exclamation of disgust and retreat a step or two.

Perhaps the aromatic leaves with which he had rubbed himself prevented Yolyos from catching that odor strongly, for he had drawn near to one of those figures and was peering into its blind-eyed face. Then he shook his head and came back to Andas.

"I have not seen their like before."

"And I have seen enough! The sooner we get back to the ship, the better. If Turpyn gets there first, he could try to take off."

"A possibility," Yolyos agreed.

"Come on then!" Andas did not move until he was sure that the Salariki was coming.

But as they went, the other still dallied, snatching a handful of leaves there, one or two blooms here, until he carried in the crook of his arm a mass of highly scented growth.

Elys still lingered ankle-deep in the pool. Her thoroughly soaked overall clung to her. But she seemed to relish that instead of finding damp clothing a discomfort.

"The ship! If we ever want to get away from here, we must make sure of the ship!" Andas tried to make his fear plain.

The other two acted as if they were drugged, each by his own form of pleasure. Finally Andas urged them on before him as a Yakkan herd hound might round up a flighty flock to keep it moving.

They retraced the route Yolyos had opened and so came to the field. The ship's ramp was still firmly planted out. Seeing that, Andas gave a sigh of relief. At least the ship was not sealed against them. Of any of the others there was no sign at all. Still that passage across the open made them targets either for an enemy in the ship or one in hiding, and it was one of the longest walks Andas felt he had ever taken. Neither of his companions was in the least hurry. Short of pushing or dragging, Andas could not make them alter their pace. Elys was singing, a low, contented hum, drawing strands of her wet hair through her webbed fingers, while Yolyos did nothing but bend his head to take long sniffs of the mingled scents of his huge bouquet. A less alert company, Andas fumed, he had yet to see. Show Elys water, Yolyos some flowers, and they would be out of a fight from the start.

There was no sign of Grasty or Tsiwon near the ramp either. They climbed that, Andas crabwise so he could keep watch on the edge of the jungle, expecting trouble and Turpyn to erupt from there. He did not accept the fact that the Veep would give up so easily.

They found Grasty standing over the bunk on which lay the Arch Chief of Naul, his eyes closed, his age-pinched face more sunken and skull-like than ever. The councilor looked up as they came in.

"About time," he wheezed as if he had not yet recovered from the blow Turpyn had dealt. "He"—he nodded to Tsiwon—"has it bad—some kind of seizure. Went down as if he were blasted."

The Arch Chief looked dead, but when Andas examined him, he found a faint slow beat of pulse. Again panic touched him. A trained medic might be able to bring the old man back to consciousness, even save that spark of life. But they had no medic. To his surprise, it was Elys, steaming with damp, who moved up to push him impatiently away.

Her hands were sure, as if she knew exactly what

she was doing, the fingers of the right just touching Tsiwon's forehead, those of the left his breast above the faltering heart. Her eyes were closed as if she concentrated or listened to what the others could not hear.

Andas was impressed by her air of assurance, enough not to disturb her. After a long moment of silence she opened her eyes.

"His heart is weak. He must go into san-sleep until we can get him to a healer."

San-sleep meant nothing to Andas, but a man with a weak heart could certainly not survive a takeoff. He said as much. Elys shook her head.

"In san-sleep he can. And here what chance has he? I do not believe you will find a healer out there." She pointed with her chin. In that she was right.

"But how do we get him in this san-sleep?" Andas wanted to know.

"I shall sing him," she answered. And having nothing better to offer, Andas agreed.

Elys shifted her position to the head of the bunk. Then using both of her hands to cup Tsiwon's head, the fingers spread to the widest extent, Elys began a low and monotonous humming note. Three times she gave that. Then looked to them.

"Go hence now. You might be caught also—if to a lesser degree."

They urged Grasty, in spite of his protests and groans, up to the control cabin, leaving Elys with her patient. As Andas went, he could hear a continuous wailing note, which made him uncomfortable.

"Do you think she can do it?" he asked as he joined the others.

Yolyos answered. "Who knows? Without a medic we shall do the best we can. It is a pity that survival techniques were not included in the past training we received. In fact, it becomes very plain that much education can be considered useless when one is faced with a situation such as this."

He had laid his untidy harvest down on the astrogator's seat and gone to the tape file, flicking it open. There were three inside, and he hooked them out with a claw. Andas saw again the symbols, save that the one for Inyanga was missing.

"Do we choose Naul now?" the Salariki wanted to know.

"No!" Grasty heaved himself up and tried to grab at the tape case. "Not Naul!"

"Now I wonder why? What do you know about Naul?" Yolyos's cat eyes were dangerously narrowed. "You made a deal with Turpyn—what do you know about Naul that you do not want to go there?"

The man picked at the waistline bulge of his coverall. His natural reddish flush was overlaid with a gray look.

"Naul—Naul is overrun by the Jauavum Empire."

"The what?" Andas stared. "But Tsiwon—he wouldn't want to head into that—"

"He—he was the one who started it all!" Grasty replied. Then in a burst of words as if he must tell it, he said, "Iylas Tsiwon gave the orders that brought the Jauavum fleet first to Naul, Everyone in the Eighth Sector knows it. He need only to say his traitor name on any world there and he'd be torn to pieces!"

"And when did this treason of his happen?" asked Yolyos.

"In 2250."

"But Tsiwon said he could not remember past 2246."

"He said!" Grasty gave a nasty laugh. "Any man who has made his name stink over half the galaxy would say anything."

"No!" Andas cut in again. "Don't you see, if Turpyn is right and we have all been put in storage so doubles could take our places, that was what must have happened. Tsiwon's double—the android—was the traitor. You," he demanded now of Grasty, "if you knew what happened in 2250, what was the last date you remember?"

"The year 2273. But you mean we could have been in that place for years?" His voice shrilled higher and higher. "But Thrisk—what has happened on Thrisk?"

"You might well ask," Yolyos said dryly, "seeing what apparently happened on Naul after Tsiwon was substituted. If that is what did happen. So we have 2273 now—"

Andas was busy with subtraction. Forty-three years galactic time! But how could a man—it must have been stass-sleep. Yes, in the earlier days before hyper space travel, men had managed to sleep for centuries in stass while the early First Ships made their blind galactic voyages. Forty-three years—and how many more? How long had Grasty been one of their company?

"Turpyn can remember 2265," Yolyos continued. "And he expected this to be a going port. Instead, there is every indication that it has not been used for a good many years. According to your dating, I myself have been in storage somewhere for seventy-three years, Elys for the longest period of all—seventy-eight. We shall, I am afraid, have to face up to the fact that whatever our absences were supposed to accomplish has long since come to pass, like Tsiwon's apparent treachery in Naul. I—I wonder what my double did for the trade mission. And you, Prince, perhaps your double now rules your empire in another's plan. We cannot be sure of anything until we learn more. But suppose you tell me, Grasty, what do you know of Sargol or Inyanga or—"

The Chief Councilor shook his head. "Nothing—I never heard of this Sargol nor Inyanga. The galaxy is too wide. A man could spend a lifetime voyaging and yet not visit a fraction of the inhabited worlds—you know that. I know about Naul because it was Eighth Sector and Thrisk is Ninth. We have had refugee ships from the Jauavum invasion."

"Well, we need not have thought that repatriation under the circumstances was going to be easy," Yolyos commented. "But we had all better be prepared to face some disaster upon our return. Do you still want to go to Inyanga, Prince?"

"Yes!" Andas supposed that the Salariki's speculations and his own fears were the truth. But still he had to know. Only what if he returned to find he was a traitor, or worse, as was old Tsiwon? More than ever he must make sure that his visit to the Triple Towers was in secret until he knew the truth.

"You'll have to find the tape first," Grasty pointed out. "It might be better to take a chance on one of those other two."

Yolyos had already clicked up the fastening of one. He brought out the coil of tape and turned it over to inspect it before returning it to its case. Then he did the same with the second. Holding that out to Andas, he pointed with claw tip to a very small symbol on its spool.

"Inyanga?"

"Yes! How did you—"

"Guess that Turpyn might have switched cases for hiding? In the tight quarters we have here, it would be the most obvious way of keeping it safe. Remember he thought he was going to set us down in territory where he had friends—he might want to use the other tape later. If our kidnaping had something originally to do with payoffs to the Guild for our disappearances, he could believe that he might hold us here and try for a second sum to dispose or deliver us—whichever paid the best."

"Then we can take off for Inyanga! But Turpyn, what about him?"

They were back now to one of the oldest and most fundamental laws of space flight. You did not abandon a fellow spacer, no matter if he was your worst enemy, on an alien world. But if Turpyn did not want to be caught, to lift off in their ship, how in the world were they going to find him? It would take days, maybe weeks, and a much larger and better-equipped search force than they could muster to find him against his will.

"Yes, Turpyn—"

"Let him rot here!" Grasty snarled.

"A fate he may well deserve," Yolyos returned. "But one we shall not grant unless he asks for it. Yet I do not think we can stay here very long waiting for him to change his mind. And we cannot hunt him tonight."

Andas looked to the visa-screen. The Salariki was right. Shadows were creeping from the jungle like dark fingers reaching for the ship. To venture into that wilderness in the dark was folly. They had no trails, no knowledge of what hostile native life might now lair in the ruins.

Elys came up to them carrying E-ration tubes from their supplies.

"Tsiwon?" Andas asked.

"He sleeps, but the life spark is very low. I do not know whether he can survive the voyage. Yet he must if he is to have any hope of a future."

Andas watched her hand around the tubes. Seventy-eight years according to their reckoning! Yet she seemed a girl his own age, maybe younger, though one could never be sure of the true age of another species. It could be a short life span or one as long as the Zacathans who had outlived empires. Should he tell her of their new discoveries or what Grasty said had happened to Naul, of how long she might have been separated from her own people? He decided against that for the present.

It was an uncomfortable night, and Andas got little sleep. They had turned on the nose light of the ship, thinking perhaps Turpyn might be honestly lost and could use that for a beacon, though they drew in the ramp as a logical protection. The visa-screen remained on, and twice Andas started up at a spark of light appearing on that, thinking maybe Turpyn had found some planet dwellers and was returning. But each time he watched the erratic actions of that spark he was forced to conclude it must mark the flight of some luminous night creature.

By morning he was even more tired than he had been when he had dropped into that astrogator's chair. But it would seem that his unrest had not been shared by his companions, for Grasty's snores and the Salariki's even breathing were those of sleepers. Andas lay for a while watching the change of view on the screen.

A dark hump moved out into the field. Andas darted a finger to a button to freeze and enlarge the scene. A man crawling? Turpyn injured? No, it was a beast coming slowly because it grazed at some small plants that had sprung up among the old burn scars. From a long, pointed muzzle a blue tongue snapped out, curled about a tuft of the growth, jerked it loose from the soil with a sharp tug, and brought it back to the waiting mouth, all with methodical regularity like a servo robot.

The humped body was shiny and dark, and the legs were very short, but its tail did not taper to the end. In fact, that reversed the usual pattern by uniting with the body in a narrow portion that then thickened and widened into a club. And the club seemed to have a coating of quills, which the creature either consciously or unconsciously flexed at intervals, so that they bristled out in an ominous display.

But it was what was caught on those quills that riveted Andas's full attention. Something fluttered, a small flag, bedraggled and stained. And that appeared also to annoy the creature, for it turned now and then (with difficulty because of its short neck and heavy shoulders) to snap out its tongue, as if it would so pull loose the rag from its quills.

Some freak of the wind finally brought it within

reach of the creature's tongue, and the animal tore it loose and mouthed it. And then, with a very readable disgust, stamped upon it and turned aside, to eat its way through another patch of vegetation.

Andas was already on the ship's ladder. He descended as fast as he could, triggered the ramp controls, and then was out in the morning, heading for that rag. It was a wet mass, but he used stems of plants to straighten it out on the ground, only to have his suspicion proved correct. Chewed, torn, muddied, it was also otherwise stained. And it was part of a coverall—Turpyn's.

The tracks of the animal were easy to read. These could be back-trailed. They must be. Andas started for the ship.

Grasty refused to go, and they overruled Elys when she volunteered. So it was Yolyos and Andas, with all the caution they could summon, who went down that trail. It led them to the buildings engulfed in the jungle. In the center of what had once been a courtyard they found what they sought.

It was not good to see, and they scooped a hurried grave, both working as swiftly as they could to get it out of sight; "it"—because what lay there had no resemblance now to a man. The Salariki kept sniffing, and when they had finished, he indicated one of the doorways that gaped about them like toothless dead mouths.

"In there—a lair—the smell is strong. He must have disturbed it. Perhaps it has young hidden. We had better move out before it returns. If I only had a blaster—"

His hands worked as if he wanted to draw that

desired weapon out of thin air. They had searched the
ship, hoping to find some cache of arms, without any
success. To be bare-handed in such a situation made
a man feel singularly naked. Andas agreed, ready to
return to the ship as quickly as possible.

"What was he hunting, do you suppose?" Had
Turpyn hoped to discover something in those dark
interiors—a weapon, a message?

"Does it matter? Death found him. And we had
better make sure it does not come sniffing after us,"
returned Yolyos.

They trotted back to the ship, watching both sides
of the trail, alert to any sound that would herald the
return of Turpyn's killer. The strength of the creature in
relation to its size must be immense. Of the efficiency
of its armament, they had had ghastly evidence.

But their problem was now solved. There was
nothing to keep them here on this forgotten world—
they could lift for Inyanga. In spite of what he had
just been doing and the horror of their find, Andas
was lighter of heart as they climbed the ramp.
He was going home! Though what he would find
there—well, there was no use hunting trouble. It
had a way of presenting itself unbidden. At least
once he was on Inyanga, he knew the kinds of
danger he would have to face. One always had
the idea one could cope with the known. It was
the unknown—like that Turpyn had met in the
dark—against which one had no defense.

"You found him?" Elys met them at the life
level.

"Dead," Andas told her, but never would he let
her know how.

"Tsiwon also," she said then. "I found him so when I went to him a little while ago."

Two of their number gone, and perhaps in the end those might be the lucky ones. But Andas was too young to accept such a view as that for more than a fleeting moment. He climbed purposefully to the control cabin. The sooner they lifted, the better. He found the Salariki there before him, the tape in his hands. But he looked to Andas searchingly before he fed it into the autopilot.

"You are sure, Prince? What if you find such a world as Tsiwon might have faced had his First Ancestress not been kind to him, as Turpyn found here?"

"At least it will be a world I know." Andas spoke his thought aloud. "And with a world I know, I have a chance. Be sure"—he faced the Salariki soberly—"that all I can do to aid you, the rest of you, to your own homes, that I shall do. As an Imperial prince—"

"If you still are an Imperial prince," Yolyos reminded him. "Count no heads until you take them and set them above your doorway. Which is a bloodstained saying of my own people, relating to barbarous customs now followed only by the wild men of the outer plains. But still perhaps it fits too well the present situation. Heads may still roll—be sure that one of them is not yours!"

Andas tried to match the slight smile of the other, but he was afraid that what he produced was closer to a wry grimace. "I shall take every precaution."

Already he was planning ahead. The trip tape would set them down without any choice of port on their part. And the public ports on Inyanga were policed. He must find some way to escape official notice until he could learn what awaited in the Triple Towers. If he had knowledge, if any of them did, of how to bring the ship in on manned controls, they could land secretly. But there was no chance of that. The one man who might have had such knowledge (though he concealed it if he did) they were leaving behind them as part of the earth of this world.

The tape was snapped into the board. But before they activated the autopilot, they had one more task. Tsiwon, wrapped in a covering from the bunk on which he had died, was carried out, to be laid in a second grave scooped out of the earth. Elys lingered as they built a cairn of such small rocks as they could find.

"I do not know in what gods or spirits or powers he may have believed," she said in a low voice. "But that one such welcomes him now, let it be so—for no man should go alone into the shadows without some belief to make smooth his road." It was as if she recited some farewell, and they stopped hunting rocks for a moment to stand, one on either side of her, and give silent farewell to the Arch Chief of Naul, of whom they knew little, but who had their good wishing on his long journey into the mystery no living creature had yet solved.

-6-

Where on Inyanga would they land? The question bit at him during all his waking moments and brought him one nightmare after another. In his dreams Andas saw the Triple Towers in ruins, even as Wenditkover had been, or else a detachment of the guard waiting to take him prisoner for some crime his double had committed in his name. Such speculations could provide almost endless possibilities, and he could make no concrete plans without knowing more. He might have worked himself into a state of unsupportable tension if Yolyos had not challenged his preoccupation with the future.

"Would you step into danger without weapons to hand?" the Salariki asked.

Andas wanted to pace, to wear off in physical exertion the tension in him. But with weightlessness he clung instead to the astrogator's seat.

"Weapons?" he repeated. "What weapons do we

have? Or"—he was suddenly more alert—"have you found an arms cache?"

"Your own weapons," Yolyos returned. "Your mind, your two hands. Accept that you cannot foresee the situation awaiting you, and do not try to be prepared in half a hundred ways when you need all your attention for one alone."

"I don't understand." Andas thought that argument had little meaning—except it was true. He could not defend himself without knowing the enemy.

"Just this—this ship has been used for illegal purposes. Of that we have simple proof. And where did Turpyn's chosen tape take us? To a base that was secret. Therefore—"

But Andas had already fastened eagerly on the suggestion and wondered why he had been so thick-witted as not to deduce it for himself. "You mean that a tape which would bring us to Inyanga might not do so to a port where the authorities would mark its arrival!" Why, that might solve so much. Then once more cold logic froze his first feeling of relief.

"That would be little better. A Guild port—with the Guild waiting—"

"Yes, but they would not be expecting our arrival. They might not even be occupying such a field at the time. Where on Inyanga might such be situated? Can you foresee a little helpfully in that direction?"

Andas closed his eyes on the control cabin and tried to mind-picture the continents of his home world. One needed certain physical attributes for a secret landing field. And Inyanga had few stretches of wilderness left to conceal such. At last he decided it was between the Kalli Desert and some hidden pocket in the Umbangai Mountains. And he said so.

"Desert or mountains," mused Yolyos. "And how well patrolled are either?"

"Not very well. There are two roads across the Kalli, but both follow old caravan routes from oasis to oasis. In fact, though there are aerial survey maps, most of the northern part has never been explored. As for the Umbangai—they lie to the north. A large section of those was once a royal hunting preserve. Now they are government conservation experimental lands. They are patrolled by rangers, but not often—they can't nose down every canyon. There is too much land, too few men."

"But of these two possibilities then, perhaps the desert is the best?"

"I trust not!" Andas could see some chance of getting transportation if they finned down in the Umbangais. But suppose they hit the Kalli at some secret but non-manned Guild field—there would be no way of getting across that blazing waste to civilization. On the other hand, he did not want to land in the midst of a Guild crew either.

He decided that Yolyos's suggestion had really done little to relieve his state of tension. It seemed that if the authorities did not loom as possible opponents, the Guild did. Andas sighed.

"You see"—Yolyos's tone was mocking, or did the Salariki get some satisfaction from ramming home the darkness of the future?—"you can plan for little either way. So the more you exhaust your mind trying to foresee, the more failure presents itself. You had better forget the whole matter."

"Easy for you to say!" flared Andas. He sulked silently, trying to remember all he had learned about the Kalli. That must surely hold their port.

Once more ship time could not be planet time, and a voyage of unknown length added to their misery. Elys again took to her bunk, unable to adjust to non-grav. And this time Grasty declared himself as unfit, swearing that the blow he had suffered had left him in permanent pain. He might be right—at least he ate far less.

At last the warning of exit from hyper came, and then they swung into landing orbit. On the visa-screen Andas saw the mottled shape of what the tape declared to be Inyanga, though he could not recognize any feature. And he wondered, with a new chill, if once more they had been deceived.

Andas felt sick, closing his eyes against a new and shattering disappointment as they went into a breaking orbit. Soon the ship would set down. In the Kalli, the Umbangai, or a port? There was no way he could alter that—he would have to accept the gamble. But he did not want to feel anything more until they three-finned on solid soil. He willed himself to that state.

He roused when Yolyos asked, "Do you know where we are?"

The Salariki had triggered the visa-screen into action, and the slowly passing landscape was indeed desolate. They had planeted in an expanse of very barren waste between two cliffs.

Where the soil was not slicked over with the glassy surface left by old rocket burns, it was red, streaked by vivid green and wine-color, marking mineral deposits. The rock walls of the cliffs were layered with

strata in red, white, and yellow. There was no sign
of any building or of another ship. They were not at
a regular port.

Then the turn of the screen showed a wide-
mouthed opening in the face of the cliff and within
that something—

"Stop!" Andas ordered, and Yolyos pressed the
button.

The scene stilled, and they were able to study it.
This was not altogether forsaken country. There were
objects well within the hang of the cliff mouth, and
they were covered with protecto sheets.

"I think nobody's home now," commented the
Salariki, "Luck is with us to that extent. But do you
recognize the country?"

Andas shook his head. "But if we are on Inyanga
and there has not been another tape substitution,
then this is the Kalli."

Sometime later he had no doubt that this was both
Inyanga and the Kalli, for upon exploration the covered objects within the cave proved to be skimmers,
made for air travel, well suited to the waste. And not
ordinary skimmers either, but master craft. Behind
them was a rack of energy units, each canister also
in protective covering.

Blown sand had gathered in pockets chance had
formed in the coverings of the skimmers. Andas
thought that good evidence that they had not been
used for some time. Any one of the craft provided
with a unit would give him transportation.

"So it would seem that fortune runs at your shoulder, Prince," the Salariki commented. "Now, do you
just take off—and in which direction?"

"If I wait until night, the stars will give me that," Andas said with assurance. As the good luck Yolyos commented on seemed to hold, he would trust it as long as he could. "I go north from here, and once I strike the Manhani Trail, then I will know where I am in reference to the Triple Towers. But—"

He rested one hand on the skimmer he had chosen, from which Yolyos had helped him strip the protecto covering, and glanced back at the ship. Now that they were down, Elys was no longer plagued with weightlessness, but she needed water. Her body once more showed signs of that drastic dehydration. And where in all Kalli would she find any moisture?

"But—" prompted Yolyos.

"Elys, the rest of you, if you stay here—"

The Salariki did not reply, only watched Andas with those brilliant blue-green eyes as if Andas must come to some decision for himself.

Andas knew that he could invade the Triple Towers in his own fashion secretly. His training in the hidden ways was the core of that belief. But to take Grasty, Elys—though he did not feel the same way about Yolyos. Somehow the Salariki from the start had impressed him as being the one of their party well able to care for himself. Andas could go on to the Triple Towers, send back for the rest as soon as he could—

But what if he never made it? Chance had put him into this company. He owed no house loyalty to any of them. But now that the moment had come to cut loose, he hesitated. Elys on a waterless desert? He remembered how light she had been when he carried her to the pools that meant her life. And Grasty with his complaint of pain—what if he had been internally injured and his whining was more than a claim for what comforts they had?

To carry more than two would crowd the skimmer, and the future was uncertain—so uncertain he did not allow himself to think too much about it so his own fears might not weaken him.

"Do you go soon?" He had not realized how long that pause had been until the Salariki asked a second question.

"Choose!" Andas rounded on Yolyos. Let them make the choice, each one of them; then the future would be as much of their own bargaining as it was of his. "Stay with the ship, or come with me."

"And them?"

"Let them do likewise."

"Good enough," the Salariki agreed. "Though we may hang like deter weights about you in the future."

"In some cases I am not certain of that," Andas answered.

So he put it to the others. There was a way to civilization out of the waste. But he was careful to lay out the fact that he was far from sure their troubles would then be over.

Elys raised herself on one elbow. Even within the short time they had been finned down here, her dehydration had grown worse. She was close to skin over small sharp bones again. Grasty nursed his paunch between his hands,

"It is a small choice," he groaned. "Stay here and die of the ache in my belly; go hence and perhaps fare as bad, if not worse. But I will go."

Elys still searched Andas's face, as if she would

read there some more hopeful sign than his words. "This is desert and no water." Her voice was weak. "I will take the chance."

It was going to be a very tight fit into the skimmer, the more so because Andas saw to rations also. But, with the coming of night, the heat, which had fitted a tight lid over the valley all day, lifted, and his guides were the stars overhead.

They lifted in the dark, Andas, a little rusty at the control, raising them in a leap that brought a harsh protest from Grasty. Then he settled the small craft into straight flight, and they winged their way north over the waste.

By dawn they had reached the scrubland that fringed the waste and spiraled down over a sluggish river, which in this season had shrunk to what was little more than a series of scummed pools. Elys must have water. Andas had grown continually more uneasy about her, though, unlike the groaning and grunting Grasty, she had asked for no aid since they had lifted her into the flier.

He brought the skimmer down on a sandbar that divided two of the drying river pools and, with Yolyos's aid, carried the now inert girl to the nearest. Using a piece of driftwood, Andas cleared off the ugly scum along the edge, and then they laid Elys in the turgid water, Andas kneeling in the stinking liquid to support her.

The cracking clay about the edge was marked with a lacework of animal tracks, but nowhere were any footprints of men to be seen. He hated to hold her in this soupy stuff, but it was all he had. She began to stir, moaned, and her eyes opened.

"Lower!" Her head twisted on his arm. "Lower!"

He hesitated. The smell and the muck of the pool were so disgusting that he did not want to obey her order. But at last he let her down so even her face was submerged in it.

Once more her recovery was quick. She wriggled from his grasp. So submerged, with the water so thick, he could not see her, though the surface was roiled with movements.

"Let her be." Yolyos caught Andas by the upper arm and pulled him out of the pool. "She knows what is best."

Andas had to accept that as he squatted on the sandbank, using that grit to rub from his body the slimy deposit the water had left. But he kept watching the pool, wondering if he should plunge back in and try to bring her to the surface even against her will.

She arose at last without his aid, her hair in dark strings about her head and shoulders, with none of the exuberance she had shown at the jungle pool on the unknown world. She spat, raking her fingers through her hair, her face betrayed her disgust at her present state.

"You could do no better," she said. "That I know. But never, do I believe, could you do worse, not even by intention. Where are we, and where do we go?" She looked around as if only now was she aware the ship was not standing by. "Where is the ship?"

"Back in the desert," Andas answered. He was suddenly very tired, wanting nothing so much as to rest. "We are on our way to the Triple Towers."

"I have been thinking." Yolyos looked up the fast-drying river. "Are those mountains?"

Andas followed the pointing finger westward.

"A spur of the Kanghali." At least he knew that much.

"There might be more water closer to them. A better place to camp? Or do you intend to keep on by day?"

Andas shook his head. If they were lucky, very lucky, they might come in after dark. In the day the skimmer would be sighted by any patrol. But Yolyos's suggestion made sense. Elys needed water, certainly a better supply than she had just dragged herself out of. And closer to the mountains they would find that.

"Yes." He did not elaborate on his agreement. They climbed back into the skimmer, Elys sitting stiffly as if she hated the very liquid that had restored her to life, and then they took off along the river westward.

By the time the sun was mid-point in the east over the horizon, they had emerged into a green land where trees stood and there was more water in the river, running with some semblance of current before the heat of the waste attacked it. In the foothills they found what they wanted, a curve of open land where the river made an arc and they could set the skimmer down.

Elys was out of its confinement before either Andas or Yolyos could move. She ran straight for the water, plunging in with a cry of joy that reached them like the call of a bird. Then she was gone, and they left her to her own devices.

She returned much later to pick up the E-ration tube that was her share of their meal, the traces of her ducking in the desert pool washed away, her spirits once more high. Grasty, on the other hand, lay in the shade the skimmer offered and grunted when anyone spoke to him, refusing food but drinking avidly from the mug Andas filled at the stream edge and offered to him. Here the free running water was chill from the mountain heights and clear so that one could see the bed sand where small things scuttled around stones or hid in burrows excavated in the clay.

They slept in turns, Elys, Yolyos, and Andas sharing watches, knowing that they could not get Grasty to aid. They waited until the twilight was well advanced before they took off again.

"You have in mind some landing place?" Yolyos asked. "I think you must want one as secluded as possible."

"The Triple Towers are built on the west bank of the Zambassi. They can be reached from Ictio only by triple bridges, one for each tower. By land, that is. On the west there is a ring of forts and outer walls. It is forbidden to fly over the royal grounds. However, if one comes in near to roof level at a point between the Koli and Kala forts, then one can set down in the section I told you of, the quarters that were once my father's. Unless there have been drastic changes in the palace, that is one of the long deserted portions with no regular inhabitants. I need only to set foot there—"

He did not continue. With Yolyos he could share the secrets of the Triple Towers. And—he might almost have also spoken of them before Elys. But Grasty he did not trust.

"What do we do?" Elys asked.

"Stay hidden. This portion of the Triple Towers is—or was—uninhabited. A man might live for a year without being found if he did not wish it."

"But you speak of a palace—is that not so?" she questioned.

"It has been added to, built on and about, for so long that all of it has not been in use for generations. The courts facing the three bridges, the traditional ones of the Emperor, the Empress, their suites, and those granted to members of the royal clan houses, are in use and have been since they were built, nearly a thousand years ago. Some of the rest were constructed for pleasure at certain seasons of the year, deserted in between. Others housed secondary wives when it was necessary for the Emperor to keep the peace by choosing mates from each of the military clans. More arose merely because some emperor was fascinated by a new form of building and wished to have an example.

"When Asaph the Second went traveling through the Fourth Sector, he gathered artists and architects as one would pick luden berries in the river woods. He set them to work to duplicate in miniature buildings on their home worlds that had taken his fancy. And before he was assassinated, ten years after his return, at least five were finished. The others, still incomplete, were abandoned. Those are now largely shunned.

"So the Triple Towers is like a great city in itself, a city in which perhaps only three out of five wards are inhabited. If we can land where I hope, we shall have our choice of hiding places."

"Hiding places!" Grasty cut in. "What of your big promises, Prince, to return us to our own worlds? What lies here that you must hide from or keep us concealed from? I think that you have not been frank with us if we must skulk in ruins in your own palace."

"If an android has taken my place," Andas pointed out, "what would it profit me—or you—to go charging in without caution. I give you all the safety I can while I make sure of what has happened in my absence." He did not add that his main fear now was just how long that absence had been. If the term of years was what it seemed at their comparing of dates—well, it was long enough to bring about a whole change of government. Surely his grandfather would long since have died. But who wore the crown of Balkis-Candace, the cloak of Ugana fur, and carried the pointless sword of Imperial justice?

The skimmer had left the foothills. Beneath them showed the wink of lights, in clusters to mark towns, singly for farms and villas. He had the power up to full speed, knowing he must reach his goal before the first graying of the dawn sky. And in so close to the palace, there would be no safe hiding place to wait for another night.

Andas picked up several reference points and knew now he was on the right course. He began to lose altitude. There would come a moment he must choose correctly, shut off the propulsion unit of the skimmer, and swoop in all the silence possible over that one strip of wall, and he mistrusted his own judgment so that now he was tense and stiff, his hands on the controls. The light glare in the sky ahead marked both the palace and Ictio on the other side of the river. Andas could count the beading of forts along the wall.

Down, down—cut speed—slacken—slacken—

He nursed the controls inch by inch, then cut off the power entirely. They swept between the two forts, over the wall, probably with hardly a handbreadth between them and it. Were they lucky, or had their passing been sighted by a sentry? There was nothing Andas could do now about that. If they could get down before any search party was out, they still had an excellent chance of playing a successful game of hide and seek. He could, in a last extremity, take them all into the passages.

Now he still had the engine off, but he dared to snap on the hover ray. Without the buildup of engine power it would not last long, just enough to cushion their descent. A loom of pallid white—Andas cut the hover and brought the skimmer to earth.

Its tail caught with a crackle, which sounded like a roll of doom drums. The light craft overbalanced and skidded ahead on its nose. Andas slammed the protecto, and its frothy jell squirted out about their bodies, thickening instantly as it met the air. By the time they had stopped, they were encased well enough to spare them more than a few bruises.

It took Andas a moment or two to realize that they had made it. And then the memory of the crash noise set him at the hatch. Surely that must have been heard in the watch towers. They would have to get under cover and fast. He half tumbled into the open and then turned to help, pull, and urge the others after him.

The skimmer, like one of the water insects it resembled, though giant-sized, was tilted forward on its nose, its battered tail upflung, looking as if it had been met in midflight by a blow from some fan of ceremony. It had earthed just where he had planned—in the Court of Seven Draks, though whether that was its rightful name he never knew. As a small boy he had called it that because of the fearsome drak statues that crowned the pillars at one end. This was one of the unfinished building enterprises of Asaph's planning—consisting mainly now of only a smooth pavement of some treated stone that resisted the passage of time.

From here Andas knew well the way into the maze he defied any guardsmen to unravel. Of course, he had not meant to crack up the skimmer. But among all the various kinds of ill fortune that might have attended them this night, that was far less than most.

"Come on!" he urged them. "We must get away from here as quickly as we can."

-7-

"Where do you take us? This is dark and smells of old evils!" Elys stood, her feet firmly planted, a little away from the opening, which was a narrow slit that Andas had just opened, thankful his memory served him so well.

"Old evils," the girl repeated. "I do not go in there!"

Before any of them could move, she drew out of reach, flitting across the bare room into which Andas had guided them, her form alternately revealed in the moonlight through the windows and hidden in the shadows between.

"Elys!" He would have taken off after her. Yolyos caught his arm.

"Leave her to me." The Salariki's voice was the throat rumble of a hunting feline. "I will see to her. There are other hiding places here beside your hidden ways. And the sooner you learn what rights you may have, the better. I shall watch Elys and Grasty. Return here when you can."

Andas wanted nothing more than to do as Yolyos urged, yet he felt a responsibility for the others. And when he did not move, the Salariki gave him a push.

"Go! I swear by the Black Fangs of the Red Gorp of Spal, I shall see to them."

With an inward sigh of relief, Andas surrendered. But before he left, he made sure that the other understood how to open the door panel. Then if danger threatened, he could, with his charges, take to the hidden ways. Andas went in, the panels slipped into place, and he was in the dark.

Always before he had carried a torch. But there had been times when, under his father's instructions, he had snapped it off and learned to advance a few steps at a time, trying to train other senses to serve him. One developed a guide sense through practice. And this part of the ruins held no unpleasant surprises.

Still he advanced with extreme caution, one hand running fingertips along the surface of the wall. Three side passages he passed, counting each in a whisper. At the fourth he turned into the new way. He should be passing now from the long deserted portion of the palace that had been erected at Asaph's orders, approaching the section in general use in his time.

In his time? How far back was that? But he must not think of that now. It could even be that while in prison their memories had been tampered with to confuse the issue should they, as they had, escape.

Far ahead he saw a very faint spot of light. Toward that Andas crept, fighting down his desire to rush heedlessly to that spy hole. He sniffed. There was a scent here now, one strong enough to battle the dank smell of the ways. Flowers?

He reached the spy hole and flattened himself to the wall to get the widest view possible of what lay beyond. It was easy to see where that scent came from. This was a bedchamber, and the floor had an overcarpeting of scented flowers and herbs fresh laid. Also the handles of several spice warmers protruded from under the bedcovers, which had been drawn up over them to contain their scented vapors.

By twisting and turning against the wall, Andas was able to get a partial view of the rest of the room's splendors. The ceiling, of which he could see only a palm's breadth, was studded with golden stars against the pale green that was Inyanga's sky tint on the fairest of days, while the floor under the herbs and flowers was a mosaic of bright color. The lower part of the wall was also a jeweled mosaic, and he focused on that. There was a line of figures in that company, all wearing dress of state. He could see four, and there was an empty space beyond the last of those as if the mural was not yet complete.

But there was no mistaking the robed and crowned man he faced the most directly. His grandfather's harshly carven features were set in the impersonal stare that was the formal "face" worn at audiences. And next to him was another—two others.

Standing on equality with the Emperor Akrama was another wearing the state diadem and robe, plainly his successor. Successor! But Akrama—dead! Andas's teeth closed painfully upon his lower lip.

If there was a new emperor—who? The face in the mosaic was familiar—he must know him—but it was not that of Anakue, Jassar, or Yuor. He could not set name to him.

A little beyond and lower than that unknown was the third portrait, this of a girl, plainly one of the Wearers of the Purple, undoubtedly a First Daughter. But her face was strange to Andas.

There was no one in the room, he could see, and he was fumbling for the release of the panel door on this side when he heard voices. The great empear shell and silver door opened, and two women, wearing the green and white of ladies of the inner chambers, backed into the room, bowing low before a third.

The newcomer was the woman whose face was pictured on the wall, save that it was not now set in the awesome, stiff pose demanded by Imperial art. She looked much younger and more human than her portrait. Her hair, like that of her attendants, was completely hidden beneath a tall, bejeweled diadem from which fine chains depended to take some of the weight of massive earrings. Her robe was of the Imperial purple much overlaid with jeweled embroidery until it made such a stiff encasing for her body that she moved very slowly under its weight.

Involuntarily Andas's shoulders twitched. He remembered only too well the weight of such garments and the way they plagued one through the long hours of some ultra-boring court ceremony. She must be glad to be in her inner chamber, able to free herself of that regalia.

She stood statue-like, stiff as her portrait, as the two ladies struggled with clasps and ties until they could bear away that robe. In her soft undergarment she looked again younger. And she continued to wait patiently as they bestowed the robe somewhere beyond Andas's line of vision and returned to take her crown. Then she raised her hands to her head and stripped off with a quick pull the tight net that had bound down her hair, allowing its wiry, curling lengths to puff up from her skull.

With the overshadowing of the crown gone, Andas could better see her features. She was no real beauty, yet there was that about her that drew a man's eyes.

"The Presence wishes—?" One of the ladies fell upon her knees, holding out a tray bearing a crystal goblet filled with a pale pink frothy drink.

The girl shook her head. "I have supped, I have drunk, past the point of feeling comfortable. One eats to forget the speeches of those who have nothing to say but recite it in a never-ending circling—" She stretched her arms wide. "Duse of the Golden Lips, how those trappings wear upon one! I think that some day when they are taken off, there will be nothing left of me but bare bone. You may go, Jacamada. Wait a little before you send my night maids. I need a moment to rest—"

"As the Presence wishes, so shall it be," intoned the lady.

Andas moved impatiently. How it all came back—this smothering life of the Triple Towers! One might speak freely—a little—as this princess had just done. But the answers from all—save a tiny number of equal rank—would never be more than the formalities frozen into a set court speech by centuries of custom. Soon he would have no more freedom, perhaps even less than she whom he watched.

If this chamber was that of one of the Imperial

princesses, he must now be on the outskirts of the
Flower Courts. Yet his memories of the inner ways
could not be that far wrong. This section of rooms
had not been in use before. They were—he probed
memory—yes, this was the court of Empress Alaha,
who had been first wife to Emperor Amurak a hundred
years ago.

Empress? No, the lady had addressed her as "Presence," which was not a ruler's title. It was safer to
assume she was First Daughter. He was trying to
imagine their relationship when he saw that she was
staring at the panel behind which he stood.

"Creeper—spy!" Her voice was cutting with its cold
anger. "Carry what tales you will, but remember two
can play at this game. And remember this also—I
have a way of knowing when you watch me. It is one
beyond your discernment since it comes from the hands
of the Voice of the Old Woman of Bones!"

Andas's astonishment for a moment was true awe.
Then the last name made the chill of fear touch him like
a hand of ice reaching into this stuffy confinement.

Old Woman of Bones—but how had a First Daughter in the heart of the guarded Triple Towers had
recourse to the Old Woman? Unless—dark rumors
of old, stories that had been many times told within
these walls, flowed from his memory. The Flower
Courts had their own intrigues, and sometimes death
had stalked there more ruthlessly even than in the
Emperors dungeons.

She raised her hand, drawing from the forefolds of
her robe a chain on which slid a ring. This she was
about to put on her finger, while her lips curved in
a small, secret smile.

"I do not think," she said, and the threat in her voice was open, "that you will return to your mistress with the same joy in life with which you left her—"

Because those old stories had a more potent influence on him than he would have believed, had it not been put to the test, Andas found the catch of the panel and watched the narrow slit open. He leaped out, his hands ready as if to meet an enemy.

He must prevent her using that ring, as the old tales said it could be used. She already had it halfway to her mouth. Let her breathe on it, activate it—

But she stared at him almost wildly, her gesture not completed. He was able to reach her, imprison her wrist, and twist it behind her back, using his other hand to cover her mouth lest she bring in guards with a scream.

She fought him, but he was able to pull her closer to the passage door. Now he released her hand long enough to grab at the ring. It was a tight fit on her finger, and he could not get it free as she battled him. Once more he tightened his hold until she could only get her breath in half-sobbing gasps.

For a moment he held her so; then she spoke.

"You have doomed yourself to the ultimate death, laying hands upon the person of the First Daughter." Her voice was calm, almost too calm after the violence of her fight seconds earlier.

"I think not." He spoke for the first time. "Look to your own safety, First Daughter, for you would have loosed the power of the Bones against the Chosen of the High Throne."

She laughed. "Your wits are gone, skulker in the dark. There is no Chosen prince. I can say that in truth. I am First Daughter, without a brother, to whom my father, the Emperor, has promised the throne to share with a husband of our mutual choosing."

"And what is the Emperor's name," Andas asked then.

She looked puzzled, but she had regained her composure. When she spoke, it was not to answer his question, but as if some other subject were far more vital.

"I do not think that Angcela sent you." She looked to the ring. "No, I have strengthened the warning with her blood and hair, she not knowing. She is not behind your coming. So, who are you—and why do you creep secretly so?"

"I asked you"—Andas shook her, hoping thus to establish some authority over her long enough to get straight answers—"Who is the Emperor?"

"Andas, son of Asalin, of the House of Kastor." She studied his face, frowning. Then she asked, "My father was in Pav in his youth, but for the rest of his years he has been ever in the Triple Towers. He took no full wife before my mother, nor was it ever known—and you cannot long keep such a secret in the Flower Courts—that he ever made a lesser choice. Yet, you might be my father in his youth. Are you some secretly gotten son of his?" And her eyes blazed with what he was sure was pure hate.

"I am myself, Andas, son of Asalin." He wondered if he could convince her, and beyond her the others, that another man ruled without right. But, she was the daughter of this false Andas! How long then—Once more he shook her.

"The year—in galactic reckoning—what is the year?"

"It is 2275."

"Forty-five years—" he said, and without his realizing it, he loosed his hold. She, ready for such a chance, tore out of his hands. But he caught her quickly again.

"I do not know what you mean. If you are some ill-got son, you have no claim on the Emperor or the throne," she spat at him.

"There is no true emperor on the throne," he got out, hardly believing it himself—though it must be true, for here he was, and he did not doubt that she was telling him the truth. In other words, she was the daughter of the android who had taken his place. But could an android father children? He had no idea—many secrets could be hidden by the Emperor's will. She might be a substitute brought in to bolster up the other's claim to humanity.

"You are mad—totally mad!" She had lost most of her assurance and began to struggle again.

"There is no Emperor Andas because I am Andas—kidnaped and hidden."

Her mouth twisted. "Have you looked into a mirror? You are a youth. My father is a man who has already had one renew-life injection. Do you think he could have deceived the medics then? You are the android—and mad in the bargain! Though the ring does not warn me, this must be some trick of Angcela's. She wants the crown so much that it has become food and drink, and she will die without it! But in you she has an imperfect tool."

Andas hardly heard her. The court intrigues she

mouthed about meant nothing. What did was that long
tale of years he could not account for—the fact that
here on Inyanga an Andas sat in power—an emperor
who was—who must be—an android! Yet, had the stass
at the prison kept him young? And if the Emperor
had had an age-arrest injection, why the medics should
know they were dealing with an android—

"I am not," he said dully.

He did not see the spark flare in her eyes. She
watched him now with a small cruel smile, like that
she had worn earlier when she had detected him in
hiding.

"Do you still doubt it? Come then, prove it! Look
into the mirror yonder and tell me truly that you are
an aging man. Come!"

She pulled at him, and hardly knowing why, he
came with her to stand before a tall mirror, which
reflected all before it with pitiless clarity.

There he stood, not quite as he had seen himself
in the past, for the torn and stained coverall was far
different from the clothes he had last worn when he
looked at himself so. But he was as he had always
been, his brown face thin, with the high bridged nose
of the royal clans, his hair springing on his head like
a dusky halo, dark eyes, teeth that shone the whiter
against his skin. On his forehead was the delicate tat-
too of the Imperial house—the Serpent of Dambo, a
crown he could never erase in his lifetime.

She stood close beside him, for he still had wit
enough to hold her beringed hand. And in this mirror
she was a slighter, more fragile copy of himself. She
could have been his sister, the relationship closely
marked—he had to admit that. Though with the

royal clans so intermated in the past, such a resemblance could well exist. Only, she was the Emperor's
daughter—that he was forced to accept. The daughter
of an emperor Andas who was not he.

He could see her in the mirror as plainly as he saw
himself. She had lost that teasing smile that promised
ill. In fact, she had changed somewhat.

"You—you are like my father in the tri-dees taken
of his coronation. You are like—too like! What sorcery
has Angcela brought into being?"

She tugged to free her hand and bent her head to
raise that ominous ring to her lips. But he held it to
him so he could see it the better. The setting was a
round stone with a heart of coiling light. Then the
light changed and made a shadow face, which grew
stronger, sharper.

"Anakue!" He hailed that tiny portrait.

The girl stared at him as if she were frightened
at last.

"Anakue the traitor! But—how comes he? I did
not summon—and he was long dead before my
birthing."

"When did he die?"

She still stared at the ring and did not answer.

"I said," Andas demanded sharply, "when did he
die?"

"When—when my father was made Chosen. He
tried to kill him. There was much trouble, and Anakue
and several of the nobles were executed. My father,
he uncovered the plot, and Anakue tried to claim that
he wanted to kill the Emperor. But no one believed
that, for my father could prove his loyalty."

The planted android—had Anakue been behind

that? But if he were the android—Andas shook his head. It was like being caught in a fog.

"Why did he show in the ring?" the girl continued. "I did not summon him! Was it because you held my hand and looked within? But the ring was not sealed to you! I saw Rixissa draw it from the fire heart, and she sealed it to me only. And you are a man, so cannot serve the Old Woman more than as a slave."

"Which you would have made me, had I let you," he said grimly. "Now—what is your name?"

"Abena, as you must well know. Yes, I would have in-tied you with the ring. It warned me that I was spied upon. I could have made you my tool against Angcela."

"I do not know who this Angcela is, and I am no servant of hers. What I am—well, that I must prove. And, Abena, this is now necessary."

His free hand rose and pressed a spot in her throat. She had no time for protest, and he caught her before she slipped to the floor. He brought her to the bed, turned back the covers, and pulled out the spicers, laying her in their place. And he lingered long enough to work that ring from her finger. He could not take her with him through the runways, but he made sure of her strongest weapon against him.

There was one way of proving, at least to himself, that he was who he claimed to be. If he were not of the authentic blood, or if he had not undergone, before his grandfather's eyes, the first of the Three Ceremonies, he could not hope to lay hands upon what he now sought. But the very fact that he could find it, hold it, would be an argument to prove his tale.

But, now he needed light. Fearing any moment to hear the scratch of a maid's warn stick on the door, he toured the room, finding what he sought in one of the window seats. They were deep enough to provide a slender set of shelves against the frames, enough to hold tri-dee tapes. And there was a small porto light there also, clumsy for a hand torch but usable.

Andas had sealed the ring into a seam pocket of his coverall. Nobody was going to see it much longer. There were a couple of wells down which it could be sent to oblivion. He paused for a moment by the bed. As she lay there, the princess looked very young and innocent. Yet the fact that she knew how to use the ring meant she had ability to draw on deep and dark knowledge that most men loathed and few women had courage to claim for their own.

Andas got back into the hidden passage and snapped the panel shut behind him. He might have a very limited time to reach what he sought—so the sooner he was on his way, the better. So far he had come by a roundabout way. Now he must seize the chance on a passage that led into the heart of the Towers—the private quarters of the Emperor. And there was no telling about the ways there—maybe the Emperor knew them.

He switched the lamp on low. If the Emperor was the android, then he must have been provided with Andas's memories—which meant that he would know all about the exploration of these ways in the old days. So he would be prepared, once he had heard Abena's story, to hunt Andas through the very passages he had confidently trusted to hide him. He could even set up ambushes!

The only deterrent to the android against putting the guard in the passages as hunting hounds would be that too many secrets would be so revealed. But what that might mean in the future had no bearing on the present. Andas had to find the Emperor's chamber as soon as he could, and he only hoped that his memory was correct.

He began to count side passages, three, four—it was the sixth one that he wanted. Yes, it was here, five almost wall to wall with six. That gave onto a flight of stairs where dampness oozed. And there was a dank smell of—what had Elys called it—evil! Yes, if evil had a smell of its own, this was where one could well find it. There had been death walking these narrow ways through the centuries before him.

Andas counted twenty steps, and then the passage leveled off. But there were slime tracks on the walls here. They glistened in the lamplight. He never remembered seeing any of the things that left such traces, nor did he want to. But he dared now to turn the lamp up full strength to shine ahead.

The pavement under foot was crossed and recrossed by thicker trails of slime. He slowed his pace a little as his sandals slipped and slid. If he remembered rightly, this was the worst section of the way, for it ran under the moat pond that surrounded the Emperor's pavilion.

Steps ahead, going up now. He turned the lamp back to low and climbed. It was like progressing out of the foul air of a swamp, for here the walls were drier, and now and then there was actually a whiff of incense or herbs wafting through the spy holes along this passage. But Andas did not pause at any of those holes. Time was important, and what he sought was at the very end of this way.

-8-

He must reach the bedroom of the Emperor, and if
it were occupied— In his day (Andas found himself
now separating past from present) there had always
been guards in the outer chamber. But the Emperor
was usually alone, even though on two sides of the
pavilion wide vista windows opened on the Garden of
Ankikas. And there were, according to custom also,
small night lights made fast to the trees out there,
illuminating moss and flowers. In addition, when the
Emperor pleased, a transparent landscape could be
thrown by concealed tri-dees on the walls, off-world
scenes. Andas recalled more details as he sped along
until at last he faced the wall where there was no
spy hole but which should contain a small pattern
of depressions.

Press—three together, then three more, then four.
A band of light outlined a door panel. But opened
no more than thumb's width. He worked his fingers

into that and exerted his strength against an ancient and apparently long-unused latch.

There was a sound, a dismal grating that froze him for an instant. But it heralded the giving way of the obstruction. The panel slid open, and he looked into the room. He more than half expected to front a blaster or else the ceremonial dagger worn by all of noble rank. There were too many times in the past when emperors had been trapped, even in their own quarters. He was a little surprised the panel opened at all. If this false Andas had his memories, he would have known about this entrance.

Luck favored him again. The room, under the soft radiance of lamps set on shoulder-high pedestals around the wall, was empty. Andas wasted no time in crossing to where there was on the wall a great mask, impressive in its solemn beauty. Three times life size, it was supposed to be the representation of Akmedu, the first emperor, he of the House of Burdo, who legend said was more than human, having great knowledge, daring even to go against the Old Woman—thus making Inyanga a world free of her bloodstained shrines.

Andas paused, looking up into those wide-set eyes, so fashioned that they lived and held his gaze with theirs, as if there were indeed a spirit yet imprisoned behind the great bronzed metal face. The full lips were curved in a very faint smile, as if what those eyes looked upon provided lazy amusement.

He brought up both hands in the salute for one facing his overlord.

"Rider of the Storm Winds, Bearer of the Whip of Ten Lightnings, Judge of Men." His head turned from right to left and back again. "He who is sought but comes only at his own will, who is desired but does not desire, who stands tall in the shadows watching those who follow in his footsteps, though their feet fill not the prints left by his mighty boots.

"He who is one with the sun, with the rain, with the cold, with the dark, with all that comes to Inyanga—look upon me, who am of royal blood, who has come here to undo a wrong, who needs that which lies in secret waiting—"

Once more Andas raised his hands as if to shield his face and his eyes from some awesome glare. And so he stood for as long as a man might count ten. Then he moved closer to the wall. There was directly below the mask a table of polished black-heart, and set into its top were various symbols in the red ivory of nurwall teeth. At mid-point there was a censer of gold from which now curled a wisp of scented smoke.

Facing him, as if to threaten, there lay on either side of that censer a weapon. Both were very old, treasures no man might touch, save after certain rites and ceremonies had been performed, for they were, according to tradition, those that Akmedu himself had carried. One was a dagger of ceremony, its blade concealed in a gemmed sheath. The other, to Andas's right, was a blaster, of a type so old that he thought its like might not now be found anywhere else in the galaxy.

But the weapons were not what he sought. It was what they and the mask symbolically guarded—that which was death for a lesser man than the Emperor or his rightful heir to lay finger on.

Raising both hands to the mask, leaning at an angle

across the table, Andas pressed his thumbs as forcibly as he could to the corners of that faintly smiling mouth. And though the mask appeared to be cast in a single unmovable piece, the mouth slowly opened. Between the lips protruded what he wanted. But again it was a case of using force on a long-untried spring. He pushed with all his strength, stretched as he was in that awkward position.

The mouth opened farther. What it held safe through the years fell with a metallic tinkle to the surface of the table, just missing the lid of the censer. Andas, with a sigh of relief, reached for what the mouth had disgorged.

He saw a key as long as the palm of his hand. The wards were intricate, the shaft a plain bar ending in curiously wrought combinations of symbols, so curled and embedded together that it would take much time and the searching eye of an expert in cyrmic script to translate, though Andas himself knew their message.

This was the heart of the empire. What it unlocked—that was not here but in the great temple of Akmedu's Shadow. Only two men had the right to hold and use the key—one was the Emperor, the other his heir.

It lay before him. Andas wiped his hands nervously back and forth across the front of his dingy coverall. He believed he had the right—he must! But to take it up would in reality prove whether he did or not. Otherwise, there would be vengeance, dealt by something above and beyond any justice of humankind. So it had happened in the historic past—there was even a visual record of such punishment.

But, he knew! If his grandfather was dead, then

there was no rightful emperor but Andas Kastor, and
he was Andas. He picked up the key. It was cold
and hard in his hand, feeling no different from any
other piece of metal. No lightnings flashed; the mask
did not denounce him with a wail of sacrilege. So,
he was Andas!

He was alive with triumph, perhaps too much so,
for he did not hear the sound until too late to retreat.
The man who had entered the room was now between
him and the panel exit. For the second time Andas
reached to the table top. He held the key in his right
hand, but his left closed about the ancient blaster.

It was like facing a strange, half-blurred reflection
in the mirror. He should have been prepared for
this after what he had learned from Abena. But it is
given to very few men, if any, to see themselves as
they would be after a long toll of years has passed.
Rejuvenation had worked in that the man facing him
was apparently in the prime of life. But his eyes were
weary and older than the face framing them. Now
Andas saw those eyes widen a little, though otherwise
the other showed no surprise.

"So"—his voice was low, almost toneless—"after all
these years Anakue is proven right. And we thought
he raved."

Andas had aimed the blaster. Its charge might
be long since exhausted. That it would even fire he
had no reassurance, but it was the only weapon to
hand. He moved along the table cautiously, always
watching the man by the bed. He hoped to get the
other to move with him and so force him away from
that line of escape. But the false emperor remained
where he was.

"Clever—" When Andas did not answer, the Emperor stood with his head a little to one side, studying the intruder with growing curiosity. "Very clever indeed. They were artists, those Mengians. Lucky indeed that Anakue cracked and betrayed it all so we could clean them out. Or did we?" His eyes narrowed a little. "You are here, and you must have been decanted somewhere. But why a replacement years out of date? I am no boy. They could not even enthrone you by claiming some miracle of rejuvenation—my basic pattern is in too many files. Now, what did you come for—or were sent for?"

"To take my throne." Andas refused to believe in that flood of words. Of course, this usurper would claim to be the rightful Andas Kastor. And apparently he had had years to build that claim into almost certainty. He had everything but what Andas held now in his right hand!

"Your throne?" The false emperor laughed. "Android doubles have no thrones—in fact, they are outlawed since the Mengian plot was uncovered during Anakue's abortive rebellion. Whoever started you on this wild venture must be mad."

"No one started me." Andas had reached the side of the bed now, but he must win around its wide expanse to reach the panel, and the other had not moved. "I am Andas Kastor. This is rightfully mine as you know—android!"

"Android? Did they program you to believe you were real then, half-man? Where did you come from?"

"Where? In the prison where you had us all kept in stass."

"Keep him talking," Andas thought. Perhaps, just

perhaps, he could hold the other's interest long enough
to make a rush. He did not trust the weapon in his
hand to fire, but there was a trick in which it could
be used.

"Us all? By the teeth of Gat, do you mean there
are more? How many Andases did they have with
which to inundate our poor empire?"

"I was not the only one of importance kidnaped.
There were others—from other worlds."

"Keep him talking!" Andas could not see that the
other had relaxed any of his air of vigilance, but there
was always a chance.

"We always thought that could be true"—the
Emperor nodded—"though the Mengians followed
their usual method of destroying their records when
threatened. But perhaps we did not get their headquarters after all since they must have had you
and these 'others' filed somewhere. But I don't
see what moved them to loose you all so late and
uselessly."

"They did not release us—we escaped." That he
was telling their story did not matter as long as he
could keep the false emperor from summoning the
guards.

"That explains it." Again the other nodded. "Well,
it is a pity that—"

"That what?" Andas held up his right hand, the
thumb across the shaft of the key against his palm,
so the other could see what he held. "That you
should be unmasked at last, android? Do you think
that anyone save him who I truly am could hold
this—and live? You know the precautions—"

The other stood very still. It was as if the sight of

the key had turned him into a statue after the nature of sorcery in the old legends. Then his lips shaped a word Andas read rather than heard.

"That!"

"Yes, that! I have it as my right."

"You are—it is impossible!" The surface of the other's calm cracked. "It is totally impossible! I am human, as has been proven many times over. Why, I have children—three daughters. Can an android breed?"

Andas smiled bleakly. "We have been told not—but by an emperor's orders children could be substituted or otherwise arranged for. We both know that in the Triple Towers there is only one law—the will of him who has the right to this!" Once more he held up the key.

"Now, call your guards if you wish. Let them see me—with the key!"

"I have guards the sight of that will not affect. Times have changed since the days of my youth. If you have been in stass, you have not been lately briefed."

His hand raised, and Andas did not try to aim the weapon he held. Instead, he threw it in a way he had learned at Pav from a mountaineer of the Umbangai. It struck the other between the eyes, and he staggered back and went down. However, he had not been rendered unconscious, but was struggling up again when Andas was on him. This time he applied nerve pressure that kept the other limp until he had him bound into a chair.

"Now"—Andas went to the open panel—"tell your guards when they come to hunt if they will. But what I hold is the heart of the empire, and I take it with me. If I fail, I shall make sure that it does not reach you again. And I shall assert my claim where it can be seen by all, in the temple of Akmedu." Then he thought of something else. With his left hand he felt for a seam pocket and brought out the ring he had taken from Abena.

"You boast of daughters, Emperor who has no right to be. You have a First one—Abena—is that not so?"

He had not gagged the other, yet he did not answer, only watched him, his eyes filled with an emotion Andas could not read. It was not hate as lie first thought, but something darker still.

"Look you at what she threatened me with, Lord of Five Suns and Ten Moons." Mockingly he used the archaic address of the court. "A ring of the Old Woman. So it would seem that filth has once more bespattered the court. A like daughter for a false lord!"

"Not so—"

"Would you see it closer to make sure? Look then!" Andas felt so much the master of the field that he took three swift strides so that he could hold out the ring at the height of the Emperor's eyes, close enough for him to make sure it was as Andas reported.

"No male can wear this, but it was against her breast when she brought it forth against me. What now of your First Daughter? Though I shall see this does not serve her again. But once one deals with the Old Woman, there is no retreat before death—or after. So, I leave you to think on that also, android, during the short time left you—"

He never finished the sentence. The wide door of the chamber opened without warning, and only his reflexes saved him, for the thing that came scuttling in was a robot, and it aimed a cloud of vapor at him.

Andas jerked back, coughing, his eyes smarting as the edge of the mist touched him. His head whirled dizzily, but he made it to the panel. And, thank the five powers of Akmedu, it snapped shut under his frantic shove. He was still coughing, reeling, not sure how long he could keep his feet, but he forced himself along back down the passage. The false emperor, if he carried all Andas's memories, could comb him out. He would have to fog his trail as well as the robot had almost fogged him! And right now he was sure of nothing, save that he had made it into the ways, that in one hand he held the key and in the other the ring. The latter he fumbled quickly back into his seam pocket. The less he had to do with it, the better.

How had he avoided the robot's attack? It would—it did—seem impossible now that he considered it, unless it was true, that other old legend, that he who rightfully carried the key had for the space that it was in his possession the strength of Akmedu!

But powers of the unseen, while they might be potent enough in the right time and place, were not to be depended upon. By all accounts they acted erratically and sometimes even turned against believers who strove to use them. He put no faith in the key except that it would do for him exactly what he planned, prove that he alone had the right to bear it into the temple and use it to unlock the secret there. And if he lived through the next few hours, when he was sure that the false emperor would exert every effort to take him, that was just what he was going to do.

The lamp—what had he done with the lamp? He could not remember now, and there was no time to return and hunt for it. But that meant he must slow his pace, not take a headlong tumble down those stairs at the under-moat section. And it was very hard to slow when every bit of him drove ahead. He must keep alive and out of captivity until he could reach the temple and prove his identity.

Beyond that he did not think. Steps—yes, he had reached the underwater way. He shrank from allowing his fingers to slide along the wall, for they crossed those trails of slime, and he had to center his will on keeping touch in spite of such defilement. He wished he had paced off this dank section and knew by counting where he was and how far he had to go. The smell, dark, and slime seemed to last forever.

Then, steps again, and with them a lift of spirit. He had the key pressed tight against him. Though its cold metal never seemed to warm any in his grasp, yet it was to his spirit now what a lamp could have been for his body. The last step—he was in a corridor comparatively free of the moat section's taint.

He had time now to think coherently, if that whiff of vapor had not left him dull-witted. To return the same way he had come would be the rankest folly. The princess might already have started the hunt. So there remained a long detour, and of all its windings he was not sure.

If only he had not the responsibility for the others, was free to pick his own route, retire into one of the more hidden ways! But if the false emperor had been schooled with all his memories— How had they accomplished this recall for their android anyway?

They must have kidnaped him first, put him in two-com—though that was risky. But it did not matter how they had done it, only that it had been done. And he could not hope to have a secret that grinning non-man back there did not share.

So, his own choice was to weave a wild pattern that would eventually bring him to the Court of the Seven Draks and those he had left. How had they fared? The hunt must have started after the crash of the skimmer. But somehow he believed that if any being could escape the guard, it would be Yolyos, though burdened with Grasty and the girl. Well, they would have to take their chances, just as he was doing.

He had had an amazing run of luck. Not that he dared build on that. Only a fool believed that fortune always turned a bright face in his direction. Count now—

He tried to make better time, but still he had to count passage openings. And he slipped into one that took him at an abrupt angle from the corridor of the princess's room. Andas cursed the loss of the lamp until he was aware of that strange little gleam from the front of his coverall. His fingers probed and found the ring.

What—? He pulled it out of hiding and was answered by a heightened glow—perhaps no greater than that of the songul's lower wing at mating time. It was nothing he could really see by, yet it heartened him. He dared not slip it on his finger—it was too charged with all he had been taught to fear from earliest childhood. Yet neither did he put it back into hiding, but held it before him between thumb and

forefinger as if it were a lamp and could give him
the sight he needed.

There was a forking of the ways at sharp angles.
Andas hesitated and then chose left. It was hard to
think of what lay above the surface and translate that
into what portion of the assemblage of buildings he
might be heading for. His only guide was memory.
This might almost be the maze in the Garden of
Scented Fronds. If one continued to choose always
the left path, it would eventually bring him out close
to the Court of the Seven Draks.

Andas had made his fourth such turn when he
stopped short and forced his breath to the lightest
possible in and out flow as he listened. No, he had
not been mistaken—sounds! Andas knew of old that
such carried through these passages in an odd fashion, sometimes sounding farther off than they were,
sometimes reversing that process. So he could not be
sure how close the trailer was.

He thought, or rather he hoped, that there were
not robots after him. Those he feared more than
any guardsman. Men could be, with luck, fooled
by someone who knew these passages. But a robot,
perhaps set to hunt for only the faint emanations
of human body heat, would track relentlessly.

If he were at all sure of his present position, and
he clung to belief that he was, there was a chance
ahead he might have an opportunity to see his hunter
from a position that would be safe for a short time.

Andas felt along the wall carefully as he went.
But it was that so-faint gleam of the ring that served
him better than he thought could happen, for with
it he caught a glint of metal and so located the first

of those loops set deeply into the stone, intended as a skeleton ladder. He tested the first by swinging his full weight on it, though that did not mean they were all as stable.

Stowing both ring and key safely within his coverall, Andas began to climb. He was well above the second floor of the palace apartment in which this was hidden as a shaft when he thought himself safe enough to brace inside that opening and wait. No robot he knew of could climb in such a narrow way as this. And long before it could broadcast his position, he could reach the roof above and strike out in the open for a while if the need arose. Now the dark below showed a glimmer of light. A robot would not carry a lamp, nor would it trail with one—too easy to alert its quarry. Guards then, so Andas felt above him for the next hoop. Still he lingered. Guards could follow him up if they saw the rungs on the wall; guards could even aim a stunner up this vent and bring him down helplessly without exerting any trouble. Guards could—

The light of the torch was very dim, yet to one who had moved through the utter dark of the ways it was bright enough. If the one who bore it was alone, Andas could leap down behind him, knock him out, and take that torch and the weapons he must be carrying. The plan built in his mind as a mason would set stone to stone for a wall, though anyone coming on this hunt alone would be a fool—unless he was playing bait—

Only one half-seen figure passed below. And the more he thought, the more desperately Andas wanted the torch and the weapons the other had. He rested his forehead against the gritty stone of the vent side and tried to picture more clearly what lay ahead.

Yes, there were two side passages not too far beyond. And if the hunter had come too far ahead of his fellows, Andas could be on him and away, giving any who followed a choice of three different routes down which to trail him. He had not been in their hands, so they had no personna reading they could feed into a trailer to follow him exactly.

He made his decision and slid down as fast as he could. The light was still ahead. He caught glimpses of it, though it was shut off from time to time by the bulk of the man who carried it. Andas listened—and then he ran lightly forward.

His hand was already aimed for a knock-out blow when he caught better sight of the man he hunted. That was enough to blunt his blow so that he did not kill, or even stun, though he carried the other before him to the floor where they lay, the attacked struggling feebly under him.

"Yolyos!" Andas pulled back. Luckily the light, a very small hand torch, had not smashed during their fall. Andas grabbed it up and turned it full on his own face.

"Yolyos!" he repeated, hardly able to believe that the Salariki was really here.

-9-

Andas switched the light from his own face to that of the Salariki, who was holding his head, giving low growls of pain. There was a dark smear of blood just above that aggressive bristle of coarse mustache, and Yolyos's ears were flattened to his skull, his eyes narrowed to warning slits.

Then Andas noticed something else. The fur-hair on one of the alien's broad shoulders was crisped and singed, a red mark rising under the blackened stubs of hair. He had had a very narrow escape from the blaster.

"Ssss—" the sound was close to a hiss. "Sssooo I have found you, or you me, Prince. And by your welcome, you expected others." The Salariki's voice had begun with that angry hiss but became more articulate.

"The others—where are they?" Andas listened intently but could pick up no other sound.

"You might well ask. But for the fact I proved faster than he expected, I might well be cooked now."

125

"Who expected? How did you come here?"

"It is something of a tale. But do we sit here while I tell it? I think by your manner of greeting you have reason to fear other life in these wall roads."

Andas was recalled to the peril at hand. "Yes!"

He arose, the Salariki with him. But Andas had to know what had happened. If it was unwise to continue back to where he had left the others, then he must revise plans.

"You were discovered? I must be sure, for if we cannot go back to the Court of the Seven Draks—"

"The idea when I left seemed to be that you would. They have a reception party waiting. No, I should advise hastening in the other direction, any other direction!"

"Elys—Grasty?"

He heard a snarling sound from Yolyos.

"Yes, our delicate little Elys, she deliberately brought this about. I think we misjudged her as badly as if we were cubs to be netted by the first pair of eyes turned in our direction. Elys who would die without water, who was to be protected, who—"

"You might tell me what happened, or do I play a guessing game?" interrupted Andas.

"I am not quite sure myself—that is the trouble. One moment I was trying out the secret fastening that controlled the door through which you had gone. I thought it well to know how to do that quickly. The next, something struck me on the side of the head, and I was on the floor. I saw more stars for a second or two then than can be sighted in the heavens of any planet I know.

"While I was still seeing double and triple, Grasty

landed his big belly on my back, and he had a force knife to my throat before I could get my wits to working—"

"A force knife! But where did he—"

"You can well ask. Perhaps Turpyn supplied it. How can we be sure how deeply that one was concerned with our kidnaping? Or maybe that she-wyvern conjured it out of midair. Grasty was only her claw man in the matter. She made that clear.

"And what she was going to do—well, she was prepared to bargain with the guard. Had it all worked out, she was sure she could appear before them, an unarmed woman, and they would not flame first and ask questions afterward. When they gave her a chance to talk, she would tell them all about you—buy their favor so. She was very sure that you were not going to achieve anything with your own actions here, and she would gain credit with the powers in control by her play of being more or less your prisoner, ready to tell all about your invasion of their palace. If you remember, she had plenty of time on board ship alone with Grasty to work out a plan to be put into action at the first chance. And Grasty's playing injured was a part of that.

"They were both sure that whoever had put up the fortune it must have cost to get you out of circulation would be most grateful to anyone who would push you back under his claws once more. Practical and logical, that is Elys. You really have to admire her straight thinking, always accepting that her ultimate goal is the preservation and aid of her own plans."

"But you got away—"

"Yes. We heard the arrival of a guard unit. I think

they were wearing anti-grav belts and had come across the roofs. So Elys ran out into the middle of the court to meet them. She raised some very pitiful screams for help. I would have believed her—you would have too, Prince.

"Grasty is no fighting man—was, I should say. He was distracted by the action in the court. Elys was doing some splendid acting, running to throw herself at the first man to set foot down. She took a chance there. He might have turned her into a cinder, but she gauged his reaction correctly.

"By that time I had my wits back in my skull, and I took action, too. Grasty, I am sure, never tangled with a Salariki before. We have our own little tricks. At any rate, I got to my feet, his wrist in my teeth, and there was no using the force blade then. He squealed, and I was trying to knock him out when a blaster flamed us. One could see the entire beauty of Elys's plan then. She wanted to get us both burned to a crisp. Then it would be her word against yours—if you lived long enough to say anything. And who would be believed?

"However, the First Ancestress was with me. Grasty took that blast. I continued to hold him as a shield and backed into your doorway, pushed him out and slammed it, hoping they did not know the trick of its opening. I went along, I can't tell you now in which direction. But I found a box with some things in it, a large torch, which was burned out, this one, a container or two, supplies, I think. They were dusty—must have been there a long time."

"One of my father's caches. He left them so when exploring sections new to him." Andas answered. He

was still bewildered by Yolyos's story. That Elys would
so turn on them—he could hardly believe it. Yet, as
the Salariki had pointed out, her actions had a cruel
logic. And, after all, what had he known of the alien
girl? Also no one could judge an alien, or even a man
of another world, by one's own standards of conduct.
What was accepted, a matter of established custom
and moral right, on one world might be high crime
on another. Elys was undoubtedly acting according
to her own ethics. Not that that made it any more
acceptable— But what of the ring in his own possession?

What that represented was evil according to his
beliefs. Yet it had been worn and used by a woman
of his own blood. So how could he sit in judgment
on Elys? It only remained that their party had been
cut to two. And inwardly he was glad that it was the
Salariki out of their number who was left to accompany him now.

"What about you?" Yolyos asked. "I would judge
you have not been too successful if you are expecting
hunters to sniff along your trail here."

Andas hesitated. The accusation made by both Abena
and the false emperor (though there was good reason
to discount them both) gnawed at him. But he could
not be the substitute! He was alive, he felt pain, he
had to eat, sleep—he was real!

"You have learned something that has clouded
your mind."

Andas was startled at those words. How had the
other guessed? Esper? But never before had the other
given hint of esper powers. And if he had concealed
such a talent, could he otherwise be trusted? Again

Andas halted and turned to flash the lamp directly at the bloodstained face.

"You—you are esper!" He made the accusation boldly, bluntly, hoping to shock the other into the truth. But how could you surprise an esper, his common sense demanded a second later. It was impossible.

"No. We do not read minds," Yolyos told him. "We read scents—"

"Scents?" What could the alien mean?

"You know how we are addicted to our scent bags? Well, those are worn not only for the purpose of enjoyment, but they are also protective. We can scent fear, danger, anger, unease of spirit—emotions. And think you what that would mean to have always in your nostrils! You would find it hard to concentrate. So we set up our own scent screens."

"But you did not scent Elys's coming betrayal."

"No, because she was alien, more so than she looked physically. To me she was always—fish!" He brought out that last word as if he were in some way at fault for not being able to penetrate the natural defenses of the girl. "Now Grasty was so filled with fear that that overlaid everything, so with him I had no warning either.

"But you I can read, for in ways your species is not too far removed from mine. We are both mammals, though our distant ancestors were dissimilar. I have seen a creature called 'cat' on one of your trading ships and have been told that such is a more primitive example of my own line. We had a creature on Sargol—now extinct—which might have been your far-off ancestor. Your emotions are not too far different from ours, save that at times they can be

overwhelmingly strong. Any of us leaving Sargol for
other worlds, even on short visits, must undergo conditioning—just as a mind-reading esper must build up
his defenses against crowds, when the burden of their
mingled thoughts could well drive them mad.

"So, yes, I can scent that you are highly disturbed,
that it is more than just the fact you are hunted by
those who have no reason to wish you well. But if you
will not share your fear"—the Salariki made a gesture
akin to a human shrug—"that is entirely your choice."

What if they were right—but they could not be!
But should he warn Yolyos? In his own world the
Salariki might face the same accusation. If he were
prepared, he could perhaps be able to prove he was
not android as Andas would use the key as proof.

So he told the alien just what happened, that a
false emperor was Andas in this place and that his
only chance of proving the truth was to reach the
temple.

"Android." Yolyos repeated the word thoughtfully.

"But it is false! I am human! I eat, I feel pain, I
need sleep—"

"What do you know of androids?" The Salariki cut
in. "It is not a science that has ever been used on
Sargol, but I am under the impression that they were
not like robots—which we also have no liking for. Is
that not true?"

"Yes. That's why they were prohibited on most
worlds long ago. It is even against all laws to make
a robot the least bit human in construction. The first
androids were destroyed by mobs whenever they were
found. Men fear anything that can resemble them and
yet be unhuman—deathless—"

"Deathless? Yet this emperor has seemed to age in the normal fashion, has had your life-prolonging injections."

"So he says. With absolute power a man can claim many things, and there are none who can prove it is not so."

"But such a deception would have to have partners, your medics—and surely at least one woman of his inner courts, perhaps more, if he has been thought to have had children. A secret is only a secret when no one shares it. I do not think that your human households are so far removed from ours. And I know that in my clan house what is known to one woman in that respect is, less than a day later, known to most others, and within two days by their mates. Do you think that a score of people could, or would, keep such secrets here?"

Andas found himself shaking his head. No, rumor and gossip had always spread, sometimes as a dark, almost destroying wave, throughout the Triple Towers. There were wild tales told of his father (he had heard some of them whispered) merely because he lived apart. And if they could so embroider invention and get it accepted as truth, what could they do in turn with explosive facts?

There could be a cold-blooded answer—that those who did know might have sudden accidents or fatal illnesses. But only a certain number of those might ensue without raising the very rumors the Emperor was trying to avoid. Andas had to accept, whether he could believe it or not, that this Andas could not cover up a medical report.

"If"—Yolyos proceeded relentlessly—"he could not

cover these matters with a lie or by his will, then they must be true. Again I ask you, what do you know of androids? You have said that among your kind they have been regarded with aversion, that they are forbidden. So, we have a form of scientific research that is under restraint. But in the past has that ever worked successfully? Can men be kept from research, their minds turned off by orders? The Mengians Turpyn spoke of—the records that we found in that prison—would that not be the very type of forsaken, hidden place where such researches could be furthered—to higher points unknown before? Suppose that the end result of such experimentation was an android that could not be told from a normal human being?

Logic—devastating logic that he could, had to, agree to at every word! The Mengians were the heirs of the Psychocrats, and the Psychocrats were men (or emotionless superendowed likenesses of men) who admittedly knew more about the human mind and body than any scientists before or since. The remains of their autocratic experiments were so widely scattered that now, two generations after men had rebelled against their yoke in the Ninth and Tenth sectors, discoveries were constantly being made of some new facet of their planning. Yes, given the Psychocrats' resources and knowledge, and unlimited chances for research, there could have been androids that were beyond the boundaries known to history.

"If we are such—" he blurted out.

"Will we ever know?" countered Yolyos. "After hearing your tale, I do not doubt my counterpart is in action somewhere, either on Sargol or engaged on some mission off-planet even as I was at the time I can still remember.

You say that you have that which will prove your case if you can reach the place to put it to the test. This I want to see, for it may also affect my future plans. But are you sure you can reach the temple? Have you any idea where we now are?"

Andas was not surprised to have Yolyos make that challenge. They had been plodding on, the dim light of the torch picking out side passages at intervals. And how long he had been in the maze he could not have told.

He was hungry, and more than that he was thirsty. Even to think of water made him draw a dry tongue tip over drier lips. They would have to find sanctuary and both food and drink soon. And all he knew was the general direction in which he had been heading since they left the vent. Not, of course, back toward the Court of Seven Draks, but into a series of ways that, if followed to the end, would bring him to the only place he recognized as home, the pavilion that had been his father's.

"I know enough to get us—" He was beginning and then paused, for the danger in his plan was suddenly clear. They knew who he was, and knowing that—if indeed the false emperor did share all his memories— what better place to lay their trap than there? No, he could not go that way. But where then?

"To get us where?" demanded the Salariki.

Andas sighed. "I am afraid not where we have been heading. They could well be waiting for us there. There is just one place—"

He had tried to push that out of mind, but he could not. Only a very desperate and reckless man would choose that path. But certainly he was desperate enough. And when all roads but one are closed, one either fought like a hopelessly cornered beast, or one took that open road. He knew what would happen if he tried to fight. They could cook him in blaster fire, pick the key from his charred body, and no one would know who he really was. But that other way—

"You are afraid, greatly afraid now."

Andas grimaced. So he smelled of fear, did he? Well, perhaps this furred alien would also if he knew as much as Andas did. But it was the only way, and unless Inyanga had changed radically since he had last walked these ways, the false emperor was going to have a very difficult time sending anyone in there after them.

"There is a place we can go," Andas said slowly, and then decided to tell the whole of it, whether the other would believe him or not. To one who did not know history, it might sound like the most primitive superstition.

"It is the Place of No Return."

"A cheerful name, that."

"Not always does it work that way. But from the earliest records of the building of the Triple Towers, there have been notations of disappearances at that place. Sometimes—in the early years—there would be four or five in a year, or less, and then a longer time when one could go and come there without harm. It was a matter of concern, for the guards' second barracks was at one side, and there were many men there on duty. The old north gate was situated near that point.

"It made no difference who the man was—sometimes a common soldier, twice officers of high rank, and then the Prince Akos. And he was seen to go! Five men, one his bodyguard and two generals, watched him dismount and start to walk across the inner court. They saw him—then he was gone!"

"There was a search, I presume?"

Again Andas ran his tongue tip across his lips. "One that turned the Triple Towers inside out. They explored more than had been done for years. On the third night they heard the calling—"

"Calling?"

"Yes, near the place where Prince Akos had vanished. Very faint and far away, as if it came from a great distance. They brought the Emperor to hear, and the Princess Amika, Akos's wife. Both swore before the altar of Akmedu later, when the final record was made, that it was truly the prince's voice they heard. For the space of two hours he called, his voice growing fainter. And he called names that all heard—first those of the men who had been with him when he had disappeared, and then, later, that of his wife. And at last his voice faded, and they never heard him again, though the Emperor stationed a constant sentry post there for two years thereafter."

"When did this happen?"

"About two hundred years ago. The Emperor had the old records searched then and counted all such disappearances. There were almost fifty—which surprised everyone as no one had completely reckoned them all before. And when, after two years, they heard nothing, found nothing more, he had that section put under ban. They closed that north gate and erected a new one. You cannot even reach that part of the palace now except by ways such as these. And I do not think guards will follow us in."

"But you have been there?"

"Once, with my father. There is a passage that reaches the inner corner of the old barracks—running to the commander's quarters. We stood in a window there and looked down on the courtyard where the prince vanished. A storm must have struck part of the enclosing wall, for stones were scattered inward, and we could see little of the pavement."

"And what explanation did they have, these people who watched your prince disappear and heard him call?"

"The ignorant spoke of night demons and sorcery. The Emperor had all the scientists called in. There was only one explanation my father thought made sense—that perhaps there was another world, one on another plane of existence, and that at intervals there was a break between that world and this, so a man might be caught. Since then I have listened to off-world travelers, and I have heard of such. Alternate time streams are spoken of, layers of worlds in which history has taken some different turn. These, they say, may exist in bands side by side, so a man knowing how to go from one to another may travel, not backward in time, nor forward, but across it."

"A most intriguing suggestion. But since that emperor closed it off, no one has gone exploring there?"

"No. That is why we will be safe there. If we do not reappear for a while, they may even think we are caught in that invisible trap."

"Always supposing we are not! But it is within the court itself that this tricky piece of ground exists. And if we stay away from that we are safe?"

"Yes." Good common sense. Andas's spirits began

to rise. It was true that they might shelter on the
edge of danger and yet avoid it. He remembered
how the empty rooms of the barracks had spread
before him on that other visit. And there was even
a small garden beyond, which had been attached to
the commander's quarters. There was a spring-fed
pool there. Water—they would have water—and there
could even be fruit growing wild—

He quickened pace, but there was still a difficult
journey ahead. In the first place, they must pass a
dangerous portion of the ways running near to his
old living quarters, for only from there could he take
direction to the Place of No Return. Time dragged
as they made that careful circuit. When he reached a
stone-walled cell into which fed four passages, Yolyos
suddenly tapped him on the shoulder. The Salariki's
lips were very close to Andas's ear as he whispered
in a hiss.

"Someone is here. There is a stink—" His broad
head swung back and forth, his nostrils wide, sucking
in the dank air. "There!" With a foreclaw he indicated
the passage to his left.

"Can you tell how far away?" Andas murmured.
That passage soon became a flight of steps leading
to a garden house where his father had enjoyed the
night blooms of the qixita.

"It is not too strong."

They could hope then, Andas believed, that the
ambush had not been set within the passage, but
rather where an unsuspecting fugitive might emerge
into the room above. But he did not have to brave
such a meeting. He was oriented enough now to find
his way. He pointed to the opening directly ahead.

Not that this way was easy. The passage dropped deeper, at such a sharp angle that they soon had to clutch at small stones set in the walls to provide steadying handholds. When they reached the foot of that incline, they were walking again underwater, as the thick trickles on the walls told them. The passage narrowed, running now beside a conduit from which the lake above drained in rainy season. And there was a slime deposit where things that had never seen the light of day crawled and bred, while from it arose a vile odor.

Andas heard a coughing grunt from his companion and thought how much worse must be the torment for the sensitive nose of the alien. But at least their way led them along above that ooze and did not run beside it for long.

Three steps up and they were in another corridor surprisingly dry. This had one wall that was a series of bars chiseled out of the stone, with narrow slits between.

"What is that place beyond?"

"A wine cellar, or used to be—when the Crystal Pavilion was the home of the Empress dowagers. We are lucky, for all this section lies close to the old north gate."

"A wine cellar. A pity that we cannot sample some of what is stored there. I am carrying a dry throat."

"There is a garden with a spring at the old barracks," Andas promised, though he spoke with more assurance than he felt. There could be many changes with the years, and he still flinched from thinking how many years had passed since he last walked this way, though, by his own reckoning, it was not more than ten. Yet Abena had told him it was forty-five. Could she have spoken the truth?

They climbed again, Andas counting steps. Once more they were in runways with peepholes, so there might once have been reason to spy on the inhabitants here.

"Where are we going?" demanded Yolyos as they began a second climb.

"To the roof. We must reach the upper ways now. The tunnel underground is closed."

That was the one danger spot if they had guards with anti-grav belts on duty aloft. But there was no other way the fugitives would go.

-10-

They emerged on a very narrow walk of stone much bespattered by generations of bird droppings, where some spindly plants had taken root in small crevices. Their doorway had been set in the wall of a chimney, and they must walk this ledge to the end, then scramble down to the eaves, from which they could swing across to the next roof, Andas hoped.

He had lost all reckoning of day and night since he had been in the wall ways. It was now early evening. There were still sun banners in the sky at his back, giving enough light for this difficult maneuver.

Something crunched under his sandals, and he glanced down at a pile of splintered bird bones. There was no marking in the green wash of moss and plants to suggest that anything save winged creatures had come this way, but he hurried along at the best speed possible, the Salariki following effortlessly.

They slid down to the eaves, Andas expecting at any moment to be sighted by some guardsman on patrol

duty aloft. That they had escaped this long seemed
to him unbelievable, though it could be that the false
emperor, knowing what Andas carried, was wary enough
to lay nets closer to their goal. Should the key be lost,
the result would be black for the empire.

It was when they reached the eaves that Andas
knew desperation. When he had made this crossing
before, his father had carried devices he had worked
out for safety during his strange explorations. They
had shot a magnetic dart across and rigged a line to
which they had snapped safety belts before they took
the leap. He had nothing and must depend upon his
own muscles.

"We go there?" Yolyos pointed to the slightly lower
roof.

"If we can make it." Andas admitted his fear. "I
only went this way once, and then we used tackle."

The Salariki crouched, drawing his legs under him in
a position that looked almost awkward. Then he took
off with speed and precision, leaving Andas gasping,
to land gracefully on the roof ahead.

Yolyos turned to look back, his mouth a little open
so that his pointed side fangs were visible in the fading light. Fading light—Andas knew he must go now,
that he could not take that leap in the dark.

"Come on!" There was impatience in Yolyos's hissed
call, as if he believed that leap of no importance and
could not see why his companion hesitated.

Trying to summon all his self-confidence, Andas
went as far back on the cramped take-off point as he
could. Before he dared have any second thoughts, he
jumped.

Hands shot out, claws ripped into his coveralls,

and he had only an instant or two to realize that, but for the alertness of Yolyos, he could have missed his goal. Then the other drew him to safety. He crouched beside the Salariki, shaking so that he could not immediately move on.

"Where now?" Yolyos gave him no respite. Andas realized later that the Salariki had been wise in that.

He steadied himself with a hand against the parapet of the roof and tried to forget the swimming sickness in his head, to concentrate on half-remembered landmarks. They were standing on the roof of the Tower of Alikias. Here were no inner ways; they must use the regular stairway and seek the ground floor before they could return to the dark warren.

They found the trap door. It took some anxious moments to force it up. Time had settled dust about it like a corking. And by the time they were on the narrow stair within, the evening had closed into night. Andas had stopped shaking, fastening his mind on what lay before and not behind. He was sure that they had, for the moment perhaps, baffled or outrun the hunters.

Even if he and the Emperor shared a common knowledge of the hidden ways, the other was still no thought reader and could not be sure in which direction Andas would head. In fact, their present path was so far away from the ultimate goal of the temple that it might not be suspected. He hoped that the false Andas and those obeying his orders would believe that their quarry would head at the fastest possible speed for the temple. It was there that they would be setting up the most intricate of their traps.

But the longer they had to do that, the less favorable Andas's chances became. Yet his tired brain saw no other plan possible.

He was tired, fatigue weighting him down with a thick smothering—just at a time when he needed to be thinking sharply, his reflexes acute. If they could reach the walled-off place, then he could rest. He said so, and Yolyos answered, his voice a purring murmur through the dark.

"True, we are not made of metal like robots. And if we are androids, it would seem that we are also heir to the ills of our prototypes."

The air in the tower smelled of dust and faintly of animals—as if some of the long-empty rooms had been used as lairs. But they did not explore any of the chambers on the levels they passed, using the limited beams of the torch to bring them into the section just below the surface of the ground outside, where once more Andas's memory found the door to the other ways.

He set the fastest pace he could maintain, needing to find refuge where he could rest, drink, perhaps find something to ease his aching stomach. This passage ran straight, with no branching ways, until they came again to one of those very narrow stairs and started to climb. It was short, taking them up past perhaps two floors. Then Andas inserted his fingers in certain slots, having first blown the dust from them, and pulled. They stepped at last into what had been the private chambers of the guard commander in the days of the old north gate.

The windows still had protective panes, so grimed by years of neglect that one could see them only as a very vague light against the velvet dark. There were sliding inner shutters, and though the runs of these were badly rusted, they beat and hammered until they got the windows covered. Only then did Andas switch the torch on the high beam and look around.

Against one wall stood the frame of a bed, so massive that it had probably been deemed too much to be moved. Their own footprints patterned the floor, together with the tracks of small creatures that had roamed the deserted barracks at will. There was nothing else.

"You mentioned water—" Yolyos said.

"There was a garden." Andas turned his head to the west wall as if he could see through it. "When we were here last, there was a spring there. There might even be a loquat vine in fruit. They live for years without tending."

"I would suggest we test the existence of both—now."

But Andas felt a reluctance to leave this shuttered room now that he had gained it. It was as if outside the walls of this one place waited all the menaces he had fled. Only the needs of his body drove him to battle that vague sensation of brooding danger.

Below the quarters of the commander stretched halls and rooms stripped now of everything that might suggest they had once harbored companies of guards. Passing these, they came out into a space between the barracks and the inner gate—to be assaulted, not by the stale, dusty air of the deserted building, but by a wave of almost overpowering fragrance, where a vine, grown wild and assertive beyond all resistance from its fellows, had run thick cables across the ground, bushes, and

intervening trees, throttling them into dead skeletons
fit only to support its vicious luxuriance.

Great white flowers burst in clusters along its stems,
almost as if their growth was as explosive as blaster
fire. And the ground was deep with rotting layers from
past bloomings. Loquat indeed. Andas stared. He had
never seen such a wild stand of the vine.

Beneath the clusters of flowers now in bloom hung
the fruit of earlier blooming, smaller than the globes
he had known, as if the strength here had gone more
to flower than fruit. But it was ripe and ready for
eating. They could eat, but however could they batter their way through that netting of leaf and stem
to find water? He had no idea in which direction
to search, and he doubted if they could get well in
without jungle knives to clear a path.

"Water? I will find it!" Yolyos had been drawing
deep lungfuls of the scent, as if the odor, well nigh
too powerful for Andas, was as much a restorative for
him as the food and drink they sought.

"That way—" He was so confident as he went that
Andas followed him without question.

The Salariki did not rip and tear at the vines as
Andas would have done. Rather he spread and pushed
with gentleness, as if he handled something he would
not harm, turning many times to hold open a space
for his companion to squeeze through. It might be
that he disliked the thought of breaking a path more
brutally.

They had lost sight of the barracks, so deep was that
growing curtain, when they at last found the spring.
Once it had been piped in to feed a pond, but that
bowl had long ago been broken by the roots of the

vine, so that now the water gathered in a few shallow cups, trickled from one to another, and formed a stream beyond.

The water was good—how good Andas did not realize until he plunged his hands into one of the depressions again and again, bringing them cupped and dripping to his parched mouth. He had tasted wine from the Emperor's finest stock in the old days that could not compare with this.

There was a constant murmur of sound in the garden, the rubbing of vine stem against stem, blown by the night wind, the cries of insects, the gurgle of the water. But he heard also the appreciative slurping of his companion as he shared that boon of a long cool drink.

Andas had mouthed two of the tart-sweet (more tart than sweet in this wilder stage) loquat globes before he thought of what might be a serious problem for the Salariki. Though his species was omnivorous, their tastes were still strongly carnivorous. But that was not the greatest difficulty—could the alien safely ingest what was Andas's native food? Anyone traveling from world to world had immunity shots. But that did not mean that they were safe from the effects of another's food—which to them might be deadly poison.

He held the bunch of fruit he had snapped free and looked to Yolyos, who in this gloom was only a shadowy bulk still dribbling his fingers in the water.

"Maybe you cannot eat these."

"There is only one way to be sure. And one does not welcome starvation if there is any form of food available," returned the other calmly. "I am duly warned, Prince."

There was a rustling, and Andas guessed the other was culling his own bunch of fruit.

"It is not bad to taste," Yolyos announced a moment later, "though that can be no warning of future trouble. Many traps are overlaid with pleasant bait. I would rather have a well-covered xar leg bone in my hand, but one does not miscall what the First Ancestress desires to set before one. So—I eat."

But Andas continued, as he fed himself, to listen for any sounds from the other to suggest that this was a deadly trap covered with pleasant bait as far as the Salariki was concerned.

"It is food, but not too filling," the alien remarked at last. "However, for the smallest favors a man in need must be thankful. That we have this private food and water is another piece of good fortune to be paid for when one is free to concern oneself again with debts to the First Ancestress."

As he tried to get up, Andas found himself dizzy. Perhaps it was the lack of rest, but it seemed to him that some of that vertigo came from the cloying scent of the flowers. Suddenly he wanted to be away from the garden. He said so sharply that he must have surprised Yolyos, for the other asked, "What danger do you feel here, Prince?"

"The flowers—that smell—I must have fresher air!" He lurched and would have fallen had the other not steadied him. In the end Yolyos had almost to carry him out of that lush growth into the sterile dustiness of the barracks. There Andas drew as deep breaths of relief as those the Salariki had taken when he had fronted the banks of perfumed bloom.

"You are all right now?" Andas heard the Salariki

rather than saw him. Out in the garden, though no moon had yet risen, the masses of white flowers seemed to give light.

He jerked free from the other's hold, feeling shame that such a thing as a flower, even in bulk, would weaken him so. "Yes. We can rest above—in the commander's room." He wanted to be near the exit he knew while in a place of such ill repute.

"You go on." Yolyos was back at the door. "To me that scent is all meat and drink. I shall come when I have had my fill."

Andas was too tired, too uneasy to argue. After all, he had warned the other. If Yolyos, knowing the danger, wanted to go and smell flowers in an overgrown garden, then let him.

Andas climbed to the upper chamber. The bed was but an empty frame. He could have brought some of the vines and grass from the garden to soften the floor. But he wanted no more of the loquats. With a sigh he stretched out on the hard surface and closed his eyes.

Dark—but with a kernel of red light that drew him, so that without knowing why, save that he must, he went toward that. Then that kernel enlarged suddenly, as if he had covered some length of distance in a single step or by willing it. There was a fire, and the weaving flames were the only illumination of a grim scene.

That fire burned not on any hearth but in the middle of a room, and not a room of four stout walls and an intact roof either, for the flames, now revealing, now dying so that they hid again, showed a ragged hole larger than any window in the wall facing him across the source of heat and light. When the fire burned higher, he could see that the roof was only partly overhead. There was little protection against a thick, creeping mist, such as Inyanga knew just before the winter came.

There was one who fed the fire, coming now and then on her hands and knees, pulling pieces of roughly broken wood to push into the flames with caution, as if she drew upon a scant supply. Andas, from his days at Pav, recognized the technique practiced in survival course, though by the looks of her she played no training game but lived life on the thin edge of survival in truth.

That she was a woman he could tell only from the hair braided tightly to her skull in the many small braids of a desert nomad, for her body was a huddle of coarse garments from which protruded arms near as thin and curveless as the sticks she handled. Her face was as close to a skull as that of any living human being could be. And, save for her eyes, she might well have been one of the dead-alive of the old, old tales.

As she fed the fire, the light it cast grew so that Andas could see the other occupant of that ruined room. He had been propped up so that he sat facing Andas across the flames. But there was something about the way his limbs were stretched before him under a tattered rug that made the prince think they were useless.

On the stranger's lap lay—was it a voice-harp? Andas could not see it clearly in this bad light, and the woman with her fire-feeding kept blocking the view. It did have some resemblance to that elegant and courtly, if very old-fashioned, musical instrument, save that from one end of it projected and then rose a fan of slender rods. Woven back and forth, uniting the rods into a transparent fan, were wires or threads that gleamed and glistened as the light touched them.

But the man did not seem to be in the act of playing. Rather he held, gripped tightly in one hand, a splinter with a wad of candle fluff on its tip, which burned with such restricted light that the holder had to bring it very close to what was in his other hand in order to see, if he could see at all.

And what he was trying under such difficulty to see was a book—not a reading tape such as had been in use over untold centuries now, but an ancient book with pages to be manually turned, words printed on them. Andas knew books. They were curiosities and brought high prices from dealers of antiquities. There were at least a dozen in the Triple Towers, among the treasures collected by dilettante emperors in the past. But those were treated as treasures, kept in gem-set boxes.

The volume that the frowning would-be reader held in this place of dark and ruin had a cover of what appeared to be thin slabs of wood, the pages as thick as plasta sheets, but yellow and tattered on the edges. The prince looked beyond the wonder of that ancient book to the face of the man who held it and—

Did he cry out, or was that sound only uttered in his mind? At least neither the reader nor the wraith woman who fed the fire were startled or looked up to see him. But that other's face, thin, with a half-healed scar upon the temple—that face was his own!

This must be a dream, yet there was a feeling of reality in it such as Andas had never known in any dream he had walked or drifted through before. Could it be true then that men lived many lives, as the priests of the half-forgotten cult of Kaissee taught? And that some men were allowed to see these past lives? That the deeds of one life, good or bad, influenced the next? If so, was he looking now upon a self that had been his in the dim past?

He could see the lips of that other Andas move, but he heard no sound. And now the reader must have said something to the woman, for she came away from the fire, hunkered down by him, and took that dreary taper into her hand, holding it close to the page of the book, while the man's right hand, now free, moved to lie on the keyboard of the harp.

The fingers pressed, one, two, three— Again Andas heard no sound. Rather there was a vibration in the air. Once more he cried out as that vibration closed about him like a net, drawing him toward the fire in spite of his struggles.

Again the fingers moved, and the vibration tightened. Now he heard sound, too, very faint and far off. But it echoed and rang in his head, a torment that could not be shaken off. The reader looked up from the book, straight at Andas. The prince saw the eyes in the thin, starved face widen. It was plain he himself was seen.

The woman started, letting fall the candle. And Andas heard another sound, a thin cry of distress.

But he was free of the net the harp had woven. And he pulled away with all the strength he had, seeking the dark that lay beyond the fire, away from the man wearing his face.

Andas opened his eyes, afraid for a moment to look about him lest he see the fire and know that he was a prisoner in that place where a man wove a spell with a harp. But the acrid smell of dust and the silence told Andas that he lay safe (if one could term his present situation safe) once again in the commander's quarters.

Had it been a dream? He tried to compare it with dreams he had known. But most of those had been very fleeting and lacking in detail after one awoke. This was a different matter, for against all reason, his instinct and his emotions told him that somewhere, or sometime, the scene he had just witnessed had been real. Perhaps his fatigue, his exposure to thirst, hunger, and the strong scent of the flowers had unlocked some unknown portion of memory and he had spied upon his own far past. But then—

Andas sat up, drawing a deep breath of wonder and then of relief. If he could believe that, if he had, as the priests of Kaissee taught, remembered another life—that was proof he was no android!

By some experiment he could have been imprinted with all the memories of a man he had been made to resemble. But he could see no possible way he could also have been made aware in deep unconscious parts of the mind of events from the other man's past life. If he could only believe in the creed of Kaissee, then his own fears were stilled. Now he could only hope.

The presence of the book—that certainly meant the scene had been in a very ancient past. Books

were treasures never to be used as that stranger had
done. And the harp, while in part it was akin to one
he himself had been taught to play as one of the
graces of his rank, was different. The past—he had
seen into the past—

Was it because he had the key? He had heard many
legends concerning that, though privately those of royal
blood discounted most of the old stories. Yet there
must be an aura of power that clung to a talisman
that had been venerated by generations upon generations, so that such objects took on a patina from that
worship until in themselves they kept shadows of the
very forces they represented.

His hand slid across the breast of his coverall,
seeking the shape of the key. But first he touched
that other thing he carried—the ring. And he jerked
his fingers away as if the fire he had looked upon
in his dream had licked them. That—that was a
thing of power and one which he had forgotten
or he would not have carried it so long. It should
be destroyed, though he had no means for doing
so. If he hid it somewhere here among the ruins,
it would still have a way to draw to it the one
to whom it had been sealed. Men might question
the power of the key, except when it was put to
the use for which it was fashioned. But there was
altogether too much proof of the influence of such
a ring. He had a duty to see to its destruction.
Luckily he could accomplish that also when he took
the key to its proper place.

Andas lay back on the stones, but he was too wide
awake to sleep again. Instead, he began to recall detail
by detail the dream, and instead of fading as such

normally would, it all became more sharply fixed, until he could remember things he had not noted at first—such as the bandage that had shown on the breast of the man when a movement of the stranger's hand on the harp had pulled aside the clumsily patched tunic he wore. There had been a crusted black-red stain on that bandage.

So it had been more perhaps than hunger and cold that had set those dark shadows under the stranger's eyes. He had the look, now that Andas had time to consider it, of a man sore hurt.

Of the ruined building in which those two had sheltered so poorly, he was not sure. It was certainly not of the Triple Towers he knew. He had seen tapes of warfare, and this dream scene reminded him strongly of such a picture taken in a refugee camp. War could reduce men to such a plight.

There had been wars in plenty on Inyanga—he could not deny that—though for the most part those had occupied only the claimants to the throne and their liegemen and had very seldom spread to the country at large. In fact, one of the pacts made by Akmedu had been that when disputes were to be settled in blood, the fighters must withdraw to the Red Waste. It had worked out very well. But the last "war" to be fought there in any force was now generations back. He himself had gone into the Red Waste from Pav—there had been nothing there like the scene he had witnessed.

"Prince!"

Roused out of his thoughts, Andas got up. He was stiff from the hardness of his bed and gave a little catch of breath at the complaint of a leg muscle.

"Yes—?" he did not need to ask who came. There was so strong an odor of loquat blossom accompanying the new arrival that the Salariki must have been rolling in a blanket of the moon-white flowers.

-11-

"There are doom dealings here!"

To Andas the words made no sense, but he could read the emotion in the other's voice, that growl he had come to identify with anger as far as the Salariki was concerned.

In spite of the shutters they had forced into place across the windows, Andas could see the dark form, and he turned on the torch to catch the other in its rays. Yolyos had his back turned. He was facing the one window that overlooked the fatal Place of No Return.

As the light centered on the alien, the prince could see the fur ridge along the other's upper arms and backbone. The hair did not lie sleek and smooth but was erect, while Yolyos's ears appeared flattened, folded in against his skull. Now the Salariki turned his head and looked at Andas over his hunched shoulder.

"It stinks of the doom here!" he growled again.

"Doom?"

"Doom—that which those who dabble in drum talk and fang work bring upon them in the Hidden Moon time." He still made no sense. "Give it what name you will then—but this is what the Death Drummer raises—death from no weapon but by stealing men's lives, sucking their breath unseen." Now he swung around to face Andas squarely, his lips flat, drawn back from his fangs, his eyes glowing as no human eyes could. "What do you here, Prince?"

In spite of himself, as if the very force of the other's suspicion drew it from him, Andas answered with the truth.

"Nothing but dream."

"Dream? But do not say that is nothing! There are true dreams and false ones. Some are sent as warnings or enticements. You have said this is a place of ill omen avoided by your kind. Now you dream. And this room has the stink of doom dealings—and you call it nothing!"

The longer the Salariki spoke, the more Andas realized that the alien was genuinely aroused, that the easy relationship between them was threatened. In turn, his own unease grew. He had not chosen Yolyos as a comrade in this wild venture. That had been thrust upon him by chance. Yet now he discovered he did not want to lose what he had in common with this warrior of another species and world.

"None of my doing," he said with, he hoped, enough force to impress. "I went to sleep and I dreamed—"

"And what manner of dream?" Yolyos relaxed none of his defensive stance. It was plain Andas had to prove himself.

Andas told him, though whether he made clear to the other what had happened, he did not know. He waited for a long moment until the Salariki spoke.

"This man wore your face?"

"With the addition of a scar," Andas amended.

"And the place, that you did not know?"

"It was too dark to see much, but I am certain I never saw it before."

"And the woman?"

"I swear to my knowledge I have never seen her, though she was of my race—a desert nomad perhaps."

There was a subtle change in Yolyos, and inwardly Andas relaxed, sure he was no longer a figure of suspicion. Now he ventured to ask a question in return.

"What is this doom of which you spoke?"

"Each race or species has its own beliefs in intangible powers—in 'magic.' We have our adepts, too. I have seen a Death Drummer—" Yolyos broke off as if that touched upon some memory he would not resummon. "As do all emotions, this dealing has a smell. My people scent things others feel. And this is a foul smell. When I came in, it was rank. I think your dream was no dream but a sending. As you tell me—this net of sound drew you toward him who made it. Whatever touched you then—" He frowned. "No, I will not set name to it here and now. Such naming can draw influences when one least wants them." Andas saw his wide nostrils expand and his head swing from side to side, as if testing the stale, dust-laden air of the room.

"Now it is gone. Whatever spear it launched at you failed. But I would not slumber here long."

"The only door to our escape is in the wall here. As far as I know, there is no other entrance to the ruins." Andas was half persuaded, yet to leave the way to such safety—poor as it was—that the wall passages promised, he could not bring himself to do.

"Then let me set such safeguards as my people know—I shall set them!" What had begun as a request was now a definite decision.

Before Andas could protest, Yolyos turned and used his unsheathed claws on the shutter they had pounded into place, levering it loose. The prince tried to stop him.

"No—we could be sighted!"

"By whom? You said this is a shunned place. We have no lights—if you will turn off the torch—even if your guards decided to fly over. I tell you this room must have protection or we do not stay in it!"

So strong was his conviction, Andas stood aside. But he did not help any as all the windows in the wall facing that ill-omened court were not only freed of the shutters but also were opened to the night. Then in the moonlight the Salariki padded back to the doorway where lay a vast mass of stuff, a mixture of vine, flower, and leaf, as if he had plundered the garden.

He picked that over, bringing forth a number of flowers, still waxy-white, though darkening bruises showed here and there on their wide petals. The best of these he proceeded to lay out on the windowsills in a pattern. When he had finished each, he held his hands in the full moonlight, cupping and flexing his fingers, as if he were actually gathering some of that wan radiance.

Then he turned palms down, opened his fingers, and murmured in the purring speech of his own people, as if he recited some charm or ritual. On each windowsill he did so. Then he stepped back, his face hidden in the dark. When he spoke, his voice had lost that threatening roughness.

"This is a potent charm of my people. If you have any you can add to it—"

Andas shook his head and then realized that the other probably could not see that gesture. "We do not believe in charms." But he made that denial conciliatory. To each species its own safeguards. And what had Yolyos said of the talisman? He had the key—though that was only a symbol.

Thinking of the key brought the ring to mind. Suppose that could be a focus for evil? Should he try to rid himself of it, if only temporarily? Yet he was determined to destroy it, and if he hid it, how did he know that he could recover it?

Yolyos spread the mass of foliage on the floor. Making a bed, Andas judged. Once more the heavy perfume of the now wilting flowers was thick, far too heavy in this room, making him dizzy. He was sleepy, too—very sleepy again, with the same eye-burning fatigue that had sent him to dreaming on the hard floor earlier. He must not sleep! In sleep, dreams could return, could reach for him, but—

It was as if he were two people. One was a prisoner watching the other surrender, ready to curl up beside the Salariki on the fragrant nest of leaves and flowers. He struggled to withstand and failed.

The moonlight through the windows made white bars of light on the floor. Half revealed in one was the huddled form of Yolyos curled about, his head pillowed on his crooked arm, his breath coming evenly. The moon was so bright that it had a glitter like ice. It was cold—

Andas stood up in the moonlight. He walked to the window, looked out and down. There was no longer any fear in him, rather a growing excitement, a tension such as filled men on the eve of a fight or some contest of skill or trial by force.

On the sill lay the pattern of blossoms Yolyos had set with such ceremony. Andas laughed silently. Did this furred barbarian think that such a stupid trick would defeat what waited out there? He swept the flowers away with his hand. Then putting both palms on the sill, he leaned out to look down.

The broken wall had spilled its upper layers well over the court. But the rubble did not cover the whole; it did not even touch upon the important section. Still, the time had not yet come, only its warning to awaken him.

He watched and waited, without any fear or surprise, save that his excitement was hard to contain. He found it very difficult to stand still and mute, not to run down there shouting aloud—very hard, but the time was not yet.

It was beginning (not visibly before his eyes, but somewhere deep within him), a beat like the beat of his heart, save that it began slow and sluggish, and then grew faster, stronger. He could hear the rasp of his own breathing as that, too, grew heavier and faster, like the gasping of a man who runs a race. But the time was not yet.

Andas stood, waiting. Then came the moment with

a signal his spirit recognized, but his ears did not hear, nor his eyes see. He left the window, passed the bed of vines, went into the hall, and threaded corridors and stairs as if they were not dark but brilliantly lighted and this was a well-known way.

Thus he came to a door that was not only closed but also fused shut. And by then the force that drew him was so strong that he hammered at the barrier, unable to think clearly. After he had battered the door for a space, the compulsion lessened. He leaned against the firmly sealed door, his bruised fists hanging by his sides.

No way through—his mind moved sluggishly. It was hard to think. No way through here, but there must be a way! Like a programed robot he turned back and retraced his path until he stood once more at the window looking down into the court, to that spot where he must be and soon.

Quickly he turned and made a dart at the vegetation that had formed their bed, on which Yolyos still slept. Andas's hands closed upon a length of vine, and he jerked it free with no thought for the sleeper. He had blanked the Salariki out. All that mattered was a way to get below. But this vine was too short! From this window, yes, but a floor below—

He heard a cry from the Salariki whom his action must have aroused, but he paid no attention. With the loop of vine about his shoulder, he ran, once more surefooted and fearless, through the dark to another room where there was another window.

That was closed, and the moonlight through it was dim and dulled by the dust. Andas looked about him wildly. There was a jumble on the floor here, as if the debris of the barracks had been pushed together to molder into dust. He scrabbled in that and came up with a bar of rust-flaking metal. But its core seemed stout enough, and with that he broke out the panes.

The bar was longer than the window was wide. It must serve as his anchor. He had no time to hunt a better one. He looped the vine about it, jammed the bar across the base of the window, and climbed out, the vine ends in his hands. At the same time there was a shout from the door of the room. He did not wait.

It was more a fall than a descent, but the vine kept him from crashing to the pavement. He no longer cared really. He must reach that spot—now!

Andas ran, vaguely hearing the thud of someone landing on the pavement behind him. Two steps more—a hand clawed at his shoulder raking his flesh painfully. Andas did not try to strike it away. There was no time. Reach the spot—that was all that was meaningful in the world now!

But there was no pavement, no bright moon, no crumbling walls. There was a time of transition through a place he could never afterwards describe, from which his memory flinched. Then he was falling, coming up against a solid object with force enough to painfully drive all the breath from his lungs in a single gasp. And propelling him forward in that dive was another struggling body.

Andas was occupied at first merely fighting to get a full breath again. But once that happened, he looked around. No moon showed. Rather a thick mist hung like a cloak, leaving cold beads of moisture on his skin. "Fool!"

Beside him another body moved. He felt the softness of fur against his arm, wiping away some of that moisture. But the voice was a warning growl of anger.

"Yolyos?"

"What is left of him, yes. And into which of the Drummer's hells have you now plunged us?"

Andas had no time to answer. The compulsion that had drawn him to the courtyard closed about him again. It was as if his transition to this place had jarred loose some tie, now once more firmly noosed about him. He scrambled to his feet, not looking for the Salariki. But as he started off, he said, "This way."

Whether Yolyos followed or not did not matter. All that did was that he, Andas Kastor, must reach that place toward which he was going. And there was a need for haste, great haste. His path led in and out among tumbled blocks of stone, many taller than his head. The mist continued—became a soaking rain. He could not tell how far he had traveled or how long. His sense of time had been disrupted by that passage through the other place. But at last he saw ahead a wink of light.

Memory stirred. Once before he had seen just that same small wink of red and yellow through the dark. Surely he had done this all before.

Fire—among ruins. The blocks around which he made his painful way were not stones, but the remains of buildings, or of a building. And those he sought were the people of his dream—the skeleton woman who fed the fire, the man who played the strange harp. He was caught again in the dream! Yet this time it carried even more the stamp of reality.

But the woman did not feed the fire now. She crouched a little behind the half-seated, half-lying man, her too-thin arm an additional prop for his shoulders, as if he needed all the support she could give him. And he held no ancient book, but instead both his hands rested on the harp and were in motion there, though Andas heard no sound, only felt that vibration, which shook and churned him and would not let him go.

He did not drift effortlessly to the fire this time—he walked on his own feet. And as he came to a halt on the other side of the now dying flames, the harper's face was filled with exultation. He spoke, and Andas heard and understood.

"The records were right. It is done well—"

The woman interrupted him. "Done, yes, but done well? Ah, dear lord, only time can answer that!"

"And I have so little time—is that what you think?" he asked half impatiently, raising his hands from the harp to press them against his chest over that encrusted bandage, as if he held there something precious and threatened. "There will be time, Shara. I have not accomplished all I have so far, not to have time to finish!"

The compulsion faded as he talked. Andas was free. Yet when he turned his head to look for some manner of escape, he was still sluggish, wrapped in the effects of that bondage.

"Yes, you are here! And you are Andas—a young Andas. Shara, show him to me clearly!"

The woman left her place at his back, moved out, took up a piece of wood, and thrust it deep into the fire's heart. When it blazed, she lifted it again and held it near enough to Andas so that he jerked his head back, the heat too strong for comfort.

"Strong, young—the rightful Andas, just as the records foretold." The stranger with Andas's face almost crooned the words, as if he sang a victory song. "An Andas for an Andas! I die—you live to fulfill all the promises—"

"Who are you? This place—where is it?"

"Andas!" But the woman did not look to him as she cried that name aloud, rather to the man on the ground. She whirled the branch around, stirring it to greater burning, and held it before her as she might a spear or sword.

There was a clatter of stone against stone.

"Prince! Give me a lead to find you!" Yolyos's voice came out of the rain and the dark.

He answered, "Here—there is a fire for a guide—"

"There is a fire to kill!" The woman menaced him with her brand so he leaped back and away. But the harper made what was plainly a painful effort, seized the edge of her shapeless outer garment, and put his waning strength into a swift backward jerk, so she staggered, almost losing her balance.

"He is not alone!" she cried. "It is a trick!"

"Not so," the harper told her. He spoke in a quiet voice, almost as one would soothe a child. "We drew him. There was another who followed, who was with him at that moment when the gate opened. He knows this one, speaks to him as to a friend. Be not so swift to judge, Shara."

The brand had burned close to her hold. She tossed it into the fire and stood empty-handed. There was an empty look on her face, too. She said nothing more, but dropped in her old place, her hands on the man's shoulders, as if she needed that contact as much as he might need her support.

She no longer even looked at Andas, but kept her head bowed, her eyes ever upon the face of the man whom she now sat beside. Nor did she even glance around as Yolyos came out of the shadows.

But there was surprise on the harper's scarred face as he saw the Salariki. He surveyed the alien with a searching stare, as if he sought to read Yolyos's thoughts and weigh them to see if he were friend or enemy.

"You are not one of us." He did not speak Basic, and Andas was sure the Salariki did not understand.

"He does not speak our tongue," he cut in swiftly. "Yes, he is an off-worlder, a Salariki—the Lord Yolyos."

"Salariki." The harper rolled the word about in his mouth as if he tasted something strange, beyond his experience. "Off-world—oh!" Once more triumph flamed fitfully in his gaze. "In your world, brother, men still seek the stars?"

"My world? What world is this—if it is not a dream?"

The man sighed, his hands slipping from his breast and the bandage there as if he could no longer find the strength to hold it so.

"This is Inyanga, part of the Empire of Dingane that was—was—was—" He repeated the verb three times, as if in doing so he tolled some bell signifying the end of a living thing. "But it is not your world, save that in some parts it is a double of perhaps that much happier life. I do not know the rights of this, brother. It would take a man much more learned than I am to explain. I only know that our twin worlds must lie very close, so that in places, or at least one place, there is a touching. Have you no tales of men—yes, and women, too"—as he said that the woman beside him stirred and raised one hand to her lips—"who have vanished suddenly and never returned?"

"Yes."

"They came here, some of them. That is how Kioga Atabi first thought of this." His hand lifted and fell upon, rather than pointed to, the harp. "I—I was his student for a short time, before the rebellion. So I knew, or thought I knew, enough to open by intention a gate which before opened only by chance, to open that and draw through the man I needed—my people needed—"

"Me?" Andas was fast losing all belief in the reality of this. Was it another vivid dream? He could not be standing here in the rain and the ruins, listening to the man-wearing-his-face saying such things.

"You because you are who you are—Andas Kastor. Just as in the world I am Andas Kastor. But I am dying, and you are alive and unhurt. You can take up the battle I must leave—carried upon my shield after the right of the royal blood, though there be none now to bear me to the Tomb of the Thousand Spears, nor any to beat the Talking Drums of Atticar at my going. Still there is a war being most bitterly fought, and my people need a leader. Thus, I summoned one they will give allegiance to without—without—" His words slowed, he swallowed visibly once, twice, then coughed, and a dark trickle crept from the corner of his mouth.

The woman exclaimed and would have moved to his aid. But with one hand he waved her back, fighting to speak again.

"I leave you now the cloak of Ugana fur, the sword of the Lion, the crown of the great queen Balkis-Candace—"

Long ago those words had lost their meaning save as a ritual so sacred and old that Andas, without thinking, responded to them. That no one knew what a "lion" was or remembered a great queen Balkis-Candace did not matter. What did was that this man, wounded to his death, invoked something so sacred, so much a part of Andas's breeding, that he went to his knees and stretched forth both his empty hands. It was a gesture he had thought to make one day, but kneeling before the altar of Akmedu, and the man saying that to him would have been a tall and glorious figure in brilliant robes, the Emperor, an old man of his own house accepting him as heir.

The harper raised both hands, though they wavered and shook. And they fell rather than were placed on Andas's hands. They tried to grip Andas's fingers, but had no strength left. It was his hold that kept them linked.

"By the rite of the crown, the spear, the shield, the Lion, the—the—"

"The thorn." Andas supplied for the faltering voice. "By the water which freshens the desert, the clouds which veil the mountains, the will of Him who is not named by lesser beings, by all these, and the blood of my heart, the strength of my arms, the will of my spirit, the thoughts of my brain, so do I accept this burden and rise under it."

He spoke steadily, the harper watching him with feverish and demanding eyes, his lips shaping the words he did not say aloud as he followed the great oath with such intensity that it was plain the whole of his being was now centered on hearing Andas intone it to the end.

"Rise under it, to serve those who look to me for bread, for water, for life itself. So rest on me this burden until the end of that time written in the stars for me, when I shall go forth on the road that no man seeth. And this do I promise by the key, which I lay hand upon." He had dropped those lax hands and fumbled at the breast of the coverall. He drew out the talisman, and the fire seemed to leap higher at that moment, giving fiery life to what lay in his grasp.

The harper looked at it, and his face contorted into a painful smile.

"Well, oh well, have we wrought, Andas Kastor that was, Andas Kastor that will be! Emperor and lord, hold well the key—the key—"

Once more he fought for words, but this time he could no longer hold fast to the last wisp of strength. His eyes closed, and he fell forward, hunching over the harp. His hands tore at it in a last struggle, and in his frenzied grasp the strings broke with a horrible discord.

-12-

Shara put both fists to her mouth as if to stifle some cry. The Salariki spoke first.

"He is dead. But what did he ask of you?"

Andas still knelt, looking at the huddled body. He answered absently in Basic.

"He put upon me the Emperor's oath, passing to me rule and reign. Though if he had the right to do so—" He glanced about at the ruins. This was no housing for one with the right to pass the oath—which was done only in an atmosphere of great richness and ceremony.

Shara tugged at the body, drawing it back so that the harper's face could be seen. Since his driving will and spirit had departed from it, that face was now a mask of endurance and despair.

"Who was he?" Andas demanded.

"Emperor and lord." She did not look at him, but continued to pull at the flaccid body, straightening it.

"Of what? By the look of him he—"

"He fought when lesser men lay down and willed the coming of death. He believed and worked for that belief!" She came alive, on fire, facing him across the body, as if she had taken into her own wasted form the energy that had held a dying man to a fearsome task. "He was the only hope of the empire. And when he knew he had taken his death blow, he held off death that he might bring one to stand for him—"

"Stand for him? But how can I do that, woman, unless I know the whole of the tale?"

Though she appeared the poorest of desert nomads, yet this Shara spoke the pure court tongue. Also he was beginning to think she was much younger than she first appeared. What was she to the dead man? Wife, Second Lady? But at least she ought to make some sense now of what had happened to Andas.

She had taken off the piece of rough material she had wound about her shoulders as a shawl, straightening it out gently over the body, covering the face that was a mask of Andas's own.

"You are right. There is a time for mourning and the beat of drums, and a time when such must be forgotten. He knew he had but hours when he came hither, so upon me he laid the burden of remaining alive, of playing guide to the one who would come.

"This is a world twin to your own. I do not know why this is so. But it is true that those from your place have come among us from time to time. It seemed they could do this by chance but could not go back. The Magi Atabi worked to discover the secret. He made many experiments. The last was this—" She pointed to the harp with the now broken strings. "It was his belief that certain sounds could open the gate between. When he was an old man, a very old man, he came to court, to beg of the Emperor a chance to put his invention to the test.

"That was when Andas saw him. His tutor was a pupil of the Magi's and took Andas to meet him. And the old man, fearful of getting no notice from the authorities (which he did not), took much time and trouble to explain to Andas what he wished to do.

"But already the shadow reached over us. He had no listeners—save a prince who was a young boy."

She paused, and she no longer surveyed the shrouded body or Andas, but rather raised her eyes to the broken wall, rapt in some vision of her own. Andas spoke to her gently and as he might to an equal in rank.

"You speak of a shadow, lady?"

"Yes. And that shadow has a name—a foul name—one to be spat upon! Kidaya—Kidaya of the Silver Tongue!" Her wan face flushed darker. "Kidaya of the House of the Nahrads."

Andas started, and she must have noticed it.

"Do you know of her then? Is your world also so cursed?"

"Of Kidaya I have not heard. But the House of Nahrad, the Nameless people of the Old Woman—yes, I have heard of them. How came one of the cursed line to your court?"

"You might well ask. Ask it of those who sing the Bones. It was decreed after the rebellion of Ashanti that none of the Nameless were to come within one day's journey of the Emperor. Yet Kidaya came to lie in his bed, to eat from his marriage plate, though she did not wear the crown. Even a man bewitched can be kept from some crimes! He took her into the Flower Courts, but he dared give her no First Honors. And for that Kidaya made him pay, and this whole empire crumbled into what you see about you—ruin and decay.

"Faction was set against faction by her cunning, and one rebel after another arose. She laid memory spells on the Emperor, so he felt hatred toward those who served him most loyally. Houses fell, their heads and all their families slain. Even Andas's life was saved only by a trick—" She laid her hand on the covered body.

"When he was of an age to take shield, he was the only true-line heir. She had seen to that by her web-spinning. The Emperor was too old, too sunk in her dreams, to be reached by those who would still save him and the empire. But she—she did not grow old! The witchcraft of the Old Woman held, so that she grew in outward beauty and in evil power as the years passed.

"But she bore no son—openly. There was a story that in secret she mothered a daughter, dedicated to the Old Woman from the first drawing of her breath, and that daughter Kidaya determined would hold the key—"

At her words Andas's hold tightened upon the talisman. There was nothing to say that a woman could not rule in her own right. Twice over in the past had there been an empress who touched what he now carried. But that anyone tainted with the forbidden knowledge would so aspire—!

"When she thought she was strong enough to move, she wrought upon the Emperor until he turned his

face from Andas. There was a silly plot uncovered,
so botched a matter that all knew it was but a sham
to give the Emperor reason for decreeing the Second
Punishment—"

Again she paused, and Andas drew a whistling
breath. In his own world the Second Punishment
existed only in the dark annals of long past history,
though it could still be used by law against any of the
royal clans who rebelled. Yet it had not been so for
more than a hundred years. To what barbaric state
had this twin world sunk that this punishment could
be once more invoked against a man?

"But his eyes—" he protested. The dead man's face
was hidden, but Andas was sure he had not been
mistaken. Those eyes had been normal—he had not
been blinded.

"He had friends still, ready to risk their lives and
more that the true line not come to an end and that
witch sit on the Triple Throne," Shara said. "But he
played a game thereafter such as few men would have
the strength to do, for he wore the mask of the Second
Punishment, and no man knew that he had not lost his
eyes. As a blinded prince he had no chance for the
throne. She could contemptuously let him crawl into
any hole he chose to hide shame and disgrace. But he
lived and so won a small victory, since she would not
send against him, blinded, such evil arts as the Old
Woman's blood-sworn knew, such as had been turned
against others. He was a nothing, a grain of dust she
had swept aside and need not remember."

"But he was not blind," Andas said slowly. A blind
prince, a cripple, one slack or injured of wits, could
not stand as emperor—an easy way in the dark old

days to sweep away a rival. But for a man to play blind so cunningly to save his life, that required such patience that he marveled at the thought of it.

"He was not blind. And he was young, very young, but his wits were old and his understanding great. He played his part very well. At first she kept him about the court, a warning and a threat to others. Also, I think, a symbol of her own triumph to please herself. But at last she discovered that pity does not die under disfavor, and she sent him to the Fortress of Kham. There she made her mistake."

"The mountaineers have never welcomed those of the Old Woman," Andas commented. Though that knowledge was of his world and not this, he saw Shara nod.

"Is that so with you as well as us? It is true. They had a spirit caller of unusual power, one sworn to peace and well versed in the inner life. He had made several miraculous cures—publicly. The commander of the fortress then was of the House of Hungang—"

"So he would be shield-up against all the Nameless." Again Andas interrupted. This was like viewing a half-remembered history tape.

"That is so. And the spirit caller wrought another cure—but on that day also the news of the Emperor's farewell flashed from the Triple Towers."

"So civil war followed? Did your Kidaya have enough of the lords to back her?"

"She had built well. Three-quarters or more of those making up the inner circle of the court were her men. She need only close her fist to crush them, as they well knew. Yes, she had backing, and there was war. But it would have been an even judgment between us had she not brought mercenaries from the stars. And they had such weapons as beat the loyal houses out into the hills like beasts. Since then all has gone wrong." Shara raised her hand and let it fall. "The mercenaries hold the center of the land. But they have had no further help from off-world since our raiding parties destroyed the call tower at Three Ports two years ago. They have already had to abandon many of their weapons for lack of ammunition or repairs.

"Also there was the choking death, and they died from it, more of them than us. It is even said that the choking death was one of their weapons that was misused, since it spread out of Zohair after they occupied it. There are other ills, though, that Kidaya has loosed—the night crawlers—"

Andas shivered. "But those are only legends—to frighten children. Sensible men—"

"Sensible men believed not—and died! What we prate of as superstition in the days of pride and safety may seem different in the dark when men hide from death. The night crawlers here are real. Then—then there was betrayal in our own small ranks!" Her voice, which had held so even and colorless, suddenly quavered. "My dear lord was so struck down. He knew that he had his death wound, though he held to life with both hands as long as he could that he might bring aid to those who had put their trust in him. For months he has sought the cache left by the Magi Atabi, hoping that in it might be some weapon strong enough to turn against the invaders now that they are weakened. But when he found it, then that secret enemy struck. I think that it was in the mind of that unknown one to take what my lord had found and use it to bargain with Kidaya.

"But my lord beat off the attack, losing in it all save me. And he would allow me only to bind his wounds and aid him here—with what he had found in the cache—for the Magi had left a writing, and my lord believed that with this strange harp he could summon from the other world one who was himself there. As he did! So he passed to your hands the power, the task—"

"But, my lady, this is not—I cannot—" For the first time Andas realized fully what he had done when, bemused by the ritual of the passing of rule, he had taken those oaths to a dying man. This quarrel was not his. He could not possibly take upon his shoulders the burden he understood so little. The first who met him would know him for an impostor.

"You are Andas, Emperor." She looked at him sternly. "I bear witness, as can this alien—whom you so foolishly brought with you—that you are. And with my swearing so, who would believe otherwise? You have his face."

"He has a scar. There is a difference," Andas was quick to point out.

"That scar was gained but a few days before the final attack in which he was wounded," she told him. "None living, save me now, knew he had it."

"And who are you that your voice will make or unmake an emperor?" Andas demanded.

He could see nothing about her that would give credence to the certainty with which she spoke—as if she held the power she allotted in her tale to Kidaya.

She was a bone-thin woman with her hair in the tight, small braids of a nomad, wearing tattered sacks as a robe of honor.

"I am Shara, the Chosen of Emperor Andas." Her chin lifted, and there was about her a pride which was as illuminating at that moment as if she did indeed stand with her feet in the slippers of gold, the pearl diadem on her dusty head. "I am of the House of Brawa-Balkis. What say you to that, son of the House of Kastor?"

Kastor was a royal house, yes. But there were older clans with the right to provide a ruler at the Triple Towers, and of them all Balkis was the fabled, the legendary one. The last daughter of Balkis had chosen to unite with Brawa. But long ago that house had dwindled and disappeared in his own world. Chance could have kept it alive here, and Andas recognized a speaking of the Blood. No one would claim such heritage unless it was the truth.

He raised his hands in the formal gesture of one veiling his eyes before a sun-bright superior. "Hail, Blood of the Blood."

"Far away and long ago that." Her voice had lost that chill pride. "But here and now I am the Chosen. Do you think that my word concerning you will not be believed? You are Andas, Emperor. And he who lies here—he must be laid secretly with only the honors we can do him in our hearts, not even knowing where he lies."

But she was moving too fast for him. Andas got to his feet and, for the first time in many moments, remembered the Salariki. He turned to look for Yolyos and could just barely make out the alien's form as the other hunkered down some distance away, facing out into the rain and the night as if he were on guard. Andas went to him.

"You now have some knowledge of what this means." Yolyos greeted him with a statement rather than a question.

Andas repeated all Shara had told him.

"So he gave you the rule. And she says that you are now the Emperor and plans to hide his death and pass you off as him. You will do this?"

Andas had been dodging the need for a decision. Perhaps that was why he had listened to her story, tried to keep his mind on the past rather than the present or the future.

But one fact was ever before him. Though he had not taken that oath in the temple or before the glitter of a court, he had given it. And all the conditioning of his life had set in one mold, that the Emperor had a duty of service. Once he had taken the oath, he was no longer so much a man as a symbol. Though that was cold and bleak, yet it was the position to which he had been born and bred.

Could he explain it so that Yolyos would understand? Andas sought to put it into words—only death now could dissolve his responsibility. He could not tell why he had been moved to answer the appeal, the determined will of that other Andas. But having done so, he was bound.

"And if you are not in truth this Andas, but an android?" Yolyos asked then as Andas stumbled through his explanation, finding his logic dwindle when he had to present it to an alien who could not understand long conditioning.

"I am Andas, Emperor, now!" He refused that other thought.

"This female tells you there is no going back. Can you believe her?"

"As she knows it, she is telling the truth. And the harp that seems to have brought us here, it is now broken."

"Conveniently, as far as they are concerned," Yolyos growled.

Andas was jolted out of his own concerns. He might be bound here, but what of the Salariki? He certainly had no duty pressed upon him by death and a ritual of words, and he would be wholly in exile.

"Perhaps there is other information kept by this Magi, to be found in the cache of which she spoke. We can—"

"Always hope?" Yolyos finished for him. "Yes. Also there is this. As you have found yourself so superseded in your time, perhaps I also have been long so. There has never come any good of counting the horns on a Kuay buck before one has shot it, nor the teeth of a gorp that escapes one's net. It is better to look to the foretrail than behind one. So we hide this emperor's body—then what?"

"She must tell us." So much would depend upon Shara's help. That she would be willing and eager to give it, he knew. And she must be able to brief him so thoroughly that he could pass as the proper Andas, even with those who knew him well. What he would do as that Andas, however, he had not even speculated.

They buried the Emperor in the ruins of the building he had chosen for a campsite, piling rubble from the walls up, over, and around him and then, at last, uniting their strength to push over a standing portion to cascade upon the mound, covering it.

Shara brought a bundle into the open when they were done. She opened a roll of mat-cloth and shared out twists of dried meat and some fruit as hard as metal pellets and tart enough to pucker the mouth.

"It would seem that your commissary does not do well, Emperor," Yolyos commented when they had managed to choke it down, washed by drafts of water they hand-scooped from hollows where the rain had gathered.

Shara tugged at Andas's sleeve. "He speaks with the tongue of the mercenaries. It is better that he learn ours as swiftly as he can."

Andas passed this suggestion along. The Salariki growled.

"Well enough, if you can teach it. But these mercenaries—are any of them Salariki?"

When Andas translated, Shara shook her head. "They are all like us, save that they have very pale skins and their hair is yellow. They wear it even on their faces—so—" She drew her finger across her upper lip. "And they speak among themselves with a sharp click-click—like a pang beetle—though they use the speech you talk in to this one also. They wear garments something like yours"—she touched Andas's sleeve—"so we shall say that you killed one of a patrol and took his robe. With supplies so few for us, this often happens. Even the enemy go ragged at times since there are no more ships setting down to bring them what they wish.

"White-skinned, yellow-haired, wearing mustaches."

Andas was trying to place the enemy. He translated for Yolyos. The other had a suggestion.

"Mercenaries are now hired from only two sectors. I have seen men of Njord among the bodyguards of the Svastian overlords who resemble your description. But how can we judge the here with our own world? Mercenaries among us are largely outlawed. It could be for a similar reason that ships have ceased coming here. Your empire may be under ban by the Patrol."

Andas had heard of such bans—of planets, even systems, so deeply embroiled in some chaotic war that they were declared off limits for any space contact. Or it might be that the plague Shara had spoken of had isolated this world. There was nothing so feared throughout the galaxy as plague, and nothing that sooner put a whole world into a quarantine that might last for generations.

But if such limited the inflow of mercenaries, perhaps this isolation was to be welcomed rather than deplored. However, it was what lay immediately to hand that mattered. Andas did not know how long they had been about the business of burying his double, but the rain had stopped and the sky was now lightening into day. The ruin they had demolished as much as they could to cover the grave was only a part of a vast, devastated area where the signs of fire, explosion, and the use of weapons that could melt and curdle stone were only too evident. He stared about him, seeing no relation to anything he had known in his own world.

Finally he asked, "What is this place?"

Shara had tied together her bundle, taking care

with the scant remnants of the unpleasant field rations she had supplied. She looked up with a strange half smile.

"This is the one-time heart of the empire, my lord. Know you not the Triple Towers?"

"The—the Triple Towers?"

He put his hand to his head as if dazed by a blow. Nor could he believe that this wilderness of riven desolation was the vast spread of palace, pavilion, hall, courtyard, and garden that he had known so well all his life.

Andas turned slowly, pivoting, to seek out some point of reference, at least one of the towers themselves, or the bulk of the temple against the sky. But the change was too great. He could not guess where they now stood as compared with that other world.

"What happened here?" he demanded.

"Ask of Kidaya," Shara replied. "We were hiding afar, back in the hills. All we saw was the flash of fire. What survivors we have met were not in the palace at all, but across the river in Ictio, and they were all suffering from radiation burns."

"But if the burn-off destroyed Kidaya—"

"I did not say that! She and those who could best serve her purposes were away before it happened. We do not know whether it came from her will or some accident—but it ended our chance of holding the heart of Inyanga. We had those planted here ready to further our cause. And could Andas have reached the temple—" She shrugged. "What might have been and is are far removed one from the other."

"The temple!" Once more Andas's hand closed upon the key. If the other Andas had had its equivalent and could have reached the temple, and if the old records were true—

Shara turned around, much as Andas had when seeking a landmark. "That way, I think. But it is high in radiation, and no one can enter without a protecto suit, which is as difficult to obtain as Kidaya's death. What want you with the temple?"

He turned the key around. But what was the use of thinking now about what that might have led him to. If the temple lay in hard radiation, it was as far removed from his penetration as the third moon of Benin.

"Nothing that matters now. But I think we would be better away from any source of radiation. Where do we go?"

"This is wasteland now." She swung her bundle under one arm. "And the only path I know is the one by which we came. It is roundabout but will bring us to the Garden of Astarte, or what is left of it. And from there we go to the mountains. It is a weary walk and one not to be taken too openly. The enemy still send out scout skimmers. I know not how effective the Old Woman's seers may be, but Kidaya has put them to good use in the past. And such events as your coming through the gate of the Magi should have set up a troubling in that spirit world and made them suspicious."

She believed in cold facts, the colder the better, Andas decided. He translated her warnings to Yolyos, and they followed behind her. It was a weaving path, swinging wide at times to avoid places Shara told them still registered high in radiation. She had a small wrist detect, which he was not sure recorded correctly, but it was their only guard against straying into deadly territory.

All through that march Andas was unable to recognize any building or part of a building that he knew. He concentrated on Yolyos's learning the new language. Except that he had a hissing accent, the Salariki fortunately proved to be quick at picking up their speech. Of necessity his answers were curtailed and very simple, but he retained words at a single repeating much better, Andas thought, than he would be able to do himself under the circumstances.

They came out at last into a place where vegetation had survived, though it was an odd color and misshapen. Pillars had been tossed back and forth, crisscrossing each other on the ground as one might toss twigs in a game. But this was, Andas knew, the Garden of Astarte.

Here they halted, sheltering belly down under a trio of fallen pillars. Shara motioned at the ground stretching before them. There was not even a bush of a size to give cover.

"By day to walk there is to be seen," she commented. "They patrol outward from the Drak Mount, which is their stronghold."

"How far do we have to go?" Andas wanted to know.

"A day's travel, plus a night more, on foot. After we reach the cache there are elklands for riding, if they have not broken free."

"Wait!" Yolyos's hand closed upon Andas's upper arm. "Listen!"

He could hear now, too, the high, faint whine from the sky. There was a skimmer aloft.

-13-

It was a scout. Andas watched it hungrily. If they could get their hands on that now— He did not relish the cross-country travel Shara had described—not in this desolate waste.

"Are you thinking with me, Prince?" Yolyos was so close beside him the slightly raised fur of the Salariki's arm brushed his sleeve. "I believe that you are."

"How do we get it to land? By wishing?" Andas scoffed at his own desire.

"They must have a scanner," speculated the other. "Therefore, they can pick up the ground on their screen. Suppose they saw something—someone they had no reason to believe could be here—"

"Such as an emperor?" questioned Andas. "Their reaction would be to trigger a flamer!"

"Not an emperor, an alien." Yolyos's claws showed. "According to this lady, there have been no off-world ships here for some time. Therefore, they would want to know what a Salariki was doing at the ruins of their once First City. They must have a prisoner, not a dead body, to learn that."

"If we had even a stunner—" breathed Andas. It was utterly mad, but sometimes a mad throw in the very face of fate paid off. Above them was not only transportation but also men who could answer his questions.

"You plan something with this furred one?" Shara's voice was hardly above a whisper, as if she expected those cruising overhead to be able to pick up their voices.

"Weapons—surely you came here armed?" Andas returned. He had seen no blaster, stunner, or even sword or dagger with the dead emperor. But they were supposed to have fought their way out of an ambush to reach the ruins, and they could not have done that empty-handed.

For a moment she hesitated. Then her hands fumbled at the neckline of her outer robe, and she drew out a slender tube, hardly thicker than a branch a man could effortlessly snap between his hands.

"This—but the charge left is very small, perhaps only enough for a single firing."

She did not hand it to Andas. And when he reached for it, for a moment he thought she would not release it. Finally she let him take it. It was an officer's sidearm—a flame-needler. But it was strictly a short-range weapon and, if the charge was nearly exhausted, not too potent.

"They could turn a stun beam on you," he said to Yolyos. "I would under the circumstances, just to be on the safe side. They might even blanket the whole area—"

"Beam, yes," the Salariki agreed. "But blanket, I think not. They would carry only hand stunners on patrol. A skimmer is too light a craft to arm. They are sent to scout, not to fight. It only remains to be seen if I can make tempting bait."

Before Andas could put out a hand to stop him, Yolyos rolled out from under their pillar cover. But he did not get to his feet. Instead, he struggled only to his one knee, the other leg stretched out as if useless. He propped on one hand to balance himself, while with the other he waved, shouting aloud in Basic for help.

"He betrays us!" Shara snatched for the weapon Andas held. He fended her off.

"Quiet!" he ordered. "Yolyos is bait in a trap." He thought their chance was very slim, however. The skimmer had only to keep on hover and report back to its base. It all depended upon the temperament of those who manned the craft and whether they were cautious or otherwise.

Andas divided his attention between the Salariki, who was giving an excellent performance of someone hailing long-hoped-for aid, and the hovering craft. The skimmer had made a swift downward swoop and hung over the place where Yolyos was flopping about. Then a rope dropped from the belly of the craft, weighted with harness.

Why had he not foreseen that? Of course, with rescue equipment the skimmer did not need to land.

Yolyos's movements slowed. He was acting as one so weakened by some injury that his efforts of the last few moments had totally exhausted him. As the harness swung down, he made a very convincing grab

at it, falling back to lie still. There was a shout from
the skimmer. Yolyos lifted a hand in a gesture of
appeal and let it flop on his chest. His other, hidden
in the shadow of his body, held the force knife he
had taken from Grasty.

The line of the harness jerked and arose to dangle
in the air. Would they draw off now? No, a figure
appeared at the belly hatch of the skimmer and
took off with the leap of an anti-grav equipped sky
trooper, spiraling down almost lazily. He made an
excellent landing beside the prone Salariki and knelt
beside him.

Yolyos moved with the speed of a trained fighting man of his own species, reacting faster than any
human. He had one arm about the trooper, pinning
his hands away from his weapon, yet holding him
across his own body as a shield.

Andas leaped out of hiding, the flame-needler
gripped between his teeth, both hands outstretched to
catch the dangling line. He caught the harness, and
his weight pulled it earthward as he began to climb.
There was another after him—Shara had copied his
run. The skimmer went out of hover into rise, or
tried to.

But the very safety precautions built into the rescue
equipment defeated the pilot. Though both Andas and
the woman were lifted well above the ground, the
harness could not be reeled in while it supported a
double load, nor might the skimmer rise higher with
the harness outside, for it had been designed for the
ultimate safety of the unfortunate in the lift.

Andas could take no thought for Shara now. He
had only moments of which he must make the most.

He climbed the swaying line above the harness, and when the hatch was directly above him, he took the needler with one hand, prepared to fight his way in. It all depended now on the number of crew the skimmer carried, though these craft were not intended for many.

He was in the hatch. Behind him the rope of the harness began to coil in on its own since Shara's weight alone could not halt it. But Andas was facing the man, who, having put the skimmer on autopilot, was just emerging from the control section. He had a blaster at ready, but Andas fired a fraction of a second earlier.

The blaster ray was close. Andas cried out at the sear of it on his neck just below his ear. But the pilot had crumpled forward. The blaster, still blazing, spun past Andas, out of the hatch. He threw himself at the downed man, but the body was inert, and he scrambled over it to reach the controls. The rope of the harness was still winding in, and until it was all within the cabin, he could not set down. So he waited, tense.

Shara's unkempt head appeared above the edge of the hatch. She clung grimly to the harness, her eyes closed, her teeth set as if she were in the midst of an ordeal she could only endure. Andas moved back, caught her robe, and heaved her in with little ceremony. He let her lie gasping as he went to the controls and thumbed the button to set them down.

Even as the skimmer settled, he could hardly believe that their wild and hopeless ruse had paid off. But he was in the skimmer, the pilot was dead, and they were in command of the situation. By the look of it, Yolyos had finished off the other crew member.

Sometime later they hunched in the shadow of the craft, ravenously eating the rations the crew had carried. Andas had always considered E-rations as totally lacking in anything but strict nutritional value. But what he mouthed now from tube and container was equal to an Imperial feast.

Before them on the ground lay their prizes of battle. There was one stunner, a blaster (the one that had pitched from the skimmer had been too badly jammed when it struck the ground to use again), and another needler, as well as fresh rounds for the one Shara had brought. The dead crew of the ship had been stowed under the overlapping pillars where they could not be sighted from the air.

"The First Ancestress," remarked Yolyos, "is always said to favor the brave, though 'reckless' and 'brave' are not always the same. When I have time, I shall offer five jars of fine essences for her delight. And what do we now? We have a ship, we have weapons—"

Andas turned to Shara. "Where do we go? The skimmer can take us fast and far."

She had not said much since she had been so unceremoniously pulled through the hatch of the skimmer after her ride aloft on the harness. It was as if she thought, reserving speech for later.

"We must return to the Place of Red Water— there lie the Imperial forces now in the field. But we cannot fly all the way in this. There are defenses about the headquarters, and we would be sky-burned before we could signal. It would be best to set down in the heights. There are places there possible. It has been long since we have had any fliers of our own."

"And this is not a cruiser," Andas commented. "She is a scout and can give us little more aid than speedy transportation."

"I wonder if there is a tracer on her. Suppose there is and they send something heavier now to look for her? Yolyos remarked. "We'd best be off quickly."

They buckled on the weapon belts they had taken, Yolyos setting the force knife in a convenient loop on his. The stunner Andas passed to Shara. He found himself a little ill at ease with her now. Such feminine women (or as he thought feminine to be) as Elys and Abena he understood—a little. But this ugly, thin bone of a woman, with her tightly knotted hair, a woman who had so quickly risked her life to insure the success of their attack, was new to him. It was as if she expected to be treated as a battle comrade. And he found himself doing just that, speaking straightly as to another man—which was contrary to all his court training.

By Shara's guidance they flew north, in order to avoid any other air patrols. North was, she told them, largely wild country now. Where once broad farmlands and grazing uplands had provided most of the food for this whole section of the continent, now there stretched a desolate waste. Some of the farmers and herders flew south, forming ragged new settlements along the very edge of the Kalli. Many more had died on their own holdings or joined the Emperor's ragged force.

Beasts gone wild in the uplands were hunted and salted for the winter. But famine was a specter at every fire. They did not know how those at Drak

Mount fared now, save that there was a rumor that stores had been laid up there before the outbreak of the war.

"The enemy must be fewer now," Shara continued. But whether that was true or she only hoped it, they could not know. "The plague was hard upon them even before the Triple Towers were destroyed. And that was years since. But the defenses at Drak Mount are such that even were it manned by dead men, the devices set on auto, we could not fight our way in."

"Then how did Andas—your Andas—ever expect to bring the war to a finish?" Andas asked.

"We have cleaned the whole of the north of the enemy," she spoke proudly. "They have really only the Drak Mount now. If they did not have such craft as this, we would not fear them at all. We reckon that they have at least two cruisers left with mounted flamers—though those we have not seen lately. My dear lord hoped to discover in the cache of the Magi some aid. Instead, he found his death."

"You spoke of treachery—"

"With good reason!" she said swiftly. "Only his own guard, three of his most trusted leaders, and perhaps the Arch Priest, knew what he would do. Also the cache was so well hidden that they did not find us there by chance. No, one of those he trusted betrayed him—for there was a party waiting in ambush. And it was only because of one of the Magi's safeguards, which my lord knew of, that we two won free. The rest died, for the safeguard was no respecter of right or wrong when it struck."

"You do not suspect one above the others?" Andas had no mind to be a second target.

"No." She answered him promptly enough.

They had set the skimmer on top speed, fleeing the vicinity of Drak Mount. Andas gave his attention now to the sweep of land below as it was recorded on the visa-screen. She was very right. One could trace the boundaries of once prosperous farms and holds, but the area was clearly under a blight, which had reduced it from wealth to scrubby half-wilderness. Nor did anything creep along the deserted roads.

Some of those roads headed to the port of Garbuka on the eastern sea, the main outlet for Ictio with the sea trade. Andas remembered those arteries in constant use.

Mountains arose—the Kumbi ranges.

Shara spoke. "Steer by the Crown of Stars."

Obediently Andas went on manuals and swung the skimmer west toward the landmark mountain. The country below was rough. Once this had been used for the systematic planting and harvesting of bluewoods, those trees esteemed by stellar trade not only for their beauty, but also for the extreme durability of the lightweight, highly polished furniture that could be fashioned from them. Andas could see now their peculiar wide-branched crowns pushing above the lower growth, very noticeable from above, where they looked like large, flat platters laid upon the uneven covering of the other woodland.

"To the north of that crag, there is a landing place." Shara pointed a grimed finger on which the nail was ragged and broken. Again he swung to her guidance.

She was right. There was a level space, enough to set down the skimmer, and they made a straight descent, though Andas wondered a little at the future difficulties with mountain winds.

"We need anchorage," he said as they climbed out.

"So, not too difficult—ropes around the rocks ought to do." Yolyos indicated large stones that had slipped down the upper slopes to make a ragged fringe along the side of the landing space.

The harness hoist supplied some anchor lines, and they found another length of tough rope in the cabin locker. With these they wove such a netting anchor as would keep the skimmer where it was in spite of a storm.

Evening clouds were gathering, and Andas eyed them dubiously. Out of the skimmer's supplies they had assembled two packs, far too small, but all they could find. He and Yolyos could carry those easily, but the ledge on which they had set down was still well above the level of the forest. And he did not fancy a descent in the dark. Nor was he sure Shara knew the road from here.

"The Place of Red Water—where?" he asked as they trudged along the rim of the plateau looking for a place to descend.

"To the west, crossing through the Pass of the Two Horns." She spoke confidently, as if she carried a map with a vocal director in her hand.

He tried to remember. The mountains, yes, he had been here—enough to recognize the Crown of Stars. But the Pass of the Two Horns—no memory supplied that, just as the Place of Red Water was a name new to him.

"We cannot travel by night," she continued. "But

that does not matter. There is a foresters' post near here. That will shelter us, and if it is manned, there will be news also."

"This way!" Yolyos gestured from where he had loped along ahead of them.

He had discovered a broken series of smaller ledges, like irregular steps, down which they could go. Andas fought his old fear of heights, keeping his eyes at a point immediately before him. But he was sweating and a little sick when they reached the scrub beginning of the woodland. Shara pushed ahead, eying the growth. A moment later she turned, much of her assurance gone.

"I can see no trail landmark that I know," she admitted frankly.

Yolyos's head was up, his nostrils dilated. "You may not see, lady," he said in his halting growl of her speech, "but smell I can! There are men—that way!"

"How does he—?" She looked to Andas.

"His species have a far better sense of smell than we do. If he says there are men that way, he is right."

Shara dropped behind Andas, to the tail of their party, as if she were so dubious about their present course that she wanted to be able to retreat in a hurry if disaster loomed.

That Yolyos was right, in at least the fact men had been here, was proven when they pushed through a screen of brush into a trail. Once in that slot Yolyos turned left. But as he went, he asked Shara, "Are your friends, lady, such as will shoot first and hail strangers afterwards? If so, how can we make sure we shall not be their targets?"

She did not answer in words but raised her head a little, testing the breeze. She pursed her lips and uttered a small fluting whistle. Three times she signaled so and then waved them on. But within ten paces she whistled again, this time twice, and, at a third time, once.

They had come to the foot of a bluewood, and her answer reached them from overhead when a vine ladder whipped down out of the foliage. Shara pushed by the others and climbed, Andas and Yolyos following.

What they came into was a very well-concealed camp. Its like had been known, mainly as curiosity, in the gardens of the Triple Towers, but here it had been put to practical use. The bluewood had branches that were inclined to grow from the tree trunk at sharp right angles. They were also relatively straight beyond that point. Use had been made of this natural peculiarity on three levels, planks laid across and fastened to form an arbor house of three stories, vine ladders leading from one to the next.

Those who sheltered here, once their entrance ladder was up, could not be sighted, for the underside of the planks that formed their springy floors had been covered with growing things, while the flatly spreading top of the tree, well overhead, was a roof no skimmer could sight through.

The man who awaited their coming was as thin as Shara, and his clothing was as coarse as hers, though it had been dyed in patches of green and brown, so that it matched woodland coloring. He had clumsy thong-bound leggings and a tight-fitting cap to which were stuck bits of leaf and vine. Andas could believe that in the woodland he could walk hidden.

"Hearth claim, master," Shara said.

He looked at her searchingly and then beyond, to Andas. When his eyes met those of the prince, his face came alive, and he dropped on one knee, both hands outstretched, palms up. His weapon, a crossbow, lay on the floor beside him.

"Sun of Dingane! That you should be here!"

"And glad for it," Andas answered. He made the traditional gesture, finger right to left on the man's palms. "We need shelter this night."

"And for once the hunting has been good!" The man's face still mirrored amazement. "I have meat, Great Lord."

Still kneeling, he waved toward the ladder to the next level. "Please to climb. There shall be food speedily. And here you may rest safely. There is none, not even the tree kangor, who dares this fort-place."

"You are named?"

"Kai-Kaus of the House of Korb, Great Lord. Once we held—"

"From the Upper Lumbo to the sea." Andas nodded. "And you will again."

"That we doubt not, Great Lord," the forester replied proudly. He was quite young, Andas saw, but there was about him the air of a man who was doing what he had to do with competence. Though he was dressed as a forester, it was apparent that he was of noble blood.

The next platform, which was the middle one of the three, was apparently the living quarters of those manning this post. There was a bed place wide enough for two, fashioned of ferns and leaves. Some calabashes with their stoppers well pounded in sat in a line, and a box had its lid thrown back to display crossbow bolts. Also there was a square of stone-rimmed clay where blackened embers showed fires burned.

Their host speedily joined them with a bundle of wood and a packet of bloodstained hide, which he unrolled to display dukker meat cut into strips and impaled with chunks of tree melon on skewers of green wood. Andas's mouth watered. This was far better than the rations from the skimmer, or the musty, dried stuff Shara had shared with them.

The forester laid his fire and brought it to life. Andas reached for the nearest skewer.

"There is no ceremony among comrades at war. We eat as one tonight."

For a moment it seemed that both Shara and the forester would protest. But when Andas held his skewer to the flames, they picked up their own. Yolyos was already pushing his to the fire.

Andas saw Kai-Kaus glancing at the Salariki. After all, now any alien would be suspect. And he must make sure Yolyos was placed above suspicion.

"This is our comrade in battle—the Lord Yolyos from off-world. He has also been a prisoner of those we hunt and are hunted by, and by his aid only have we come through a great peril. He is thus named Lion Friend and Shield Upon the Left." From old tales Andas dragged those titles, the meaning of which might be forgotten, but would still be honored by those loyal to the Emperor. He remembered that his grandfather had once named a warrior so who had saved his son's life. And thereafter the court gave that man, though a commoner, the honor due a first house lord.

"To the Lord Yolyos, greeting—" The forester raised his hand in salute.

Yolyos looked up from the skewer he was tending so carefully. "To Kai-Kaus, greeting. It is a good hunter who can provide so well for unexpected guests."

The boy shifted. "It has been a lucky day. Some fear sent the herd on the move down trail. I was able to pick off five before they stampeded. They have grown so wary from our hunting that it is seldom we can find them so. It is perhaps by the will of Akmedu that this happened so I would have food for my lord—"

"Or something else. If a thing is not natural, it is suspect!" cut in Shara.

"That is so, lady. And the reason why I am alone here. Ikiui, who is a trained scout, has gone to see what set the herd moving. There are no hunters now except us, and I do not think the enemy would venture into the wilderness."

"Never underestimate an enemy." Yolyos had withdrawn his skewer, though to Andas's eye the meat on it was hardly cooked. He used thumb and forefinger to jerk the end lump from it, waved the bite for a moment in the air, and then popped it into his mouth, chewing with the noisy good manners of his people.

-14-

There were no lamps to be lit in this tree house, and even the coals of fire were covered at the coming of full dusk by an earthen bowl. The forester swung down to the lower platform and crouched there, listening, and now the dark was such they could hardly see him.

Yolyos, once his hunger was satisfied, sought the same vantage point. And now Andas dropped down the ladder also.

"What do you listen for?" He stood beside Kai-Kaus.

"Ikiui. He has not returned. Yet we do not walk the forest trails at night."

"So?" The Salariki moved closer. "And why not?"

"The tree cats hunt by night, as do the great serpents. And lately, there are other things—" His voice trailed away, and Andas suspected he did not want to discuss those "other things."

But that very suspicion led him to press for information.

"Those being?"

"Nothing any man has seen—and lived."

"But some have seen—and died?"

"Yes. Four men of the southern range, Great Lord. Their bodies, two of them, were found in the trail easy to see—left as a warning, we believe. They had met the night crawlers—"

Andas froze. But legends could not live! The horrific tales that gave children pleasurable shivers up the spine had no base in real life.

"They were," Kai-Kaus continued in a low voice, as if by telling the story at all he could be invoking the evil he described, "drained of blood. We have found forest animals treated so, also, twice plainly hung on bushes to be seen—but those were earlier. Ikiui, he feared that the stampede might have been caused by such an attack."

The forester was so certain of his facts that Andas's disbelief was shaken. After all, the events of his own immediate past were enough to prove that anything was possible.

"The night crawlers serve her," Kai-Kaus whispered. "And that she-rat of the Drak Mount is her voice, as she has sworn openly. Also that one has danced the Bones before the eyes of the living and promised that all beyond her cloak of safety will be the meat of the Old Woman."

Danced the Bones! That anyone had dared so drastic a ritual—this Inyanga was indeed a bedeviled land. Andas's hand went to the seam pocket wherein lay the ring. Did these women know wherein they dabbled? Or was their hunger for power so great that they did not care?

He recalled those tales he had considered fiction. Remembering one thing after another, he shivered. The ring—he must rid himself of that talisman if Kai-Kaus spoke the truth and that which should never be named now crawled this forest land.

Where to get rid of the ring? It must be lost in some place where no follower of the Old Woman could sniff it out, for by all accounts those who had taken such oaths were attuned to these things and they could be drawn. Perhaps even to carry it with him now would make them a focal point of attack.

"There is trouble—" Yolyos's growl was subdued to a rumble hardly louder than Kai-Kaus's whisper. "I can smell it on the wind."

"What kind of trouble? Someone coming?"

"Not so. This is the doom thing again." He made a spitting sound of disgust. "Evil. It stinks worse than the rotting hole of a gorp's nest. Also"—he was silent a moment and then added swiftly—"one flees before it. And his fear is as great a stench as that which follows him."

Andas listened. He could hear nothing. Only, out of the dark, came Kai-Kaus's hand to close about his arm.

"Lord, I am your man to defend you to the death. Get up into the fort level, taking the ladder with you. What comes may be only seeking hunters—"

"Before I was an emperor, liege man," Andas answered, "I was a warrior, taking blood oath. And among the words of that oath is a promise of shield rights in battle. I do not let others fight my wars for me."

"An emperor has no choice, Great Lord. That other men die for his life is the pattern of things, for with the head of state dead, the state itself crumbles into nothingness. When you became Emperor, you put aside the rights and duties of a warrior to take on a greater burden.

Andas had to recognize the truth by which he had been reared. An emperor was no longer a man—he was the embodiment of all that made the empire, and his life must be bought, if that need arose, by the blood of others. Yet he was not going to let this begin here and now.

"Not yet," he said. "Yolyos, what else can you tell us?"

"He who runs is close. That which follows is yet a space away. But the runner is near the end of his endurance."

Even as he spoke, there was a rustling that was not wind. It came from below—someone was trying to attract attention.

"The ladder—drop it!" Andas ordered.

"He will have to go hence so that you be not endangered."

"Emperor or no, I do not reign in the Triple Towers," Andas burst out. "Nor may I ever. Those rules about the Lion in Glory do not stand now." He could not be responsible for this. Groping across the floor, he found the ladder and dropped it before Kai-Kaus could stop him. The vine lines were taut—the fugitive was already on his way up.

Andas could hear the heavy gasping breath of the climber. He did not need Yolyos to assure him that the man came with death breathing at his heels.

"Kai-Kaus! The man crawled over the edge. "Night crawlers—"

"Quiet! cried the other forester fiercely out of the dark.

Andas's hands closed on the man's heaving shoulders as he sprawled up onto the platform. He dragged him away from the hole and pulled up the ladder as fast as he could. Perhaps whatever hunted would be baffled at the disappearance of its prey aloft and go on. He did not regret his decision. Emperor or not, he was not and perhaps never would be able to accept such sacrifices. He must walk his own road. Perhaps that other Andas had chosen poorly when he had summoned him through the gate; perhaps he would have been a failure himself had he indeed been crowned in his own world. It might be that he was not the material of which emperors were made, unbending, infallible to those about them. Well, he must be himself or be utterly lost.

"Close—" Yolyos's warning was a thread of sound.

Andas dropped belly down on the platform, his head over the ladder opening, staring at the dark below. Here and there he saw the flitting of huge ghost moths, their almost transparent wings outlined and ribbed with fluorescence. And there were some small plants that had the same eerie radiance, using that lure to attract prey. But there was something else—

Yolyos spoke of smells, stenches. Now Andas put his hand to his nose, trying to shut out the odor wafted to his post. This must be pure torment to the Salariki with its sensitivity. It was decay, old death. Though he had never smelled either, he thought of both now.

And there was a wan light also, like that of the ghostly moths, yet unclean. If such a stink could have light, this was it.

With his other hand Andas worked the needler free of his belt and drew it forward. He did not know what hunted below, but he had never seen anything yet that could survive a needler attack at full strength. And having reloaded it, he could set it on that.

The thing coming along the trail moved swiftly, but it did not seem to walk or run on normal feet. He aimed and fired at the fat bulk.

The burst of needler ray lit up the trail. He heard a wailing that screeched up the scale until human ears could no longer detect it. But his body, his head, was pierced through and through by the sonic vibrations the thing was now emitting. He fired again, though this time, tormented by that vibration, he could not be sure he aimed true.

It threshed about, beating at the growth, flattening and tearing at bushes in its agony. Then that terrible sound ended, and it lay still, though Andas had caution enough not to believe it was yet dead.

"You have a needler!" Kai-Kaus had crowded beside him. "We have not seen one for seasons now."

If crossbows were the best armament the loyal forces had in plenty, Andas did not wonder at the other's pessimistic attitude toward fighting the monster below.

"I'll lay another shot—" He was aiming when Yolyos spoke.

"The thing is dead. Have you a torch? We had better look upon this enemy so that we know it again," he said to Kai-Kaus.

"Here is your light." They turned their heads. Halfway down the ladder from the sleeping platform was Shara, in one hand a brand glowing red. She twirled this a little, and the fire came alive, giving them a source of light in the dark.

"My thanks, lady!" Kai-Kaus caught the brand from her.

"Is there anything else waiting down there?" Andas asked Yolyos.

"The stink overlays much. But I pick up nothing save the life forms that are harmless. I think this thing hunted alone."

Kai-Kaus made no objection when Andas descended the ladder behind him. The realization that the new-comers had the superior weapons had done much to allay his sense of responsibility for his ruler.

On the ground the smell was so terrible that Yolyos held his nose, gasping. Almost, if with lesser reason, Andas could have duplicated that gesture. But he forced himself to prod the white thing now curled into a half ball in its final convulsion.

He stared down as Kai-Kaus swung the torch close, and then he backed away, his shoulders heaving in a rising nausea he could not control. Thus, he leaned against a sapling along the trail and lost all his earlier supper.

Yolyos reeled away in turn. Andas saw him run for the ladder and pull himself up, as if the thing had come alive. Nor were the two foresters long behind him, though they waited at the ladder foot, urging Andas up before them.

The sight of that—that thing—had been such as to almost paralyze his mind for moments. Anyone familiar

with tapes made by star travelers (and his father had
had a fine collection of such, which he had known
from childhood) was aware that there were many
strange—even horrifying—life forms in the galaxy. But
never had Andas seen anything to equal what lay in
the forest of his own world.

Unclean? It was more than unclean. It was so
heavy with evil and filth that it seemed impossible
for it to have held life. Yet there was a teasing sense
that he had viewed something like it before—not
exactly like, but near enough that this tantalizing
resemblance now made him uneasy.

From whence it had come, he had no clue. Was
it even native to any of the planets of the empire?
He hoped not. He trusted that such spawn had never
developed under the sun he knew. Yet, there was that
familiarity—

"In the name of the First Ancestress"—Yolyos's
voice was a little muffled by the hands still clapped
across his nose, as if he could so strain the stench
from the night air—"what is that thing?"

"I do not know—" Andas was beginning when a
memory far buried came to the surface of his mind.
"An eloplan—but it can't be!"

"An eloplan from the garden of the Old Woman."
Shara cut across his denial. "An eloplan and something
else—worse. She has more than gardeners serving her.
She has the Nessi Magi—"

After seeing that dead thing, he could believe anything. But that any Magi, no matter how far from the
true light, could serve the Old Woman—that was a
contradiction of terms. The Magi were male, and their
training forced them to keep to their own sex all their

knowledge. The Old Woman could and would receive only the worship of women, women who had such natures that they were known as hers almost from their birth hours. Magi and the Old Woman—no!

"The Nessi Magi"—Shara could have been reading his thoughts—"are apart. They entered into an alliance with the Old Woman just after Kidaya began her ensorcellment of the Emperor. They acted truly as if their minds were turned about in their skulls, so they thought entirely differently. It was one of those three who brought about the death of the Emperor. And twice have they tried to set a sending on you. Do you not remember that, my lord?" Her voice was a warning, and he was aware that this was one of the things he must appear to know.

"With Nessi knowledge, creatures such as the night crawlers could be bred. We have no information concerning what they were, are, able to do. It was always research that interested the Nessi."

Andas forced himself to consider what he had seen dead as rationally as he could in the light of her suggestion. An eloplan—mobile at certain times of the year, able to travel from one favorable rooting ground to another—was a vegetable curiosity. He had seen small captive ones in the exotic palace gardens.

But this had been no plant—it had had a head. Andas clamped his teeth together and willed fiercely not to be sick again. This had been partly—horribly— human! And if the Nessi Magi were responsible for such, they must be rooted out, exterminated, and all their unholy knowledge eradicated with them.

"You said night crawlers," he said to Kai-Kaus. "There are more of these things?"

It was Ikiui who answered. He had been eying Andas with awed recognition as the prince stood in the light of the torch, and he saluted as he spoke.

"Lord, there are at least four loosed in the forest this night. All the warm-blooded creatures flee before them. They are driving out the game."

"And you know from whence they come?"

"Only that they move from the east. Nor do they turn aside, save to feed. Also, they are, I think, directed."

"How so?"

"There was a water loffin they surprised, and it ran past them east. One of the crawlers started after it. I—" He put his hands to his head as if in memory of some hurt. "In my head there was a pain. The crawler reared and cried out as if it were angry, yet it came back from the loffin trail."

"And where were you to watch this?"

"In the vineways above. I would not have been trailed, but there was a place where the vines did not run. When I came to earth, that one hunted me."

"As if you might have been sighted and that creature sent to make sure of you? There was a skimmer overhead then?"

"No. And if so, no one aboard could have seen through the veil of trees. Whatever spy is used was closer than the air above the forest."

"Close indeed." Yolyos still held his nose with one hand so his speech sounded odd. "Prince, that is not a good thing to look upon, but I think you should examine it again. I caught a glimpse of something—though I may not have seen aright."

The last thing Andas wanted was to approach the

kill again, but he did not disdain the importance of
Yolyos's suggestion. Very reluctantly he descended,
Kai-Kaus coming with the torch. The Salariki remained
behind at Andas's order—this ordeal was doubly hard
for him.

That fat worm body still lay in the coil it had
assumed upon death, but not so tightly. Andas took
the torch from Kai-Kaus and forced himself to view
the thing with searching intensity, though he gulped
and fought nausea.

The light held steady on the round of body just
behind the head. Luckily the head itself had dropped
forward, to lie face down, so he did not have to view
that. He spoke to Kai-Kaus.

"Hold steady, and give me your skinning knife!"

It took every bit of resolution Andas could summon to work with the knife, hacking free what was
embedded in the fetid flesh, until he could stand it no
longer and ripped and pulled in a frenzy that brought
loose a bespattered device, trailing horribly befouled
wiring from the body of the creature.

Andas set his trophy on the ground and grabbed
at leaves and grass to wipe it off as best he could.
But he would have to take it with him, and his flesh
shrank from touching it. Still he would not ask Kai-
Kaus to do it for him.

At length he managed to wrap leaves about it and
carried it up to the tree fort. Laid out on the floor,
it proved to be a complex machine, probably of the
electronic order. And his knowledge of such was less
than adequate. He looked inquiringly to Yolyos, but
the Salariki made a gesture of denial.

"I am no tech, Prince. But I would venture to say

this is no simple thing. And undoubtedly it was used to control the creature."

"Could it be something of the mercenaries?" Andas asked.

"More likely Nessi," Shara returned. "But I would not believe they could make such a device now with most of the empire in ruins. Such technology is the result of highly specialized manufacturing. We have no factories or labs left. And I do not believe that the Drak Mount has either—it is a place given wholly to war."

"What of the Valley of Bones?" Andas had been poking at the box with the point of the hunting knife, taking care not to touch it directly.

He heard a whistle of breath from the others. One did not mention that name directly. It was so great a taboo that for him to break it was almost as if he shouted a curse in a place of honor.

"Kidaya is of the Old Woman's kin," he said slowly, making that a statement rather than a question, but watching Shara to make sure he did not make a mistake. "Perhaps it was she who brought the Nessi and her mistress together. And what better place would they find in which to hide their misbegotten experiments than the valley? I begin to think that it is not to the Drak Mount we should face, but in another direction!"

"My lord"—Kai-Kaus spoke up then—"we cannot stand against the Old Woman."

"So have we always been taught," agreed Andas. "And there was method in that teaching. The Old Woman is a woman's thing, and they have mysteries no male can understand. But if such mysteries now shadow this land, we must do as Akmedu did in his time—carry war to that heart."

He was still staring at the box that might mean so much, yet he was aware that all save Yolyos had withdrawn from him a step or two. Pledged they might be to the Emperor's cause, still he might discover that there were none to back him in this. But in his mind it was proven as true, as if he had tapes to support the idea that he was right—the war spread from the fortress held by the off-worlders, but it fed upon the flaw in his own people, from their clinging to custom, their long conditioning.

There had always been a strong strain of mysticism in his race. In some this took the form of formal religion, or a delving into philosophy, or experimentation with esper. With others it followed a darker trend—to such things as the worship of the Old Woman, the researches of the Nessi. It was in him, too—when he had reacted to the ring he had taken from Abena.

But he would have to set aside beliefs and fears if he was going into this battle. Men—and women—who had been ground down to the extremity of these foresters, of Shara, half starved as she was, perhaps did not have the inner will to break old bounds. They would be easy prey for such devil's tricks as the crawlers.

Perhaps because he was not fully one with them— and he had Yolyos who was not of them at all—he would have a chance. But it might be that he would be forced to take that chance alone.

Andas dropped the knife. He reached within his coverall and brought out the key. It shown ruddily in the torch light. And he kept it in his right hand. But with the left he freed the ring and drew it from that pocket in his closed fist, holding it well away from the key—for they still stood in his mind as opposite poles of light and dark, good and evil.

Then he gave an exclamation, for the cool metal circlet in his fist was not cool any longer. He opened his hand. On his palm lay the ring. And it glowed—but from no reflected torchlight. It was the gleam of life. And at the same time the device he had dug out of the crawler gave a spark of flame and began a low humming.

-15-

"A seer ring!" Shara drew away farther yet.

At her cry the others, except for the Salariki, stared at him.

"A seer ring." Deliberately Andas confirmed her identification. "One I took from a handmaiden of the Old Woman when she sought to use it to my betrayal. But think you that I could also hold this"—he raised the key so that they could see it clearly—"if I had surrendered my will to such a ring?"

Perhaps the foresters did not know the key, but Shara would surely understand. She had witnessed the other Andas's reaction to it.

"He is right," she said after a moment. "This is the key to the heart. But to bear it together with the ring—"

"The ring must be destroyed. But how can that be done until I find a place in which it can be forever hid?" Andas countered. "Bury it in the ground, throw it into a chasm or lake, and can you say that there

217

will not be those whose nature will draw them to it? Also, perhaps it can be made to aid us—"

"Look at it!" Shara had been watching the ring. Andas did indeed look.

The milky-white setting showed a thickening swirl of color—something was coming through! But he had done nothing to summon—Andas raised the key between him and the ring as a protection, the only one he could think of.

"Back," he ordered, "out of line with this!"

The others were only too ready to obey, pulling away as if he had a live flamer in his hand, one about to spew destruction.

"Throw it away!" Shara cried. "My lord, meddle not with the things of that she-devil!"

Every instinct in Andas agreed with her. Yet he held tight command over his desires and continued to hold the ring. At that moment it spelled contact with the core of the enemy force. And all he could learn would be to his advantage. But he did flip the glowing circlet about so that he was not looking into the setting, but rather down from above, while it was focused on the device from the crawler.

In addition to sputtering sparks from that device, the wires he had ripped loose came alive, writhing on the floor as if they still governed movements in the body from which they had been pulled. The ring was now yellow-green, and in it moved, not the picture he had expected, but a series of spark impulses that made tiny patterns. But those came and vanished so quickly that he could not be sure of any.

"The question is"—Yolyos had not withdrawn as the others and now squatted on his heels by Andas, watching those sparks—"is that broadcasting or receiving? Does the ring activate that device, or the unit the ring? And can such a broadcast be picked up elsewhere?"

He was interrupted by Ikiui. "Listen, my lord!"

He need not have warned them, for it was plain to hear—that wailing that could be heard in the night, yet rang in one's head.

"Crawlers—more than one!" Kai-Kaus had gone on hands and knees to the entrance for the ladder. "They are coming—"

"The ring! Perhaps it called them!" cried Shara.

Andas closed his fist again about it and almost cried out at the heat radiating from the metal. He slipped it back in hiding.

"Perhaps this is for the best." Yolyos had drawn his needler. "I would rather meet those things on a field of my choosing than loose in the woods. Summon them in and pick them off—as we do the gorp in the great hunts!"

"You are right!" With only crossbows for defense, the crawling horrors might seem menaces to the foresters. But faced with superior weapons, they could be disposed of with what appeared now to Andas as ease. And to have them gathered in one place for slaughter—

He dropped a hand on Kai-Kaus's shoulder. "Is there a way we can set an ambush above that trail—pick them off as they come?"

"For us perhaps, my lord. But you are not trained so—"

"Just show me a stable perch."

"If we have time." There was a new eagerness in

Kai-Kaus's face. Their triumph over one of the weird beasts had given him confidence.

Shara moved into Andas's path. "My lord, you bear the ring, and you would go to meet those things which answer to it. I beg of you, do not leave with what may be a break in your defenses! You do not know how that acts, only that it has been alerted by the device which directs the crawlers. What if it can compel you to meet them on their own ground?"

"It did not before."

"Then, my lord, you had not deliberately exposed it. It was not 'alive'—not until you held it before that device. But alive it has powers."

Was it the old superstition working in her, or was her warning a legitimate one? Before he could decide, Yolyos closed in on the other side.

"A suggestion, Prince. If that ring is bait, let it be bait indeed. Set it or suspend it so as to pull them to our best advantage."

Andas was reluctant to let the ring out of his control. From the first he had feared that if he loosed it, it might escape him altogether. But Shara's warning influenced him somewhat. After all, to battle enemy forces holding that which might prove traitor was folly. And Yolyos's suggestion had good logic.

"The stranger lord is right, my lord," Ikiui agreed. "Use it for bait."

Andas left it to the foresters to select the proper ambush, and they moved swiftly. The wailing, which had only been a faint cry at first, was growing louder. Also the forest itself had come alive about them, its inhabitants fleeing a common doom as they might have run before a fire. Bushes threshed, flying things cried with small hoots and flutings, and there was a scurrying on the ground beneath their trees.

The prince discovered that the foresters were indeed right in mistrusting his ability aloft. He had to be pushed and shoved along one of the tree branches that supported the platform to reach another lower limb, which was not so comfortable and swayed under him. Kai-Kaus passed him a length of vine rope made fast to the tree trunk, so that he had a lifeline.

He was slightly irritated to learn that the Salariki was far more surefooted in his limb travel, having little or no difficulty in scrambling aloft in another tree across the trail. Andas knotted the ring, testing the fastening over and over again, before he allowed the vine end to which it was tied to drop. The glow of the set increased in color as it swayed back and forth. And now that wailing was silenced.

Andas turned to Kai-Kaus, not too far away on the same leafy perch.

"They are—?" he began when a faint hiss warned him into silence.

He balanced as well as he could, waiting, though the interval was not long, for out of the brush pushed the white mass of a crawler. It came at a pace faster than he would have allowed for its bulk to squat below the ring. The forepart of its half-seen body, visible because of its paleness in the general gloom, reared as it tried apparently to reach the ring.

Its repeated failures did not seem to matter. It kept on rearing, even though at best it was well below the dangling treasure it sought. And it was still single-mindedly busy when a second of its kind appeared.

The monsters took no notice of each other. It was

as if their world had narrowed to the ring. The smaller
rocked against the larger as they both reared, sending
it off balance. There was a sharp grunt, and the head
of the larger swung around to butt its companion
away from the bait.

Since the smaller accepted the challenge, they were
striking at each other when a third and greater one
arrived, plowing up and over the struggling bodies
of the other two, aiming at the ring. Its questing
forelimbs (if you could call them such) came close
to achieving the goal. Andas, afraid that a second try
might be successful, fired. He had given no warning
to Yolyos. But at the same instant his needler rayed
out, the other fired also, so that the twisting bodies
below were caught in a cross fire that was fatal.

Were there any more? And would the lure of the
ring suffice to draw them even though some signal of
their companions' ending might have been broadcast?
The men waited in the branches above for what seemed
to Andas such a stretch of time as must comprise half
the night. But no more crawlers appeared, nor did
they hear any wailing.

At last, Andas, stiff from his unaccustomed position
and wondering if he could cope as well with a second
attack, hooked in the vine and loosed the ring, to stow
it away safely. Evil token it might be, but tonight it
had served them well. And there was a chance that
they might continue to use its calling powers for their
own ends. He was more confident about the future
since they had won this engagement. First they had
taken the skimmer by wild chance and now defeated
these monsters.

When they were back again in the tree fort, Andas

was willing enough to stretch out on the bed place. His body ached from that cramping vigil in the tree-top, and he could not remember sleeping since that abortive try in the commander's quarters.

Green light sifted down through the branches when he awoke. At least it was day, but what hour he could not tell. He rolled over to see that he had shared his bed. Shara's head was pillowed beside his. Her sunken eyes were closed, but he thought she looked a shade less gaunt now and younger—

How old was she? She had announced herself the Chosen of the Emperor. There had been cases in the past of marked disparity of ages for dynastic reasons, but he began to believe that she was no worn woman as she had first appeared—haggard with the hardships of her hunted life—but a girl instead. And he was still searching her face for some clue as to the truth of that when her eyes opened.

There was instant awareness in those eyes. She was like a trained warrior who wakes at once to any alarm. But she said nothing, only returned his study, surveying his face with the same intensity he turned upon her.

They were alone on the bed platform of the tree as he saw when, embarrassed, he sat up, a little ashamed he had been detected spying on her as she slept.

"You are the Emperor's Chosen." He was at some loss as how to approach the matter of his own feelings.

"But not yours." Her voice was the faintest murmur of sound, meant to carry to his ears only. "My choosing was a matter of state—or began so—"

For once imagination told him what he guessed was the truth. "But later it became otherwise between you two?" Inwardly he was now doubly ashamed at his own blindness. The death of that other Andas might have ended part of her world for her, but it had meant nothing but a burden for him. In his self-centeredness he must have been cruel where he should have been kind. He had thought only what events meant to him and inwardly struggled against enmeshment, resentful of the man who had committed him to this life. That the other Andas had been devoted to duty and had taken the only way left to save his plans, he did not doubt. But he, too, had been selfish, or he would not have sentenced a stranger to this.

"It became otherwise." Again her light whisper wrenched him from his thoughts to consider her. But she did not enlarge upon that admission.

The Chosen of the Emperor—his wife, though not his empress, until he could crown her publicly. He had a wife in the sight of his loyal followers and one he could not possibly disown.

That thought bothered him. His father's solitary life, which he had shared, had been devoid of feminine company. They had not even had a woman servant. And when Andas had been drawn into the life of the court, he had shortly thereafter gone to Pav for warrior training, again a world without women. There had been ladies enough at court on his return ready to toss him their flower bracelets. But he had been too shy, too ill at ease in such company, to react to their invitations. And there had been no official marriage made for him before that night when he had gone to bed in the palace—to awaken in the prison on another planet.

Since then, there had been Elys for whom he

had been sorry, judging her by his own fears and feelings, only to learn that she had been more alien than the furred Salariki. And he had seen the Princess Abena—he smiled wryly at the memory of that meeting. Abena was supposedly his daughter. Now here was this frail-looking yet tough wraith, with her drab barbaric dress, who claimed to have been the other Andas's Chosen. How closely would she expect him to carry out that previous relationship?

He had no feelings about her, save a kind of impatient pity—impatient because she was part of the new life he could not discard. Could it be that lack of emotion was the sign of an android? The old fear bubbled in him. If he only knew more about androids! They had been forbidden for so long that the references he had were mainly hearsay. But could they have made an android so physically human that he could deceive a medic, even father children? But if the false emperor was not false—then he, Andas, was android!

"Your thoughts are troubled." He had risen to his feet, but she only sat up on the bough bed. "I do not claim more from you than you can give, save that before others we must make a pretence, for the truth shall be kept. For his sake will I keep it!" And the concern in her voice became a warning.

"Before others I shall play my part as best I can. And I can play it better if you will tell me more."

She nodded. "This is a good time for such talk. We are alone. Even that furred one you speak of as friend has gone with the hunters. With the crawlers dead, there is a chance hunting will improve. And any chance to increase our food supply must be seized.

"The headquarters of your forces are at the Place of Red Water. You have four first captains now. There is Kwayn Makenagen. He is the oldest, once Governor of the North Marches, a tall man but a little stooped, and he has a habit of pulling on his lower lip so"—she demonstrated—"when he is thinking deeply or is at some disadvantage. He is none too fast at that thinking, but once he sets upon a matter, he does not drop it until the end.

"Next is Patopir Ishan. He is younger, a valiant fighter, but reckless, and needs the curb hand. He limps from an old wound, but is very soft-spoken and charms women as much as if he wore a love mirror about his throat. His face is handsome, and he laughs much, but he is also shrewd. Only his reckless impulses to action keep him from being truly great.

"The third captain is the Lady Bahyua Banokue."

"A woman!"

"Just so." Shara made a reproof of his two words with her tone. "When her lord fell at the battle of Ninemarr, she took command of the forces and stopped the rout. She is very shrewd in council and brings years of experience, for she is of middle life and had four sons in your service. Only one remains alive.

"And the fourth and last of your leaders, my lord, is one Shara. I have led my house since we broke out of the fire ring at Tortu and my elder brother covered our retreat.

"These are the ones with whom you will deal mostly, but there are others you must learn to recognize." She continued patiently, and he strove to memorize the details about men and a few women whom, upon meeting in the future, he must be able to greet as old comrades in arms.

Andras discovered that he was more proficient at this study than he would have believed. But he was a little surprised when Shara stopped suddenly and sat looking down at her hands.

"There is one other." Her reluctance was so visible that it was as if she spoke under duress. "That is the Arch Priest Kelemake."

"Kelemake!" Andas was surprised, though why should he be, he thought a moment later. If he, Andas, had had a counterpart here, surely others he knew must also. That he recognized none of the names Shara had recited earlier meant nothing. There had been a vast upheaval here. People who normally might never have come to the Emperor's notice were now in direct contact with him.

"You speak as if you know him—"

"There is a Kelemake in my world, though he is not an arch priest there. He was a court historian and taught me for a while."

She fastened at once on the explanation he had already guessed. "If there was an Andas to match an Andas, perhaps there is a Kelemake to match a Kelemake. Of what manner was the man you knew?" Now that they were alone, she spoke as equal to equal with none of that subtle deference she showed in company. And her directness made him more at ease with her.

"He was a man difficult to know—of deep learning, but little interested in anything beyond his work. He kept apart from the court, staying in the archives. In the end, the Emperor, my grandfather, appointed him keeper of the archives. He was not a man of religion, yet he knew more of its forms than many devoted priests, just as he knew much of other things but never exercised his knowledge. In spite of it all, he was no Magi—he never went through their training. Yet I would have thought that was what would have attracted his temperament the most."

"Knowing the forms of religion and learning rooted more in the past than the present—both these things could be said of our Kelemake also. He is a man who rules the temple brotherhood with a firm hand and has proved steadfast in support. Yet, I do not like him. And Andas, also, found him such that he could not bring himself to appoint him to the inner council. This I think was resented as a slight, though Kelemake has said nothing. But those who gather about him have tried to change Andas on this matter. My lord said that in him he sensed a flaw he could not put name to. And, let me tell you, there are some men—yes, and women—to whom if the need arose, I would tell our present deception. But Kelemake would be the last. Watch him with care—I cannot honestly tell you why. But in such a life as we lead, shadows can be worse than substance, for substance can be faced boldly and fought, but shadows slip away, only to return, always waiting for our courage to fail and our reason to falter in some time of need and despair."

"I am warned. And never has an emperor had more reason to lean upon his Chosen," he said deliberately, for he was moved again by her inner strength, by the fact that she could so set herself to preparing another to take the place of the man she had loved. That she had loved Andas but kept it within her, making no parade of her emotions, he had no doubt.

"As I am Chosen, so were you also," she said quietly.

He held out his hand. "Therefore, let us be hand-fasted anew."

When they had begun this talk, the last thing in the world Andas would have thought of doing was to offer her his hand so. Yet now the act came very easily and naturally, though there was nothing more in it for them both, he was sure, than the comrade tie existing between good friends—such friends as he had never before had the fortune to know.

"Prince!" Yolyos hailed from the lower level.

Andas stepped back from the girl and went to look down. The Salariki smiled up at him.

"The hunting is good, so good that your foresters need aid. They urge us to go on to the pass and have a message sent for transport, for this meat should get to the smokers as soon as possible. And you should be at your headquarters, also."

So they traveled trails that led them out of the woodlands, no longer haunted, at least for a space, by the obscene creeping horrors the enemy had unleashed there. It had been noon when they began that journey, but the way was easy enough, so they reached the pass before sundown.

The small garrison there greeted them warmly. Shara had privately informed him that none of the men stationed there had been of his close following. They greeted him with a respect he could meet easily.

Ten of them were sent down the back trail to pack in the unexpected bounty of meat.

"Lord, there are rumors of the crawlers out—" the commander had ventured before they left.

"They are out no longer." Andas told him of their own adventure and found the officer staring at him wide-eyed.

"Four—four crawlers killed! Lord, this is almost as good news as learning that the Drak Mount is breached. With the forest free, we can harvest game to push back the black fear of famine. If we but had our old weapons—what we might not do in our own behalf!"

"We have a skimmer also." Andas gave a terse account of their great luck in that encounter. "We dared not fly it in lest we be shot by our own defenses—"

"You need not fear, my lord. Perhaps we no longer possess the coms of the old days, but here we have that which serves us in a like manner, if less speedily. We can send your message, and you can fly back to headquarters. Marcher"—he spoke to the door sentry—"summon Dullah with his swiftest fliers."

Then he spoke once more to Andas. "Lord, inscribe what message you wish. It will be in the hands of your first captains before moonset, for Dullah is a master breeder of horn hawks, and his messengers have never been bested for speed or accuracy."

"Give me leave, lord," Shara offered. "I will send the message you require, while you gain from this captain knowledge of affairs along the mountains." So swiftly had she taken the matter into her hands that Andas knew he could make no wrong guess.

He admired the horn hawks when their breeder-trainer brought them in, message carriers already clipped to slender legs, two dispatched for safety.

They were not as heavy as the birds of that breed he had known in his own world, and they were wider of wing. Their plumage was gray, deepening into black, and would make them invisible at night, while their heads, bearing these "horns" of ridged quills, held bright eyes, used to darkness. In their natural state they were nocturnal.

Shara busied herself with a sheet of tough, light skin the captain produced, printing terse script thereon with a fire pen. As she wrote, Andas turned again to the captain.

"Tell me how it goes along the mountains." He was very ready to add to his information, needed if he were going to continue in the role of commander in chief.

-16-

The light was bright enough for Andas to study the faces of those seated at the table. Shara had done well. He had known each of them at once from her description and was able to greet them without hesitation. Kwayn Makenagen sat at his left hand in the place of greatest seniority. Beyond him was Patopir Ishan, facing him the Lady Bahyua Banokue, and to his right, Shara.

They had welcomed him earlier with open relief, in which he could detect no sign of consternation. Yet with Shara's warning he was alert. That was why Yolyos sat now at the end of that council table facing Andas. He did not know how much the alien's strange warning sense could do to unmask a traitor, but it was a safeguard of a sort.

It was Ishan who spoke first, eagerly. "It must be the truth, my lord. This fellow was well-nigh dead when my scouts found him after his skimmer had crashed. They heard his story and went to the Drak Mount. There are no signs of life to be seen."

"Tricks!" Makenagen returned as forcibly, favoring his colleague with a glare. "Bait to get us into a trap."

"The Arch Priest reports"—it was the Lady Banokue who spoke, in a low, calm voice—"that this prisoner is speaking the truth. He has tested him under hypnosis. The plague has spread widely through the Drak Mount. And what has fought us for the past months have been robots set on auto controls. Now those are going inert for want of tending."

"Inert!" Makenagen snorted. "They were in working order enough to blow a hole through our last land crawler. And that but ten days ago while we were hunting you, my lord." He directed his words to Andas. "I tell you, to venture into the land around the mount is fatal. No, this is a trap. Let the Arch Priest talk of the truth—we all know that in the old days a man could have his memory tampered with, be implanted with a false past. It was against the law, but it was done. They could have implanted this wretch—they still have machines while we are reduced to crossbows and the riding of elklands!"

Andas inclined his head to acknowledge the bitter logic of his captain's reasoning. What he had seen of this barren headquarters did not encourage a man. The spirit of those who held it was far higher than their ability to carry on war against those they admitted still held weapons of so-called civilization. It was as if they expected some of the old hero legends to work in their behalf, letting the "right" win by the favor of some supernatural force. But to depend upon a supernatural force—Suddenly his thoughts turned to what had lain at the back of his mind since their ordeal in the forest.

"Most dead or dying, said this prisoner?" he asked Ishan.

"Many so. There are some among them who appear immune. But those form only a skeleton force, unable now to defend the mount to any purpose. We can move in—"

"And among these dead was Kidaya?" Andas interrupted.

He saw the eager look fade on Ishan's face. "Now. This man was but a squad leader—he had no contact with the superior officers. But he said that a month ago, perhaps a little more—he was so dazed by the trials he had been through that he was vague on time—the lords who had declared for Kidaya and she herself took the last of the cruisers and departed."

"I suppose he did not know where?"

"There could be only one place she would seek," Shara said in her usual toneless voice. "She would go to the Valley of Bones where there is a power to help her."

They were silent. Ishan stared at the girl, and the Lady Banokue looked down at her folded hands on the table top, hands a little plump, with the rings of her rank cutting into her flesh as if she had worn them so long that they were a part of her. Makenagen plucked at his lower lip. As Yolyos relaxed in his seat, Andas thought he saw the Salariki's nostrils expand as if he tested some scent in the air.

"If the off-world mercenaries are alone and those who hired them have, in a manner of speaking, deserted them"—Andas spoke first—"then perhaps we can persuade them that they are contract broke. And if we offer terms, they may surrender in honor."

"It is a trap!"

"That we have a means of testing. We have the skimmer. Suppose we return this prisoner to the mount by it and then await results? Mercenaries do not take kindly to contract breaking on alien worlds. It will depend upon what promises have been made them."

"Shara nodded. "And do not think that such have not been made. There is good reason to believe that oaths have been taken to hold these men even as they died. The heart of the rebellion is not Drak Mount now—it is the Valley of Bones."

"But to get to the valley, I must have something I am sure lies within the mount."

"You have a plan, my lord?" asked Makenagen.

"I have this." Andas showed his hand on the table top. Across the flat of his palm lay the key.

"But you cannot—the temple is under deadly radiation!" Ishan cried.

"Not deadly if one has a radiation suit. I know what I would seek. I can find it wearing such protection."

"No!" Makenagen brought his fist down on the table with force enough to make the blow audible. "You would die. This is too great a risk, and if we have not you, then Kidaya has won and we might as well all put knives to our own throats and have done with it!"

"What do we then?" Andas asked. "Do we wait here until Kidaya and that demon crew think up another evil to send against us? Have we not slipped down far enough into the dark of barbarism? We need what is in the mount, and we need it now! You all know what this means, what force it is said to unlock." He held the key now between thumb and forefinger as a pointer aiming it down the length of the table.

"The temple is impossible," Makenagen repeated. His eyes were on the key, but his head shook stubbornly back and forth, denying any promise it might have.

Andas wished he could accept that as firmly as did this noble. What he held to as the only plan he could formulate was nothing he wanted to do. He was no hero willing to die to accomplish some task that might or might not save the situation. But it was part of the burden laid on him. Only the rightful emperor or his proclaimed heir could hold the key and set it in the place it was meant to go. And he was not even sure what he would unlock if he could accomplish that much, save that he did believe to the full that it would give him the ultimate answer to the life of the empire. And it would seem that the hour had come when they must have that answer or go down to defeat.

If Drak Mount was the well-equipped fortress they claimed, there must be radiation suits there. Wearing one of those, he could enter the temple or its ruins and then—"Take one step at a time," Andas cautioned himself—these were formidable steps.

"Let the prisoner be brought," he ordered Ishan, knowing the longer they sat in council, the less they would decide, and to act was important.

In appearance the man proved to be like those from whom they had captured the skimmer, save that he had lost all self-confidence. But his training held, and he came to attention before Andas.

"You have told us a tale of your troubles," the prince began. To him the prisoner seemed broken in spirit. He could well believe that they had pumped out of him all that was to be learned. But perhaps Yolyos could learn more.

"The plague, Your Mightiness—"

"Just so. And I have also heard that your employer or employers broke faith—is this not so?"

The man looked startled, as if that question had penetrated through his own misery.

"Broke faith, Mightiness?"

"Did not the false rebel Kidaya and her lords withdraw, leaving you, whom she had brought hither to fight for her, to die alone? To the mind of an honest man, soldier, that is breaking contract. Have you not thought of it so?"

"Nothing has been said, Mightiness. We hold to duty."

"Needlessly. Now, soldier, there is that you can do, not only in your own behalf, but also for your whole company—what is left of them by now. You can take our terms to whomever remains of your leaders with authority enough to agree to surrender. We shall grant mercenaries' terms with full honors, oath pledge for that. This is now no battle of yours, for you shall see no pay from those who fled."

"Mightiness, no one can return overland to the mount. I came forth on a skimmer, which failed me. The heavy arms are all on auto and locked there, by the Lady Kidaya's orders. There can be no way for me to get in."

"You came by skimmer—you can return by skimmer. Or have the air defenses also been locked on auto?"

The soldier licked his lips, but his eyes did not shift under Andas's level regard.

"No, Mightiness. It was thought that—that those of your command no longer had any air power. And it was also said, Mightiness, that you yourself were dead, or soon to be so!"

"Yet I am not, nor are we lacking in air power. You will be taken to the top of Drak Mount and there dropped with your grav belt—" Andas turned to Ishan. "He was wearing a grav belt?"

At the captain's nod, the prince continued. "You will carry to your commander our terms. We shall give him the space of a day to consider them. If he accepts, he and at least two of the highest ranking officers under him shall signal from the top of the mount. A skimmer will be sent to bring them to me to give truce oath. Do you understand?"

"Yes, Mightiness."

"Have him ready to go," Andas told Ishan.

"They will not yield." But Makenagen did not sound as emphatic as he had earlier.

"I think that they will. The mercenaries sell loyalty, but it must work both ways. If they believe that contract is broken, they will surrender on mercenary terms. Since we cannot ship them off-world, we shall take their paroles until we can."

"You put faith in their oaths?" Makenagen still fought a rear-guard action.

"You know the breed, do you not?"

"Yes. If they will take trust oath."

"One thing waits upon another." Andas fell into the more formal court speech. "The day grows near, my captains—the audience is ended." For the first time he stepped from battle commander to emperor with that dismissal. They went, save for Yolyos, to whom he made a gesture, and Shara.

"What did you learn?" Andas hardly waited before they had gone to ask.

"First, your traitor is not here. Second, you read that prisoner aright. I think he will do exactly as you wish. Let us hope his superiors do likewise. But what do you intend to do, Prince—or should it be 'Emperor?'"

"I believe that which this opens"—Andas stowed the key once more within his clothing (he had shed at last the grimed and badly worn coverall and been fitted with tunic, breeches, and boots)—"will give us the answer to Kidaya at long last. It is the mightiest weapon our race ever knew. We are pledged never to call upon it until the last extremity. And to my judging, we have reached that point. We can wait out the fall of the Drak Mount, and that may take centuries with their defenses on auto—those will run until the energy is exhausted.

"But it is not the Drak Mount that matters so much as the Valley of Bones. For as long as the empire has existed, the Old Woman has menaced it. How does the warning go?" He looked to Shara, who replied.

> "Dark spawns dark, evil gives root to evil.
> What man has wrought, man can destroy.
> But that is the way of man.
> For the other, it is waiting, watching—
> And in the end triumph over all.
> Night will fall, day comes not again.
> Winter's cold knows no spring.
> And the dried bones will lie in rows,

But none shall weep,
For there will be no eyes to hold the tears."

"A mournful enough saying," the Salariki commented. "This has some meaning beyond its gloomy surface words?"

"The Old Woman negates all we believe is life. She wears many faces. Sometimes she has sunk to become a bogey with which to frighten children; other times we see her followers walk proudly with power. But there was always the warning of an ultimate confrontation between the power invested in him who can use the key and the Old Woman. I think the time has come—here and now."

"And Kidaya was sent into the world to induce that coming?" Shara mused. "Then all the evil she has wrought here falls into a pattern that one can understand, for if it had been the Empress's crown she wanted, she could have gained her ends without wreaking such destruction on friend and foe alike. She has had choices, and always her choice has fallen in a way to bring more chaos. So you take the weapon of the key. And where do you bear it—to the Valley of Bones?"

Andas suddenly felt very weary, like a man pushed to the edge of endurance who must yet stoop and add another burden to a load he already carried. "Where else?" he asked her simply. He had never wanted to do more than what now seemed light and pleasant duty in his own time. But there was no turning back. From the moment he had laid hand on the key, he had chosen the path that led straight here, and he could not turn aside, even if he would.

"But not alone," she protested.

He was too tired to argue. Sometimes when he was alone (which seemed to be very seldom now), he would close his eyes and rub his fingers across the lids, as if to so rub away all the light and sound about. Without Shara he could not have played his part for an hour. Sometimes he wished she would let him blunder into self-betrayal so he could be free.

Now he went to the window of the small room to which the rule of the empire had shrunk. For a space action was out of his hands. All hung now on the surrender of Drak Mount.

"Emperor"—Yolyos gave him the title without any of the accompanying honorifics his own people used—"there is someone coming and"—he had faced around, his nostrils dilated—"this is not right—"

Andas had no chance to ask for explanations, for the door sentry looped back the blanket that served as a curtain.

"Lord, it is the Arch Priest with tidings of urgency."

"Let him enter."

The man whom came in was twin to the Kelemake Andas remembered. He had not followed the universal habit of eradicating his beard, but sprouted a small growth on his chin, trimmed into an aggressive point. His voluminous robe was not as shabby as the garments of the rest of the garrison and was the russet-red of the temple. And he also had the conical, pointed miter of his rank, though this was not jeweled in regal splendor, but merely carried on its front a silver representation of the key. A like replica depended on a long chain about his neck.

Andas had seen him twice since he had come to the fort. But both times it had been a purely formal meeting in company. It seemed to him that the Arch Priest, instead of making a point to welcome his emperor back, had, as unobtrusively as possible, chosen to escape any direct communication with his leader. But he was here now and seemed eager for an interview.

"Pride of Balkis-Candace"—his voice was that of a man who had learned to use it effectively with audiences—"the message is that we move on Drak Mount."

"After a fashion," Andas agreed. "An offer for surrender—"

"These off-worlders, these evil ones—they should not be allowed parole!" There was a glint in the priest's eyes now. How much dared Andas judge this double by the man he had known? Of old such a look meant that Kelemake, the scholar, was preparing to rip to shreds some long-held belief.

"They are mercenaries. We shall offer them the usual peace by oath."

"When such as they have despoiled this world, brought the empire to dust? Pride of Balkis-Candace, those who have passed beyond will not be honored by such mistaken mercy. I pray you think again before you offer terms to drinkers of blood. Let them stay and die in the hole into which they have sealed themselves."

"Much the easier way." Andas hoped that he sounded reasonable. The priest's attitude was a little strange. Theirs was not usually a cry for revenge. "Save that it may take years. And we do not have years to go on starving out our own existence. If this struggle can be brought to an end, then the oaths are worth it."

"There will be no peace with Kidaya!" Kelemake fairly spat. "And she is not at the mount."

"No. She is where we must seek her."

Kelemake showed his teeth in what might be a smile, savoring of contempt. "Doubtless with weapons taken from the mount. Which perhaps might be a worthy plan, save that those with whom she shelters now have such weapons as can put to naught any taken from Drak."

"Not at all." Andas's hand went to his tunic breast beneath which lay the key. "There is this." On some impulse he did not understand, he drew forth his heritage. Again it seemed that the light in the room gathered to it.

The change in Kelemake was astounding. His hand had been resting on his own silver key, the badge of his office. Now he twisted that up and out as if thus he held a cutting weapon. But whatever he intended was never completed, for Yolyos sprang. The Salariki had been edging to the side, and his sudden attack beat the priest of his knees. A second chop from the alien's hand collapsed him. Yolyos stopped and jerked loose the key, examined it, and a moment later uttered a deep growl.

"A fine toy indeed for a priest, Emperor. Behold!" Holding the key as Kelemake had done, he moved closer to the table. There was a click, and in the wood of its top quivered a tiny dart hardly as long as a cloak pin, which must have been fitted snugly into the shaft of the key.

"Do not touch it!" Yolyos swept out an arm to keep

Andas back. "There is a very suspicious smear on it. But I will tell you something else. This"—he stirred the body of the priest with a boot toe—"was not a man—not as we know men."

"Android?" Andas jumped to the one conclusion ever with him.

"No, he was human once. What he is now, perhaps your followers of the old Woman can best name. But this is your traitor or I never have sniffed one with more of such stink!"

"Kelemake!" breathed Shara. "But the priests, they are armored against the Old Woman. They have to be, or they could not function as priests."

"But how long has it been since there was a temple with protective safeguards to uncover such?" Andas asked. "You smelt his treachery?"

"I picked up a foulness like those woods creepers, enough to know he had kinship with them. And he came here to kill you, which suggests one thing—that those you would face hold you in fear. Perhaps this last plan of yours is what they dislike."

"But how would they know—we have only just discussed it?"

"Did not you show me those eye and ear holes in that palace of yours? If there are not such in the walls hereabouts, then this one had his spies. He must have been worried indeed to risk killing you before witnesses and so betraying himself. Either he planned to kill us also, or else he has served his master—or mistress—as much as he can and was due to be discarded. How better quit the service than in a blaze of glory, removing the chief threat with you?"

Andas knelt beside the priest, turning the body over. He did not expect to find Kelamake dead. Surely Yolyos had not struck that hard. But he was, and Andas searched the man. He did not know what he sought, save that there might be some link between this traitor and the enemy. And he found it at last in the interior of the miter, lying directly behind the key symbol. It was a tiny device, which, when he tried to rip it free, proved to have a whole network of very fine wires buried in the sides of the headgear where they might touch the skull of the wearer.

That skull was shaved as was customary among priests. Yolyos squatted down on the other side, looking first at the cap and then at the skull. Suddenly he put forth a hand, extending the claws on two fingers to their greatest extent, and made a savage pass across the skin, tearing it open. No blood flowed, and they could all see the glint of metal that ripping had uncovered. The priest wore a metal plate as part of his skull.

"More of your Nessi dealings," Yolyos commented. "They appear to temper their magic with science, if one can call it that."

Andas stood up. "The sooner we visit the Valley of Bones, the better," he said between set teeth.

-17-

Andas paced back and forth. The rooms in this small fort, never meant to serve as more than an outpost, were not intended for pacing. He could cover the space in about four medium strides. But he could not sit still with the thoughts that clawed at his mind, even as the Salariki had clawed free the Arch Priest's secret. How many more of those gathered at this heart of the command were more—or less—than they seemed to be? He had only Yolyos's talent to "smell" out the enemy.

Dark old tales came unbidden to his mind. Once his people had worshiped gods who turned their faces from the light, who were to be appeased only with blood sacrifices. Only the Old Woman existed still from that time. Then kings had kept about their persons "witch doctors," men and women supposedly with the gift of literally sniffing out prospective enemies. The result had depended upon the whim of those doctors. And the innocent must have suffered with the guilty many

246

times over. Yet Andas could not believe that those of human breed had ever been gifted with Yolyos's talent. And he should be thanking Akmedu that not only had the Salariki followed him into this waking nightmare, but that he was also comrade in arms.

The alien sat now, cross-legged, in a deep window seat, watching Andas. He had refused the clothing of the Imperial forces, save for breeches, boots, and a cape. Apparently to cover his furred upper body caused him discomfort. And he held to his nose a wilted green ball he had clung to ever since they had left the woodland, though the aroma of those herbs and leaves had faded considerably since they had been gathered.

Shara sat in the single chair. Her torn and grimed garments had been changed for male clothing. Only the intricate braiding of her hair betrayed her sex, for otherwise she might have been a boy. She sat quietly enough, her heavy-lidded eyes not turned on Andas at all, but fixed as if she looked inward and not outward.

"How many—" Andas flung around to face both of them. "How many such can there be among us?"

"None, among those I have seen—save that devil-priest," Yolyos replied calmly. "Be sure I would know. He was a puppet jerking to the will of another, like the shadow people of our entertainers. None else I have met are so."

"But where one has entered—"

"In the very ancient days of our people"—Shara spoke from the same memories as Andas had—"such searchers were known. The king would summon all his people to a meeting and send out his witch-finders to run about among them. Those they touched with their wands were killed. But—"

"That was savagery," Andas said. "Disclosure of the king's enemies depended upon the whim of men who had private hates and quarrels to avenge. If there are any here, Yolyos can sniff them out; I think we may be safe for the present. But we must move against the Valley of Bones before it looses worst against us!"

There was a polite scratching at the doorframe outside the curtain. At Andas's call, Ishan entered. He was smiling broadly.

"Lord, your wisdom read aright these sulkers in the Drak Mount. They have agreed to a meeting. The skimmer has been sent to bring them as far as the Tooth Craig, even as you ordered."

Andas felt a small leap of hope. At least this far he had judged the situation aright. In spite of the priest whose body had been dragged out hours earlier, he had made the first move of his complicated game, and it was successful.

"Let us go then." He was already heading for the door. Yolyos swung from his seat, the girl close behind. There were elklands waiting, the smaller, surer-footed breed of the mountains. Their best pace was a raking trot, and they continually bobbed their heavily horned heads up and down. Now and then one voiced a bellow, to be echoed by the rest.

Andas, Shara, Yolyos, Ishan, and a squad of the latter's own shield men made up their swift-riding band. The Tooth Craig was at least two hours' steady riding away. They must travel ever alert as this was wild and broken land. And, after the unmasking of Kelemake, Andas trusted nothing.

They made a rough camp at the crag, Andas and his leaders a little apart. Down before them stretched the raw land of the waste, a northernmost arm of that in which they had landed the drone ship in that other Inyanga. Andas wondered fleetingly if Elys had told her story and what the false emperor had made of it.

"They are coming." Shara touched his arm.

A skimmer showed against the sky like an insect. Ishan spoke, and half of his men vanished on the rocky hillside about their appointed meeting place. Andas was startled at their skill at taking cover. But these had been part of a hard-beleaguered guerrilla force for years. Those who had not learned were long since dead. They had been given orders not to move unless treachery was offered.

There was barely enough level ground for the skimmer to alight on. It moved sluggishly, carrying an overload of passengers. Four men in mercenary uniforms disembarked. They wore their side arms, as by custom they could, but carried no larger weapons. Their heads were concealed with helmets on which the protecto visors were down. But as they exited from the craft, each deliberately snapped that visor up and removed his helmet to stand bareheaded.

Two were young, aides or squad captains. But those they escorted were older, men plainly well established in their business of war. The one in the lead held up his hand in a peace salute to which Andas responded.

"Commander-in-Arms Modan Sullock," he introduced himself brusquely. Then he indicated his followers. "Captains Masquid, Herihor, Samson."

"The Imperial son of Balkis-Candace"—Ishan spoke

formally—"his Chosen, the Lady Shara, his comrade in arms, Lord Yolyos."

Sullock's attention for Andas and Shara was fleeting compared to the measuring stare he gave to the Salariki!

"Salariki!" His surprise was unconcealed. But he recovered his aplomb quickly. Once more his hand raised, this time in a full salute to Andas.

Under the circumstances it was a waste of time to stand on ceremony. Andas came directly to the point.

"You have our terms, Commander-in-Arms, and you must have considered them seriously or you would not be here. They are simple—your contract was broken when she who employed you fled, leaving you to the plague death. We offer you parole with honor. And though we cannot give you off-world withdrawal, since ships no longer fin down here, we offer you the best we can. This has never been any quarrel of yours, save that you used your fighting ability to aid a usurper. You have your choice—stay pent in the Drak Mount and let the plague and time end you. Or surrender the fortress to us on honorable terms. We do not seek you, who are but tools, but her who brought this ruin upon us."

Sullock studied Andas for a long moment before he answered. "Since you know so much about us, then you must also know that it is beyond our power to surrender the mount entirely. Many of its heavy defenses are on auto, and that has been tampered with so it cannot be shut off again. There is no way to reach the mount safely overlands."

Andas shrugged. "Let it stand, so, a monument to

the evil that used it. We have a skimmer. Do you have any?"

"Two, recalled from scout duty. No cruisers—your Lady Kidaya took the last in commission."

"Let those ferry your men out to a place we shall appoint. They will bring with them rations and only the side arms that by law are theirs. There is but one thing you must give me and that as soon as your exodus begins."

"That being?"

"A radiation suit that will fit me. And the best you have at the mount. Those are our terms. Do you wish to confer with your men at Drak before you give us one word or another?"

"You will accept truce oath and parole us then after interplanetary custom?"

"We will," answered Andas promptly. Whether they would believe him after all these years of bitter struggle, he did not know. It must seem that he was utterly confident now.

"I am empowered by custom also," returned Sullock that, "to agree to terms. And we shall accept. Our contract is broken." From his tunic he brought forth a sealed tape, tossed it to the ground, and set his heel upon it, grinding it, case and tape together, into a mass that could never be read again. "When shall we come forth?"

"You can begin as soon as you return to the mount. But I want that suit at once, so I shall go with you. Your men can stay here."

Andas saw Ishan start forward as if to protest, but he waved him back, giving him no chance to speak.

"Each shuttle taking your men out will bring a

selected party of ours in," he continued. "We shall clear out supplies and arms—"

"The plague!" Shara spoke in warning.

Sullock looked to her. "Lady, the plague died four tens of days ago. There have been no new cases since. It went when those we served left."

"But why?" she demanded. "Why should Kidaya seek to kill those who served her?"

"Your suspicion is quick, lady." Sullock grimaced. "Now it took us a little longer to spell out the truth. Well do you say, lord"—he turned to Andas—"that our contract was broken. There came a messenger to that one who hired us. She was in a fury of excitement thereafter, and she left, taking her own with her, and an evil lot they were. As for why she would be rid of us—well, the defenses were on auto in the mount and the food was limited. We cannot lift off-world now, and we had become an embarrassment to her. She relies now on other methods of warfare. And she would have left us to death-haunt that hold, in truth, had not our first medic found the herbs in the water system and removed them. She is a woman in form, but within—she is not human!"

"No plague but poison!" Shara exclaimed. "But she could use plague, the threat of it, to isolate us, keep out any from the stars. In truth, what is she, Andas, who plans so?"

"She serves that other. And, it would seem, well. The more reason to strike to the heart of that dark, and soon."

So they took truce oath with the mercenaries, and the ferrying of those within the Drak Mount began, moving them to a long valley to the north of the Place of Red Water. There they set up camp with what rations they brought out of the mount. Andas did not mistrust the men who had surrendered. Their custom of standing by their parole was known galaxy-wide.

Since there were no ships now lifting from Inyanga, he wondered whether he might later follow with them an old method of his people, offering them soldier land for settlement. They could so provide the core of a new army, since soldier land could only be inherited in each new generation by service in the forces. But that would come later—a decision for the future. What faced him now was not months away, but in the immediate hours—or days ahead.

It was Sullock who ordered the radiation suits brought out of storage for Andas's inspection. Though they had not been used, perhaps in years, the prince knew them for models he had seen in his own time as adequate for heavy duty. He had no tech among his own force to test them, so he had to depend upon the aid of such among the mercenaries. That expert reported that four were in working condition.

Andas chose the one closest to a good fit, though it was a little large. By the advice of the first medic among Sullock's men, his body, before he dressed in the suit, was given an additional shielding of those plasta bandages used in radiation treatment. The binding made him more clumsy, but it was further insurance against painful death.

To the last, Shara demanded to share his desperate venture. Andas was adamant in his refusal. Only one man could do this, and by the choice of fate, that one was he. He persuaded her at last that the safeguards in the temple were such that, even if she went with him, she could not accompany him all the way and would only be a burden for him.

The only addition he insisted upon being made was a com unit that would allow his voice to be projected beyond the suit. The lock that he would have to deal with was partly controlled by certain sound waves.

Whether the temple, being in the midst of the ruins, was intact enough so he could enter it, he did not know, since no one had penetrated to it since the blow-up. He wondered whether the destruction had been done deliberately for that reason, not just to wipe out the palace and its defenses. If the Old Woman was as powerful as she seemed, then those who served her might well know of the existence of that which he sought.

It took them a full night of labor to install the com in the suit. Andas willed himself to sleep in the commander's quarters of the Drak Mount, taking what rest he could.

"If I do not return," he said to Shara and Yloyos the next morning, "then to you, Shara, the rule. My lord"—he looked then to the Salariki—"this is not your world, and it may be that you cannot leave it again, nor is it your war. But if you would serve this lady with your talent, as you have aided me, then I shall be content, for no man ever had a better comrade in arms in any undertaking. I know not what form friendship takes among your people, but among mine this feeling is such I name you 'brother.'"

Somewhere in the mount the Salariki had found a small bag of spices, which he kept at hand, sniffing it often. But now he let that drop so it dangled from the cord that bound it to his wrist, and he put out both his hands, claws sheathed, so Andas laid his own in them.

Delicately the claw on each forefinger extended and dug into Andas's brown flesh until a drop of blood showed.

"Lady," said the Salariki then, "since this, my brother, has no nature-given claws to mark me, do you take the knife at your belt and do to my hands as I have done to his."

Shara did so without question, using the point of her belt knife as delicately as Yolyos had his claws.

When drops of blood showed on his hands also, still holding Andas's hands, he raised them to his lips and touched tongue tip to the blood. Then Andas followed his example in a twin gesture that brought Yolyos's blood to his own mouth.

"Blood to blood," said the alien. "We are clan kin now, brother. Go content that I shall stand where protection is needed for your First Lady."

So it was that with the salt-sweet taste of Yolyos's blood still on his tongue, Andas pulled on the heavy helmet of the suit and allowed the tech to fasten it. And then he clumped in the thick boots to the skimmer, taking his place in the rear by the harness that would lower him as close to his goal as the craft could get.

As they neared the site of the ruins, Andas was appalled by the task of identification here. All those towers and buildings that should have served as landmarks had been leveled, toppled, or had disappeared in craters. The skimmer circled as the pilot waited for Andas's choice of landing site. In this awkward suit he could not climb far among the debris below. He would have to be put down only a short distance away from his goal. But where was the temple?

Then he was able to trace what he thought was the Gate of Nine Victories. He waved the pilot eastward. There he saw the broken pillars of what could only be the colonnade of the temple terrace. Andas signaled, hooking the descent line to the belt already buckled about him. The hatch in the belly of the skimmer opened as the machine went on hover, and Andas clambered through.

The lowering cord played out slowly and evenly, and it continued to reel on as, twisting and turning, he descended to what had once been the entrance to the temple. As he went, Andas studied what lay below, trying to locate the points of reference he needed. The closer he approached, the more the temple showed its hurts. Walls had collapsed, but there seemed to be open spaces enough to enter.

His boots touched pavement, and he moved his gloved fingers to free the belt hooks. Then the line snaked speedily aloft, to descend again, this time weighted with the one other thing he had taken from the mount, a blaster. With that he hoped to open any blocked way.

From ground level the mounded mass of the temple was almost threatening. If it had been congealed with the fire of the blast, he could never have made the attempt to enter. But now he started toward a promising opening.

Luckily he did not have to penetrate the main part, but rather work north to the other end of the terrace. There was the Emperor's Gate through which even he would have passed on only two occasions in his life,

when he went for his crowning and when the urn of
his ashes on a cart, which would run of its own voli-
tion, would pass after his death ceremony.

The barrier of carved metal was a crumble of broken bits. Andas used the blaster with care, cutting a
passage until he stood on the block he sought, where
the Emperor's death carriage would halt for a long
moment coming and going. There was no chance in
this welter of ruin to hunt for the spring that would
release what lay beneath. He applied the blaster on
half voltage, cutting around the block. Then putting
aside the tool, he used a bar of twisted metal to lever
out the freed stone.

Below was a dark opening into which he flashed
his torch. Steps showed, seemingly uninjured in spite
of the wreckage above. But his suit was too bulky to
pass through the hole. He used the blaster again to
nibble around the edges and enlarge the space. Then
he started down.

There were ten steps, steeper than those of a
normal stair. The whir of his radiation counter was
a constant buzz, but he tried to forget that warning.
There was no way he could help it, so he must not
let it alarm him into carelessness. The freeing of the
blocked passage was only the beginning.

There was a passage leading on from the foot
of the stairs, running in toward the heart of the
temple. What he sought had been placed directly
below the throne whereon the Emperor sat at all
state services.

Andas's torch showed him only blank walls of
stone, nothing to suggest the importance of this crypt.
Now—a door. But before him was only another blank

wall putting an end to the way. He had expected this. Now, if only—

Andas ran his tongue across his lips. He raised his gloved hand but did not quite touch the com. It had been adjusted as well as the tech could do it. He could not alter it any.

He spoke. The words were very old, in a language he did not understand. He doubted if any, even like Kelemake, who had made a study of the ancient records, could translate them. Nor did he know their meaning, only that they must be intoned slowly, with pauses between their groupings, in this place.

There was no answer. No door opened—the wall did not fall. He tried a second time, sure that he gave the right accents in the proper places, without result.

It must be the com at fault. That probably distorted some tonal quality that was of major importance. He would have to unhelm to recite the words properly or fail. But with the radiation counter buzzing—unhelm here?

When there is only one answer you accept it—or retreat. And he had come too far; this was too important to retreat. Nor could he ruthlessly burn through the wall. It was provided with safeguards against that. What he sought would be destroyed at the first alarm.

Andas placed the blaster against the wall, and his gloved hands loosened the face plate of his helmet. The air was dead, with an acrid, burning smell that filled his nose. Yet he could not hold his breath and recite at the same time. He spoke the formula for the third time and knew that this must be his last try.

He closed the plate of the helmet, coughing. Then,

the wall split down the center, the halves slipping back into the corridor. It had worked!

He was still coughing as he faced, a couple of paces farther on, a grill of metal that glistened in his torchlight as if it had been recently polished. The center of that grill was worked into a design he knew, the legendary "lion"—a fabulous beast sacred to the Emperor. The open mouth of the creature was his keyhole.

Now, would the key from one world fit the lock of another? This was no time to lose confidence. It slid in easily enough.

Turn to the left—it opened! The lock was the same. At his push the grill swung in, and he shuffled on. There was a pedestal in the very center and on it a box. This also showed a keyhole, but Andas did not wait to try his key. He had plucked that out of the grill and fastened it to his belt. Now he slid his hands under the box and lifted it.

He had expected it to be heavy, but it was lighter than the blaster, and he could carry it easily under one arm as he turned to retrace his way, making the best speed he could.

Though he no longer coughed, his throat was dry and his eyes smarted. Whether he had taken such a dose of radiation as would doom him, he dared not think. He must take what he had found to those who might be able to use it, even if he brought his own death with it.

Up the steps he went, back into the open where the skimmer had dropped him. Though it was very hard, encased in such armor, to tilt his head back, Andas managed it far enough to see the skimmer on hover. He raised his arm in signal.

The ascent rope came tumbling down. Andas pitched the blaster from him. He needed that no longer. Still holding the box close, he made fast the hoist cord and gave the signal to rise.

The hoist jerked as it took the strain of his weight. He was hauled up, hoping that the pilot had taken the precautions in which they had drilled him, erecting a force screen between him and his passenger. No one would dare to approach Andas now until they had used every method of decontamination. But he had done it. He had their greatest weapon now in his two hands!

-18-

Having gone through the most rigid decontamination processes the medico and techs of the mercenaries could devise, Andas sat alone before the box. He thought only of what must be done now, rather than of the results of the tests they had forced on him. He had known that his quest might well be fatal, though it is hard for any man to face directly the fact of death, of ending all that he knows, feels, is—They had told him the truth, that the tests had shown a higher degree of radiation than the body could survive.

So, he had made his payment in advance. What he bought must be worth it. Andas inserted the key and turned it.

Surprisingly, though it must have been locked for centuries of time, the lid arose easily. And in the interior, bedded down in a thick layer of spongy material, were two things, one a roll of what seemed to be thin leather, the other a length of metal links, the metal dark and dull, studded with small bosses in

no decorative pattern. He drew that out and straight-
ened it to full length on the table. Disappointment
choked him.

Indifferently he took up the roll, slipped off the
ring that kept it tight, and flattened it out. The inner
side was printed with signs and drawings, meaningless
to him at first.

To have bought so little with his life! Then the
promises of legends were worthless. Perhaps they
had never intended to do more than to give a prop
to the emperors, a confidence in knowing that if the
worst came, there awaited a way out. And they were
expected to find their own solutions first, not to fall
back upon this deception.

Yet all the precautions—would such have been
taken to preserve a fake? Yes, if the fact that it was
a fake was never to be unmasked, that the belief in
it was its only power.

Andas looked down at the script he could not
read, at the diagrams that blurred as he stared at
them. Unless—

It was a moment or two before, sunk in his despair
and disappointment, Andas realized that he was able
to read a word here and there. Those long hours with
Kelemake, when the archivist had been so immersed
in his own studies that, needing a sounding board,
he had expounded them to a boy, were paying off.
Intently Andas shaped the archaic symbols with his
lips and traced diagrams by fingertip. There was
much he did not understand, but enough—perhaps
just enough—that he could!

He drew the length of metal links to him and let it
slip through his fingers as if counting them. But what

he quested for were those bosses that had a meaning. An hour later he leaned back in his chair. Around his waist those links made a belt. He had done what he could without fully understanding the preparations. But the old tale had not failed him.

There was only one reason for life left, to carry what he held—or rather take what he now was—to the Valley of Bones and there fight the last battle, which would decide the fate of the empire one way or the other.

Andas came out of the room. Shara sat on a stool against the wall. Beyond her Yolyos lounged, inspecting the inner workings of one of the hand weapons from the mount. They turned to him, but he raised his hand to warn them off. How deadly he himself might be now was a matter of some concern. There was that in their faces which warmed him, even through the ice that had encased him since he had heard those test readings.

"No. I have now what may be the salvation of the empire," he said hurriedly. How long did he have before the final illness began? "You have the skimmer ready?"

"Andas." Shara spoke only his name and reached out her hand to him.

"No," he repeated. "This thing was laid to me. He gave his life to begin it and bound upon me the oath to finish it."

He looked then to Yolyos. "It has been good," he said simply. "I never had a brother, nor anyone save my father whom I could trust. It has been good to know such a one, even for a short time."

Yolyos nodded. "It has been good," he answered,

his voice a low purr. "Go, brother, knowing that one
stands to do here what must be done."

At his orders they cleared the short hall between
the room and the outer courtyard where the skimmer
waited—the craft already contaminated by his flight
to the temple. But there was the garrison drawn
up, and, as he went, for the first time in his life he
heard the full-throat roar of those hailing him as the
Emperor.

"Lion, Pride of Balkis-Candace, Lord of Spears—
hail!"

Andas dared not look either right or left to see
those who shouted, knowing that pride alone would
help him to finish that march with dignity. Somehow
he reached the hatch of the skimmer and climbed
into the pilot's seat. Still he could not allow himself to
look back. He touched the rise and was above them
in a leap, the force of which made him breathless
for an instant. Then the flier was on course, heading
toward the last battle of all.

Andas had only one guide to the Valley of Bones
(save the general directions he had been able to piece
together from old accounts), and that was the ring, for
it was united, he was sure, to the source of its power.
He had it wired to the control board of the skimmer
and watched it for any variation in the set.

His course was not a straight one after he topped
the mountains, but a zigzag to pick up a trail for
the ring. And before midday it had proven to be a
guide, for the dull set glowed, took on rippling Life,
and grew the brighter as he flew on in the direction
it indicated.

There were more heights ahead, the sere spur

range of the Ualloga, once a chain of volcanoes making a blazing girdle for the continent. Their broken cones now were sided by such cliffs as not even the wild cam sheep knew, a riven and waterless land that repelled man and animal alike. In his own Inyanga the range had seldom been penetrated and many of the peaks never explored.

The stone glowed, flashed as he had never seen it do before. It pointed directly into this land. How much longer did he have, Andas wondered, before death attacked his body? The thought made him shift to top speed.

Thus he overshot his goal and was aware of it only when the gem signaled it. He circled about, also intent on what the visa-screen showed of the land below.

It was no true valley the ring brought him to, but the hollow of a giant crater. And, as he went on hover, Andas was aware of something else. About him the linked belt was warming, rousing in answer to some energy, while through his body he began to feel a vibration, almost as painful as the one that had accompanied the crawlers.

He put the skimmer on descend. There was no need to take any precaution over his arrival. Andas did not in the least doubt that those who sheltered in this hole knew of his coming. But he watched the screen carefully.

The very heart of the crater was a lake, though the waters there did not mirror the sky above, but were a dead slate gray. Around its shores there was vegetation. It had a withered, dead look, lacking the brilliant color and shadow one saw in normal plants.

Farther away from the water were heaps of some

gray-white material set in loose order. And while
they resembled no buildings he had ever seen, Andas
believed them to be shelters for those who made this
dismal mountain cup their home.

He brought the skimmer down on the only nearly
level space he sighted. The visa-screen showed him
that and a portion of sand and gravel beyond, as well
as scraps of blighted vegetation—but no one moved.
If there was a reception party, it was in hiding.

With care he unwired the ring, being careful
not to touch the band itself. That he dared not do
while he wore the belt, for their powers were so
opposed, one to the other, that he believed such a
connection might be fatal to him. Into the ring he
inserted the end of an officer's baton, which Yolyos
had smoothed down to serve that purpose. And
holding this before him, he left the skimmer.

The nearest of the shelters was close enough to see
clearly, and he was startled at its material. There was
no mistaking the nature of the loglike objects piled
to form its walls—bones—huge bones! He had never
heard of an animal large enough to yield such. But
why not—was not this the Valley of Bones—though
that was a literal statement he had not known.

Andas's right hand hovered about his belt but did
not quite touch it. With his left he held the baton
well away from his body. The glow of the ring was
torch-like through the gloom of the valley.

Again he looked about for some sign his arrival
was known—that they were prepared to move against
him. Nothing stirred. There were no sounds. If bird
or insect lived in this gloom, it was silent now.
There was a feeling of waiting that made him want

to linger by the open hatch of the skimmer as his only refuge.

Perhaps all his race was conditioned to expect the worst here. There were too many old terror tales about the ruler of this pocket—and of much more when she wished to reach out and touch this one or that to be her follower. But the fact that he knew he was a walking dead man was armor. Fear of dissolution was now longer hers to threaten.

So Andas walked away from the skimmer, from all the world that he knew, carrying the ring as a torch. And since the huts of bones seemed the logical place to start searching for whoever dwelt here, he went to those.

Sometime later he reached the end of that line of weird dwellings, having found each empty, though there was good evidence that they were occupied. But where were those he sought? That sense of expectancy, of being on the brink of action, had never left him. Yet no movement, no sound, indicated that he was not alone in the valley.

Would the ring continue to lead him? He could try an experiment. Andas loosed his grasp on the baton until he held it by only the lightest of grips. Then he spoke for the first time. Though he purposely kept his voice low, yet his words rang unusually loud in his own ears.

"To thy mistress, go!"

The baton quivered, moved. He tried not to hold it too tightly lest he hinder that movement, yet he must not drop it. It turned at a sharp angle left. And he pivoted to face that way. The baton stiffened to point, and he found he could not make it waver.

Away from the bone-walled huts it led him, from the lake, from the skimmer. It was like a spear aimed at the steep side of the crater.

Then he saw that he walked a marked way, sided by stumpy pillars, first knee high, then waist, and finally topping his shoulders, and these were also bones.

So walled in, Andas came to an opening in the cliff. As he paused, there was a flash within, a leap of greenish flame. He smelled a stench that was worse than the odor of the crawlers.

Then a voice called, "You have sought us out, Emperor. Have you then come to seek your crown? But your hour is past—even as the crown has passed to one who can better wear it!"

In the green of the flames he saw the gathered company. Back against the wall on either side were a sprinkling of men, who stood, staring in a kind of despair and complete surrender, as if all their strength had been drained. But in the center was a group of women, and behind them another, enthroned.

Andas raised his eyes to the face of that one. On her head was the Imperial crown, the sacred one worn only when the ruler took his oath of allegiance. It was death for a lesser man to touch it. At the sight of that in this place, anger blazed hot in him.

The head on which it rested was held high with an arrogance he thought not even an empress in her own right could have shown. Her face had the perfection of a soulless, emotionless statue, with only the eyes and a cruel curl of mouth betraying life.

Her body was bare of any robe, but she held on her knees, so that it covered her to the base of her throat, a huge mask. That mask was demonic, yet not ugly. Rather it seemed great beauty had been twisted to serve great evil, so that it was degraded and debased.

"Andas." He saw the cruel smile grows as she spoke. "Emperor that wished to be. Behold your empress! Give homage as it is due!"

As she spoke, the mask before her looked at him also with a compelling stare. He shivered, knowing that it, too, had life—or was in some way an extension of a life force that had no human connection, more to be feared than merely alien.

"Homage, Andas, humble homage—" She made a chant of the words. And that chant was taken up by the women gathered at the foot of the throne until it beat in his head. But he stood erect and did not answer.

It appeared that she was not expecting such defiance, for now she ran tongue tip across her lips and ceased that chant. But a moment later she spoke again.

"You cannot stand against me any longer, Emperor of rags and tatters, of a ruined empire. If you have come to surrender—"

"I have not come to surrender, witch." Andas spoke for the first time, and his words cut across hers as swords might clang blade on blade in a duel.

"Yet you bear our emblem as a banner!" She laughed, pointing with her chin to the ring.

"Not as a truce flag, Kidaya, but as a torch to show me your path."

"And you have walked it—to your end, Emperor of ashes and dead men!"

"Not yet!" From whence came that flash of inspiration he never afterward knew. It was like an order

sent ringing through his head by the will of a power
beyond his own knowledge.

He readied the baton as if it were a throwing spear,
such as a man uses for skill hunting. And he hurled
it, so that the ring at its tip entered straight into the
mouth of the mask.

Then he saw the lips move, close upon the wand
and snap it. The portion bearing the ring, with the
ring, vanished.

"To like fares like!" he cried, and the words also
came from somewhere outside his own mind.

There was a moan running through the company.
But Andas was no longer aware of them—he saw
only Kidaya. Now, as her mask of confidence broke
and she allowed emotion to show fleetingly upon her
face—consuming hate—he traced a likeness to the
Princess Abena, faint though it was. The princess was
at the beginning of a crooked and shadowed road. This
woman had walked the full way to stand at its end.

She laughed. "My poor littling! Now you have
thrown away what small protection you ever had.
As the Old Woman has eaten your safeguard, so
shall she now eat you." She fell then to crooning,
rubbing her hands caressingly along the sides of
the mask, so that Andas could see that she did not
need to steady the thing on her knees, but that it
rested there of itself.

Kidaya crooned, and the mask began to grow larger
and larger until it hid all of her, save her slender feet
and the hands that still gentled it. If this was illusion,
the hallucinatory power behind it was very great.

The eyes were alive, and they looked upon him
with a stare as if to draw him forward to death, while

the mouth opened and a great tongue used its tip to beckon him.

Andas could feel the urge, the need to reach that mouth. But what he wore about him kept him steady, though the pull was nigh unbearable. And all the time the mask grew.

Still Andas waited for the signal he was sure would come. Move too soon and that which manifested itself in the mask would not be drawn far enough into this plane of existence to be destroyed. Wait! But the need to go to it— He swayed as he stood, torn between the witchery of the mask and the counter force about his body.

He could not stand it much longer—he would be torn apart!

The signal he waited for came with a flash of energy filling his whole body. Andas raised his hands and began to trace in the air the contours of the mask. From his lips poured the ancient chant he had learned at the fort. It was the sound and tone of those words that should release the energy now filling his entire being and aim it as he made of himself a vessel of destruction.

His whole body quivered and shook with what filled it. Andas believed he could actually see faint threads of light shooting from the tips of his fingers. And then he obeyed the call of the mask, leaping up to meet it as if he were its prisoner at last.

There was—

But no man could—would—be allowed to remember what came then. There was nothingness and the dark.

He was cold. He had never been so cold in his life. Life? No, this was death, which had been his

burden and finally finished him. But could one smell
in death? Could one feel? If so, then old speculations
were at fault. Smell, feel, hear—for there was moaning he could hear.

See? Andas opened his eyes. He lay on rock, looking at blasted, blackened stone, so stained it might
have been worked upon by blaster fire.

Stone? Memory came back. So, he was not dead.
He levered himself to his knees and swung his head
slowly from side to side. And what he saw sickened
him somewhat but did not pierce far, for it was as if
the cold he felt created an ice barrier between him
and the world.

He could not get to his feet, but he crawled out of
that hollow until he crouched in the open between the
bone walls of the pathway. He was no sooner in the
open than there was a resounding crash from within.
A great billow of gritty dust puffed out, so he cried
aloud and threw up his arms to cover his face. But
afterward there was no moaning in the dark.

Andas crawled on, and the stones and gravel cut
his hands and knees. He felt no pain, for the cold
kept him' in its hold, and no other sensation could
pass it. Finally he came to the skimmer.

It took the last of his strength to crawl within and
tumble into the pilot's seat. He had to raise two bleeding hands to set the controls, nor was he fully aware
as the craft raised from the valley and swung around
on the recorded tape that would take it home.

For a while he was limp, inert, preserved from
all feeling. That he had accomplished what he had
gone to do, that what occupied the mask had been
destroyed in this world, at least for a space, and with

it those who had served it, he knew. But he felt no
triumph. It was like watching a taped story in which
one was not personally involved.

He had hoped to die swiftly and cleanly in that
final moment when he made of himself the ultimate
weapon. But it seemed that the very power he had
invoked had preserved him, to die more horribly
and lingeringly. That, too, he was able to face with
detachment, which he dimly hoped would continue
to hold. If the energy had burned out of him all fear
and emotion, so much the better.

At last he either lapsed into a stupor or slept while
the skimmer bore him away from those ominous
mountains toward a land waiting to be reborn.

When Andas awoke, he was not in the skimmer, but
lying on a cot bed, and around him were the walls
of the fort. So he had made it back after all—or the
skimmer had made it for him on tape command. But
again there was no feeling of triumph in him, only a
vast weariness. He wanted to close his eyes and sleep.
Perhaps this was the first symptom he must endure
before the end.

Someone moved into his line of vision. Shara stood
there—but with a difference about her. Those tight
braids were gone. Her hair made a soft halo about a
face that was still far too thin and drawn. Again the
years had fallen from her. She was young, and in her
burned a light that made her far different from the
woman who had wept over the dying emperor. But
though she did not weep for him, she would watch a
second emperor die. Suddenly feeling broke through
the cold that encased him. There was no one to weep
for him. And the desolate loneliness was more than

he could bear. Andas closed his eyes. But it seemed she would spare him nothing.

"Andas! Andas!"

Reluctantly he looked at her once more. She was on her knees beside his bed so her face was close. There were tears in her eyes after all. One spilled over to form a clear droplet on her brown cheek.

"Andas—"

"It is done," he told her. "The Old Woman—is destroyed—perhaps forever. Rule in safety, Empress!"

"Only with an emperor!" she replied. "Andas, the medic—he could not find any radiation deterioration. You will not die, not now!"

He continued to stare at her. She was telling the truth. He could read it in her face. Not die? With radiation readings such as they had told him? It was impossible that any human being could survive.

Any human being! Did he have at last the answer to his one moving question? Was he Andas—the false emperor, the android? This was the proof.

"I am not what you think—no emperor, not even a real Andas." He must tell her now, before she went on building on something which did not exist. She would perhaps have some kindness in her, but being human, she could not but repudiate him for what he truly was.

"You are Andas!" she told him firmly. Her hands closed upon his with a grip he could not find the will to fight. She held them, imprisoned in hers, against her breast. "You are Emperor Andas, of that there is no question."

How could he make her understand? There was only the stark truth left.

"I am an android—made to look like the other Andas in my own world. But I thought that I was real!"

"You are real! You are Andas—"

"No!" His energy seemed to grow with his need to deny, to make her realize what he was. "This proves it. I am an android. A human being could not have survived such radiation. Don't you understand? I am not human!"

"Brother." A hand with fur growing down its back came out of nowhere to rest lightly on his shoulder. Andas turned his head to see Yolyos.

"Tell her," he appealed to the Salariki. "Tell her the whole story. She must not go on believing—"

"He has told me, Andas! When you went as we thought to your death, he told me. Do you think the medics would not have known that you were android? They believe that you were healed by the force you used to destroy the Old Woman, that it might have killed you instead if you had not been already exposed to the radiation, but that one balanced the other, to your saving."

"Yet neither would have affected an android—"

"No one could make so human an android. You are a man. Believe—accept it—" she entreated him.

But he looked to Yolyos. The Salariki smiled. "If you are android, so am I, but we are near enough human, it seems, to be human. Why should it then matter, brother? If it has saved your life twice over, be glad for it."

"Be glad—" Shara leaned closer. Her lips were warm and comforting on his.

He surrendered. Near enough human to be human. He would believe—he had to now.

WRAITHS OF TIME

For Esther Turner,
Renee Damone,
and Carol Cross,
all of whom have had their
own struggles to prove
themselves against odds
in a hostile world.

-1-

The box was placed in the exact center of the desk.
Under the full beam of light Jason Robbins had turned
on it, its eighteen inches of age-yellowed ivory glowed
as might polished wood. Or was she only imagining
that, Tallahassee wondered. This artifact had a quality
of—she searched for the right word, then knew it
was one she would not use aloud—enchantment, that
was it. There was a golden inlay on the lid, as well
as four other disks, inlaid with gold, one on each
side. She could guess without touching that they
had been fashioned of that pure, soft gold used in
ancient times.

"Well"—the grey-haired man, apparently in charge
here, leaned forward a little—"can you give us any
lead, Miss Mitford?"

Tallahassee found difficulty in turning away from
the box at which she had stared from the moment
Jason had snapped on the desk lamp.

"I don't know." She spoke the truth. "There are

279

elements of African design, yes. See." She pointed a finger, nearly as ivory in color as the time-darkened box itself, at the gold inlay on the lid which formed a strip curved like a snake to travel the length of the ivory. Yet the spiral had no real head, rather there was a strip of precious metal bent at right angles—not unlike a stylized hunting knife. "That really combines two known devices of old kingship. This device at the top is the 'plow' which we believe was carried by the rulers of Meroë. The rest is of a later period, perhaps, a symbolic sword blade in the form of a snake. But these two forms have never, to my knowledge, been found so linked before. The Meroë dynasties borrowed greatly from Egypt, and there the snake was a sign of royalty, usually a part of the crown. These"—her finger moved to the disks at the sides—"are again symbolic. They resemble very closely those gold badges that were worn by the 'soul-washers' of the Ashanti, the attendants of the king whose duty it was to ward off any danger of contamination from general evil. Yet—though it combines symbols from two, maybe three, periods of African history, it is very old—"

"Would you say a museum piece, then?" The man Jason had introduced as Roger Nye persisted. His tone was impatient, as if he had expected some instant snap judgment from her. And his tone aroused in Tallahassee her own, sometimes militant, stubbornness.

"Mr. Nye, I am a student of archaeology, employed at present to help catalogue the Lewis Brooke collection. There are many tests that would have to be made to date this artifact, tests for which one needs certain equipment. But I will say that the workmanship . . ." She paused before she asked a question of her own:

"Have you seen the rod of office in the Brooke collection?"

"What's that got to do with it? Or are you saying that this"—Nye indicated the box—"could be a part of that collection?"

"If it is," she was careful in her answer, "it was not included in the official customs inventory. However, there is something . . ." Tallahassee shook her head. "You do not want guesses, you want certainties. Dr. Roman Carey will be here tonight. He is coming to study the collection. I would advise you to let him see this. At present he is the greatest authority on art of the Sudan."

"You are sure it is Sudanese?" Now it was Jason who asked the question.

Tallahassee made a small gesture. "I told you, I cannot be sure of anything. I would say it is old, very old. As to its general point of origin I would believe Africa. But the combination of symbols I have not seen before. If I may . . ." She put out a hand toward the box, only to have Nye's hand close tightly about her wrist in a lightning-quick movement.

She looked at him in open amazement and then irritated dislike.

"You don't understand." Jason broke in again, speaking very swiftly as if he were afraid she could keep no better rein on her temper now than she could when they were children. "The thing is hot!"

"Hot?"

"It radiates some form of energy." Nye studied her with those measuring eyes. "That was how it was found, really. It was by sheer chance." He freed her hand, and she jerked it back to her lap. "One of our field men went to put his kit in a locker at the airport. He had a geiger counter with him and it started to register. He was quick to use it and located the source of radiation in a nearby locker. Then he called me. We got the port key for the locker. This was the only thing inside."

"Radioactive," Tallahassee murmured. "But how . . ."

Nye shook his head. "Not atomic, though a counter can pick it up. It's something new, but the lab boys did not want to take it to pieces—"

"I should say not!" Tallahassee was thoroughly aroused at the suggestion of such vandalism. "It may be unique. Has it been opened?"

Nye shook his head. "There is no visible fastening. And it seemed better not to handle it too much until we were sure of what we had. Now what about this rod of office you mentioned, what is it and where was it found?"

"There was a strong belief in the old African kingdoms that the soul of a nation could be enclosed in some precious artifact. The Ashanti war with England a hundred years ago came about because an English governor demanded the King's stool to sit on as a sign of the transferal of rulership. But even the King could not sit on that. Sitting on a floor mat, he might only lean a portion of his arm upon it while making some very important decree or when assuming the kingship. To the Ashanti people the stool contained the power of all the tribal ancestors and was holy; it possessed a deeply religious as well as a political significance—which the English did not attempt to find out before they made their demands.

"Other tribes had similar symbols of divine contact with their ancestors and their gods. Sometimes at the death of a king such symbols were retired to a special house from which they were brought to 'listen' when there was need for a grave change in some law or the demand for a decision involving the future of the people as a whole. These artifacts were very precious, and among some tribes were never seen at all except by priests or priestesses.

"The rod of office which Lewis Brooke found is believed to be one of these tokens. And because he discovered it in a place that has some very odd legends, it is of double value."

"He found it in the Sudan then?"

"No, much farther west. It was nearer to Lake Chad. There is an old legend that when the Arab-Ethiopian kingdom of Axum overran Meroë, the royal clan—and they themselves were the descendents of Egyptian Pharaohs and held jealously to much of the very ancient beliefs—fled west and were supposed to have established a refuge near Lake Chad. There has never been any real proof of this, not until Doctor Brooke made his spectacular find—an unplundered tomb containing many artifacts and a sarcophagus, though the latter was empty, and there was evidence that no body had ever been within it. Instead the rod of office rested there."

"The soul of the nation buried," Jason said softly.

Tallahassee nodded. "Perhaps. There were inscriptions, but, though they used Egyptian hieroglyphics, the later Meroë tongue has never been translated, so they could not be deciphered. Dr. Brooke's unfortunate accidental death last year has delayed the work on the whole project of arranging and identifying the artifacts."

"I am surprised," Nye commented, "that he was allowed to take anything out of the country to bring here. The new nations are doubly jealous of losing any of their treasures—especially to us."

"We were surprised, too," Tallahassee admitted. "But he had full permission." She hesitated and then added: "There was something odd about the whole matter, as if they wanted to get rid of all the finds for some reason of their own."

Jason's eyes narrowed. "A threatened uprising, perhaps, using the old rod of office for a rallying point?"

Nye's attention swung from the girl to the young man. "You believe that?"

Jason shrugged. "Rebellions have been started on lesser excuses. Remember the Ashanti and their stool."

"But you say yourself that was a hundred years ago!" Nye protested.

"Africa is very old. It has seen the rise and fall of three waves of civilization—maybe more, for who has actually identified those who ruled at Zimbabwe or in the intricate fortifications of Iyanga? Men remember well in Africa. The later kings might not have any scribes, but just like the Celtic lords of Europe who had no written language, they had trained memory banks among their own kind—men who could stand up in council and recite facts, genealogies, laws reaching back three and four hundred years. Such skills do not die easily among such people."

Inwardly Tallahassee was ready to laugh. Jason was

drawing on her own knowledge now, though he had often enough in the past shrugged at her comments and conversation as being deadly dull. Who cared what happened two thousand years ago anyway? The best time was here and now.

"Hmmm." Nye leaned back in the chair behind the desk. He was not focusing on either of the young people, nor even on the box now. Instead his eyes were half-closed as if he were thinking deeply.

Tallahassee broke that moment of silence. "I would suggest—" she said boldly. After all no one had made plain just what this Nye's authority was in the matter (though she judged from Jason's hurried call which had first brought her here that he was some VIP of the type who is never identified publicly, if he can help it). "I would suggest that you put that"—she gestured at the box—"in the museum safe. There is perhaps only one man, Dr. Carey, who can make a true identification if that is what you need."

Nye opened his eyes wide then in a long stare turned on her, as if he could unlock her thoughts by merely looking at her intently. The girl lifted her chin a fraction of an inch and met his gaze with one as steady.

"All right," he decided. "And I want to see this 'rod' of yours into the bargain. But not right now. We've got to think about who planted this—here. Robbins, you go with her . . ." He glanced at the watch on his wrist.

"It's nearly closing time for the museum, I take it. Better make it fast—we don't want any action which can be noted as out of the ordinary, not if this thing has any political overtones."

He had brought out a briefcase, snapped it open. To Tallahassee's surprise the interior had been metal lined. Now Nye produced a pair of tongs from the inner cover of the case and used them to slide the box into it. As Tallahassee stood up, Nye handed the case to Robbins.

"Yes, it's lead-lined, Miss Mitford. We're taking no chances about the radiation, even if it is a new one to us. Robbins had better carry this. When does Carey get in?"

"He should be there already."

"Good enough. Ask him to call this number"—Nye scrawled some figures on a card and pushed it to her—"as soon as he can. And thank you, Miss Mitford. Put the case and its contents in the safe. Robbins will drive you."

He turned to pick up a phone as if Tallahassee had already dissolved into thin air. The girl waited until the door of the office had closed behind them before she spoke again.

"Who's that playing James Bond?"

Jason shook his head. "Don't ask me, girl. All I know is that the Big Chief himself couldn't get better service if he showed his face in these parts. I'm small fry, but I got asked in 'cause somewhere along the line since that was found yesterday somebody said, 'Oh, my, now just maybe that's African!' I guess then somebody went and asked the computer who locally could tell them the truth and I got punched out. But I saw it wasn't modern—so I called you."

"Jason, do you really think this is political? I know that finding the rod in the sarcophagus was odd, and it does make some sense about it being a 'soul' burial. But this thing . . ."

"It was you, Tally, my dear, who tied this to your rod, remember?"

"Because there is something alike in them"—she watched him stow the heavy case in the car—"only I can't just put a finger to it. It's more a feeling than anything else." She bit her lip. There she went again, one of her hunches. Someday she was going to be proved very wrong, and when she was—

"One of those feelings of yours, eh?" Jason's left eyebrow slid up. "Still having them?"

"Well, a lot of times they've paid off!" Tallahassee retorted. "You know they have."

"You've been lucky," was Jason's verdict as he edged the car into the heavy traffic of the beginning rush hour. "Will we make it before they close up that repository of dead knowledge for the night?"

"They close to the public at four, but the back door is for staff and I have a key. The alarms won't go on until Hawes has made sure everyone is out of the offices and that those are shut for the night. Dr. Carey should be there."

Jason concentrated on his driving, Tallahassee was content to sit quietly. She tried to understand the odd emotion inside of her which she had been aware of ever since she had gotten into the car. Twice she had actually turned her head to glance into the narrow back seat of Jason's bug. No one there. Yet the sensation of another presence was growing so acute it made her nervous, and she had to exert more and more control not to squirm around again and again.

The thought was strong in her now that what they

carried was important. Not, she believed, exactly for the reasons that the mysterious Mr. Nye might think, but for some other reason. That was probably her "hunch" busy working overtime, and she tried to dismiss all thought of what they carried, of the museum even. Her vacation—it started next Monday. She had had to wait for the coming of Dr. Carey . . .

Not that it was a real vacation and she was going to utterly escape her job. But to fly to Egypt and join the Matraki party! Egypt—Meroë . . . She could not keep her thoughts on vacation plans. That nagging feeling persisted. But she was not going to give in to it!

The traffic was lighter now as Jason swung off the expressway and started through the series of streets to get to the museum. It was darker than usual—a lot of clouds piling up—maybe a storm later on.

When the car pulled into the narrow back way used by delivery trucks, Tallahassee got out quickly. She had fitted her key and had the door open when Jason followed her, his arm dragged down under the weight of the case.

"Who's there?" There was a light only at the far end of the hall, and it seemed twice as dark as usual.

Then the upper lights flashed on, and she could see the chief guard.

"Oh, you, Miss Mitford. 'Bout ready to lock up."

"We have something for the safe, Mr. Hawes. This is my cousin, Mr. Robbins. He's with the FBI here."

"Saw your picture, Mr. Robbins, in the paper last week. That sure was a good haul you fellows made, pickin' up all them drug smugglers."

Jason smiled. "The boss says just routine. But I'm

glad that the public appreciates our efforts now and then."

"Did Dr. Carey come?" Tallahassee wanted to get rid of that case, put the building and this day out of her life for now.

"Yes, ma'am. He's in that extra office of Dr. Green-ley's, fifth floor. The back elevator's on, faster for you than the stairs."

"I left my car just out there," Jason pointed. "Be back as quick as I can."

"That's all right, Mr. Robbins. Nobody'll bother it there."

Tallahassee hurried around a corner and into an elevator. Jason had to take long strides to keep up with her.

"You're in a rush all of a sudden," he commented.

"I want to get that in the safe," she said with an emphasis she regretted a moment later when again his left eyebrow arose in question.

"Well," she added in her own defense, "I can't help what I feel. There—there's something wrong."

She saw the eyes in Jason's brown face go suddenly sober.

"All right. I'll accept your hunch as real. This has been a queer one from the start. Where's this safe?"

"In Dr. Greenley's office."

"There's one thing—don't forget to tell this Carey about Nye wanting to hear from him."

She had almost forgotten Nye; now she hoped she could find that card in her purse. The urgency that gripped her had absolutely no base in anything but her nerves. But she felt if she did not manage to get rid

of the case and out of here something dreadful was
going to happen. And so acute was that feeling she
dared not let Jason know the force of it. He would
think she had lost her mind.

In the fifth floor the hall lights were still on, and
their footsteps on the marble floor were audible.
But Tallahassee found herself straining to pick up
another sound, perhaps a third set of heel taps. That
belief—no, it could not be a belief—that they had
an invisible companion was intensifying. Tallahassee
caught her lower lip between her teeth and held it
so, using all her self-control to keep her eyes straight
ahead, refusing to look over her shoulder where nothing could possibly be.

She reached the door of the director's office with
a sigh of relief and pulled it open, her hand reaching
out to snap on the light switch. Before that gesture
was completed she gave a little cry. Then a burst of
light filled the room to display how silly she had been.
Of course no one had passed her. There was no one
here but herself and Jason, who was now closing the
door behind them.

"What is it?" he demanded.

Tallahassee forced a laugh. "I guess it is all this secret
business. I thought I saw a shadow move . . ."

"Only the Shadow knows . . ." intoned Jason sol-
emnly. "You are nervy tonight, Tally. Get your work
done, and I'll take you out for dinner."

"Some place cheerful," she found herself saying,
"with lots of lights—"

"I beg your pardon."

With another gasp Tallahassee swung around. The
inside door between this and the neighboring office

had opened. A slender man who must be at least an inch or so shorter than herself—which was not unusual: when a girl stands five-eleven-and-a-half shoeless, she does not look up to many males—was eyeing her in manifest disapproval.

He was thin featured, his nose sharp-pointed, his mouth turning down with a sour twist. And his sandy hair had been combed back with care over a pink scalp, which showed only too readily through those thin strands, to touch his collar in the back.

"I believe this is Dr. Greenley's office—" His thin lips shaped each word as if he broke them off as he spoke them.

"I am Tallahassee Mitford, Dr. Greenley's assistant in the African division."

He surveyed her, Tallahassee realized, with actual distaste, and she could sense his resentment. Was he one of those who disliked and downgraded any woman with a pretense of knowledge in their own field? She had met several of that ilk.

"You are quite young," he commented in a way which made the observation vaguely offensive. "But surely you are aware that this place is not a proper one for social contacts."

He had looked beyond her at Jason. And if he was implying what she thought he was—Tallahassee had to subdue her flaring temper with every bit of control she could muster. After all, she would have to work with this man (whether either of them liked it or not) until the Brooke collection was catalogued.

"We have something to put in the safe." She hated herself for even explaining that much, but she knew she had to. "And—" She opened her purse. For once luck was with her. That card was right on top, and she did not have to waste any time delving around in sometimes jumbled floating contents to find it. "I was given this. It is for you to call as soon as possible."

She laid the card down on the edge of Dr. Greenley's overflowing desk and did not look at the man again as she went to the safe. As long as Hawes had not yet snapped on the night alarms she could open it.

Jason, his mouth set in a way she well knew (he had his own temper, even if he had learned long ago how to keep it under), came around the other side of the desk with the case ready. She did not know nor care at the moment whether Dr. Carey had his precious phone number or not. As the door came open at her pull Jason slipped the case in. Tallahassee slammed the door, spun the dial. Still ignoring Dr. Carey, she walked to the phone and punched the number of Dr. Greenley's home.

"Is Dr. Joe in?" she asked as she heard Mrs. Greenley's deep, pleasant voice. "Yes, it's Tally. Oh. Well, when he comes in, tell him there's something in the safe. It was picked up—by the FBI."

She had Jason's nod to reassure her that she could keep to that story.

"Yes. They want an opinion on it. They'll contact him tomorrow. No, I don't know much more. But it's terribly important. No, I'm not going home right away—Jason's in town and we're going to eat out. Thank you. I'll ask him. Good-bye."

She set the phone down and smiled with angry brightness at Jason. "Mrs. Greenley says if you have time before you leave, do stop in and see her. Now—" she swung back to the man who had made no attempt not to listen in—"you have the reason for my being here, Dr. Carey. If you care to check on me, you need only call the Greenleys."

"Not so fast," he said, as she turned away. "As you have been working on the Brooke files, I want you here the first thing in the morning. They must be completely rechecked, of course."

"Of course," Tallahassee said softly. "You have your own methods of working—"

"I certainly do!" he snapped.

It came to her that he was watching her with a kind of outrage—as if the mere fact that she existed and must be a part of his daily round in the future was an insult which he found hard to bear. And his hostility was so patent that she began to lose her own control, but also grew curious at what had so forcibly triggered this seemingly instant dislike for her.

As she and Jason went down in the elevator she was aware of something else. That feeling of a third person was gone, even her queer hunch was fading. Maybe she had left it all back in the safe and, if it did have any effect, let it bother Dr. Carey—it might do him some good.

-2-

Tallahassee sighed contentedly and Jason laughed. "For a black woman you sure do put away a Chinese dinner in a competent manner," he commented.

"I like Foo Kong's, I like sweet-sour pork, I like—"

"Fortune cookies?" He broke open one and unrolled the paper slip inside with the air of a judge about to pronounce sentence.

"Well, well, this is apt enough. 'Food cures hunger, study cures ignorance.' What weighty thought lies in yours?"

Tallahassee produced her own. "That's odd . . ."

"What's odd? They put the bill for this feast in yours, Tally?"

"No," she answered a little absently and read: "Dragon begets Dragon, Phoenix begets Phoenix."

"I don't see anything odd about that. Just another way of saying 'like begets like.'"

"It could have another meaning, too. The dragon

was the Emperor's symbol—no one else dared use it.
And the phoenix was that of the Empress. It could
mean that royalty begets only royalty."

"Which is just what I said, isn't it?" queried Jason,
watching her intently.

"I don't know—oh, I guess it is." But why had she
had that odd momentary feeling that the message of
a fortune cookie, which was simply some old proverb,
had a special significance for her?

"Look here, I didn't say anything because I had a
hunch you didn't want to talk about it." Jason broke
across her thought. "But what are you going to do
about this Carey? It's plain he's going to make a brute
of himself if he can. I wonder why?"

Tallahassee had tried to keep their encounter with
Dr. Carey out of her mind all through dinner. But
she would have to face it sooner or later, and she
might as well do so now that Jason had brought it
into the open.

"It could be," she returned frankly, "because I'm
black. But I think mostly because I'm a woman.
There're a lot of Ph.D.'s floating around, and not
all of them are whites either, who resent any female
daring to crowd into their own particular field.
Which is one reason, my dear, that we're pushing
for equality—and you hear about Amazons giving the
cry the matriarchy shall rise again! Oddly enough,
matriarchy of a sort did persist, and right in Africa,
too, for a long time. When a queen in Europe could
be pushed around like a chess-woman on some
plotter's board, queens well to the south were leading
their own armies and wielding such influence as no
white skin dared dream of. Each kingdom had three

dominant women, if not more—the queen mother, not necessarily the ruling king's mother, but rather the most important royal woman of the preceding generation; the king's sister, because only she could produce a royal heir—the king's sons mostly didn't count; and his first wife. Why, in Ashanti, the king's wives had the duty of collecting all the taxes and had their own very efficient guards, attendants and the like, to do just that."

"So—if Carey is the expert on African history he's supposed to be," commented Jason, "he ought to know all this. Maybe that's why he wants to cut you down before you take over your natural-born ruler-ship of his department. But"—Jason turned serious now—"look out for him, Tally. I think he could be an ugly customer if he sets out to be."

She nodded. "I know, and nothing can be deadlier than department politics. Luckily, Dr. Greenley has seen me work long enough to know what I can do. Jason, it's nearly nine-thirty!" She had glanced at her watch.

"The knife flaying the elephant does not have to be large, only sharp!"

She gazed at Jason. "Now just what does that mean?"

"We had some wisdom of the East." He gestured to the discarded scraps from the cookies. "I was merely supplying some from our own native stock. In other words, watch your step."

"I'll probably be doing that so steadily I'll trip over my own feet," she agreed as she stood up. "The Greenleys are pets, I won't rock any boats to make trouble for Dr. Joe."

Jason was unlocking her apartment door for her when they heard the steady shrill of the telephone inside. "Oh!" She sent the door spinning with a hard push and crossed the dark living room in a rush to catch up the phone which gave one last demanding ring.

"Tallahassee?" It was Dr. Joe, and he sounded odd, his voice strained.

"Yes—"

"Thank goodness I got you. Can you come down right now to the museum? I wouldn't ask except it is of the utmost importance." Then the line clicked off so suddenly she stood there, startled. This was not Dr. Greenley's way . . .

"What is it?"

"Dr. Greenley." She put the phone down. "He just told me to come down to the museum—at this hour!—and hung up. Something's happened! It must have!"

"I'll take you." Jason moved behind her to shut the door, taking out the key to hand to her. She felt a little dazed. In her two years of work—first as a junior assistant, then as a full-fledged assistant—this had never happened. She could feel the uneasiness now even as she had felt that shadow of a third presence, which, of course, had never been there, accompanying her through the museum.

"There's something terribly wrong," she murmured as Jason settled beside her in the car and started to work his way out of the parking lot.

"Sure, that Carey," he returned.

But what could Dr. Carey have done or said to make Dr. Joe call her down to the museum at night? She could not think of anything and was still bewildered when Jason brought her to the same back door they had entered some hours earlier. There was a light in the hall now and just inside the door was Hawes. He swung it open.

"Go right on up, Miss Mitford. The elevator's waiting."

Jason had moved out but Tallahassee turned. "No, you stay here, Jas—if it's department business I'll do more than put a foot wrong to bring a stranger into it."

"You sure?" He looked both concerned and doubtful.

She nodded vigorously enough, she hoped, to satisfy him.

"I'm sure. And if it's going to be a long session I'll phone down and Mr. Hawes can tell you. I know you have to take the early plane out. That all right, Mr. Hawes?"

"Sure thing, Miss."

As Tallahassee entered the elevator, she half expected to feel that other presence. But there was nothing, except the rather eerie sensation that was always part of the museum when it was closed to the public and most of the staff was gone, intensified perhaps by the fact this was night. The storm which had promised earlier had not yet broken, but the sky outside was still overclouded and now she heard, even through the thickness of the walls about her, a roll of what could only be distant thunder.

Thunder of drums—somehow that phrase slipped into her mind as she shifted from one foot to the other impatiently, waiting for the elevator to reach the fifth floor. Drums meant so much in Africa—the famous "talking drums" whose expertly induced sounds could actually mimic tribal tongues so that they could be understood. . . .

The elevator door opened, and she looked into the open hall. There was a light on behind the frosted glass of Dr. Greenley's door. Tallahassee found herself breathing as swiftly as if she had been running. Deliberately she made herself walk more slowly. She was not going to burst into Dr. Joe's office as if she had been called from play like some forgetful child.

When she knocked and heard his muffled voice in answer, she worked to summon full control. And a moment later she was facing him across a desk that was no longer stacked with papers as it had been all the length of time she had known him. Those had been swept to the floor, a snowstorm of littered pages, books, magazines. The office was in such wild confusion that she halted just within the door and gasped. It could look no worse, she believed, if a small hurricane had gone to work here.

"What—what happened?"

Dr. Joe's jaw was set. "That's what we are trying to find out, Tallahassee. Someone was undoubtedly hunting something; to the best of my knowledge there was nothing here worth this effort."

"No?" That supercilious voice came from the corner. Dr. Carey sat on a chair, looking about him with a satisfaction he could not hide from Tallahassee's narrowed eyes. "Ask this Miss Mitford of yours what she and her boyfriend so conveniently locked in your safe tonight."

Dr. Joe did not even look at him. "Tallahassee, if

you have any explanation at all of this, I would be grateful for it."

Tallahassee made her account brief. "I was called to the airport this afternoon, late. Jason sent for me. They had found something curious in one of the lockers there and wanted an identification. I—well, I thought the artifact looked a little like the rod of office in the Brooke Collection. So the head man—by the way," she turned now to Dr. Carey, "did you call that number he sent? He could have explained it all—"

"What number?" Dr. Joe looked puzzled.

"I told this Mr. Nye that Dr. Carey was coming to evaluate the Brooke Collection. He wrote a number on a card and asked for him to get in touch as soon as possible."

"Carey?" Dr. Joe turned his head.

The other showed no sign of discomfiture. "I did not know the man. If he wanted my services he need only approach me directly—which he did not. No, I did not call."

Why, wondered Tallahassee? The man seemed almost to take the suggestion as an insult.

"But you put this artifact in the safe?" Dr. Joe asked.

"Yes. It was in a lead-lined case—which is why Jason brought it up for me."

"Lead-lined?" Dr. Joe was plainly bewildered.

"They said that the artifact gave off some unidentified type of radiation. They were taking every precaution."

"It was African—a real artifact?"

"Look and see." Tallahassee, shaken as she had

been by the sight of the office, now felt a rising
irritation.

She put her hand to the safe dial, and then remembered the night alarms. But Dr. Joe had already antici-
pated her request and was on the phone to call Hawes
and have those cut off. When the door opened, she
brought out the case which was heavy enough that she
needed both hands to swing it to the top of the desk.
Flicking open the catch she lifted the cover. There the
box lay as Dr. Joe went forward eagerly.

Tallahassee took the tongs at the top and lifted out
the find with care. To her surprise, Dr. Carey did not
join them by the desk. She glanced at him once and
saw that he only sat there calmly, a faint, satirical
smile on his thin lips, watching them as if they were
edging into some trouble that he had no intention of
warning them against. His attitude was stranger than
ever, strange enough to awaken Tallahassee's feeling
of something lurking here, waiting . . .

Dr. Joe had taken the tongs from her eagerly, was
moving the box slowly around.

"Yes, yes! But, what? The style is a mixture—old,
though, undoubtedly very old. And just left in a locker!
We must run a test on it. Carey, what do you think
it is—what culture?"

Dr. Carey got up. He moved swiftly, oddly. His eyes
were now fastened avidly on the box and the malicious
look was gone. With two strides he reached the desk,
elbowing Tallahassee roughly to one side. Reaching
forward before either of the other two could prevent
it, for they were not prepared for his sudden move,
he put one hand at either side of the box.

There was no sound, but when Dr. Carey lifted

his hands, half the box came away. Inside was a small bundle wrapped in yellowed material.

"Don't!" Tallahassee caught at Carey's elbow. "The radiation!"

He did not even look at her. Instead he dropped the lid with a clatter to the desk and caught at the bundle. Dr. Joe attempted to snatch it away, his expression one of complete amazement.

Dr. Carey eluded him, just as he had jerked free from Tallahassee. He was tearing at the wrapping of the bundle frenziedly. The material peeled off in bits, as if the stuff had been weakened by age. What he held, after a second or two of fighting the covering, was an object about a foot long. And the shape was familiar to them all. This was an ankh—that very ancient key to all life which every representative of an Egyptian god or goddess carried in one hand. It had been carved of some crystalline-appearing substance and showed no fracture or erosion.

Dr. Carey dropped it to the desk top.

"What? Why?" He was wiping his hands up and down the front of his coat as if something he feared and hated clung to them. And now his face was pinched and drawn. "Why? . . ." he repeated in a voice higher than usual as if he needed an answer from them as to the reason for his actions.

At that moment there was a burst of thunder which seemed so close overhead that the roof itself might have been shattered. Tallahassee cowered and screamed, she could not help it. A second later the lights went out, and they stood in darkness.

"No! No! No!" Someone was crying out—the sound growing fainter with every denial.

"Dr. Joe." Somehow Tallahassee found her voice. "Dr. Joe!" She tried to get around the table and ran into a chair, nearly losing her balance. Then she stood still.

There was light in the room. But it did not come from any bulb, any lamp she knew. It rayed out from the ankh on the table. The thing glowed.

And that glow drew her—just as she knew again that the presence she had sensed earlier was back, stronger than ever.

The ankh arose from the desk top. It was moving— and it was drawing her along after it. She tried to call out, to catch at the chair, at the wall, at anything that could serve as an anchorage. But there was nothing she could do.

"Dr. Joe!" This time her plea came as a faint whisper; the ability to say more had left her. That—that presence controlled her better than if someone had laid hands upon her shoulders and was pushing her ahead.

Frightened as she had never been before in her life, Tallahassee followed the floating, ghostly ankh one reluctant step at a time. They were in the outer hall now, she and the thing she could not see but well knew was with her, willing her to some task.

Here there was no light, either, but that given off by the ankh. However, it seemed to glow the brighter, so she could see the stairwell. Holding to the banister she went down and down, always that compulsion pushing her.

She found herself praying, not even in a whisper, because she could no longer voice even that much, but in her mind. This—this will that held her—it was a nightmare. This thing could not be happening—it could not! Yet it was.

They reached the fourth floor, the ankh swung into the hall there. Dimly, through her fear, Tallahassee realized where they were going—toward the three rooms that held the Brooke Collection. She had somehow surrendered part of herself. This was happening and apparently there was nothing she could do to prevent it.

"Tallahassee!"

Her name echoed hollowly from the stairwell behind. Dr. Joe! But he was too late—too late. . . . Too late for what, a part of her mind asked dully?

There was another roar of thunder but under it something else which pulsed even as the thunder died. Drums—the calling drums. Tallahassee forced her hands up over her ears, but she could not shut out that faint, demanding vibration of sound. And now there was added a tinkling, as if small bits of crystal were shaken one against another. That, too, she identified from a single moment of the past, the sistrum of the temple priestesses of old Egypt. They once had duplicated one in class and tried to use it as it must have been swung to summon the attention of the ancient gods.

She was going mad!

But she was not! Tallahassee's strong mind and intelligence began to rally. There was some logical explanation for all this. There must be! Part of her—that part which controlled her own movements—was in bondage to the influence of the presence. Her mind was still free.

They were at the door of the third and last room.

Light greeted them. But not the normal light Tallahassee knew. This was a beam shooting from the depths of the main case in the room. She was not surprised at its source. The crystalline head of the rod of office held a fainter glow maybe, but one which matched, in part, that given off by the ankh floating ahead.

Then the ankh stopped, held in the air as if the girl herself supported it at the level of her breast. The compulsion changed. A new order had been given her, one she was no more able to resist than she had the unvoiced command that had brought her here.

Her hands moved out, willed by that other, to seek the lock of the case. But it resisted her efforts. Now the compulsion strengthened, beat down upon her as physical blows might have done. The other will demanded that she free the rod. But she could not, it was locked. There was no way, no way at all. . . . The part of her mind that was free argued silently with the unseen, even as her body actually swayed back and forth under that beating command.

Out of the dark rang a voice. For one wild, hopeful moment Tallahassee thought either Dr. Joe or Hawes must have come to her rescue. Then she realized she could not understand a word of that impassioned speech. It was hot with anger, the emotion as strong as the will behind and about her. Yet it was not issuing from the presence that had brought her here.

A part of the control over her failed. As it withdrew, she somehow understood the rage that had gripped it, in turn, at the sound of that voice. But if it could reply it did not.

Now those words fell into the cadence of a strange

chant, the rhythm of which was accented by a distant
roll of drums. Tallahassee no longer wondered how
she heard what she did, nor from whence it came.
She only cowered before the display case in which
the light-crowned rod lay, wanting to creep away from
the site of battle. For the will that had brought her
here was now facing another, and they were joined
in struggle.

Tallahassee was suddenly caught up and hurled
viciously against the case. She screamed, throwing her
arms up over her face, fearing that the glass would
shatter and cut her flesh to ribbons. But though she
struck with bruising force, it was not enough to smash
the case and accomplish the purpose of that will.

It withdrew, meshed again in a struggle with the
invisible other.

More than one voice chanted now. She was sure
of that as she clung where the attack had left her,
spread-eagled against the case. Her mind whirled. She
felt sick with vertigo as forces beyond her knowledge
or description stirred into a mad swirl about her.
Then the ankh swung over her shoulder, hung directly
above the case.

Wide-eyed, she watched the rod stir, rise until it
stood vertical, without any support. It leaped upward,
its glowing head thumped against the top of the case,
while the ankh swooped downward to meet it at just
the same point.

The glass cracked, shattered and fell. And the lib-
erated rod spun through the air. Shadows gathered
around it in a hectic dance, as it tipped, fell to the
floor.

Above it, the ankh hovered as if trying to spur

the staff to another effort. Was that the shadow of a hand—a hand so tenuous that it was only outlined in the glow of the ankh? It was something, of that Tallahassee was sure, and it was reaching for the rod. But before it settled close enough to grasp it, the rod itself shifted. Not upward again, but, snakelike for all its stiffness, across the floor.

Again the will seized upon Tallahassee, whirled her about, and gave her what amounted to a vicious shove after the slithering rod. The ankh flew up at her, as if to dash itself into her face and was warded off by what she could not see, so that it hovered, making effectual darts as she was forced to obey the orders of her strange captor. She must get the rod into her hands—that was the imperative now filling her whole mind.

Again a voice called out. And Tallahassee realized dimly that the chanting had ceased. The ankh swung away from her, skimmed through the air, to remain poised in one corner of the room toward which the rod was moving with Tallahassee stumbling after it. Since she moved puppetwise by the other will, she was clumsy, slow, trying always to break away from that hold.

But the will was implacable and its hate hot. Not that the hate was turned wholly against her, as a very inept tool it must make use of, but rather more at the enemy it fronted. She saw now that the rod lay quiet.

Once more, a ghostly outline moved across the glow at its head. Meanwhile the will hurled her forward. She tripped and fell as her outstretched hand closed on the other end of the rod just as it was plucked

upward. Tallahassee held as she was commanded and
forced to. Wraith-like that grasping hand might be—if
hand it was—but there was strength in its hold upon
the rod. The ankh dipped and touched the gleaming
head of the staff.

It was like being caught in an explosion. There
followed light, heat, pain, and such a noise as deafened Tallahassee. The girl had a terrifying sensation
of being swung out over a vast void of nothingness.
That other presence was left behind. Her hands were
no longer glued to the rod by its command. But she
kept her grasp for her very life's sake. In her welled
the knowledge that, should she let go, the answer
was death—a death that was unnatural enough to be
worse than any her kind had feared since their first
beginnings.

She centered every bit of the force and strength
left in her to retain her hold. There was nothing
around her, a nothingness so negative as to tear at
her sanity. Hold—ON!

Then the nothingness closed about her in a vast
and horrible wrapping of utter blackness. Despairing,
she lost consciousness.

-3-

It was hot, as if she lay on the hearth of some furnace breathing in the stifling heat of the blast. Tallahassee tried to edge away from that heat, unaware as yet of anything else. She opened her eyes.

Sun—so blazing that it made an instant glare about her. With a little cry, Tallahassee shrank back, her hands over her eyes to shield them. It was hot, and she was lying under the sun—where? Her thoughts began to stir feebly, throwing off the torpor left from those last nightmare minutes.

Still shielding her eyes, she dug her elbows painfully against a hard surface on which she lay, levering up the forepart of her body, making herself look around.

Immediately before her was an outcrop of rock. And on its surface she could pick out a pattern deep-eroded by time into just faint lines. She crawled to that rock, lifting sand-encrusted hands for its support in order to gain her feet. Then she turned, giddy and sick, feeling as if each labored movement might send

her sailing out again into that dark void. Her dulled
mind jibbed at even thinking of that—place.

More rocks beyond. Or were those long-ago quar-
ried stones built into a piece of tumbled wall? But
at their foot. . . .

Tallahassee stifled the scream in her throat, made
herself blink, and blink again, to be sure she really
saw that body stretched out on rock and sand.

The stranger lay face down, arms flung out above
the head. In one hand was grasped the ankh, in the
other the rod. They no longer pulsed with light. Or
perhaps, in this blinding sunlight, their auras of radiation could not be distinguished.

Tallahassee inched along the rock which was her
support. Was the stranger unconscious? And who—and
what—and where? . . . She felt as if she were going
mad, or had passed the border of sanity during the
time that the rod had drawn her on.

There was a thin, almost gossamer cotton robe
on the body, so finely woven that one could see the
gleam of darker flesh through it. It was simply made,
reaching from armpit to ankle, with two broad straps
of the same material holding it over the shoulders, a
belt which gave off glints of gemlike color against the
dead white of the garment. The stranger's shoulder-
length hair had been woven into many tiny braids,
each tipped with a bead of gold, and there was another
band of the same precious metal forming a narrow
diadem to hold those braids in confinement.

Tallahassee was reminded of something. She moved
a fraction closer, fearing to stoop lest her present
vertigo send her toppling against the stranger. Instead
she dropped carefully to her knees and put out a hand

to the shoulder where the brown skin was a shade or so darker than her own.

With an effort she rolled the stranger over, the body limply slack in her hold. She was sure somehow that this was death. But, as the other's face came into view, Tallahassee screamed and flinched away.

Sand was matted on the generous lips, caught in eyebrows that had been darkened and extended by the use of a heavy cosmetic. But the face itself—NO!

Save for the slight difference in the color of their skins, she was looking down at the same features she saw every time she stood before a mirror! Oh, there were differences—the brows artificially lengthened toward the temples and darkened, thick lines drawn under the now-closed eyes, while the headband rose in front to the likeness of a striking serpent.

"Egypt—" Tallahassee whispered. "Egypt and royal . . ." For that serpent diadem could be worn only by a woman of the Blood, and one placed very close to the throne itself.

She scuttled back on her hands and knees. The girl was dead, she was certain of that. Now she looked around wildly. . . .

They were in a place where sand had been scoured away, perhaps by the wind of some dune-lashing storm, perhaps by human effort. There were ruins all about, stones pitted and defaced by those same grit-filled winds. And she was nowhere on the earth she knew! Shaking with a growing fear, she crouched against the rock that had earlier supported her and tried to understand what had happened. There was no sane explanation for this, none at all!

She was still locked in rising panic when she caught

sounds, first faint and then growing louder. It was such
chanting as she had heard just before this unbelievable thing had happened to her. Only now it rang
far more clear and distinct. It—they—were coming!
She tried to force herself once more to her feet, but
she literally did not have the strength to move. She
could only huddle where she was as the nightmare
went on and on.

There was no word in that rise of sound which she
could understand. But she began to believe she could
detect more than a single voice. Once more Tallahassee
made a desperate effort. She must hide! Only, under
this blistering sun, in this waste of stone and sand,
there was no place of concealment she could see.

The voices ceased suddenly. Now came the ringing
of a sistrum. Tallahassee gave a weak laugh. Egypt!
But why was her unconscious (which certainly must
be directing this weird dream) so set on reproduc-
ing Egypt?

And she was so hot, thirsty. Perhaps back in her
own world she was burning with a fever. Or—a scrap
of memory flipped through her thoughts—did radiation, an overdose of the strange radiation from the
ankh, lie at the bottom of this?

She heard a sharp cry and turned her head. The
figure coming between the broken bits of walls was
all of a piece with the rest. A woman, who from
Tallahassee's present squatting position looked super-
naturally tall, was running toward them. Her figure,
covered by the same kind of white dress as the dead
girl wore, was human and female.

Only, on her shoulders instead of a human head,
rested the golden head of a lioness wearing a diadem

of two metal feathers, spine to spine, standing tall and straight from the top of the lioness's rounded skull.

The creature sped toward the sprawled body of the girl. Then she caught sight of Tallahassee for the first time and stopped almost in mid-stride. There was no change of expression on the set features of the golden beast-face. But, though the lips did not move, there came a series of words which held the inflection of a question.

Tallahassee slowly shook her head. As the lioness head faced her more closely she could see now that it was a mask, for the eyes were holes through which the wearer must look. Swiftly, the other turned from Tallahassee to the dead girl. She knelt by the body, her masked head moving slowly back and forth, looking first at the painted face against the sand and then to Tallahassee. Almost reluctantly she put out her hand and picked up the ankh. But the rod she left lying where the dead had dropped it.

Twice she stretched out her hand tentatively as if to grasp it but did not complete the motion. Then—Tallahassee started—there came a gust of wind so cold that in this sun-soaked place it was like a blow. The woman arose, faced in the direction from which that wind blew. Tallahassee saw a strange movement in the air, as if some shadowy thing whirled about and about.

The lioness-masked woman swung up the ankh. From behind her mask came a series of explosive words carrying with them the force of a curse. With the ankh she swiftly drew a series of crosses back and forth in the air as if so erecting a wall of defense against whatever struggled there to come to them.

A feeble thrust of the will that had held Tallahassee and made her obey strove again to enter her mind. However, this time she could stand firm. Far off—very faintly—did she then hear an angry cry? She was not sure.

But the movement of the air grew less, vanished. The woman waited for a long moment, the eyes of the mask turned to the place where the disturbance had been. Then Tallahassee saw the rigid tenseness of her body relax. Whatever had striven to reach them had failed.

Now the mask swung once more in Tallahassee's direction and she who wore it made a sharp, commanding gesture.

Though she did not want to, Tallahassee crawled away from her rock and reached for the rod, obeying that deftly signed order. Once more her fingers clutched at its smooth surface and she raised it upright. The masked one stood as still as might the image of some goddess in an ancient temple.

Then once more her voice broke the heated air. At her peremptory call, two more women came running lightly into view. Both were dressed in the same plain white garments, their hair braided into the same design favored by the dead girl, squared off at the shoulders, their eyes rimmed and lengthened by strokes of black. But the headdresses they wore were bands of material, each centered over the forehead by a medallion of gold worked into the likeness of a lioness, matching the mask of their superior.

They showed signs of shock and excitement at what they found. But at the sharp-voiced command of their leader they gathered up the body of the dead. Tallahassee was beckoned to follow them.

In the heat, her long skirt and blouse clung stickily to her skin as she tottered along with the women, mainly because she could see nothing else to do. Where was she? How she had come here? She felt that she must force all save the immediate present to the back of her mind or she would become insane.

The bleak ruins were, she discovered as she rounded the largest rock where she had taken refuge, on the edge of a slope. There were outcrops of parts of walls, a series of small, sharp-pointed pyramids, the caps of many of them missing, a dry dead land going down to a single large and pillared building which appeared to be in some state of repair.

But it was the sight of those small pyramids that drew a gasp from Tallahassee. She could close her eyes and mind-picture a series of photographs she knew very well, indeed.

Not Egypt, but its darker, lesser sister—Meroë of the Nubians. Meroë where had gathered the last, faded remnants of the glory of old Egypt, which had indeed provided, at a later time, three Pharaohs to conquer northward, to rule the whole of the near-extinguished land of ancient Khem and become wearers of the proud double crown. Meroë about which so little was known, so many guesses made. Was it Meroë that lay now before her? But how—how had she come here?

The two women she followed carried their burden toward that single great building. Tallahassee did not turn her head to see, but she was well aware that behind her stalked the lioness-priestess—for priestess she must be.

Meroë had worshipped a lion god—Apedemek. There had been no lioness, unless one remembered Shekmet, the war goddess, of the more northern lands.

Again she moved under a measure of compulsion, though it was not as great as that which had sent her through the museum corridors. She might even challenge it if she wished, Tallahassee believed. But to what purpose? It was far better to keep with these until she could somehow discover what had happened. The rod of office slipped in her sweaty hand, she took a firmer grip upon it. Why had the priestess given it to her? It must be highly important to these people, whoever they might be, yet she had been ordered to carry it. Tallahassee could only believe that they were afraid of it in some manner. If it was what had brought her here—then she could understand that. On the other hand, if that was the truth, then it might just be a way of breaking this strange dream and returning to her own time and world. Thus the closer she kept to it now the better.

They passed from the glare of the sun and its draining heat into the temple. Fronting them was Apedemek himself wearing the double crown, in one hand the symbolic plow of the kings and queens of Meroë. The stone face was very old, eroded, but there was majesty in it—an aura of confident power that was not quite arrogance.

At the feet of the ten-foot statue the women laid down the body of the girl, smoothing her robe about her slender legs, crossing her hands to lie palms down and open on her motionless breast. Then one of them knelt at her head and one at her feet and began to wail.

Another sharp command from the priestess silenced them. She motioned Tallahassee to go on, past Apedemek, into an inner room of the temple. Here were signs of occupancy—though Tallahassee thought this was only temporary. Four thick rolls of padding might form beds at night, and there were cushions covered with brightly patterned material on the strips of matting that cloaked the floor. Baskets and two tall jars occupied one corner. But what was opposite those, across the room, brought Tallahassee's instant attention. Three plates of metal glistening black, over which played a sheen of faint rainbow colors, formed a small, flat-topped pyramid. Set upright on that was an object which certainly had no place among the signs of ancient past which lay all about.

It was an oblong of glass and yet opaque, milk-white. Up and down the three surfaces she could see ran a ripple of ever-changing color, to outshine the rainbows on the stand. The oblong was perhaps two feet in height, and from it came a soft hum that Tallahassee could only associate with smooth-running machinery. But this was so anachronistic in comparison with all about it, she could only stare and wonder.

She had come into the room obeying the priestess's gestures. But none of the others followed her. Instead the priestess laid the ankh carefully on the threshold and raised her masked head, making a firm sign that Tallahassee was to remain where she was. Then she stepped back into the main portion of the temple.

The girl made a circuit of the chamber. She discovered that the tall jars in the corner were covered,

and when she slipped the lid off the nearest she
could see water in it. Instantly, as if the sight of the
liquid had triggered her response, she was so thirsty
that she longed to raise the whole jar and let its
contents take the taste of sand grit from her. There
was a cup resting on a pile of plates nearby and she
seized that.

The drinking of that water more than anything else
roused her out of the bewilderment that had held her
since she had awakened among the ruins. She did not
remember ever drinking or eating (for now she had
reached for a date lying with others in a sticky little
pool on a plate, above which was a transparent cover
easy enough to lift) in any dream before.

The date was very sticky, for it must have been
steeped in honey. Too sweet, she had to wash the taste
of it from her mouth with another gulp of lukewarm
water. Food, water, the mats to sleep on—and that
thing in the corner which certainly was not of Meroë,
nor of Egypt either.

The steady hum it had emitted vanished in a flash
of brighter light that rose, not in random lines now,
but in a well-marked spiral on the front panel. At the
same time, there came a crackle of sound that grew
louder and more insistent with every second.

Tallahassee approached the thing carefully. It was
eerie, mainly because it was alien to all the rest in
this room, all that she had seen outside, enough so
to make one wary. However, as quickly as it had
appeared, the brilliant spiral of light vanished, leaving
again only the vibrant hum.

There was only one door to the room, but high on
the walls some stones had fallen out, so that the sun

made bright, light patches here and there. Tallahassee, oddly reluctant to turn her back on the pillar thing, crept softly to the door. She had no idea of the plan of this temple. And now, from what must be the outer shrine, she heard once more the tinkle of the sistrum, a murmur of voices chanting in a tone hardly above a whisper.

Could she slip out? Tallahassee studied the ankh lying in the doorway. It was enough in the shadows to show once again a small shimmer of radiance about it. When she tried to edge past it, it was like meeting a solid surface—not hard and stationary, like a wall, but a barrier that gave a little and then repelled.

Retreating to one of the cushions on the floor, the girl sat cross-legged and tried to assess her position. Now she deliberately did what she had kept herself from doing earlier, attempted to trace this unbelievable situation back to the very beginning.

She had indeed been forced along after the ankh to the room of the Brooke Collection. There had been a seeming confrontation there between two invisible wills—perhaps personalities. Then had followed her own compulsion to capture the rod, her full awakening in the sand and ruins.

This was all too vividly real and had lasted far too long to be just a dream. She was not and had never been into drugs. But perhaps this was the sort of thing a user might imagine when high.

The evidences of the past, she knew, could be drawn from her own memory. Only, to refute that, there was that thing in the corner which was plainly not of any Meroë she knew through her studies. If she was not drugged, nor dreaming—what had happened to her? And why did the dead girl have Tallahassee's own features, features which could not be disguised even by the exotic eye makeup, the difference in skin shade?

What was she?

There was no logical, nor acceptable answer for what had happened: none that she could muster anyway.

It was hot, so hot, in spite of the thick walls of masonry. A flicker on the wall caught her eye. A lizard ran swiftly into nowhere before she had more than glimpsed it. She could hear a shuffling sound and watched the doorway, alerted, as the priestess entered, having stooped to pick up the ankh which so efficiently had locked in her captive.

One of the other women came behind her and, paying no attention to Tallahassee, went directly to a woven basket with a lid. This she raised. Through the dead air of the place, Tallahassee caught a spicy scent as the woman shook out a white robe similar to those they all wore. She laid it to one side and stooped to dip once more into the basket, this time to come up with a pair of sandals having thongs to slide between great toes and the rest, ties to lash about the ankles. Last of all she brought out a stand on which was a wig, the hair of which had been arranged in the many small gold-tipped braids such as the dead girl had worn. On this she carefully fitted what the priestess now handed her—the circlet bearing the striking snake.

Having overseen the assembling of this wardrobe, the priestess now turned to Tallahassee, making unmistakable gestures for her to shed her present clothing. When the girl did not comply the priestess raised the

ankh, her threat plain. If Tallahassee did not obey of
her free will, the forces the priestess could employ
would be called upon.

Slowly Tallahassee did as commanded. As she let
fall her last garment, she found that the lesser priestess was beside her carrying a small pot. Using some
greasy but spicy substance from that container, she
began to smear it, with even strokes, over Tallahassee's
arms and shoulders.

She worked quickly and expertly. And, when she
had done, Tallahassee saw that her skin had been
completely matched to the shade of the women with
her. She was helped into the shift dress: a gemmed
girdle, which she was sure she had seen on the dead
girl, was hooked about her. Then they motioned her to
kneel and the lesser priestess hacked at Tallahassee's
hair with a knife, shearing it closer to the skull.

Her eyes were encircled by brush strokes from
another cosmetic pot. And, at last, the wig bearing
the diadem was carefully fitted on. The lesser priestess drew back as the masked one surveyed the result
of her labors—critically, Tallahassee guessed. She did
not doubt that she was being deliberately disguised
to take the place of the dead.

Once more the bewilderment receded. This time
she felt a small excitement rising in her. Dream, hal-
lucination, no matter what this was—her curiosity was
now firmly engaged. Meroë's fragmentary history had
always interested her. Now she wanted to know how
long her illusion was going to last, how far it would
take her. Oddly enough, she wanted, somehow, to go
along with the play (for play it seemed to her to be),
as long as she could.

When she stood once more, the rod (which none had touched, but which the priestess had gestured her to take up again) in her hand, she longed to know what kind of an appearance she made. The priestess stood very still. Tallahassee could not see the eyes behind the mask holes, but she did not doubt they were now sweeping her from head to foot, an inspection that was broken only when there came a loud crackle from the lighted block in the corner.

She saw the priestess start as if in amazement. Then she hurried over, to drop to her knees before that column of spiralling color which filled the front panel. That she listened to something which made sense to her, Tallahassee guessed. There came a hastily smothered gasp from the other woman who sped to the door and was gone.

Tallahassee's curiosity rose like a fever. If she only understood, could really know what all this meant!

The crackle stopped. However, now the priestess reached forth her hand and made a sweeping, wiping motion across the block. The spiral vanished. What formed in its turn was a symbol Tallahassee knew, the Eye of Horus. As it held there steady, the priestess brought back her mask even closer to the surface of the block and spoke—in soft, sputtery sounds Tallahassee thought were not the same used in the chanting she had earlier heard.

The eye blinked out of sight. Once more there was only a loose play of unformed color, the hum of the machine. The priestess rose to approach Tallahassee. At this short distance, the girl could well see the dark human irises within the eye pits of the mask. She felt the other's pressing need for communication though how she realized that was what the other wanted, she could not have said.

"What do you want of me?" Tallahassee asked.

The other pointed to the doorway and then to herself and to Tallahassee. From the heavy front panel of her girdle she drew a long knife and aimed it first toward her own breast and then toward Tallahassee, again pointing to the doorway when she had done—this time with an almost vicious thrust through the air itself.

The girl made a guess she believed was not too wild. "Danger—for us both," she said aloud.

Once more, those eyes surveyed her steadily and searchingly. Then the lioness mask nodded only a fraction, as if to do more might send the whole thing spinning from its wearer's head.

The priestess pointed from her knife to the rod, and then to the knife again. Was she trying to say that the rod was as much of a weapon as the blade she had drawn, Tallahassee wondered. But a weapon to be used against what—or whom?

Her own head jerked as she heard a sound ujoverhead—a sound that grew louder. Again it was familiar in part, though not in any world where Meroë ruled. Unless Tallahassee was completely mistaken that was an aircraft of some sort, and it sounded as if it were coming in for a landing!

-4-

The priestess made no move, save to turn her head slightly toward the door, as if all her attention was given to what might be happening without. After what seemed only seconds, Tallahassee heard the voices of men, raised in anger, she believed. Now the priestess stepped forward beside Tallahassee, so they were ranged together facing the door.

There came a sharp crack, enough to make Tallahassee start. She could not be sure, but that had sounded very much like a shot! Like the lighted block in the corner, the thought of modern weapons here was anachronistic. Fingers touched her arm. The priestess made a small gesture, one that urged Tallahassee to raise the rod before her. She remembered of old the common stance of most of the Egyptian statues, ankh, flail, crook so upheld.

The other women backed into the room, their voices raised in hot protest. Herding them so came three men.

Seeing them, the belief she had somehow returned to the ancient past vanished for Tallahassee. By rights these newcomers should have worn kilts, carried spears or bows. Instead, the newcomers were closer to her own world in their dress, for each wore a one-piece uniform, cut off at elbows and knees.

The garment was a dull green in color, relieved only by a mask of Apedemek on the shoulder. Incongruously, their headgear, striped in two shades of green, did resemble the ancient sphinx head-dress of the Egyptian fighting man. For the rest, they each carried what was manifestly a weapon, like and yet unlike, Tallahassee believed, the guns of her time. These were neither rifle nor handgun, but between those two in length. And the short barrels pointed along their own forearms, as they held them ready to fire.

On catching sight of Tallahassee they halted—their eyes went wide. Shock or mere surprise? She could not be sure. The priestess beside her broke into speech. Never had Tallahassee longed so much to know what was going on than at this moment.

The two men behind the leader took a couple of steps backward, their discomfiture plain to read. What or who they had expected to find here, it was not those they fronted now. The priestess raised her ankh and spoke commandingly, while the leader of the trio scowled at her. A scar, which split his right cheek from temple to chin, did not add to any suggestion of mercy in his expression. He gave no ground, only glowered at the lioness-masked woman.

The rod! Tallahassee decided to try a small experi-ment. She held the staff a little aslant so that its

top crystal now inclined toward the man. He quickly
shifted gaze from the priestess to the girl. She saw
the change in his eyes.

He was afraid! Afraid of either her or the rod, and
she believed it the latter. Now an expression of sullen
defeat warped his scarred features. Tallahassee took
one step forward and then another. He retreated, but
not as fast as his two followers, who broke and ran
as the girl approached them.

Their leader was not giving in easily. Tallahassee
sensed danger building in this man. She had always
been able somehow to pick up emotional reactions
of others to herself, knowing when she was accepted,
tolerated, or disliked. But it was no dislike this man
radiated, rather it was hate. She was as certain of that
as if he had shouted curses in her face.

Driving him this way might be the worst move
she could make. Yet the two women stepped quickly
aside, and she was aware that the priestess walked
steadily behind her. They wanted her to do just as
she was doing!

The soldier growled under his breath, a hostile mut-
ter, yet he backed step by slow step, as she advanced.
Now they passed into the outer chamber of the temple
with the statue of Apedemek looming behind the man's
shoulder. Back and back again—outside into the white
blare of the desert sun, the furnace heat.

She caught a glimpse of something standing not
too far away. But she could not look at it closely. It
was necessary instead to keep her eyes on the man
before her. Back still more until they were at the very
edge of the temple pavement. Suddenly he swung his
weapon by its strap up across his shoulder and spoke

a last sharp sentence in which she could read menace without understanding the words.

He seemed reluctant to turn his back on her. His withdrawal was rather crablike, glancing at her with a side look as he descended the wide outer steps and stalked away—his whole body expressing his angry impotence—to a flyer.

To Tallahassee's eyes that vehicle possessed some of the attributes of a helicopter, save there were no whirling blades on top. Rather, once the man had made his way to the opening in its side and climbed within, it arose in a cloud of grit and sand by a method she did not understand.

There had been an insignia painted on the flyer's side but those markings had no meaning for the girl. Again a touch on her wrist, and the priestess made that small inclination of her masked head, suggesting their return to the interior of the temple ruin. One of the women behind spoke and then spat outward in the direction of the vanished flyer. The roar of its withdrawal was already fading.

The priestess wasted no more time. Instead she moved at a pace that closely approached a run, Tallahassee hurrying after, to reach the inner chamber. There the masked woman, once more on her knees before the lighted block, spoke to it with an imperative burst of words.

Tallahassee moved closer to the woman who had spat after the retreating soldiers.

"Who?" She tried to get into that word of her own language the sound of inquiry as she pointed to the outside.

For a moment it would seem that the woman

was not going to answer, if indeed she understood
Tallahassee's query. Then she spoke slowly and deliberately one word:

"Userkof." At least it sounded like that.

The part of Tallahassee's knowledge that had already
found the small, disturbing, familiar hints in this
place seized upon the sound. Userkof—Nubian of
the past—or Egyptian? She was sure it was a man's
name. But was it that of the leading intruder, or of
one who had sent him? If she only knew. Her ignorance made her want to hurl the rod at the wall and
then do a little therapeutic screaming. When would
she ever find out what had happened, where she was,
and why? The "why" might outweigh all the other
points, she suspected.

They had made her up to play a part. Apparently,
she was someone who, with the rod in hand, had
authority to banish armed men who had certainly
not come here for anything but trouble. And she had
only a single name—Userkof—on which to build an
answer.

Names? Names were important. Among some
people the personal name held such great importance
that they never revealed it to strangers, lest that give
another some psychic hold over them. She could
begin with names—the first stumbling exchange in
any language.

With her thumb she energetically thumped her
own breast and asked again:

"Who?"

The woman glanced first at the priestess still busy
crooning to the slab. This time her hesitation was
even more marked. Yet she answered at last:

"Ashake."

"Ashake," Tallahassee repeated, striving to give the word the same pronunciation. Now she indicated the priestess:

"Who?"

"Jayta." This time the pause was not long. Perhaps the woman found that, since the sky had not fallen the first time, she dared be more helpful.

"Jayta." Now the girl's finger pointed to the woman. "Who?"

"Makeda."

The other woman was identified as Idia. Tallahassee was faintly encouraged. If they just cooperated a little she might be able to find out something.

"Where?" She moved her hand about in a gesture that she hoped would be intelligible to the other, who watched her very closely. But the three words she then got in answer meant nothing at all. And it was hard to be baffled again just when she had made progress, no matter how small.

The priestess arose from before the slab and uttered what could only be a string of orders. Both the other women hurried to draw together the pallets on the floor, pile them in a corner. They paid no attention to anything else but the basket from which they had taken the clothes Tallahassee now wore. That they carried out into the shadow of Apedemek's statue.

Jayta was busy with the slab, pressing her fingers carefully about the lowest of the three square blocks on which it was positioned. As if that had released some mounting, she picked it up and the light now vanished from its surface. An inclination of her head sent Tallahassee before her. It was plain they were making preparations to leave the temple. Leaving for where?

If she could only see more than just the priestess's eyes through the mask. One could learn much from an expression if one was attentive.

But she tried once more, waving her hand toward the outside and asking:

"Where?"

Again came more than one word, and those meant nothing at all. Yet Tallahassee believed that they were not the same Makeda had uttered earlier. Their destination? And how were they to travel?

That was answered soon enough by a second roar from the air. The invaders back with new forces? Tallahassee took a closer grip on the rod. A second party might not be so easily cowed.

Once more a flyer set down, spinning sand and grit in a murky cloud, wide enough to hide the whole entrance to the temple. As that settled, figures dropped from the machine, came trotting toward them. Uniforms again, but not the dull green of the first party. These were of a red shade, close to rust. And those wearing them were unmistakably women.

At the sight of Tallahassee, three of them dropped to their knees and raised one hand palm out, but with the other hand held ready the same type of weapon the men had borne. Their leader did not kneel, merely raised one hand to Tallahassee, and then broke into a spate of excited speech.

The priestess made a sharp answer, waved them on toward the waiting flyer. Tallahassee went with a faint reluctance. She had come into this world at this point. If she left here—was there any way she could find her way back to her own place? For she was convinced now, in spite of herself, that this could not be a dream. And she had no reason to think she was hallucinating, unless the unknown radiation given off by the ankh had induced it.

Within the flyer, quarters were somewhat cramped. The priestess and Tallahassee were given a double seat while the temple women and the Amazons settled down on the flooring, drawing webbing belts over them. Tallahassee could see another uniformed woman at the controls. She was given little time to examine her surroundings before the flyer lifted with a jerk that made her feel unpleasantly like being caught in a runaway elevator.

She was not next to the small window, so could not catch any glimpse of the terrain over which they flew. But she had a sensation of speed which was surely greater than that of the helicopters of her own world.

This situation was like facing a giant puzzle, or rather two puzzles, where all pieces had been arbitrarily mixed so that one could make no sense out of either. The masked priestess, the ruins—those she could better accept somehow than a flyer. She had seen the like of the former throughout the years of her study, if only in pictures. But what had ancient Egypt or Nubia to do with unfamiliar weapons and vehicles?

Her head ached under the weight of the wig they had forced on her. She longed to jerk it off, yet somehow knew that even so small an act of independence might bring serious consequences. The leader of the soldiers opened a small compartment set against the wall of the pilot's cubby and brought out a metal flask and some handleless cups. In spite of the unsteadiness of the flyer she poured a measure of liquid into a cup, about half-full, and handed it carefully to the priestess, who in turn, with a show of ceremony, held it out to Tallahassee.

She accepted with a murmur of thanks and drank. The contents were tart, and so cold that she had a momentary shock. She drank thirstily, realizing again that her body needed this though she had not been aware of that until she drank.

Another cup was offered to the priestess, but she declined. Tallahassee began to wonder how the woman could endure wearing the mask so continually, and why she did so. At the temple it might have been for some reasons of ceremony, but why did she cling to it now?

Then abruptly, they spiraled earthward, to set down with a slight jar. The Amazon officer made haste to open the door, scramble out, with her three followers, as if expecting some trouble against which they must guard. Jayta, if Jayta the priestess really was, touched Tallahassee gently on the arm and signed for her to go next.

She moved rather awkwardly, for though the priestess matched her in height as did the leader of the soldiers, the others were at least four or five inches shorter and the flyer had manifestly been designed to their norm instead of hers. As the girl came into the open down the single step, she was no longer in the desert. The sere stone and sand, the blank walls of the ruins were gone.

Here was a lush green that rested her eyes. A few feet away a path of stones set in colorful mosaic patterns led into a tunnel walled by palm trees and brilliantly flowered bushes. She sniffed the perfume of flowers, heavy, almost cloying to the senses, saw bits of what could only be a building of at least three stories engulfed by the lush greenery.

The Amazons stood at stiff attention, two on either side. As Tallahassee moved slowly and hesitantly down the walk, they fell in behind, leaving only the priestess a step or two to the rear as they went.

This was going it blind all right. She did not have the least idea of where she was heading, or what she was to do here. But it was a vast relief to get into the shadow of the palms and the tall branches of the bushes. There was a flash along the path toward her and Tallahassee froze, then gave a small laugh of embarrassment. For the newcomers were two kittens. Very superior kittens, since each had a gold ring in the right ear near the tip and wore in addition a collar with small tinkling bells.

The kittens halted, their baby heads up at an angle, watching her with that unblinking stare that cats use to make humans uneasy. If they were the dead girl's cats—then the imposture Tallahassee had been ordered to. . . . She stooped and held out her hand. All depended now on them. Suppose they unmasked her as a stranger, what would the Amazons behind her do? If Ashake were a princess, as the diadem on her stifling wig signified—well, what might be the penalty for impersonating her? The larger of the kittens advanced hesitantly to sniff at Tallahassee's fingers. Sniffed a second time, then made a quick dab with a rough little tongue tip against her flesh.

The young cat uttered a sound which was not quite
a mew and bounded at its companion. With a cuff of
a paw it passed, streaking once more down the walk,
its brother or sister now in wild pursuit.

Tallahassee gave a sigh of relief she hoped was
not audible. She did not ask about her role, but
she certainly wanted to be sure that she was not
going to be unmasked at a time most dangerous
to her.

Jayta spoke, addressing Tallahassee with deference
she had not paid before. She gestured to the building only half seen among the thick growth, plainly
urging the girl on.

They passed through a thicker growth which appeared
to mark a hedge between a garden and the landing
field. Now the building before them showed clearly
above the carefully tended flower beds. Massive pillars
flanked the front, supporting an overhang of the roof.
And the pillars, like the ruins, were familiar. These
were not the columns the western world had inherited from the Greeks. Rather they were designed to
resemble thick stalks of flowers, formalized half-open
buds forming their crowns.

The door they guarded was very wide, and gave,
not on a hallway or room, but rather on an inner
court, the center of which was occupied by a long
pool in which living lotus plants fringed the sides.
Guards by the door snapped to attention, Amazons
again. Beyond, waited a group of white-clad women
who scattered at an order from the priestess, though
they went reluctantly, many looking at Tallahassee as
if they expected her to countermand Jayta. A second
order sent the two women who had come with them

from the temple, to one side and ahead, carrying between them the dress basket.

As those two passed through one of the doors that lined the four sides of the inner court, Tallahassee caught the hint. Clever of Jayta—she now knew just where she was to go and would make no betraying slip in choosing her room. As an embroidered door hanging fell behind her she looked curiously about these new quarters.

The walls were painted with a stylized pattern of lotus blossoms, bordering the head of a lioness which matched the mask her companion wore. Here was a narrow bed, the four legs of which had been inlaid to suggest a leopard's legs and paws. Folding tables stood beside two straight-backed, feline-footed chairs. And there was a padded bench before a more massive piece of furniture which consisted of two sets of drawers, an open space between, topped by a slab of inlaid wood on which stood a mirror, together with a number of small and fancifully carved and inlaid boxes and pots. As Tallahassee came a step or so farther into the chamber she caught full sight of herself in the mirror and gasped.

She faced a stranger. The thick makeup about her eyes—the lines of which extended well back to the edge of the wig—were almost as concealing as a mask. Her darker skin, the wig itself—she might have walked out from some painted tomb wall in Thebes or Memphis!

"Ashake!" She was not aware she had said that name aloud until she heard herself.

It was hard to turn away from that stranger on the mirrored surface. She—she was not Ashake.

Suddenly her hands began to shake. She might even have dropped the rod had not a quick exclamation of warning made her look away from that deceiving reflection.

One of the temple women approached bearing a long case covered with gold, in raised design upon it those same spirit-protecting medallions she had pointed out on the box—where, how long ago? The priestess pressed fingers at two places to lift the lid. Inside, a soft cushioning carried an impression, a hollow long and narrow, meant undoubtedly to contain the rod. Thankfully Tallahassee fitted that within and saw the box shut and laid upon the bed.

Then Jayta's hands went to the back of her own head, pressed at the nape of her neck much as she had on the case for the rod. A moment later the mask fell into two parts which one of the women took from her.

Tallahassee found herself facing a woman who had no claim to beauty. Her nose was a hawk's proud beak, her chin pointed and seeming (when seen in profile) to curve up to meet that same beak. The hair, close-cropped to her skull, was silvered, and she wore no makeup to enlarge her eyes or to give more color to her full lips. It was the face of one who had her orders obeyed and swiftly. Yet the strength in it, Tallahassee thought, was not marred by any touch of cruelty. Had she, in her own mind, ever built up an idea of justice personified, the answer could have come close to Jayta.

Now the priestess studied Tallahassee closely in turn, even as an artist might minutely examine some product of his hands, searching ruthlessly for the slightest fault.

The other women retreated to the door, raised their hands in salute, and were gone. Tallahassee drew a deep breath and allowed herself to sit on one of the two chairs. Jayta continued to stand until Tallahassee, guessing at the cause, waved her companion to the other. Though this room was infinitely cooler than the ruined temple, she wanted to throw off the wig, rid herself of the grit that clung to her stained skin. Yet now she needed communication most.

There was a movement by the door and Idia slipped in again, almost furtively. She held a covered basket in her hands which she offered to Jayta. What the priestess lifted out was a box from which dangled two cords. Idia hurriedly pushed one of the tables closer and Jayta settled the box on that. She picked up one of the cords and inserted the hard tip of it in her ear, signaling for Tallahassee to do the same with the other.

The girl nearly jerked free again when she felt the result. Telepathy? No, for this exchange apparently needed the box. But she had indeed received a message—not from lip to ear, but mind to mind.

"Do not fear, Lady."

Tallahassee half lifted her hand to pull out the cord, then forced her nerves under better control. This was what she wanted most: communication—explanation.

"Who are you? Where am I? How did I get here?" She asked her questions in a quick whisper.

"Do not speak—not until you know our tongue, Lady. There are far too many shadows who have ears and mouths to whisper in the wrong places what those ears have picked up. I am the Daughter-of-Apedemek, though many of our people have regretfully

turned aside from the True Learning in these years.
As to where you are—that I cannot say more than
this is the Empire of Amun in the two thousandth
year since the parting of North and South. It is
not your world. As to how you got here—now that
is a tale which must be made short for we have
so little time. But it follows this pattern as a cub
follows its dam.

"What lies there"—she gestured to the now encased
rod—"is the soul of our nation. Oh,"—she made a
grimace as if she had bitten upon something very
sour—"there are many nowadays who do not believe in
the teachings that made Amun great under our Lord,
the Sun. They lean upon the work of their own hands,
say that what is born of their thoughts is theirs only
and comes not from the teaching of One greater than
themselves. Yet even those loose thinkers know that
without the Rod in her hands no order the Candace
gives will be obeyed. Without it she is nothing, for
in the Rod is all the strength of her Blood. And only
one of the Blood may hold it."

"Candace!" Tallahassee forgot the other's warning. "That was the title of the ancient Queens of
Meroë!"

The eyes turned toward her, narrowed. "Who are
you who speak of the Place of the Dead?" The demand
was like a pain in her head, sharp enough to bring
her hand up to her forehead. And there was a note
of hostility in it. . . .

-5-

Tallahassee hesitated. Where she was became more the question she wanted answered. "Empire of Amun" meant nothing. Yet Jayta obviously reacted quickly to the mention of Meroë. Now she tried to frame her counter-question with care.

"I do not know the Empire of Amun." She made her admission first. "To my knowledge very long ago—perhaps two thousand years—there was a kingdom of Meroë whose people held even Egypt for a short space. But that was swept away long ago, leaving only ruins and a few names of kings and queens of whom we know little else than those names, today. So—I ask you—of your charity, Daughter-of-Apedemek, where am I now?"

Now it was Jayta's turn to wait for a moment which stretched even longer for Tallahassee. She thought out her reply slowly at last:

"I do not know how much knowledge you may have of what can be done by the ancient powers. It is only

339

within my own lifetime that certain of us who are trained to the Far Sight and the Command of the Upper Way have come to be sure of what I tell you now. And if you need proof that we speak the truth take your own presence here for that.

"We have ceaselessly through centuries wrought with certain mind skills that are very old. You spoke of Egypt—do you mean the Land of Khem, of the Two Crowns?"

Tallahassee nodded.

"Ah, then you must also know that those of the Inner Teaching there, too, had talents beyond those of ordinary men. When the invaders broke Khem, these initiates, together with some of the Blood, fled southward, coming into Kush where even the Men of the Bow recognized them for what they were and gave them refuge. More and more they strove to set their learning to the use of the Inner Ways. Then Kush itself in time was assaulted—by the new barbarians in the north, by the greedy traders of Axum who would reduce our power to naught and gather into their hands all the wealth that flowed through Meroë.

"Again must a core of the Learned and those of the Blood flee—this time west, into a land that had never been linked with Khem and where they were strangers, indeed. But in those days they had harvested enough from their experiments to give them the power to win rulership over the natives of that land who were unenlightened and took the Talent for a magic they could not themselves command.

"It continued a long time, this searching for knowledge. And there were years when our rulership was disputed, sometimes when only a scarce handful of us held the secrets we had been so long in winning. Around us the world changed, sometimes slowly, sometimes swiftly when there would arise a leader of superior ability. Of these some had the Power, and then we came out of hiding and wrought as much as we could. Others taught that man must depend upon his hands and the work of those, instead of upon his inner spirit and the controls of that. And then we were not listened to.

"But this we learned not long ago—that time moves not only in one dimension, passing us by like a ribbon drawn too fast for our catching. No, time embraces much more, so that this world in which we move lies close to other worlds existing in the same space, yet separated from us by the walls of this other kind of time. So that there are worlds in which Amun does not exist—as you tell me it does not in your world."

"Space-time continuums!" Tallahassee stared at Jayta. "But that theory is only fiction, used in stories of my time for imaginative entertainment!"

"However you may think of it, we have proved it true. Are you not here in Amun?"

Tallahassee ran her tongue over lips that seemed suddenly dry. Fantastic, insane? . . . What other words could she find to explain such a suggestion? Yet it was plain Jayta was entirely serious.

"Accept that it is so," continued the Priestess, "and know that a year ago Khasti found a way to breach the wall of that time—for the purpose of ruining Amun itself!"

Her deepset eyes sparked fire, and she seemed even in her mind-to-mind speech to spit forth the name "Khasti" as if it were an obscenity.

"Two treasures have we possessed from the earliest days when we first fled to Kush, we of the most ancient people. This is the truth—an object upon which the Power has been so long focused becomes in turn a reservoir of that force, sometimes to the extent that only those, by training and blood immune to it, can touch it and live."

"The Rod." Tallahassee glanced at the case on the bed.

"The Rod into which has entered the centuries of thought-force of those of the Blood. Even I, who can control the Key-to-Life, dare not lay bare hand on that."

"Then why can I?" challenged Tallahassee.

"That I do not know, though I have two guesses, the first being that in your world you are the same as the Princess Ashake, she who gave her life to regain that which had been stolen. The other is that because you are from that world, your inner force is of a different nature, repelling rather than attracting the Power that is bound within this. But that is another matter. I must tell you what else you should know and quickly—we may not have time, much time. And there are those who will be alerted once they know that the Rod has returned.

"It was taken by a creature of Khasti because Khasti himself stands behind the late Pharoah's son, Userkof. We have had many queens, and they rule by their own right, not under the will of any man. If they take a husband he is one apart and cannot command in their name. Nor can this Userkof, which is a sore thing to him. For our Candace was the eldest child of King Pahfor's sister and thus the heir.

"The new people among us—those who are restless and would put away the heritage of our past—they strive to follow foreign ways. And Idieze, she who is chief wife to Userkof, would be queen. Thus she plays for power with Khasti and his knowledge.

"The creature of Khasti was sent into the world beyond the time wall and there he was to hide the Rod. There he was freed to draw upon the strength of those of Khasti's own way of thought—those who hated the rule of women—for his energy and aid. Thus the Candace could not come before the people at the Half-Year Feasting with it in her hand. And because of that theft, she could be lied into the loss of her throne. But, Khasti was not as secret as he thought and, when the Rod indeed disappeared, there was a way of learning what he had done and why. However, it took us much searching and experimenting before we could ourselves dare to hope to unlock the same door. And the Key, which we held—that, at a last moment, was itself taken—with dead guards left to mark that we had once held it. For the Key and the Rod are linked, and one can point always the way to the other.

"It was made plain to us that one with power to hold the Rod and to mind-search for it must also breach the door of parallel time—though this was a desperate and perhaps deadly thing. And the Princess Ashake, she whose form you wear, swore that it was her venture alone. For the Candace could not be risked, and there is no other of the whole Blood in this generation, so thin have our ranks now become. Thus we went to the most holy place where the vibrations of the Power had long been, and there she threw herself into the unknown. There she must also have met the full force of some hate like unto Khasti's."

Carey? Tallahassee's thought caught and held upon the man who had made so plain his dislike. . . . It could well be Carey, influenced beyond his knowledge or belief, had been the hostile focus.

"When she returned"—Jayta paused, and then went on—"it would seem that because you, too, had laid hand on the Rod, she must draw you with her. And this was too great a strain on the Talent we had summoned to our backing. Thus she was gone from us, even as she fulfilled the mighty task she had bent herself to do. Also—there was that creature of Khasti's who would have followed her—perhaps it was necessary for her to strive with him also in your time. For he came after—but"—there was complete satisfaction in Jayta's thought now—"him I was able to seal outside now that Key and Rod had returned. I know not if his master has managed to draw him back by whatever unhallowed means he employs, but if he has—then Khasti knows what we have done. Also Userkof knows, for it was the personal guards of his household who broke in upon us at Meroë and were forced to acknowledge that they had no right of intrusion upon the Daughter of the Blood."

At least there was logic in Jayta's explanation, wild as it might seem to Tallahassee. If she could accept this all as reality, then the fact of her sudden transportation here was true.

"What do you want of me?" she asked.

An expression of surprise altered the harsh cast of Jayta's features for a moment.

"Need you ask? The Candace, who knows all of

this—save of Ashake's death (though word of that is already on the way to her) is in the north on a state visit to the People of the Sea. She will return in time for the Half-Year Feast. We must then have the Rod ready for her hand. But to all others you must be Ashake! Those who were with us at Meroë are of the second circle of Believers and servers. They are sworn to a still tongue on this business for I needed their united power with mine to light the way for Ashake's return. But in Amun you are the Princess Heir and must be—"

"And if I choose not to aid your plans? I was drawn into this through no will of my own—"

"How?" countered Jayta.

Tallahassee found herself telling of the wild night's work in the museum and how she had been compelled to follow the ankh to the rod, of the presences she had felt during that strange struggle of wills.

"Khasti's creature. It was he who stole the Key and hid it so. It was he who hoped to reach the Rod before the Princess broke through to claim it. It was he who had you lay hand upon it, and so brought her to her death."

"You say his 'creature'. What do you mean?" Tallahassee asked.

For a moment or two she believed that Jayta was not going to answer. Then the message came with obvious reluctance.

"We do not know by what means Khasti has learned of this thing, or how he projected his servant with the Rod into this other world of yours and in turn sent the Key after it. He has set up shields about his work of a kind we cannot pierce. And those who are of our Talent dare not try to spy on him, for they can be instantly detected by some trick of his own kind of power, as we discovered when the Rod vanished. To be unmasked by Khasti is death—we think—for none we sent returned, and neither could we after pick them up by persona-scanner. They—they simply vanished. But his servant who did this thing—he, she, or it—could not have been of the Talent. For that, too, would have registered on those devices our mind-watchers maintain. We do know only that there must have been some alteration in the messenger-thief he sent. You say that the Princess you saw only as a shadow, and this other was also a shadow—a wraith in your world. Well"—again there was satisfaction in Jayta's voice—"that other remains a wraith, since the Key has been turned against the creature's return!"

"If I play this part you wish"—Tallahassee stared straight into the woman's eyes as she formulated that thought with all the force she could summon—"then when it is done and your Queen safe once more, can you return me to my own time?"

"I give you the truth. As it stands now, I am uncertain. But if Userkof is vanquished and all is safe—it may be that the Candace herself can do this thing. If so—she will have the backing in power of all of us who command the Talent."

"But you are not sure?" persisted the girl.

"I am not sure," agreed the priestess. "What we can do, that we shall. There is this—we must do something, or all we have accomplished so far will be lost."

There was a strong determination in that, and Tallahassee felt a new wariness.

"What?"

"You must become Ashake—not only outwardly, as you are now, but inwardly—owning her memories and knowledge."

Tallahassee could see the sense of that, but it would take some time, and how good would she be at learning the language, all the small details of the life of the girl she had replaced? Did they have weeks?

"It will take some time—"

Jayta shook her head. "We cannot give you the Talent if you are not born with it. But all else can be shifted mind-to-mind from our archives—"

"The what?"

"The storehouse of knowledge possessed by all those who follow the way of Power, also those of the Blood who come to rule. The Rod." She gestured to the box. "That is theirs by right, but it does not enrich their memories. Rather do all of us with the Talent come twice yearly to the shrine and there cast our memories into the lap of the Great Power. Thus if I must know what the Daughter-of-Apedemek who was before me at an earlier time understood, I go to this storehouse and draw forth the memory of one who may have lived two lifetimes ago and wore the Golden Mask. What the Princess Ashake knew, you must have—"

"Computer memory banks!" Tallahassee interrupted, excited that she could make such an identification with her own time.

"I do not understand," Jayta returned. "The picture in your mind—it is strange—like unto those things which Khasti has turned to. But in another time-world, who knows what form knowledge takes? There is one

more whom we must admit to your secret, since only
he will have power enough to use my seal and unlock
for use Ashake's recordings. I have already summoned
him, and if luck favors us he will be here before
daybreak. Now I urge you—eat, sleep, rest well, for
what lies before you is no little task. We use such
recordings only for a few facts. You must absorb many
upon many and those as quickly as possible."

Jayta took the button from her own ear, coiled
the line, and laid it neatly upon the top of the box
sitting between them. At a clap of her hands, Idia
entered and bowed.

Tallahassee was at last able to shed the wig, her
head feeling curiously light without its stifling weight.
But when she glanced at her shorn skull in the mirror, she was a little startled. Did she really look that
bad without hair? She wished that the ladies of Amun
had not held to that particular legacy from Egypt.
Another curtained door gave upon a bath wherein
she was glad to plunge, washing way the remaining
grit of the desert, though she noted that the skin dye
they had laid on her in the temple did not disappear
in turn. When she had wrapped around her a loose,
long square of soft cotton and gone back to the other
room, she found Idia setting out a tray of dishes that
contained a small roasted bird, some fruit which Tallahassee identified as slices of melon and small, reddish
bananas, and bread which came in thin sheets spread
with what could only be a conserve of dates.

It was dark now and, with the coming of the darkness, there glowed two candle-shaped sticks of light,
on which no flames danced. Instead, radiance was
diffused from along their length. Idia left her alone,

and Tallahassee had time to think as she ate. If she could accept this first premise of sidewise trips by an unorthodox theory of time travel, then all else did fall into place. But now the thoughts of taking on Ashake's carefully preserved memories made her uneasy. It was true that to learn the language would be a vast help. And if she could play the part of princess better by being able to recognize the proper people and places, she would be safer than she was now. But it remained to be seen just how she took this crash course and how it would change her own mind.

Dare she really risk any such meddling? She would demand from Jayta a complete summary of what such an action would entail when she saw the priestess again. Finishing the meal, Tallahassee moved slowly around the room, studying the fittings on the dressing table. Once she put out her hand to open one of the drawers and then refrained. She did not feel, for all her curiosity concerning the girl she was now supposed to be, that she had any right to pry in this way.

There was a soft "puurtt" and under the edge of the outer door curtain padded first one and then the other of the kittens she had met in the garden. They seemed at home here, falling into a follow-the-leader game of leaping on the bed, prancing around it, then jumping from its end to the top of the dressing table where they landed with ease, threading in and out, with the air of long practice, among the bottles and jars there. At last they returned to the bed and curled up, one of them eyeing Tallahassee sleepily over the other's rounded back as if asking why she did not join them.

But she felt far from sleepy. The length of cloth she had found lying on the bench beside the bath

was hardly attire to go venturing forth in. And she
had no wish to assume again the wig which now sat
on a stand before the mirror—the lifted cobra head
of the diadem seeming to watch her knowingly with
small, jeweled eyes. When Idia returned for the supper tray, she smiled at Tallahassee reassuringly and
held out one hand to cup the candle lamp, though
her flesh did not touch its radiant surface. As she
drew her fingers downward along it, the light faded.
Tallahassee understood the pantomimed instruction,
smiled in return, and nodded.

All at once she did begin to feel sleepy. It had
been a long day—or maybe days. For the first time
she wondered, as she slipped out of the cloth and
into the bed, trying not to disturb the kittens, what
had happened back in her own time and place. What
excuse would they have for her being missing? Could
they think she had taken both their mysterious find
and the rod? Dr. Carey, for one, she believed would
never credit what had happened. Perhaps it was better
for her that she had come through and not been left
to face him with the wild story she would have had to
tell when the real Ashake did her disappearing act.

One of the kittens shifted position and laid its head
on her leg as if that were a pillow. This was real,
here and now, she could never deny that any more.
And so she drifted into sleep more quickly than she
would have believed possible.

Tallahassee awoke with a weight on her chest and
opened her eyes a little dazedly to look upward into
a kitten face. The small mouth shaped an impatient
mew, and she saw that sunlight entered the room
in broad shafts from under the door curtain. Only a

moment later Makeda came in. It was plain she was
disturbed for she began to gesture as soon as she saw
that Tallahassee was watching her, making the motions
of getting up as if there was some need for hurry.

The kitten hissed as the girl put it gently to one
side to slip out of bed. Makeda gestured again—this
time to the door of the bath. Again Tallahassee found
water drawn, this time with petals of flowers strewn
upon its surface, and two open pots standing nearby,
each giving off a strange, sweet scent. She bathed
and dried herself on the towel Makeda produced and
then, at the other's direction, scooped up fingers of
the creamy, scented lotion from the pot she liked
best and rubbed it into her darkened skin. The odor
once applied was not so strong, but fragrant enough
to please.

This time the robe Makeda held ready for her was
not the austere white slip of a priestess, but rather
resembled in style the caftan popular in her own
world. The color was clear rose pink, the borders of
the wide sleeves worked about six inches deep with
gold thread, a girdle of gold links settling about her
slim hips to mold the folds closer to her body.

Makeda set to work deftly, applying the heavy eye
make-up. But Tallahassee was glad to see that she did
not reach again for the thick, smothering wig. Instead
the other produced from one of the drawers of the
dressing table a small, turban-like cap of gold net and
with it a box from which she took a wide collar that
extended nearly to shoulder point on either side and
well down Tallahassee's breast. This was fashioned of
rows of small flowers, rose quartz, clear crystal, and
enameled metal, the whole set in gold.

Tallahassee studied the result of their combined labors for the perfect toilet of a princess as Makeda stood back, having clasped the necklace-collar. Barbaric? Not quite, she decided. More like a sophisticated playing at barbarianism, something akin to those fads that swept the time she knew, drawing on African, South American, Mayan designs, in part, for their source. The necklace was a heavy weight, and she shifted her shoulders, trying to adjust to its presence.

"Ashake!"

A man's voice just outside the door curtain. Makeda's hand had flown to her lips, her expression was one of consternation.

"Ashake!" There was a rising impatience in that hail, and Tallahassee decided that whoever stood there was not in the mood to be put off. Who would have the familiarity to hail a Princess of the Blood in such a fashion? The cousin who had his eye on the throne? Drawing a quick breath, Tallahassee arose. There was no use in lingering here—sooner or later she was going to have to face whoever impatiently demanded her presence.

She moved to the door. Makeda made a small gesture of defeat. Yet the girl, looking closely at the under-priestess as she passed, thought she did not detect any fear. Or would she be afraid if it was Userkof? Apparently she now agreed with Tallahassee that the stranger must be faced, for she went to sweep aside the door curtain.

Tallahassee, seeing who stood there, froze, but was startled into voicing a name:

"Jason!"

-6-

But even as Tallahassee spoke that name she knew that this was not the Jason she had known all her life. He wore Jason's features right enough, but he could not be Jason.

"Ashake?" Now he made of her name not a request for her instant company, but rather a question as he stared at her, his expression of pleasure fading into one of puzzlement.

It was hard to believe that the man was not Jason, though the garments he wore, which resembled those of the soldiers who had first invaded the temple (yet were of a different color, a rust-brown, and had embellishments of brilliant gold on the collar and a lion's head on the chest), were certainly nothing pertaining to her Jason. Nor were the wide bands of gold about his wrists, the belt with a precious-metal-hilted dagger riding on one hip.

"Herihor!"

Jayta came skimming down the arched passage that

flanked the pool. Like Tallahassee, her head was now
covered with a small turban, but she still wore the
plain white shift of her office.

He turned his head, and then sketched a salute, as
if to the office the older woman held, before bursting
into speech which Jayta's upheld hand hastily silenced,
as she glanced around as if to make sure that no other
listener save Makeda was nearby.

Then she beckoned imperatively, and both Jason
(no, Herihor) and Tallahassee followed. They went
along beside the pool into another room that held a
table piled with sheets of thick paper, some of which
were in rolls. While around the walls. . . . Tallahassee
under other circumstances would have been eager to
explore. Outside of a museum she had never seen
such an array of artifacts as lay or stood on shelves
that covered the walls from near floor level to ceiling.
Jayta indicated a chair to Tallahassee and pushed two
stools forward.

The priestess's speech was quick, staccato, and
Tallahassee could guess by the slight changes in the
man's expression what she must be doing, retelling
the events of the immediate past.

At first the girl thought that he refused to accept
what he heard. Then he stared at Tallahassee so
measuringly that she was certain he did now believe
the priestess's account. Perhaps in this world such
things were not uncommon. And as his expression
changed, he became less and less like Jason. There
was a grimness in the set of his mouth that she had
never seen her cousin wear. Twice his hand snapped,
as if instinctively, to the hilt of the dagger at his belt,
as if he could hardly control the urge to draw that

weapon. To use against her? There had been a note in his voice, when first he hailed her, that suggested some emotional tie with the Ashake who had been.

Now he listened so intently to what Jayta said that her words might have been a verdict affecting him deeply. When the priestess had done he answered in an even, cold voice, never glancing at Tallahassee. Then he arose and stalked from the room, again bringing her a fleeting memory of a Jason who also had just such an expressive way of holding his shoulders when he was annoyed, whether he might give voice to that annoyance or not.

Jayta watched him go, half raising her hand as if to stop him. Then she shook her head, seemingly at her own thoughts, and once more beckoned to Tallahassee.

Back they went to the girl's own room where Makeda and Idia had moved two of the small tables together beside the bed, in order to support a box from which led covered wire cords. This was not the same equipment that they had used for communication, for both cords this time were attached to a single circlet. Jayta motioned Tallahassee to the bed and reached out herself to take off the small turban before the girl was well aware of what she would do.

Tallahassee eyed the circlet warily. She did not care for the idea of using it as apparently the priestess meant it to be used. But did she honestly have any choice? She could not go on blindly here. And if this arrangement would fill in facts for her, give her the knowledge she lacked, then she did not really dare to refuse it. Only she wanted to get away even as Jayta adjusted the band about her forehead and pushed her down on the narrow bed.

From Makeda, the priestess took a very small bottle and thrust a pin into one end sealed with a covering of taut skin. With one swift gesture, before Tallahassee could elude her, she swung the bottle under the girl's nose. Queer aromatic smell . . .

Tallahassee brought no one clear memory out of that induced sleep when she opened her eyes to see Idia seated on a stool near the head of the bed. The—there had been something on her head, hadn't there? But it was gone now. . . .

The memory inducer!

"The dream is over, Great Lady."

"It is." Then Tallahassee realized that she answered in the same tongue as the question had been asked.

She was—she was Ashake of the Blood. But she was someone else, too. She frowned as she tried to fit one memory to another. Idia had hurried away, beyond the curtain. That machine, it was gone.

This was—she sat up on the bed, discovering an odd weakness in her body, as if she had been ill and was just trying out her legs, having been bed-bound for some time. This was her room. She could look upon each item in it as old and long familiar, some cherished because of past associations. But those were of Ashake's memories, not hers, another part of her mind made haste to report. At least one fear she had held had not been realized—she, herself, had not lost her own identity, no matter how clearly she could now call upon a dead woman's past recollections.

Only . . . her head ached and she held it. So much . . . she needed time—time to sort out what lay there. And there had come fear with those memories, no longer for herself, but that fear which had been the Princess's, the fear that had, at last, driven Ashake to take the dangerous venture which ended in her death.

"It is done?" It was not a statement but a question. Jayta entered the chamber with her swift, gliding step.

"I remember—too much . . ." Tallahassee replied.

"There cannot be too much, Great Lady. For you have a part to play, not only before those who love you and wish you well, but also those who watch for that which can be used against you. We have less time than we thought. Also, there has been a spy beam set upon us, cutting us off from contact with the temple at New Napata. While the news the Prince General brought . . ."

She paced up and down as might the lioness, which she had seemed in part to be at their first meeting, might do when pent within a cage. There was more than impatience in her expression. There rested there now an urgency approaching distress.

"You must listen to the Prince." She turned abruptly once more to Tallahassee. "His spies have brought him news that is worse than ever we dreamed."

Herihor, Ashake's memory identified the Prince. Not Jason—Herihor. He was of the Blood, but lesser, a leader of men who was general of the border forces to the north. And—he had been betrothed to Ashake from the time they were very young, though they could not wed until those of the Greater Learning allowed the Princess to retire from that service.

"I—I cannot think clearly," Tallahassee protested,

rubbing the forehead of her aching head with the palms of both hands as if she could so banish the pain.

"Makeda brings a healing draught. Drink it all, Great Lady. I wish you might indeed rest away this day. But time passes—we cannot now know what happens elsewhere while we are here. The Candace—there is a message that out-of-season storms in the desert lands prevent her flight back. She may be so late that the Half-Year Feast will be upon us before she arrives. The Prince General has sent two of his most trusted officers with messages for her. Neither has reported back. We are told all communications are affected by these storms. But those who handle the sending may well already be creatures of Userkof. May the jaws of Set open wide for him!"

The under-priestess returned carrying a goblet and knelt to hand it to Tallahassee. She sniffed doubtfully at the odor of the colorless liquid, but memory sustained her guess that this was only a restorative.

And Jason—Herihor—came even as she drank deeply, making a face at the bitter taste. His expression was set, and he did not meet her eyes, gazing over and beyond her. If he really cared for Ashake, and memory now insisted that he had, he must resent her. Tallahassee felt a faint regret about that as he swept so swiftly into speech, she believed he wanted to say what must be said and then get quickly away from sight of her.

"I cannot break the spy beam," he began tersely. "But there is no mistake, it comes from the southwest. And the Fourth Ashanti force lies between us and Napata."

Out of her memory sprang a name. "Itua?" Tallahassee asked.

Herihor nodded. "Itua and perhaps Ukaya also. I know not how far the rot has extended. There was a certainty that Khasti had a meeting—secretly—with both our esteemed relatives and a picked handful of the army. It was noted that they did not summon General Shabaoko or Marshal Nastasen. Nor did Colonel Namlia know until too late to station any of her guards. They dared to enter the South Palace without proper authority. And"—he shrugged—"they had something that repelled any of our devices. Khasti has promised much in the way of new equipment, and he may now be producing it. Two of my best men sent to keep an eye on them have vanished—even their persona check does not suggest where they are—"

"Dead?" Tallahassee fought to call upon the proper memories to understand what he was saying.

"No—at least the persona has not erased them. And I have had the best looker in search on this plane."

A looker, Ashake's memory supplied, was one trained in the strange and, to Tallahassee, non-understandable lore of the temples, wherein apparently psychometry, hardly yet understood in her world, could be put to definite and concrete use to locate people.

"I went to Zyhlarz." Now Herihor was pacing back and forth in the same caged fashion the priestess had earlier shown. "He says that what Khasti is using does not fit any device born from the Great Knowledge, and that even with the accented Power, he, himself, cannot catch the minds, now, of more than half of the suspected officers and councillors."

There was an exclamation from Jayta. "What has

this one of Set done that he can stand against the
Greater Knowledge?"

"That is within your province, not mine, Daughter-
of-Apedemek," Herihor snapped. "I only know that
three flyers striving to hover over the South Palace
crashed. And their pilots were dead when we found
them. I have done everything, save call out what
troops I am sure of. Those are mainly the Candace's
own guard and the north forces. We may have to
try such action officially before the end of this—to
batter down the gate by force of arms, though to do
so might well bring down upon us the very revolt we
fear. Naldamak must return. I have alerted the Guard.
But what Khasti has . . ." He flung out his hands. "He
might even be able to bring down the flyer carrying
her, though we have been testing with that thought in
view these past two days. It would seem that whatever
influence he has under his control, its range of force
is yet limited. We were fools not to keep a better
guard on him from the start. Fools!" He drove one
fist into the palm of his other hand.

"That is what comes"—he rounded on Jayta as if
he was accusing her of some crime—"of believing too
much in one way of Power. Khasti has gone beyond
the Great Knowledge, I will swear to that!"

"He depends upon the work of men's hands." Jayta
looked as angry as the Prince. "Man cannot stand alone
without the aid of that which is beyond."

"No? Tell that to my dead men, Daughter-of-
Apedemek. They are dead, thrown out of the air
as if they were leaves whirled off in a storm. And
it was not a power of the Greater Knowledge that
did that! Nor can Zyhlarz, who is supposed to draw

to him the height of your knowledge, explain it even to himself. Khasti must be stopped—but tell me how? I will not send more men uselessly into a death trap."

Jayta appeared to have controlled her momentary flash of temper. "We have done what we came to do. The Rod and the Key are safe in our hands—"

"At the cost of another death!" he flung at her.

"If it would cost us all the Circle of the Talent, still we must have so spent their lives," she replied calmly.

"I know," he said in a low voice. "I know why she had to go. But that makes her loss no easier to bear. And what if the Key and the Rod are not the answer? What if whatever Khasti has discovered is greater—"

"No!" Jayta's voice rang out fiercely. "A hundred centuries of years have we wrought within ourselves to achieve what we know. I will not believe that there is some thing of metal that can counter the Greater Knowledge, wherein we work with that which powers this world itself! If this man tries such—"

"I am not of the Temple, Daughter-of-Apedemek," Herihor answered curtly. "And I have seen in the past what the Belief of the Chosen Ones can accomplish. Have they not made the desert bloom and bear fruit, strengthened our race until we stand staunch against the barbarians, north and south? No man denies that this has been done, is being done. But if Khasti has made himself master of something else, then we must accept that perhaps even the Great Knowledge can be threatened."

The Greater Knowledge. Tentatively Tallahassee,

listening only a little to the dispute before her, tried to tap memory (or series of memories) concerning the nature of that. But while the life of Amun and her place in it came clearly to the surface when she called it, this other. . . . No, to summon it was like trying to catch wisps of flying shadows between her hands. Perhaps the Princess did not record that, it might be considered too secret to have where such might be drawn upon.

She could pick out the history of this time level from her memory induction. Egypt, which in her own world had been rumored by so many cults to be the fountainhead of occult knowledge, had, on this plane, indeed discovered and perfected a type of mental control and general ESP (centered in a trained priesthood and the royal family) which did approach that ability the cults argued it once had had.

Though Egypt had fallen to invaders, first Greek and then Roman, even as in her own world's history, it had not been lost. Retreating south to Kush, the modern Sudan, those of the Hierarchy who had survived again brought their civilization to a peak, favoring their own teaching. Arabs had attempted to invade from modern Ethiopia but they had been driven off during a war that had again depleted the hard core of the priesthood—for the strained use of their powers had brought death or mental collapse to many. So Meroë had fallen, while the handful of refugees—the royal family and what was left of those with the Knowledge—had fled westward.

There were very few in any following generation who showed ability for the training that the closed Circle of the Talented kept alive. Thus their ranks of late were thin, though a generation after their westward flight a king of unusual ability had come to the throne. After the custom of those of the Blood from the most ancient of days, he married his half sister, one who had passed three of the four stages toward becoming a major wielder of the Power. Together they had laid the foundations for the Empire. It seemed an auspicious time, now looked back upon as a golden age, for there had been then, for a short interval, a number of births of those having the Talent, and several of these were also rulers of provinces that the outspreading Empire occupied.

There followed a peak of prosperity and success that lasted for nearly two centuries. But what favored their safety was the fact that in this world there had arisen no Muhammed, no way of Islam to drown in blood the central African states, as had happened in the history Tallahassee knew.

Coptic Christianity spread slowly among the lower classes, but the hard inner core of the rulers and administrators remained almost fanatically tied to the Great Knowledge. And in the royal family a strain of those who had the Talent continued.

Europe, Tallahassee had learned from her new foster memory, had not meddled. Though trading ships from Portugal, Spain, and England visited Empire ports, the northerners had not dared to attempt that conquest which had brought the curse of the slave trade to this continent. For by the time Europeans made their appearances, the Empire was close-locked with India, China, and the Far East in bonds of trade. Since there was no interruption of the Meroë-Egyptian civilization, their own inventions and defenses equalled if not topped those of the traders.

Cunning metal workers always, and led by the Great Knowledge that planned and experimented, those of Amun had developed a modern civilization on a par with any of the emerging African nations of the world, yet far more stable because of the core of belief on which they had drawn for centuries. Now at last, they were being threatened, not from without, but from within. Again, there had been a marked recession of Talented births. Ashake had been the only one of the royal line to possess the Power for two generations. And, because such were weak in numbers, there came suggestions that the rulers of Amun apply other means for their defense.

Tradition here was a power in itself, so, at first, Khasti found few to listen to him. It was the envy of Userkof and the real hatred of his chief wife for his royal cousins—whose attainments were higher than she dared to hope to equal—that gave Khasti his chance. His own background was obscure, for he had only appeared several years ago, shunning the temple but prevailing on Userkof for support.

Jayta drew herself up proudly. "No work of any mind not endowed with the grace of That Which is Beyond Measurement can stand. Where it is used, there will it break the tie between us and the earth. Look at those to the north with the tie between us and the earth. Look at those to the north with their constant warring, their famines, their plagues. . . . Have the people of Amun faced such in a hundred hundred years? We open our hearts to all life about us, and through us, then, the spirit of life flows into the hands of the farmer who tends the grain, the herdsmen with his flocks. Our people dream beauty, and it comes alive under their fingers. Do we plant a tree and leave it to live or die—no. He who plants draws into him the spirit of life which he wills outward again to aid the growing roots under the soil. We are builders and not destroyers—and if we turn from the truth we shall indeed be lost."

"How many have now the Great Knowledge?" Herihor flung the question at her. "How many children are born in these days who can be brought to temple care and nurtured to the use of the Talent? What if we grow too old, our blood too thin? What if there comes a time when this life-spirit cannot be summoned?"

"There are ebbs and flows of the tide," Jayta returned. "If we stand now at an ebb, there will come a flow. But it is now that those who believe against us will strike. For it is as you say, our numbers are not great. Therefore, we must attack first, root out this Khasti and the abominations with which he busies himself."

"If we can," Herihor commented darkly.

"Look upon what we have already done," Jayta said sharply. "Were we sure we could find where the Rod was hidden? Yet that we did, even though the Key was also stolen. It is back in our hold. And I tell you, my Prince, that the Rod is far more than many believe it to be."

"Just what do you mean by that? It is a symbol of authority, and it seems true that no one not of the true line of the Blood can hold it. But what else is it?" he demanded.

"We do not know yet," she told him frankly. "But there was a power unleashed in it even as we drew it

back that we do not yet understand. Or perhaps"—she
looked to Tallahassee sitting silent on the bed—"that
was the doing of someone else."

"I have nothing of your Talent," the girl quickly
denied. "You have given me enough of her memory
so I know what I lack."

Herihor glanced from her to Jayta and back again,
his eyes now searching Tallahassee's painted face as
if beneath that cosmetic mask he could find a truth
he must have.

"Yes, Daughter-of-Apedemek—your number of sup-
porters lacks now the one I think you esteemed the
highest of all. By so much are you the loser." There
was bitterness in his voice, and his eyes were cold, his
expression closed. Did he really hate her? Tallahassee
was sure that that must be the truth.

"We do not know what we face." Jayta seemed
to temporize. "It is only true that above all else we
must hold in safety the Rod and the Key and pray
that the Candace finds a quick way home. Since the
spy ray holds us mute, perhaps it is better to send
some messenger directly to the Temple to speak with
Zyhlarz. And guards—"

"I know my trade. I brought the Ibex Regiment
with me when I came. And two messages have gone
to those commanders I can still trust in full. One
answered while I was still airborne. He is moving
overland to keep open the north road—if he can. For
if Khasti extends this power of his, who knows what
evil surprises we shall have to face."

He gave a quick nod of his head, divided between
the two of them, and was gone before the priestess could speak again. Tallahassee broke the silence

between them with a question she was herself surprised to hear, even as she asked it:

"Did he love her very much?"

For a second or two Jayta appeared so buried in
some thought of her own that it did not register. Then
she started, stared at Tallahassee, so that the girl had
a queer, shamed feeling, as if the question she had
asked broke some important rule of politeness.

"The Prince Herihor was chosen as consort for the
Princess," Jayta's tone was very remote and forbidding, "since he was not of the pure Blood. It was
believed that perhaps a mixture of such heritage
would strengthen anew the line for the next generation. It is—was—Ashake's child who would wear the
next crown."

A marriage of convenience and state, then. Yet
Tallahassee thought that that greeting shouted outside her bedroom earlier had held something else,
a warmth of feeling. But she could not judge these
people, she told herself firmly. She might have Ashake's
memories filtered through their recall machine, but she
did not possess any concerning Herihor that seemed
especially close. In fact, she was now engrossed by
a discovery she had just made—there were no overtones of emotion raised by any of those memories
she had yet sampled. She was not aware that Jayta,
having watched her closely for a breath or two, went
silently out of the room. For Tallahassee was testing,
after a fashion, those memories, drawing to the fore
of her mind each of the people she was supposed to
be closely allied with, to wait some response, a yes
or no of liking—no matter how faint. And still she
could detect none at all.

-7-

Tallahassee's headache dulled, she was able to eat all of the meal Idia brought her later and knew her energy was flowing back. In fact she felt almost euphoric, a condition that aroused suspicion in her mind. Had the restorative also been a drug of sorts to tie her more closely to Jayta's will? She could not detect a ground for such suspicion in the Ashake memories she could tap. But it was well not to depend too much on those for present assurance.

She went out beside the pool and sat on a bench, gazing into the water where the lotus blossoms spread wide their pointed petals. This was her own villa, or Ashake's, she knew now, a private retreat where the Princess had many times withdrawn for study and meditation in the past. Within it she was as secure—as long as she was Ashake—as she could be anywhere in this world.

The kittens came leaping out of nowhere to jump up beside her. One spoke in feline fashion at some length, staring straight up into Tallahassee's face as if delivering some message. When she put out her hand, it nipped delicately at her fingertips, while the other small mouth yawned wide, as, sleepy-eyed, it settled down for a nap.

This was soothing. She could almost push away that feeling of displacement. Would Ashake grow stronger in her and become dominant? Tallahassee stirred uneasily. How much dared she give open passage in her mind to those implanted memories?

There was—

Tallahassee stiffened, tense. Both cats roused, turned on the bench to stare at some point behind her. Both wrinkled their lips in silent snarls. The girl's hand went to the hilt of the dagger at her waist. Behind her—now—was danger.

She made herself rise slowly as if unaware. A call would bring one of the Amazon guard. Only there was something. . . . This she had felt before, not as a Princess of Amun but rather as herself, Tallahassee Mitford.

Slowly she turned to face what lurked there. Though this was day and not in a dark building in another time and world, there was again that presence—no better could she describe it. Only she could see nothing. . . .

Nothing? No! In the doorway of that chamber where Jayta had her rolls of wisdom—there flickered a shadow. And that shadow . . .

Tallahassee could not define it as more than a kind of blurring of her own sight, a blurring confined to that one area. Drawing upon every bit of courage she possessed, the girl started toward it. Her hand moved, not by her will, but directed by the Ashake memory, in a gesture, to draw in the air the outline of the Key.

There was—not menace, she realized, as her own controlled fear began to ebb. Here was a need that reached her fleetingly. And then that blur was gone. As if a door had closed. What kind of a door and why? Ashake was dead. It could not have been the Princess's shadow-self that invaded Tallahassee's world and lingered here now. Both memories assured her that was impossible.

But there had been that other one. The curdling in the air among the ruins when Jayta had sent such a presence away. The other one—he or she who had been dispatched by this Khasti to steal and hide the greatest defense of Amun—could such be the lurker? If so—they might face a danger now that even all the vaunted Ancient Knowledge could not handle. For when an enemy is invisible . . .

Tallahassee made herself go to that doorway, gaze into the room beyond. But she knew the thing had gone. The cold chill of fear that it could bring with it was already fading. However, that it went did not mean it would not return.

"Great Lady?"

Tallahassee was so startled by a voice from behind that she nearly cried out. But she mastered her loss of self-control before she turned to face Colonel Namlia herself.

"Warrior-of-the-lion." The old, old acknowledgment came unbidden from the second memory.

"There is one who has come—the Princess Idieze. She would have speech with the Great Lady."

Idieze—the wife of Userkof—she whose jealousy
had brought on much of this trouble here. But why
did she come?

"You may admit her to the presence, but summon
also the Daughter-of-Apedemek and Prince General
Herihor."

"As it is commanded, so it is done." The Amazon
gave the formal response.

Tallahassee moved back to the bench, deliberately
seated herself. She guessed that Idieze might come
so boldly on a kind of "fishing" expedition. She had
both the cunning and the arrogance to take such
action. Ashake's memory supplied much concerning
Idieze and little or none of it good.

There was a stir at the main door at the far end
of the pool as a slender woman wearing a garment of
saffron yellow and a small travel wig came determinedly
forward, those escorting her lingering by the gate.
Tallahassee did not rise to greet her. Ashake's rank
was far higher than that of this upstart female. In the
old days, before the smothering etiquette of the court
had been revised, this one would have approached on
hands and knees and kissed the sandal strip of the
Princess. None of the Blood ran in her veins.

If no emotion had broken through from the memories Tallahassee had earlier sifted, she had been wrong
in feeling that none such existed. For the very sight
of Idieze's smooth, painted face brought to life now
a flare of hot anger.

The woman was very beautiful, her lips finely chiseled, her features well cut. Though she was small
and dainty, yet she had excellent carriage and she
held herself with that inborn assurance which beauty

breeds in a woman. Even as contemptuous as Ashake's memories were, Tallahassee knew that the Princess had always understood the appeal Idieze had for her weakling cousin, and how this perfection in flesh could mold him easily to her purpose.

"I see you, Idieze." Tallahassee-Ashake gave greeting, not of intimate to intimate, equal to equal, but rather of the Blood to the lesser. And she saw the swiftly hidden spark in Idieze's eyes. It was as if something in Tallahassee now fed triumphantly on the hate the other projected.

"The Great Lady receives her servant." The other's voice was soft, carrying no hint of anger. Idieze was a superb actress, Tallahassee had to admit.

There was the sound of sandals and boots on the pavement behind. The girl did not need to look around to know that Namlia had carried out orders. Jayta and Herihor were coming. She wanted no confrontation with this—this viper that was not witnessed by those she could trust.

"Greeting, Daughter-of-Apedemek," Idieze continued. "And to you, General of the North." She smiled gently. "Has some emergency arisen that you are called from your station when the Glorious-in-the-Sun Naldamak is not with us?"

"I did not realize, Lady, that your interest in military matters was so marked." Herihor's voice was cool.

She only smiled, warmly and graciously. "Is not my Lord, also, of the defenses of our land?" she countered sweetly. "As his wife, I have learned much."

That you have, Tallahassee thought, or perhaps should it not more rightly be that he has learned from you!

Impatience stirred in her. Idieze would not come here without a purpose. Let them get to the point quickly. Though she could trust her implanted memory, yet there was something about this female that was a threat she could well do without and speedily. It might not follow the rules of formality and custom, but she decided now to dispense with those.

"You have sought me out, Idieze," Tallahassee said bluntly, "and for that there must be a reason."

"Concern for your welfare, Great Lady. It has been rumored in New Napata that you have been grievously ill—"

"So?" Tallahassee was aware of that searching glance the other gave her. She wondered what had really been told Idieze, what had been the result on the enemies' side of that invasion into the other world? Had they even suspected the real result—Ashake's death? If so, Idieze must be confounded now, through she showed no trace of surprise.

"Rumor," she continued deliberately, "often is fathered and mothered by false reports. As you see, my health is good. As one of the Talented I withdraw to renew my spirit—as all know must be done at intervals."

"When the Graciousness-in-the-Sun and her sister of the Blood are both gone, and none is delegated to hold the Rod, there is uneasiness." Idieze still smiled with her mouth, kept her voice low and gentle, but Tallahassee wished she could see more clearly into those downcast eyes.

"And to whom would the Rod pass," Tallahassee asked in a voice she hoped was as deceptively mild as the other's, "seeing that there are none of the pure Blood to set hand to it?"

The smile was gone now, the lips set straightly together, as if the other had an answer that prudence alone kept her from saying aloud.

"But"—Tallahassee was being forced to this because Ashake's memory warned her that she dared not trespass too deeply on a field of action adverse to the ways of the court—"since you have come in your concern, you are greeted. The way to New Napata is long, and it is close to evening. You are bidden to dine, to sleep within these walls, you and your people."

It did not sound very gracious, and she did not mean it to. Also she heard a slight stir from the direction of Herihor, behind her left shoulder, and she knew that perhaps he was not pleased with what she had done. But to send Idieze forth now would mean an open break that perhaps they could not afford. Tallahassee clapped her hands, and as two maid servants appeared she gave orders.

"Escort the Lady Idieze to the guest quarters. See also that those who serve her are made at ease."

Idieze smiled again, and at the sight of that a small doubt arose in Tallahassee. The woman wanted to stay, she had come here for no other reason. Why? Now she made a graceful gesture of homage and withdrew, walking down the other side of the pool toward rooms at the back of the villa, her people coming from the gateway to follow her. Two maids and another woman, older and somewhat hunched of back, who hobbled along leaning on a cane. Yes, that was the old crone Idieze had ever about her. Some said she was the ancient nurse who had tended her as a child—others retailed more fantastic suggestions.

"She comes for a purpose." Herihor spoke first,

staring after that ordered withdrawal as Tallahassee arose and turned to face the other two.

"Better," Jayta remembered, "that she be under our own eyes now. Our Lady could not turn her from the door, even though there lies no friendship between them. It may be that we can learn what has brought her here."

"Learn anything from that one?" Herihor laughed harshly. "She is like the scorpion hiding beneath a rock, her sting raised—yet the shadow of the rock ever hides her threat. I do not like it."

"Neither do I," returned Tallahassee as frankly. "But, as Jayta says, what else could be done with her? We do not yet court an open break with her party. Let the Daughter-of-Apedemek deal with the matter; there is perhaps something that can be done by the Talent to learn more."

Jayta nodded. "Yes. For now, we must be content with the matter as it stands. It would be well to acquaint Colonel Namlia with a suggestion that the guard of honor be doubled tonight—"

"With special emphasis on the outer part of the guest quarters." When Herihor's left brow slid up as Jason's had so often, for a moment Tallahassee's heart lifted. If he only were Jason! If she could have confidence that he did not hold any grudge against her, that he was not just serving her because it was his duty!

"We must all do our best," were the only words that came to her lips. She was not looking forward to this disturbing night wherein she must fence with Idieze across food she had now little desire to taste.

At least they did not share the same table, and there was nearly the width of the room between them. For it seemed that the household at the villa followed the old Egyptian custom of food being served on small, separate tables, each placed beside a chair. Tallahassee, Herihor, Jayta, and Idieze were grouped at one end of the room, while members of the household of sufficient rank were a little apart. Among the latter there was easy if low-voiced conversation, though it did not include the hunched form near the opposite door—Idieze's crone attendant. But among those of rank there was a general silence as if each were only too-well occupied with his or her own thoughts.

Once or twice Tallahassee had that shivering sensation of being overlooked. She saw Jayta stir, glance over her shoulder at the painted expanse of the wall at their backs. Did the priestess also pick up that feeling that there was something hovering about them? The girl longed for the meal to be done, for Idieze to be gone, so she could share with the Daughter-of-Apedemek her curious experience beside the pool.

Only Idieze showed no sign of wanting yet to withdraw. She had finished her meal. Now one of the maids standing along the wall ready to give service brought forward a carved box from which the Princess selected a slender brown stick, putting it to her lips, waiting for the maid to touch a flame to its tip. Smoke rose in needle-thin curls from the stick when Idieze drew deeply upon it, so that a tiny spot of flame flared.

"It is sad that you who followed the Upper Path, Great Lady," she said, "are forbidden so many of the luxuries of life. These pleasant dream sticks can be most soothing to the nerves."

A tendril of the smoke floated in Tallahassee's

direction. It was sickly-sweet and, without thinking, she fanned it away.

"Lady," it was Jayta who spoke, "this is a house for those who do follow the Upper Path. Such—"

"Cannot be defiled by my dream stick?" Idieze laughed. "I am rebuked." She thrust the glowing tip into the dregs of wine in her goblet. "Forgive me, Daughter-of-Apedemek. We of the outer world are not so constrained in our life. The old ways"—she gave a dainty shrug—"they fasten chains upon one, and it is so unnecessary. For much can be learned by an open will and mind."

She was insolent, being deliberately so, Tallahassee realized. And why did Idieze feel so free to speak thus—here?

Herihor set down his goblet, his eyes were on Idieze with that narrowed intentness that had been— was—Jason's when he was considering some problem. Tallahassee could believe that he was now as alert as she was to the danger of Idieze and her real purpose in coming here.

It was as if Idieze herself could read that thought. Her lazy smile was gone. Now she leaned forward a little in her chair.

"Great Lady, there is a matter that must be discussed. But, privately . . ." And her eyes shifted to those in the other part of the room.

"So we had guessed," Tallahassee returned. "Let us to the poolside, then."

Herihor was almost instantly at her side, holding out his arm so she could touch fingers to his wrist. As she arose, Tallahassee bowed her head to Jayta, but gave no such courtesy to Idieze. The sooner that one spat

out whatever poison she had brought hither, the better.
For Ashake, memory was only too clear in reminding
what Idieze could do.

Colonel Namlia was by the door as Tallahassee and
Herihor reached it. And Tallahassee gave her order.

"We speak in private—by the pool. See that we
are undisturbed."

"On my head be it, Great Lady." The Colonel raised
her hand to touch the lion emblem to the fore of her
linen sphinx headdress.

Two of her Amazons were waved to draw another
bench near to the one where Tallahassee had rested
earlier. Then they took their places well out of earshot,
their backs to the four who sat there, Tallahassee
between Herihor and Jayta, Idieze on the smaller
bench facing the three bound in what she must see
was open hostility against her.

"You would speak, I see you," Tallahassee said.

"Princess, Priestess, General"—Idieze looked slowly
from one face to another—"and all so ready to beware
one unarmed woman—me. You grant me stature I do
not have, Great Lady."

"Be glad then that you do not, for the wrath of
the Blood is not a light thing to face." Out of Ashake
memory came the words. Yet Idieze was smiling once
more, and now she laughed, low and sweetly.

"Such ponderous language, Great Lady. One would
think that the Blood was about to pronounce one of
those Seven Curses which, we are told, could wither
flesh, break bones. It does not matter that I am hated
here, but truly I have come out of concern. The
Blood has held power a very long time—by ways so
ancient that the very accounts are now dreary dust.

To everything there comes an end, have you ever thought of that, Great Lady? Those of the Blood, of the Upper Way are very few now, a handful against perhaps more than half a nation.

"There is no cure for narrowness of mind; that leads only to stagnation and defeat. The end of your road is very near, Great Lady, and if one does not heed the branching of another path ahead, there can follow chaos. None of us wants to see Amun rent by a war of brother against brother, sister against sister. But the branch of the tree which gives not to pull of the storm wind breaks and is gone."

"A warning, Lady?" Tallahassee cut into this spate of metaphors. "So you think you are strong enough to give a warning? That in itself is interesting indeed."

Idieze's smile set a fraction. "You here have had no news from New Napata, I believe, for some hours. There can be many changes in even a small portion of such a space of time, Great Lady."

"And what momentous happening has there been at New Napata in those hours?"

"Changes, Great Lady. Not all love the past. It is said that the Temple of Light is now closed so that none go in or come out again. Rumor can whip the people to violence. And rumor spreads that the Son-of-Apedemek, Zyhlarz himself, has been struck mad so that he howls like a desert jackal and looses upon those of his own people death from the mind. Do not discount rumor, Great Lady, it often holds a core of truth. And do not discount what I have to offer. The turn in the road will not be open for long."

"That turn being a way for Userkof?" Tallahassee asked. "From such a change there could come

only trouble. He is not of the direct descent and his
get—though I believe you have not yet provided our
lord with any to call him father—cannot sit in the
Lion's seat."

"So there is no heir save you, Royal Daughter? Ah,
but you are also barred from the throne now since
you profess the celibacy of those who strive to follow
the Upper Way. And this valiant lord has waited so
long for you that already he looks elsewhere!"

She swung on Herihor. There was a sharpness in
her features that carried the threat of an aimed dagger. Tallahassee did not doubt that Idieze was about
to spew forth something she thought to be true.

"In the old days, General Prince Herihor, our
men took more than one wife. Does this Great Lady
betrothed to you know the rumors of a white skin
from the north who now confidently expects to wear
jewels of your bestowing?"

Herihor made a slight movement but his face was
smooth of any telltale expression. "Your servants have
been busy, Lady. But if I were you, I would subject
their reports to a closer study. Such who spy upon
command often relate only what their mistress wishes
most to hear."

"Perhaps, Lord Prince." She shot a sly, searching
glance at Tallahassee, as if to judge the effect of her
revelation.

If she expected to light a fire with that! After all,
though the Prince had not uttered a denial of Idieze's
malicious accusation, Tallahassee was scornful of any
statement from that source. In fact she could imagine
several reasons why Herihor might be on good and
even confidential terms with a woman of the north

through whom information affecting the border might flow. Did the Princess believe she dealt now with utter fools? When Tallahassee looked to the General Prince, she saw Jason, and Jason had had his secrets into which she had never thought to pry.

"The loose talk of servants has never been of interest to me. But your warning is now delivered. I have seen you, Idieze." Tallahassee deliberately used the dismissal for an inferior and was queerly glad to see the other's lips tighten into a grimace.

As she stood up, Idieze, too, was forced to rise, and by court custom she could not speak again. But as she withdrew, Tallahassee spoke swiftly to Herihor, hoping to convey by her very order her trust in him: "See that she is watched. Also I want her and her spying servants away from here as soon as possible. She came more to see than to warn, or so I think."

"She wears a mind-shield," Jayta said in a low voice. "It is not of her Talent. Also she would not dare speak of the affairs of the Temple, as she did, was this not a fact."

"But Zyhlarz—" Herihor protested.

"Yes, Zyhlarz, he who is Son-of-Apedemek in our time." Jayta's voice was strained. She stared after Idieze, already nearly lost in the shadows at the other end of the pool. "This is worse, far worse. Great Lady—we must know!"

"Herihor? . . ." Tallahassee made a question of his name.

"Be sure if there is any way possible, we shall know and soon. I have an officer with me—I left him in charge of the outer guard. He has undertaken such duties in the past; he will again. I have your permission to try?"

"You have my will on it!"

Then he was gone. Tallahassee put out her hand to the Priestess. "There is something else, there was a presence; one such as I felt in the other world . . ." Hurriedly she told of her experience before the arrival of Idieze.

"Yes, that can be the wraith of him who stole the Rod and the Key. He strove to follow you through the corridor Ashake opened to reach your world. We have sealed that. But that he has still the strength to follow you. . . . We shall set safeguards anew!"

It was late when Tallahassee finally went to bed. She had had discussions with Jayta, later again with Herihor who had sent his officer out. And the report came that Idieze and those who followed her were safely pent in their chambers, a guard set to watch.

As she stretched out on the bed, the faintly purring kittens against beside her, she was so tired that she felt wrung free of any emotion at all. Idieze had meant that gossip concerning Herihor's barbarian woman to be devastating. But then she could not know that Herihor was—was like—Jason—a companion-brother—a . . .

There was a faint trouble born of that thought, but she was too tired to strive to examine the source of her uneasiness.

She roused at the growl of a kitten. Her room was dark. Only a faint light shone around the edge of the door curtain. Only—there was an intruder here. She did not need the growling to know that someone stood beside her bed.

Tallahassee opened her mouth to shout for the guard. There was a spray of liquid, stinging on her lips and in her eyes, wet on her cheeks. She fell away, sick and dizzy, into dark nothingness.

-8-

Tallahassee was drowning, there was water about her and nothing to hold onto. Waves lapped over her head as she fought for air for her lungs. She was drowning! However, the waves were receding, though she could still feel them beat through her exhausted body. Not a sea—not water, yet she could feel movement and hear sound. The beat of an engine!

Her mind stirred sluggishly, but there was a spark of caution awakening, too. Recollection of what had happened came slowly. She had been in her bed and then—? The few moments of awareness, that spray in her face. . . .

She was certainly not in her bed now, nor in the villa. So where was she? Though she ought by this time, she thought, with a queer desire to laugh, to be accustomed to unbelievable changes of scene.

Though Tallahassee did not open her eyes (let whoever was near her believe she was still unconscious), she tensed her arms enough to know that they had been securely bound to her sides, her feet and legs immobilized in the same painstaking fashion. The bonds were not about her wrists or ankles, rather she was enveloped in some wrapping like a cocoon, though they had left her head free.

So, she was a prisoner and on a flyer. How they had gotten her away from the well-guarded villa was a question. Unless they (whoever they were) had methodically trotted about spraying all the guards and inhabitants with that handy little gadget they had used so efficiently on her. Idieze was behind them, she was sure of that. What utter fools they had been to even let her in.

When Tallahassee's thoughts drew upon the Ashake memory, she could find no hint that such an attack had ever been known before. Idieze had sat there and warned them. . . . Tallahassee's temper flared. She had dared—dared! Ashake memory burned at the thought she had dared to lay hands on one of the Blood! They would see what payment would be extracted for this outrage.

But who were "they" in this instance—beside Idieze, of course, and her servants? Userkof, probably, and beyond him, Khasti—that man of mystery. At the rise of that name in her mind Tallahassee knew a wariness that dampened but did not extinguish her anger. She must learn all she could.

First, she depended on her ears. There was the constant beat of the engines. She must be lying flat on the floor of the cabin, which she realized was very hard and unyielding. There must be a pilot, and . . . she tried to remember how many had accompanied Idieze. Two maids, she believed, and that crone of a nurse.

But the wife of Userkof had never come without a squad of her own personal guard. Idieze would cling to that prestige no matter how supposedly private her visit.

None of the guard had showed up in the villa. Naturally not, the Amazons would not have allowed that. Even all of Herihor's men, save a single aide, had been restricted to the barracks beyond the landing strip. The villa was a house of women, as was correct for the unwed Daughter-of-the-Sun-in-Height.

There could be half a dozen enemies now about her, so the longer they thought her unconscious, and helpless, the better. Now that her ears had identified the sound of the engines she heard words, always pitched so that she could not quite catch them. Her sense of smell was an aid, too; she could pick up perfume—to her left—Idieze perhaps. And with that—yes, a whiff of that sickly sweetness from such a tube as the Princess had begun to smoke at the villa.

Farther away—another scent, vaguely unpleasant. But around her they were all very quiet. Perhaps this was how a mouse might feel trapped in a corner with a cat lazily on guard.

There had been a change in the flyer's rhythm, they were losing altitude, she thought, though she could not be sure. Then came a jar—landing. The engine cut off. Suddenly air puffed across her face, carrying not the freshness of the breeze at the villa, but rather a combination of odors that aroused the Tallahassee part of memory—that was like the tainted breeze of home—the smell of a city.

She was nudged in the side by someone walking past her. But no one came to lift her out—not yet.

Very slowly she raised her eyelids a fraction. Her field of vision was very limited, but not so much so that she did not see a soldier in dull green. And in his hands—the case of the ROD!

She almost betrayed herself in that moment. What had they wrought at the villa to have that in their hold again? Could they have killed? She felt sick as she made herself face that thought. If they had reduced the others to impotency as easily as they had her, then it might well be that death had followed, leaving her entirely on her own in the hands of those who had little use for her.

Only one use in fact—that she alone in the absence of the Empress could handle the Rod. Did they have the Key also? She could guess that they would not overlook that. Within the wrappings that bound her she felt cold as she added up a sum and found the answer was probably complete disaster. What had she left for weapons? The memory—partial—of a dead girl, memory, but not the power that girl had commanded, and such courage and resourcefulness as were her own birthright. The Rod—she could hold it, she had proved that. But could she command what it symbolized? Tallahassee was not sure if that Ashake memory tape had been edited before it was forced upon her, but she believed that it had been. Naturally—they would do that for their own protection. What did Jayta know about Tallahassee Mitford that would lead the Priestess to allow her the full memory of her predecessor? Therefore she could not fight on Ashake's level, she could only bluff. And any bluff can be so easily called.

There was a tramp of feet again. Resolutely Tallahassee closed her eyes entirely. She was jerked upward, still lying prone. She must be on a stretcher as they did not touch her body. Now the stretcher dipped so she might have slid off, but there was a band about her waist on the outside of the wrappings to hold her steady.

Once more she peeked beneath three-quarter-closed lids: lights, and beyond them a scrap of night sky, also a back with wide shoulders, covered by a green uniform. Those vanished suddenly as the stretcher on which she lay was pushed into a dark, confined place. And she heard a noise like the slam of a door, whereupon all light vanished.

A motor started up, they were moving again. But there were no openings to give her any hints of where they might have brought her. Odd that she was making this part of the trip alone. Then something slid across the floor on which the stretcher so uncomfortably rested and banged against the side. Could that be the Rod box? With the inborn awe with which most of the empire regarded that artifact, Tallahassee did not believe that they would be comfortable with it close to them.

She tried to fit together the facts she had. There was no doubting she had been kidnapped, brazenly taken from her own home. And no one would have dared such action had the one giving the orders not believed he or she was invincible against any retaliation. The person of the Heir was sacred, even though in these latter years much of the ancient beliefs had worn thin enough.

To expect any help from Jayta or Herihor—no.

Somehow it was very hard to believe that those who had taken her would leave any such strong opponents alive. So, she was on her own now, with only Ashake's edited memories to draw upon. However, what she felt at present was no longer fear, but Tallahassee's own temper on the boil. She had had to learn self-control early, yet her emotions were no less strong for that suppression. Now she must make the anger work for her as she had several times in the past, to bolster her own determination to succeed and uphold the courage to back that determination.

Idieze, Userkof, Khasti—She began methodically to summon to her mind all Ashake memories concerning those three. Userkof—he was perhaps the weak link. In a monarchy, which was firmly built on matriarchal inheritance, a king's son held little power. If he had wed Ashake—then he could have hoped for the crown. But he had never had a chance at that.

The Blood married by duty and not by choice, at least their first and official marriages were arranged so, though queens regnant had had their favorites, kings their concubines, often enough. And in this generation it had been decided that fresh strains must be interbred, with hope that the infusion would lead to a new generation with the Talent. The Empress Naldamak had been married in her early youth to a very distant cousin who had been killed two years later in the crash of a flyer. And there had been no issue of that marriage, nor could there be of another, for the physicians had pronounced the Empress sterile. Thus furtherance of the line depended on Ashake—if she lived.

And if she did not live? Userkof—perhaps.

Idieze was only the daughter of a provincial governor and had in addition a trace of overseas barbarian blood—since her province was that of the sea coast where the carefully supervised trade with outlanders was conducted. That she would be empress in fact and not just consort, should Userkof come to the throne, Ashake had known for years.

Reluctantly she drew on the memory for Khasti. Here were rulership and power, and sometimes one was not a part of the other. One could choose to stand behind the Emperor and wield through him true power. That was what was suspected of Khasti. And it would seem that suspicions were true.

If Naldamak returned at the Half-Year Feast, to appear enthroned in the ritual ceremonies of that time without the Rod in her hands . . . that was what they had tried to accomplish from the first. Now they had both the Rod and Ashake! Or the seeming of that princess. From the memory she probed, Tallahassee discovered that Khasti was the least known, the most suspected.

And what Idieze had reported—that the High Priest Zyhlarz was imprisoned in his temple—was a forewarning that he could not be called upon. No, she had better depend only on herself, Tallahassee, rather than upon the infused memory from the dead or any aid from outside.

Though that was of little reassurance.

The vehicle in which she was a prisoner came to a halt. She closed her eyes. Ears only now . . .

She heard the clang of a latch at the back of the carrier. And then fresh air—this time a little less tainted with the effluence of a city—as the stretcher on which she lay was drawn out. Now she was being carried, and her bearers were in haste, moving at a trot. There was more light which she caught through the very narrow slit she allowed for sight.

"To the Red Chamber." For the first time she caught clear words. "And summon my Lord." That was Idieze speaking.

The Red Chamber? Yes, it was the South Palace— that center which Herihor's men had been unable to penetrate—to which the suspected rebel leaders had been summoned. And that room had a gruesome enough history, for within it a hundred years ago, brother had slain brother in a battle for the throne and the hand of a half sister who had already chosen her consort.

Even the Talent had not kept the line free from the taint of ambition and greed. Perhaps that was why it ran so thin in this generation. Misused, or forced, that kind of power was lost. Perverted, it could turn upon the very one who tried to make it weapon or tool. Perhaps Idieze had chosen that shrine of infamy now with good reason. In such places, where emotion to a high degree had been released in some desperate and bloody action, there was wont to cling, even for generations, a residue of evil that could obstruct the clear sight of the Talented, leave them open to an invasion that was to be feared above all things. Only she was not Ashake, so such an invasion need not be feared.

Her bearers turned a corner, then another. Finally the stretcher was set down, not on the floor, but apparently on a couch, for the surface gave a little under Tallahassee's weight. She heard them retreat, yet she was certain that she was not alone. And she strained her ears to catch the faintest sound.

"Ashake?" No "Great Lady" now. Idieze might have been addressing one in house bondage.

Close upon that call of name came a vicious, open-handed slap which Tallahassee had not been expecting. Without thinking she opened her eyes. Idieze leaned over her, smiling, her own eyes very wide and alive.

"I thought so," she observed. "Khasti said that the sleep-spray would not hold you too long. You have been trying to play a game, but the time is past for games, Sister." She stressed the last word. "You would never grant me that name, would you, Ashake? Nor stretch out your hand in any welcome. You 'saw me' when I came to you. Now I see you!"

Her lips parted in what was nearer a snarl than smile, showing small pointed teeth, very white against the red of her lips.

"I see you," she repeated, lingering over those words, as if from the saying of them she achieved some manner of contentment. "But will anyone continue to see you for long? Think on that, Sister!"

Tallahassee made her face as impassive as she could and gave no answer. Idieze's spite might be a weakness. And any weakness she must note and ready herself to use.

Idieze had turned and now approached a table as Tallahassee moved her head so she could watch. She had been right. The Rod had been brought with her. There lay the case in which she had placed it at Jayta's bidding. Idieze's fingers rested for a moment on the lid, but she made no effort to open it. She only looked back over her shoulder at her captive.

"You see—this too we have, in spite of all your struggles to keep it to hand. And very easy it was to take both you—and it. I have heard so much prating of the Power, the Talent. All my life people have been in awe of this thing, the force of which could not be proven. See how easy it was for us to defeat you?" She laughed. "I spoke of other roads, Sister—now we walk them. And there is nothing you can do to retrace time and change that, nothing!"

She ran her hand in a greedy gesture down the length of the case. Tallahassee thought that for all Idieze's spoken disdain for the Talent, she was still wary enough to let the Rod remain hidden; she was not so sure inwardly of the freedom of her other path as she would have the world believe. Tallahassee could sense the other's aching desire, the wish that it might be her own hand which could lift that symbol from its bed, that she need not work through Userkof.

Even as Tallahassee's mind pictured Ashake's cousin, so did he suddenly come into view. He lacked the height of Herihor and, though those two might have matched year-to-year in age, Userkof's flabby body and petulant expression seemed to add a toll of extra time. He did not wear a uniform, but rather loose trousers, fastened at the ankle, and a sleeveless over-jacket of white, much covered with elaborate embroidery. Also, his head was bare of the wig preferred by the court. Instead, he had a twist of flaming red scarf about his skull, which was a mistake, for it accented somehow the loose gaping of his thick lips, those jowls that softened and weakened his jawline.

"Maskaq said . . ."

Then his eyes went beyond Idieze and he saw
Tallahassee. First they widened in what she could
only believe was real surprise, then he laughed, a
low chuckle.

"So you did it!"

Idieze was watching him closely, and Tallahassee
did not miss the shadow of contempt in her face as
she answered:

"My Lord, did you then so doubt the success of
our plan?"

"There were many obstacles. She was in her own
palace—guarded," he answered. Now he advanced to
where Tallahassee lay and stared down at her before
he laughed again.

"Greetings, Cousin."

Idieze came to his side. "She does not answer. But
she will learn, will she not, my Lord?"

His tongue crept out, swept over his loose lower
lip. He might have been reaching into a dish that
held some sweetmeat he savored.

"Oh, yes, she will answer!" he agreed.

He reached out a thick-fingered hand and flicked
Tallahassee's chin. There was something about him of
a small boy who had been dared to some act and
must carry through. Idieze must be full of triumph
at this moment, but Userkof, for all his seething
malice and spite, was still uncertain of success.

"My Lord." Idieze's hand on his arm drew him
away from their prisoner, back toward the table. "See
what lies here, ready for your hand!"

Her fingers went to the box and she loosened the
catches, throwing back the lid to display the Rod. The
pleased malice faded from her husband's face as he

looked down. Instead he drew a breath so deep even Tallahassee could hear the faint hiss of it.

"It is yours, take it!" Idieze's expression held more than a shadow of contempt now, which Userkof did not see. He was too intent upon the Rod.

"I have—have not the Talent . . ." he said, not as if he spoke to the eager woman, but rather as if he drew some warning from his own thoughts.

"Talent!" spat Idieze. "What need have you for that, my Lord! Has not Khasti given us and will give us yet again, much more force than these superstitious, meddling priests can conceive of controlling? You are of the Blood, you have only to pick up this, and you can command the Empire. Are you such a nothing"—her voice grew shriller, shrewish—"that you cannot do even this one small thing to gain a throne? You say you are a man, at least prove that in this much."

He had sucked in his bulbous lips, now he wiped his hands down the front of his jerkin as if they were wet and he might not be able to grip anything in them tightly enough.

"Khasti is coming." Idieze moved the Rod box a fraction closer to Userkof. "Meet him with the Rod. Do you now see what that will mean? He thinks too well of himself, even though his plan for getting this was a failure. You must make him understand that you are of the Blood."

Once more Userkof wiped his hands down his sides. He glanced uncertainly at Idieze, then back to the box and what it held.

"Show him," she hissed. "This you must do—or he will not be the tool we need. Rather will he think and plan for himself! He failed, but we have succeeded.

Prove that to him, husband—and then you shall hold him in the hollow of your hand. For there must not be two minds and two wills when you come to power—only one!"

Yes, yours, Tallahassee thought. However much Idieze urged, it would seem that Userkof was haunted by fear. As well he might be, Ashake's memory prompted. No one, not even of the Blood, could master the Rod unless there was that within them which answered to the undefinable thing that kept the ancient belief strong through all these centuries of study and testing.

Userkof put out one hand, and Tallahassee noted that it shook. How strong Idieze's will must be to bring him to such an action. She was not sure what the result might be, but that it would benefit Userkof—no.

Perhaps he had screwed up his small store of courage to its greatest point for he made a sudden grab with his right hand, wrapping his fingers about the staff a handsbreadth below the lion mask, snatching the Rod from the padded box.

For a single moment he held it before him, even as Tallahassee had done when the soldiers had broken into the ruin. Then—he screamed, high and shrill, more like a woman than a man. The Rod fell from his hold, struck against the floor and rolled.

But Userkof's hand—still held stiffly before him . . . The skin on his fingers was as red as if blood had been drawn. Slowly the flesh faded to an ashy grey. He screamed again as his fingers thinned into claws, fused so that he could not flex them.

Idieze shrank back, her face open for the first time to terror, staring at that horror of a hand, while

Userkof's screams became peals of mindless agony. His wife nearly stumbled over the Rod, started to kick out at it, and then stopped, as if she feared now with a deathly terror any contact with the thing. Userkof sank to his knees, his body shaking. He still screamed even as he slid completely to the floor.

People burst into the room—guards first, their hand weapons drawn and ready. But when they saw what lay beside their master on the floor, looked at the ruin of his hand, they backed away. Their withdrawal cleared a path for another man.

Khasti!

He was as tall as Jason and spare of figure. His features were finer than Userkof's—he might well be a son of the Blood, though who he was remained an unsolved mystery. He could be traced no farther back than ten years when he had been discovered by a desert patrol beside a dead camel, himself barely alive. But he was of Empire stock and not a northern barbarian, and on his recovery he had managed to so impress the Commander of the fortress to which he had been taken that that officer sent him to New Napata with a recommendation to General Nemos.

From his first coming fortune seemed to have favored him. In spite of the fact that he made no close friends, nor confided in anyone, when he wished he could bind men to him. And no one denied the quick dexterity of his mind. Not even Zyhlarz could probe the extent of his intelligence. From the beginning of his life in New Napata, he shunned all that was of the Temple. Also, he allowed others in time to see that he disdained and held of small account what he deemed unprovable superstition, an attitude that attracted and

soothed the egos of those who could not hope to ever
enter the ruling center of the Empire.

Now he knelt beside Userkof, putting out his hand
to clasp the wrist of that shriveled horror. Having
given the claw fingers what seemed a single searching glance, he turned his attention to the man whose
screams had died into a whimpering. Stooping, he
stared straight into Userkof's distended eyes and murmured something so low-voiced that only the injured
man might have heard. The rest of that company,
including Idieze, kept well distant, as if the Prince
was truly cursed, and that curse in turn might well
envelop them all.

Userkof's eyelids slowly closed. Then his head
rolled limply to one side, his mouth slack, a thread
of drool dripping from his open lips. Khasti took
quick command.

"Take him to his chamber!" He snapped fingers at
the guards who were very plainly loath to approach
at all, but could not disobey. It was only when they
bore the Prince from the room that Khasti looked
about—at Idieze, at the Rod, and finally and most
piercingly at Tallahassee.

There was nothing to be read in that stare he turned
on her. And that very fact began to arouse within
her the fear she thought she controlled. He showed
no emotion, she could not guess at his thoughts. It
was as if she were an object, not a living being. That
quality in him was what Ashake had feared most in
Khasti—now Tallahassee found it gripped her also.

-9-

"So, princess. . . ." Though he still looked to Tallahassee it was Idieze he addressed. "You have been busy, it would seem."

Perhaps that cool note of superiority that was plain in his voice snapped Idieze out of her state of shock. Her lips tightened as she drew herself up, once more self-controlled.

"We have succeeded," she returned. "There lies what your aide was sent to fetch and did not." With her foot rather than her hand she indicated the Rod.

"With what seems an unhappy result. My lord Prince has not managed to control it."

Khasti knelt on one knee again to inspect the Rod, bringing from the breast of his long grey robe something so small that he could conceal it in the palm of his hand. This he passed down the length of the staff, being careful, Tallahassee noted, not to come within touching distance. Twice he made that passage, up and down, and then opened his fist for an intent examination of a metal object no larger than the matchbox of her own time.

A single frown line deepened between his brows as he continued to study what he held.

"Radiation." The word he uttered was more for himself than his hearers. "But what? . . ."

Khasti gained his feet in a single lithe movement, came to Tallahassee's side with one stride. Now his hands loosed the bonds that had kept her captive.

"What would you do?" Idieze was beside him. "She—"

"It would seem, if all accounts are the truth," and this time his arrogant disdain of Idieze was very plain, "that the Princess Ashake can handle this symbol of might and show no harm therefrom. I would have proof of that here and now. Or would you, Princess, care to raise it from the floor?"

The last of her wrappings gone, Tallahassee sat up, only the thin night garment flimsy about her. She was stiff, and her back ached from her long imprisonment in one position. But she swung her feet to the floor, keeping her face as carefully blank as she could.

"Can you pick that up?" Khasti came directly to the point.

"I am of the Blood and the Upper Way," she returned obliquely. Tallahassee was not sure what method of control they might exert on her. But suppose she got the Rod in her hands, she might then be able to exert pressure on them in implied threat, though Ashake memory gave her only a very hazy and incomplete hint of how that symbol of authority was put into use.

"Do not! She will curse us and we shall die!" Idieze

caught at his arm, dragged him back a little. "You have freed her—with the Rod in her hand you do not know what she can do!"

"She will do very little," Khasti returned calmly. "I will see to that. Now!"

In one hand he still held the object he had used to examine the Rod, but in the other he had, with the speed of a conjuror, produced something else, a glittering disk he spun out through the air, twirling it on the end of a chain. Against her will Tallahassee's eyes were drawn to that. Over her dropped the same compulsion that had held her to another's will back in the museum.

So compelled, she arose jerkily, not even mistress of her own body, and then stooped to close her hand on the Rod. The shaft felt warm, almost alive in her grasp. There was something she could do—should do—but Ashake memory was not strong enough to tell her. No, as Khasti's prisoner she must take up the Rod and carry it, three—four tottering steps forward, to place it once more within the guarding case.

"Well done, Great Lady." He made a sneer of her title as he leaned forward to push down the lid, seal the Rod from sight. "So it is true, you have some control over that thing." Now he swung the box up before her, holding it steady at her heart level and watching its surface. Once more the frown line appeared and he shook his head, perhaps denying the path of his own thoughts.

"You see, Princess," he said to Idieze, "how the new knowledge confronts and vanquishes the old? She is now as obedient to my control as might be a hunting leopard in leash."

"She is dangerous, too. She can be our deaths," Idieze retorted.

"Quite so. Yet it was you who brought her here, Princess."

"Because we must have a hostage until our plans are full ripe. They deem her the Heir, they will not want to lose her."

"So you have thought it all out?" Khasti smiled—coldly. "There is no need for the old methods of hostages and bargains. Did we not agree, Princess, that the time has come to sweep away the past and strike out anew, unburdened by age-old superstition and custom?"

"We have not yet the strength—"

"We have all we need—for the present. If more must be sought, we know well where to discover it."

Idieze gazed at him in open bitterness. Maybe she was beginning to realize now, Tallahassee suspected, that the power behind the Emperor Userkof would not be his wife after all, but this other.

"Then what do we do with her?" She stabbed a finger at their prisoner as if she wished it were steel aimed to take the other's life.

"She will be very safe, Princess—with me." As he uttered those words Khasti let the whirling disk grow still, thrust it back into the folds of his robe. But before Tallahassee, released from that compulsion, could move to save herself, his hand came into the open again holding a cylinder. Once more there was discharged into her face the same narcotic spray that had brought her prisoner here. She remembered crumpling forward and that was all.

She roused slowly, but now she played no game

of trying to confuse her captors concerning her state, for she had an idea that she could achieve nothing by that a second time. Around her shone light, bright enough to make her blink, and she heard odd sounds she found hard to identify.

The surface under her was level and hard as she levered herself up on her arms to look about. She was—caged! There was indeed a mesh of netting secured to four stout posts which kept her in one section of a very large chamber. But there was far more than her own cage here.

Tallahassee had no difficulty in identifying objects that would have been totally strange to Ashake. This was a laboratory of sorts, hardly differing from those in which she had once been a student. To her left stood a clicking box which reached nearly to the ceiling, but elsewhere there were two long tables crowded with retorts, bottles, instruments. And the air was slightly acrid with the fumes of chemicals.

On the nearest table there stood a much smaller cage, fashioned exactly like hers but of slightly different shape, and in that lay the Rod, out of its box again. Even in this strong light Tallahassee believed she saw a shimmer of radiance about the gem that was its head. Beside it lay something else—the Key—or at least an ankh which was enough like the one she had seen in Jayta's hand to be its twin. Yet it had not been displayed earlier as part of Idieze's loot.

There was something—a sudden small spark of Ashake memory stirred at the sight of it. But it faded quickly when Tallahassee tried to define it more clearly. She was left with the feeling that with the Rod and the Key together something could be done for her own defense and perhaps return attack against those responsible for bringing her here.

The cage did not have any visible door, and when she tentatively reached out her hand toward the mesh there was a warning reflex that made her wary of touching it. She would not sacrifice her single garment, but the cloth about her head might be used.

Carefully Tallahassee twisted it into a hard knot and then gingerly touched one end—holding it as far from her fingers as she could—to the screen wall. There came an instant flare as Tallahassee froze. What if her hand or arm had come in contact with that? Now she sat cross-legged in the middle of her cage and tried to see ahead—though the future was more than unpredictable.

Her thoughts were unpleasant and led nowhere, but it was some time before she began to realize that she was not alone in this room. Though she arose to her feet and turned slowly around, giving a long and searching survey to every portion of the long room, there was no one else. And the room itself was very open, with no screened corners or places she could not view.

But—she was not alone!

Some spy device? Tallahassee could well believe that such might be turned on her. Only she could not sense such a thing! That would be impossible. Therefore the identity was of another kind. Identity—yes, this was the same sensation she had had in her own—or Ashake's home—that there was a definite personality, unseen, perhaps unhearable (if it was trying to communicate), yet none the less present.

Slowly Tallahassee settled back on the floor of the

cage. She was attempting something now that was very new to her. How does one locate a thing that is invisible (for this time there was not the least hint of the shadows she thought she had previously seen on such occasions) but which is here?

She set about methodically quartering the room, studying each part with a painful intensity, trying to "listen," if one might term it that, with her mind. Not there, nor there—nor there . . . Bit by bit she became somehow convinced that each judgment, ruling out a portion of the chamber, was correct.

In the end—she knew!

It hung close to the other cage, the cage where lay the Rod and the Key.

Who? Idieze had spoken of using her as a hostage, a term that presupposed there were those left who might bargain for her life. Naldamak, perhaps, on her return? The Followers of the Upper Way, locked now within their city temple? Or Jayta and Herihor? But had there not been that clean sweep of death at the villa which she had made herself halfway accept? She remembered that Khasti had pushed aside the suggestion of hostages as of little account. And this was Khasti's own stronghold—Tallahassee had no doubt of that at all.

They had sought always, those of the Upper Way, for things that might be termed of the spirit—for control over their own minds, the sharpening and lessoning of their own talents. Khasti was plainly one who was achieving, outside himself, something of their same ends. That he had succeeded in part was why she was here. Hypnotism, that must be the answer to that swinging disk that had compelled her to his will.

Also there was the chemical which rendered one so speedily unconscious, as well the initial stealing and hiding of the Rod and the Key in another plane of consciousness, the one that was her own. What other weapons and tools had he devised?

It was still there, that thing. Now and again she tested her strange sense of awareness and always found the same answer. Was it the identity of the messenger who had wrought Khasti's will in transporting the Key and the Rod and then been "locked out" by Jayta's quick action in the desert? Could she communicate with it or him? Would she dare to try? Now that Khasti had the two symbols of power in his hold he might well free his messenger—or could he?

Tallahassee's hands balled into fists. There was so much she wanted to—had to—know. And all she could reach were guesses.

There came a sharp sound at the far end of the room. Here there were no hanging curtains such as she had seen at the villa, but rather a door of the kind she had known most of her life. Khasti, his long grey robe exchanged for a sleeveless, knee-long smock of white, came purposefully down the aisle between the two lengthy tables of equipment to face her.

He must have noted at once the burned edge of the cloth knot which she had thrown down beside her, for now he smiled.

"You have already realized the folly of any thought of escape; you were quick," he commented. "How did you guess that there might lie some such danger in the walls about you?"

"I knew," she returned with all the calm she could

command. "Just as," something made her add, "I know that we are not alone here now."

He looked around quickly, even a little startled, which displayed a small sense of unease in him that Tallahassee had not believed he would show. She marked it in her mind as a chink in his facade of complete authority.

Now he laughed. "Spirits of the air, Great Lady? Or the shadow of Apedemek Himself waxing strong to give freedom to His Chosen?"

"What is here, barbarian"—deliberately she gave to that word all the opprobrium it held among the nobility—"is not of Apedemek, nor of the Way, but of your dealing. It hangs now above the Things of Power." She pointed to the caged Rod and Key as if she could indeed see some shadow there. "It was sent by you, so it returns to you."

He had turned his head to look in the direction she had pointed. Once more he laughed.

"Do you seek to enweb me with your ancient follies? I know better than to believe such."

Tallahassee shrugged. "Believe or not, Khasti—but Akini is here." From whence had come that name into her mind? She could not have told, she had only said it aloud as if it had been that moment whispered into her ear—or called to her despairingly from a long, long distance.

His eyes swung back to her. "You know much, Great Lady. But it will do you no good to use the name of a dead man to make me believe in your 'Power.' Such a name could well be known already to those who have served your cause. I say that that cause is dead, just as you are dead when and if I will it so.

Do you believe me? Yes, in the innermost part of you, you do. Good, now we understand each other. And I have yet to meet the man or woman who will not bargain for life itself.

"If you will give me your knowledge—such as how you blasted that weak fool Userkof without laying finger on him—of the energy that abides in this"—he waved to the caged Rod—"then we can deal together. Did you think that I would make any lasting compact with Userkof and that she-leopard who moves him about at her whim? They have been of use. Now they are no longer. One can wipe them away as dust from the hands."

"You want the Old Knowledge, yet you say it is no longer of any worth," Tallahassee returned. "It seems with your own speech you contradict yourself."

"Do I? Not so, Great Lady. That there is a portion of the unexplained, and perhaps the usable, in your knowledge, that I am willing to concede. Amun has endured a long time, and before that was Meroë, and earlier still Egypt. What you possess now must be only the near-worn-out crumbs of what was once a vast alien science. And there are other ways of achieving a return to that day—shorter and straighter ways. Let me learn the secret of such power as these can generate"—again he pointed to the smaller cage—"and there is nothing I cannot aspire to! Would you rise to set foot upon the very moon above us, Great Lady? Who knows that that might not be done!"

Though enthusiasm colored his voice, she sensed his falseness. This was how he wooed those dissatisfied with the past to join in his dream of the future. Did he think that one with the Talent could not read him for what he was—one who would rule, draw power into his hands, until he believed himself Lord of Life and Death?

The girl did not answer, only locked stares with him. One small part of her senses told her that whatever had brooded above the caged talismans now had drawn closer to him.

"Does Akini whisper in your ear, Khasti? He stands close enough now to lay hand upon your shoulder."

"So—you loose your witchcraft? Well, do not believe that it will do aught for you here. I have had secrets out of brains in plenty, Great Lady. Do not think that I will suffer yours to escape me. See—I shall give you but a small taste of what can be done."

He strode to the click box, pushed with his forefinger upon a certain place. Tallahassee jerked. It was as if a band had settled about her head, was closing, squeezing inward. Fear brought a sour taste to her mouth.

Then Ashake memory came without her tapping it. This is what he wishes, do thus and thus. All life is a state of mind, use your mind as a tool. . . .

It was as if she were able to retreat into herself, passing swiftly over some well-known path into a place of safety where no pain or fear could reach, a castle where the core of her identity could hold the walls against all assault.

She had believed that she could not find in Ashake memory those portions that dealt with the Power—yet this was such a one. Perhaps it was fear of that which had turned the proper key to let her in.

Thus—and thus—and thus!

She saw shadows, the very cage that held her became

a wispy thing, like a cobweb, to be struck lazily away if such was her will. And Khasti—he was not a man, but rather a beam of light, pulsing a lurid red-purple, the color of arrogance and self-belief which no man should hold within himself. For all knowledge comes from the Fountain of Life, and such as Khasti deliberately deny that Fount and say it is naught.

There was a snap, a sharp return to the focus of normality. Khasti was himself again, standing by the machine, studying her with the frown line very deep carven between his eyes. Now he smiled, slowly, as had Idieze in her time, with the same tasting of a sweet that he would prolong to the utmost.

"So you are a little more perhaps than I had thought," he said. "Yet, in the end, we shall come to terms, my terms. And, because of your stubbornness, those terms will grow harsher the longer you withstand me."

He strode away, as if he had set her completely out of mind. Tallahassee drew a long breath and then another. But her attention was all for Khasti's back. Not because she feared his return or another attack, but because behind him, though he walked under the direct lighting of this place, which could support no shadow and did not, there trailed a tenuous something that she now could see. That which had kept watch above the Rod had now materialized farther, to cling to Khasti almost like a tattered cloak.

He paused at the far end of the room to bend over a table. Tallahassee thought she could see a sheet of paper laid there on which he was concentrating his gaze. The wraith hung about, seeming to nudge first one of the man's unyielding shoulders and then the other, striving to draw attention to itself, or so the girl believed. Yet Khasti displayed no sign that he knew of its presence. And the girl thought that that was the truth.

She waited for it to come drifting back to the cage of the Rod, as Khasti set aside the sheet of paper and now busied himself with the apparatus on the table. Instead it seemed to slip back into the air and was lost, nor could she sense its presence any longer. But she knew its name—Akini. And, knowing that, by the very ancient lore, she had a small bit of control over it, or would, if she remembered the proper ritual.

Now she was left to consider what had happened to her during that period of time when Khasti had striven to bring her to heel with his machine. He had failed in whatever purpose he had worked to gain. But she was still a prisoner, and so were the Rod and Key. Tallahassee did not expect any help from the outside to come thundering in to her rescue, even though she continued to doubt that Khasti had things as well under his control as he would have her believe.

There was one point he had openly made—that he was no longer, if he ever was, working to set up Userkof as Emperor. Tallahassee was not certain of the temper of the people. Would they accept a commander, a ruler not of the Blood? They appeared to have accepted the closure of the Temple, which was against all right and law and which once would have brought out a mob, squalling and fighting to get at the blasphemer who had ordered such a move.

He had offered to bargain with her, but more rightly he would in the end go straight to the source and bargain with Naldamak, the Empress. The woman

who wore the triple crown was not now the same girl
Ashake had called sister in the long ago. By delibera-
tion, and through sorrow and loss, the woman in her
had sunk so deep into the ruler that now she was
forever remote and gave the impression of one who
thought first of abstractions, and only last of human
emotion, liking, hating, fearing.

Against such could Khasti use that strange weapon of
hypnotism (for that surely was what the whirling disk
was) and so make Naldamak his dupe? Then outwardly
their world would continue the same, while inwardly
he wrought a different life, overtaking the old.

Naldamak had been too set apart—Ashake memories
had only the outward appearance, some guesses, to
offer. This could indeed happen and very logically.
Then why had Khasti suggested a bargain, attempted
to force it on her—the Heir?

Because she was who she was. Naldamak had taken
solemn oath she would not marry again, nor could
she under the law now when her sterility had been
judged complete. But with her Heir . . .

Tallahassee nodded. Even situated as she now was,
she could find a wry smile for Idieze's fallen hopes.
The wife of Userkof, instead of furthering her own
cause, had played neatly into Khasti's hands by bringing the Heir within his reach. She wondered if Idieze
realized that; certainly she was not stupid enough to
believe that she could command her one-time ally
any more.

Khasti poured greenish liquid from one beaker
into another and brought it closer, to add the contents, drop by careful drop, to a bowl upon the table
only a little beyond the cage of the Rod. There was

a nasty smell, so irritating that Tallahassee coughed in spite of her efforts to remain quiet.

Having finished his task the man raised his head to look at her, as he picked up the bowl in one hand.

"Perhaps a chance"—he held the bowl up so she could not miss seeing it—"to forestall the imminent death of our dear Prince. A rather slim chance, I believe. But since I am called upon for miracles, so will I do my best. The Princess Idieze . . ." He shook his head mockingly. "Alas, Great Lady, since she cannot call for your blood openly, I think she will try most energetically to obtain it in other and more hidden ways. Not because she loves her dear Lord, but because a crown she thought very firm, if invisible, upon her brow has been dashed away.

"Well, it is a hope. As for you, Great Lady, occupy yourself with thoughts also—namely how long can even one who is Temple-trained lie pent without food or water. Food—maybe the longer. They say that those having the Talent are nourished rather than exhausted by fasting. But water is another thing."

And as if his words had been a key to open the door for the demands of her body, Tallahassee's tongue moved within a mouth that seemed suddenly parched. The mental image of water brought a terrible thirst to rack her.

-10-

The thirst induced by that suggestion from Khasti became a torment. Tallahassee rested her head upon her arms folded over her knees as she hunched in the cage. He had reached her once with the whirling disk that had put her under his command; had he done it more subtly again by words alone? She fought to control her thoughts—to shut away mind pictures of running water, of cups full and waiting for her to pick them up.

Did Khasti believe he could set her at the screen in a frenzy of thirst and so be rid of her? Drip—drip— A sound hammered at her control. Slowly she raised her head, peered at the laboratory beyond. There was a sink fashioned of heavy stone, fed by a pipe. And from that the liquid was falling drop by drop, though she had not noticed nor heard that before. Was this but a refinement of torture arranged by Khasti?

She closed her eyes again, tried to shut her ears to that sound, monotonous, somehow deadly to her control. That Khasti had meant exactly what he said, she had no doubt. He would use her body to get at her mind . . .

Panic lashed at her. She covered her mouth swiftly with both hands lest she scream out in fear. That was his weapon—fear. But her defense was the anger she nurtured in herself as a wall against her own despair.

Drip—drip—

She shook her head wildly, as if by that gesture she could shut out the sound. But that was not the way to fight. Her best weapon lay in one place, of that she was sure, Ashake memory. As she had done earlier she began to test, to draw on that knowledge, becoming more and more aware of the tatters in it—the blanks which, if filled, might have served her.

Ashake had gone through the long ordeals of the Temple, had learned there control of the natural processes of her own body that were only rumored as possible in Tallahassee's own world. Therefore somewhere there must lie an answer to this. . . .

The palms of her hands were wet with sweat as if the cage once more was heating, around her, yet the mesh wires remained dull and fireless. She forced herself to breathe slowly, evenly. Thus—thus . . .

Again, it was as if she had broken through a wall, tapped a new reserve of strength she had not known existed. But—hold—do not be too quickly sure. As if she crept along some very slippery path with extinction waiting on either side, Tallahassee explored, to hold, finally to use, that bit of memory. The sensation of thirst receded. It was still there, yes, but it no longer made an unthinking creature of her.

She opened her eyes, tested her control by watching the drip of the pipe. For now—yes—she could hold!

But, the door beyond that pipe was opening slowly, as if by stealth. A moment later a figure slipped through, shut that portal quickly. Idieze hurried down the aisle between the tables, came to front the cage.

For a moment she only stood, surveying Tallahassee. However, this time there was no glint of malice in her eyes, no mocking smile to see her enemy so entrapped.

"Listen." She moved within touching distance of the wire netting. "You have powers. Even though that one has entrapped you, still he dares not put finger to that for himself." She pointed to the Rod. "He—he thinks to use you to accomplish his desire—"

"That being," Tallahassee commented dryly, "the rule of Amun for himself."

"Yes." Idieze's lips were tight against her teeth. "He says he will try to cure my Lord—I think he lies."

"And he has no more use for you?"

Idieze's expression became one of blazing fury. "This—this barbarian—and more than barbarian. He is not even human, not of this world! Oh, he thinks that is safely hidden, but there was the knowledge Zyhlarz gained. He came into this world through some demon-opened door. Where think you he learned this?" Her outflung hand indicated the laboratory.

"You were willing enough to accept his help, demon-inspired or not," Tallahassee pointed out.

Idieze laughed. "Why not? We thought then that he lived by our favor alone. We could expose him for what he was—something that had no right to live. He promised us—showed us . . ."

"Enough to make you believe, but not enough to warn you," Tallahassee continued for her. "It was his idea, was it not, to hide the Rod and Key out of time?"

Idieze brushed her hand across her forehead dislodging the set of her formal wig, but making no attempt to adjust it.

"Yes. But that did not serve, for you returned them. Yet if he can open such a door once, it can be done again—and he can draw through those to serve him."

"You have not the mind of a child, Idieze, nor are you one whose thoughts have been emptied by the Greater Evil. Surely you knew that this would come of? . . ."

Idieze bit the knuckles of her clenched fist. Tallahassee wanted to laugh. Did Idieze think she could so deceive one with the Talent? (The Talent? queried another part of her mind which she did not take time to answer.) The woman's complete reversal of purpose was not to be trusted, of course. This was another ploy, probably set by Khasti for the purpose of weakening Tallahassee's own will. But if he believed that she could be won by such as this, what a very low estimate he must hold of her.

"He . . ." Idieze did not answer her question but switched to another track entirely. "He is not like other men, I tell you. He believes that all women are weak of will and purpose. He despises secretly our people because they will listen to women, be ruled by them!"

"Yet you believed he would listen to you, be controlled by you," Tallahassee pointed out. "So I ask again—why?"

"Because I did not know!" Her voice was shrill and high as if that question had in some way goaded her beyond endurance. "It was not until my Lord was struck down that he revealed himself truly—"

"You are contradicting yourself now. Have you not said that you had already learned he was not of our kind?"

"I do not know what I say!" Her hands, made into fists, were lifted as if to beat in the wire of the cage, perhaps reach Tallahassee. "We knew he was different, but not how different. He spoke to me—me—as if I were a barbarian slave. He—there was that in him which he had not dared show me before."

"Not dared—or not cared?" Tallahassee asked. "But why come you now to me? You have seen me safely imprisoned by his device. What can I accomplish?"

Idieze shook her head from side to side. "I do not know. But you are learned of the Upper Way, surely there is something you can do."

"Perhaps. Reach out and bring me the Key and the Rod—" Tallahassee challenged her. "Then we shall see."

Idieze actually turned as if to catch up those talismans. Then she shrank back.

"If I touch what holds them, I die."

"So I have thought," Tallahassee commented dryly. "Thus you are caught in your own fine trap. But what of the others—those in the Temple? Have you appealed to Zyhlarz?"

"There is a guard on the temple—not of men—but

of one of his things. No one has come forth for three days."

"And those who were my own guards—did you make them sleep and then cut their throats perhaps?" Tallahassee forced her voice to an even tone, just as she had forced control on her body.

"No!" Idieze stared at her. "To sleep, yes, when we took you. And maybe for a day thereafter. But they cannot come. Khasti has set his guards upon the city itself, so only those of his following may enter and none can leave. He waits to entrap the Empress so."

"So having safely taken New Napata he can do all—"

"No! There is one thing he cannot do!" Idieze interrupted. "He cannot take up the Rod. He tried it when it came into his hands before and failed. That was why he sought to hide it in a place he thought no other could reach. He cannot hold the Rod any more than could Userkof."

"You saw him try?" demanded Tallahassee.

"Yes. In his hand he held a box—so small a box. That he passed over the Rod and from it came a clicking, so that swiftly he snatched it away. But he had one who served him—whom he held by the strength of his eye and his will—and that one took the Rod—and vanished!"

"But that one did not suffer from the Rod?"

"Khasti put on his hands gloves that were very heavy. With those he gripped the Rod so no hurt came to him."

"He can banish the Rod again, can he not? And, if he can do many strange and wonderful things, can he not rule without it?"

Idieze stared at her now. "But you know whereof the Rod is made. It is the heart of our nation—our people! Without it we are finished. Why do you say that the Rod is naught and Khasti can rule without it?"

A bad mistake, Tallahassee realized instantly. Those of Amun were conditioned by the centuries to that belief. And if indeed the Rod were taken from them they would crumble as a state, die out as a people, because they believe this would be so.

"Yet he took and hid it," she pointed out.

"Only for a space was that to be. He had knowledge of where it lay—and only four knew that it was gone. Until you and Jayta divined it!"

"But you took it—and me."

Idieze pounded her fists together. "Userkof is of the Blood, none has denied it. The Empress does not wed, she has withdrawn much from the world. And you—you are of the Upper Path. What have you to do with ruling? Userkof was the Emperor's own son. Why should he not be ruler here?" Her words tripped over one another in a rush. "In other nations it is the king's own son who follows him—"

"Among the barbarians," Tallahassee pointed out. "Of them you have more intimate knowledge than do I. You speak of the Rod as being the heart of our nation. Well, to it are wedded our own customs in turn. We do not follow barbarian ways."

"Throw my blood against me if you will! Yes, my grandmother was of the western sea people—but she was none the less for that. She was the daughter of a king—the which you are also."

So their suspicion of Idieze's blood mixture had been the truth. Not that that mattered to Tallahassee.

"What matters now whose blood runs in our veins? It is enough that Khasti has been turned loose to do his will. And since you know him better than do I, what do you propose then?" She brought them back to the main matter. And she indeed wished to have Idieze's answer to that.

When the other hesitated, Tallahassee asked another question. "How is this cage in which I sit controlled? I have learned there is energy in its sides so I cannot hope to batter my way out."

Idieze shook her head. "I do not know. I have been in this room only once before. And then Khasti said that death lay all around for the unwary and not to touch aught that was here."

"Then why did you come?" persisted Tallahassee. "To tell me how hopeless it is to struggle against this barbarian you sought to use as a tool, who now turns easily in your hand to threaten you?"

"I came because—because for all Khasti has said— the Talent is. And there is that in the Upper Way which is as powerful as his machines—to urge you to use that against him before it is too late!"

Tallahassee observed her through narrowed eyes. She had begun this interview by believing Idieze's arrival a subtle attack or feint against her, doubtless set in action by Khasti. But that new sense of hers was able to pick up now that the other was indeed afraid, that she might be quite close to meaning exactly what she said. Though of old the truth was not in this woman, now fear itself was forcing it out.

"I think you mean that—but it would seem too

late," Tallahassee observed. "There is this you can do—alert those who would rise to crush Khasti, open a way for Jayta and Herihor—"

Idieze was already shaking her head. "I have told you—he has his own guards on Napata—"

"Guards can be—" began Tallahassee, when the other interrupted.

"Not these guards—for they are not men, as I said, but rather things he has wrought within this place. We know not how to command them, any more than I can release you from this cage. His ways are not ours."

"Perhaps not." Tallahassee eyed the block wherefrom came that steady clicking, where Khasti's adjustments had brought upon her that searing attempt to master her mind. "It is that"—she pointed—"that, I believe, controls this cage. What can you see on its fore?" The thing sat just at the wrong angle for her to be sure of the front panel.

Idieze moved to stand before it, her fingers laced behind her as if she dreaded above all else any contact with the thing.

"There is a panel; upon it burns a small red light. Below that is a row of buttons."

"How many buttons?"

"Four."

Four, and the farthest one controlled the agony with which Khasti had attacked her. Would any of the other three release her? It was a slim chance but Tallahassee dared not let it go.

"Do not touch the one that lies the farthest to your right. But try the one farthest to your left."

"It is death to touch. He said so!" Idieze made no move to lift her hand.

"If you did not come to aid me—then why?"

"Use your own powers," Idieze returned. "You of the Upper Way have in the past said that so much can be done in that fashion. I have given you warning, but I will not touch this thing born out of demon knowledge."

Then she wheeled and ran, as if she were pursued by some horror. Tallahassee watched her go. Use her own powers indeed. Was Idieze really moved by panic, or had all her talk been a deception, a need for knowing what Tallahassee, with the vaunted Talent, could do? Her conviction that the other had been truthful in her fear was shaken. Truth and falsehood could be skillfully mingled so that one could not be sifted free of the other.

But she was haunted by those four buttons. If she could only have talked Idieze into trying them! She stared at the block to her left as if by will alone she could manipulate its secret, win her freedom.

Will alone! Ashake memory responded with another fragment. Unluckily one on which she could build nothing. She only knew that Ashake herself had once witnessed such a feat of telekinesis. But it had been performed by several adepts acting together, joining their powers. And it was not common.

She closed her eyes, to shut out the here and now, to better catch any hint from that second and mutilated memory. Some details were so clear that she could believe she herself had done such things. Others—they blurred, faded, when she tried to fasten on them. An animal could be mind-touched, brought into control, made to perform any task within its physical ability. But such manipulation of other life forms was not to be indulged in. For all life was to be respected and man should make no slave of any species. Also, where in this room was she to find anything she could influence, even if she might have the power to do so?

Where . . .

Tallahassee grew tense. That—that presence—for which the name Akini stood—it was back. She opened her eyes and looked to the cage of the Rod above which it again hovered.

But—Akini—it—was not alone!

She could see nothing, only sense that there was more than one presence here now. Still she watched, hardly daring to draw a deep breath.

"Akini . . ." Tallahassee moistened her lips, spoke the name aloud.

There fell a queer kind of stillness—as if what she had not seen had halted, was listening intently, that now these presences were focusing on her.

"Akini." Again she spoke the name, this time with a certainty that she was heard.

There was a flow of emotion, striking her suddenly as a wave might batter a cliff—anger, fear—but not aimed toward her. No, that emotion flooded out for her to receive merely because she was present and in some way had established a thread of contact with the identity that generated it.

But the contact seemed all on one side. If it— Akini—knew her or did respond as she thought was happening, he—it—could not reply.

Save that there was a wavering in the air, a shadow, a wraith—like a cloudy outline with a blob for a head, stick arms, legs, a cylinder body. . . . It writhed, as if striving to set what might be suggestions of feet on the floor, still it wavered and floated. Save that somehow it could control its movements enough to front her cage.

Emotion again—a pleading—a voiceless cry for help.

"Akini." She summoned up all her control, for the wavering thing held for her a growing horror, and she had to force herself to look at it. "I am a prisoner—I cannot help you—now."

Did it—he—understand? There was plainly a struggle to hold to even the slight visibility it had. And then one of those stick arms began to stretch, pulling into itself the gossamer material of which the whole was fashioned, until there swam in the air restless coils of what might have been a great serpent—very thin in diameter but long. It looped about the cage from which Tallahassee watched it wide-eyed. She had been able to accept in part the wraith she had first seen, but this was something else again, and still it was spinning out its substance, refining it down and down to threadlike size dimensions.

The thread end poised before the screen of the cage. Tallahassee threw up her hands before her face. She knew what would happen. It strove now to enter between the wires of the deadly mesh! To reach her! Her control snapped. With a cry she sank down, her face against her knees, her arms laced protectingly over her head—though there was no protection, she was certain, that could hold against what hunted her now.

There came a touch, cold, sending a tingle up her arm from the wrist where it had met her flesh. She tried to ball herself more closely together, moaning softly, with no thought now but the need for escape.

Then—it was gone!

Tallahassee need not look up, out into the laboratory, to know that. Its snuffing-out was a mental not a physical thing. For the moment she was only thankful for its withdrawal, for her escape—though what she feared from it she could not have said.

There came the sound of a closing door. Idieze returning? She above all must not see Tallahassee reduced to these straits. The girl fought for control of her shivering body, of her scattered, half-dazed thoughts, and drew on the dregs of her energy to raise her head.

"How is it with you, Great Lady?"

Tallahassee's blurred sight cleared. Khasti! But at this moment Khasti, though he had entrapped her, was safe compared to what had hung in the air, tried to reach her through the netting of her prison walls.

"Do you wish to drink?" he asked with malicious mockery, crossing from the side of the cage to the sink to twist the end of the dripping pipe. A gush of water answered him.

"Water, Great Lady. At this moment I would say you would find this sweeter to the taste than the rarest of wines. Is that not so? . . ."

She shook her head, not so much in denial, as rather to clear her thoughts. Khasti was a man, that other thing . . . She shivered.

"No water? They have trained you well." He turned from the pipe flow and began to swing the disk once more on its glittering chain. But this time she was forewarned and closed her eyes. He could not hypnotize her a second time.

"Stupid female!"

"Was Akini stupid too?" she asked.

"Akini! Where got you that name? Your spies have been busy." There was a new harshness in his voice. By the sound of it, he had moved away from the sink, was coming closer to the cage.

It was as if a hand were laid warningly over her lips. For a second out of time that other was here again. There was anger—toward Khasti—a sharp hint of silence for her.

"As yours must have been in their turn," she answered. But she did not open her eyes, even though she believed she could no longer hear the thin swish of the chain passing through the air.

"It does not matter." He was master of himself once again. "You might wish to know, since he is your kin. Userkof did not 'depart for the west'—as your people so euphemistically put it. He will live—a cripple—and no more thankful to you for that than any man would be. As for you, I leave you to your dreams, Great Lady—and I do not think that this night they will be pleasant ones!"

She could hear the scrape of his sandals on the floor. He had passed her cage, was going to that block bearing the buttons. Another assault upon her mind? She was too worn now—she could not hold—she could not. . . .

Did she or did she not catch the faint click of a button? There was a hum, soft but persistent, walling her in, as if the wires of the mesh were being plucked as might be the strings of a harp—singing—lulling . . . Her head fell forward once more so that her forehead rested on her knees. She tried to prod her will into keeping her awake, but she could not. . . .

There was no cage—instead she walked down a
corridor and she knew what lay at the end. This was
the trial of a novice who must face death and then
rebirth or never tread the Upper Way. Fear walked at
her shoulder, matching step to step with her, but she
did not turn her head to see what form it took. She
fought to breathe evenly, slowly, as one does when
fully relaxed, to make each pace as measured as the
next. Behind her lay years of the Temple training,
before her only this last ordeal, and then she could
prove her right to the Power which she felt struggling
now within her, seeking the outlet that only the initiate could truly give.

There hung the dark curtain of death-in-life and
beyond it was life-in-death to be fronted. Ashake held
high her head as if she already wore the initiate's crown
of victory. Her hand moved, closed upon the curtain
and drew it aside. With the courage of a warrior she
stepped out into the deep dark.

-11-

This was her last trial. By years of training, or learning to know herself and the depths of her thoughts even when they were unpleasant to face, she had been prepared for this moment, to be pitted against the fears from which those thoughts were born. For none can wield the Power until they can command themselves fully.

She was ready. . . .

But something else struggled in her. Not her fear, no. This was urgent, a warning. Ashake hesitated within that all-enveloping dark, tried to understand.

This—this she had done before! She was being made to relive the past by some force outside herself. And that force had only one reason, that through her it could learn secrets which none who knew them must ever reveal.

What was truth, what was a dream? Was this a false warning sent to her as a test? She had no real knowledge of what an initiate faced, save that it

would try her to the utmost. And was the beginning
of such a test the suggestion that it was not the truth
but a lie?

She raised her hands to her head, knew that they
were shaking with the tension building in her.

Truth—lie? Which, oh, which?

Panic—she must not panic! She was Ashake of the
Blood, one destined since birth to walk this path.
Therefore, the truth must be tested by the one way
she had been taught. She disciplined her mind, forced
away the panic, sought those guides that should stand
ready at her call.

They were clear as she pictured them. But, they
were not there! Once more she tried. There was
nothing, nothing at all, nor could she sense that
ingathering of Power which should have drawn
about her.

So, this was not as it should be. But—what had
happened? She swayed as she stood, fighting the force
that would have moved her on—that coercion came
from without, was not born of her own will!

She was Ashake. Who dared play such a perilous
game with one of the Blood? Who dared challenge
the Rod and the Key?

She was Ashake . . . she was . . . she was . . .

Identify itself blurred. Ashake? No, then who? She
thought she moaned, and yet did not hear her cry
ring through this utter dark.

She was Ashake! She must be, for if she set aside
Ashake—then there would be a stranger, and one
could not live as a stranger. No, this assault was part
of something that sought to spy, through her, on the
secrets of the Upper Way. And with that answer, a

steadiness spread through her giddy mind. Who dared use her so? There was only one—Khasti!

As if his name in her mind shattered some spell, the dark, the ritual hallway disappeared. She stood now in the open under the hot sun of the northern desert. Before her lay the battered walls of the oldest shrine. She hurried (or seemed to skim the ground as if she flew rather than touched foot to the sand and grit) toward that.

Here was the temple, battered by time and by the ancient enemies, yet still it stood. Apedemek, whom the ignorant claimed she and her clan worshipped, yet whose great statue stood as only a reminder of something else that could never be caught and held in any stone, no matter how skillful the artist, stood facing her.

The blind eyes stared out above her head, the hands grasping Rod and Key were above her too. Yet the talismans were not stone. They glowed with life, pulsed with force. She had only to reach out and grasp them. Then all that was of the dark would not dare to contain her. Up she reached, straining farther and farther, yet her fingertips could not even touch the end of the Rod. Furiously she struggled, knowing in her mind just how the power of the Rod must be wedded to the power of the Key by the initiate and what would come of such a mating.

She was Ashake, she alone had the right to touch the things of the Past. Within her the Power swelled, as she knowingly drew upon it, for it would seem that as she used it in her need, so did it grow and flow. She was Ashake.

Now the shrine wavered before her eyes as if it were

a painting on fabric. Vast rents appeared from side to side. It tore and was gone, leaving her facing—nothing, an emptiness—that strove to invade her mind, wash free all she knew, even her own identity. No!

She drew upon the Power, pulled it about her as one might pull a cloak against the force of a storm. The emptiness could not reach her. For she was Ashake.

She saw that emptiness in turn break, not tear slowly, as had the shrine, but shatter in an instant. Objects faced her. She was neither in the hall of the temple, nor in the northern desert, she was—

The cage!

And beyond that barrier, Khasti watched her narrow-eyed.

Tallahassee was a little dazed. Still she knew what he had tried to do to her. He would have learned the sacred, the forbidden, by making her relive her initiation in a dream. That he could have sent her so far as he had into the past was frightening—but she had won!

"You are stronger than I thought," he said slowly. "But not too strong. This time I took you to the threshold, the next you shall step across it. Let thirst and hunger weaken your body, and you cannot so well hold out against me."

She made him no answer. Why should she? He stated the terms of their struggle and those she must face.

"I wonder . . ." he continued musingly. "There is something in you that I do not yet understand, and it is not born of your nature. For this thing registers in spite of your stubbornness. Listen well, Great Lady,

I have resources beyond any you can comprehend in this world—"

For the first time she spoke then. "This world? Are you then of another world, Khasti?"

He frowned. Perhaps he had made a mistake. If he had, he decided quickly it did not matter, for he answered her.

"There are worlds upon worlds, Great Lady. Does not your own 'learning' "—and he made of that word a sneer—"hint at such?"

"We all know there are worlds beyond. Look upon the stars which are suns. Many of those warm worlds we cannot see," she returned calmly. But she was inwardly uncertain, he was getting too close, too close to Tallahassee, who had slept while Ashake had fought her dream battle, but she was now awake.

"Your legends," Khasti continued thoughtfully. "What say they of such worlds, Great Lady?"

Ashake shrugged. "Why ask me, Khasti? You must have made yourself familiar with those long ago. Would you tell me now that you come from such a world? Do you expect me to look upon you as a god because you might have knowledge such as we have not? Knowledge varies, it is of many kinds, comes from different sources. Yours is built on what lies about us in this room. It is not ours, nor would any man of our kin be fitted to use it. Therefore, I can believe that it may be unearthly—"

His frown had deepened as he looked at her.

"Such a thought does not alarm you then?"

"Why should it?" she returned. "Did you believe that I would say you were a demon as might those unlearned? There is that in you which is not kin—nor are you like

anything we have heard of among the barbarians. Thus
you must have come from a place we know not, the
proof being that you stand here and now to meddle
dangerously in our affairs." Again she shrugged.

"Meddle dangerously in your affairs." He caught
up her phrase. "Yes, that is how you would see it, I
suppose. But what if I have much to offer you—"

"No merchant offers trade upon the point of a
sword," she snapped and was pleased to see the
answering flash from his eyes. Ah, she had indeed
pricked him then. "You want not a bargain with us,
you want the Empire. For what reason I do not
know yet, unless there is such a boiling of desire to
rule within you that you must seize all you can, as a
greedy beggar stuffs his mouth with both hands and
then reaches quickly for more. Why are you now so
frank with me, Khasti? Is it because you have not
broken me as quickly as you thought to do? Is there
some time limit on your meddling?"

He was silent and she knew a small surge of triumph. If that guess were only right! What time limit,
and set by whom, and for what purpose? She had the
questions, but who would give her the answers? For
she believed in this exchange she had brought more
out of him than any other in Amun knew.

She had angered him, but she did not care.

"For a female you are quick with words, bold
words—"

"Among your kin then, Khasti, are those of my sex
considered the lesser? That is a barbarian belief. I hear
that their women in the north are wed to become the
possessions of the men. With us it is not so. Does
that anger you a little?"

"It angers me not at all. It merely amazes me that your men are such spiritless fools as to allow such a way of life to continue," he said coldly, in spite of the anger she sensed in him. "It is well known that the female mind is inferior—"

"Inferior to what, Khasti?" She had the last word with that, for he did not answer, but turned and strode away. She waited until the door closed behind him, alert to any other move he might make toward the box. It had been the force of the box that had drawn her to the brink of remembering her initiation, thus almost supplying him with some knowledge he pried for.

She was alone once more. He had left the water trickling from the pipe in the sink. Her mouth was dry. Now also her stomach begun to proclaim its emptiness. She folded both arms across it, hugging herself, as if by touch alone she could persuade herself that she was not hungry.

If she could only have talked Idieze into trying that row of buttons. One of the four must release the cage. She remained sealed here at Khasti's pleasure. She tried to occupy her mind with the hints he had dropped. Was he really from off-world? Ashake memory had produced some very ancient tales of "Sky Lords" of incredible learning who had visited Khem to the Two Lands thousands of years ago. Tallahassee's memory was ready to babble less intelligently of flying saucers, and the speculations concerning ancient spacemen giving impetus to the beginnings of civilization in that time and world.

Or could Khasti have slipped through another rift in spacetime such as had entrapped her, merely stepped from another world like this, but one that had followed a different pattern of history? It did not really matter—he was not only here, but well prepared to engraft on Amun his own pattern of living.

She was thirsty! The trickling of the water . . . And she was empty enough to feel weak. How long could she stand up to this? She could not even be sure how long she had been here. That period of induced unconsciousness might have been prolonged past her judgment of time. How long could she last?

Her headache came from the strong light as well as lack of food. And it would seem that her brave fight against the demands of her body was nearly lost. Once more she rested her forehead on arms crossed over her upheld knees. She was very close to the sleep of complete exhaustion.

There was a cold touch on one elbow, a tingling that spread from that point of contact up her arm. She had felt something like that before. Her mind seemed sluggish. What? . . .

She made herself look up. This time her extra sense had been too dulled to alert her. Outside the cage coiled that serpent thing, and it had again inserted a tendril to make contact with her.

Even her fear arose slowly, and she could not make the effort to avoid the thing. It clung to her flesh. And now it seemed no longer so wispy, so tenuous. In dull horror, Tallahassee watched the thread turn milky and opaque. At the same time she realized that it was drawing strength from her in some way. Down that thread traveled the opaque suggestion of new solidity. She reached out her other hand desperately trying to break its hold on her. But she could not. It remained, sucking, sucking.

Tallahassee began to cry weakly. For all her brave words to Khasti, her struggle to remain herself, this she could not fight any longer. She was too worn from the earlier struggle to defend herself.

She crumpled on the floor, moaning a little. Still the thing fed—if you could call this vampire-draining feeding. Then, before she blacked out entirely, it loosed hold. Wonderingly, she saw something else appear in the air before that shimmer, which she identified with Akini. It was milky white and it was a hand. A hand that ended at the wrist. Its fingers were now being flexed as if about to be put to use.

Her mouth open a little in astonishment, Tallahassee pulled herself up on her knees. The hand was moving away from her, propelled through the air as if it had been given some task it must do. The outline kept changing, as if to hold it in shape was almost too great a task.

But it was before the cabinet now—nearing the row of buttons. Another dream? Perhaps one evoked by Khasti to further torment her and drain her obstinate strength so that he could make her wholly his tool?

The hand darted forward. She could not see from her cage just what it had done. But certainly there was no change in the wire mesh around her and, for a moment, she knew a deep disappointment. If the hand thing had not intended to kill, she had hoped a little that it might be here to help. Only—nothing had happened. She was as securely pent as ever.

While the hand was fading, the strange stuff of

which it was formed sloughed away from the shape
of fingers into wisps. It was moving again, shapeless
though it was, not back toward her cage, but rather
to the near table. For a moment, as long as it took
her to blink twice, it hung above the smaller cage
that imprisoned the Rod and Key.

Could it be? . . .

Tallahassee's heart lurched within her. Perhaps she
was not free—as yet—but that other . . . She watched
the shifting blob, which the hand had melted into,
pass through the mesh of the smaller cage, make a
dart at the Rod and as swiftly recoil, not only recoil
but become dispersed into nothingness.

There was a feeling of shock in the air. Akini was
gone, driven away by the very force he—it—had
attempted to use. But what had he done at the control
box? Perhaps turned off whatever unseen defensive
mechanism Khasti had set up to protect what had
been stolen?

Ashake—Ashake knew what could be done. If
Tallahassee surrendered completely to Ashake there
might be a chance. But if she so surrendered could
she ever regain herself?

Only—now she believed that even such a loss as
that was worth a chance to escape. She closed her
eyes, summoned Ashake memory defiantly, opened
her mind to what the other had to give.

Ashake crouched down. Her body was feeble, it was
true, but she could still draw upon some inner energy,
enough, she prayed, to do what must be done. She
fixed her stare on the jeweled head of the Rod.

"Come to me!" she commanded with all the strength
left at her command. "Come to me!"

Slowly the Rod arose from the surface on which it lay, the lighter end sloping upward ahead of the heavy, begemmed top. Now it was pointing upward at a sharp angle, the tip aimed at the woven wires of its cage.

"Come to me!"

The tip touched the cage mesh. There was no reaction. Sweat streamed down Ashake's face, lay wet in her armpits, on the palms of her hands.

"Come to me!"

The tip of the Rod exerted more and more force against the cage. Ashake fought to give it all she had in her. Then the cage tilted, fell to one side with a clatter. And, since it was bottomless, the Rod was free. It whirled around and swooped through the air, aiming straight at Ashake as she called it.

Like a lance it struck the side of her own cage. There was a brilliant flare, which made her cry out as the backlash of radiance struck her. But she had had time to shield her eyes. When she dared to look again she saw that the Rod lay on the floor. But where it had dashed against the cage there was a black patch in which holes appeared to spread. The metal was rotting swiftly as might a broken fungus.

Now she looked beyond that growing hole to the Key and raised a hand weakly.

"Come!" she called for the fifth time.

The Key arose, slower and more sluggishly, since she called now from the very dregs of her failing strength. But it obeyed her, moving in jerks through the air and settling at last in the trembling palm she held out to it.

The hole in the screen was open enough to let her

through. And at the touch of the Key new strength flowed into her. She crawled out into the open, stooped to pick up the Rod, and then, with her weapons in hand, stood to her full height and looked around.

Such a use of the Power had set up a troubling in the whole atmosphere. If there were any within this building who possessed a scrap of the Talent, they would be warned. She waited, using the force renewed in her from the talismans of her people, to listen, with not her ears, but her mind.

She could pick up no instant response to the waves of energy she had projected. But she owed a debt, whether the other had meant to save her or had only been working to liberate the Rod. And debts, for one of those who walked the Upper Ways, lay heavy.

"Akini?" With mind, not voice, she sought the creature who had come to her rescue. She did not know what he wanted with Rod or Key. But manifestly it was not to put them in Khasti's hands, for all that labor had been to free them.

But there was only mind-silence. When Akini had striven to reach the Rod had he—it—been blasted forth to extinction? Somehow Ashake did not believe it.

She tottered toward the sink with its trickle of water from the pipe. Gathering both Rod and Key into a single hand, she held the other under that less-than-finger-wide stream. It filled the hollow of her palm, and she brought the liquid to her lips, sucking carefully, doing this many times until her thirst was at last quenched.

Hunger was still with her but that must wait until she could find food. Purposefully now she started for the door, waveringly at first because of weakness, but each moment that she held the precious talismans it decreased a little, so at last she walked with much of her old, determined stride.

There seemed to be no catch or knob on this inner side. Well, she could use more of the charge of the Rod to burn her way through. But that she would rather not do. She did not want to further deplete its energy.

However, when she set flat palm to the door, its surface shifted slightly so that she inched it forward, listening all the while, hardly daring to breathe lest that faint sound cloud her hearing.

Now that the crack was wide enough, she could see a slice of darkness beyond. After waiting a very long moment more to make sure there was no sound at all, she slipped through.

There was darkness facing her and not too far away, but both Key and Rod radiated light enough for her to see that she was now in a narrow hallway that ran into deeper darkness both left and right beyond the range of the talismans' glow.

She had two choices and no guide as to where each might lead. Not only was there no sound, but, Ashake decided, there was a peculiar emptiness here, as if all that which made life as she knew it had been barred.

Left—right. . . . Her head turned as she quested for some guide as to which way would lead her back to the world she knew. Finally she faced right, holding the Rod and Key before her to give the best light possible, and started on.

-12-

There was no other break in the wall after she left the door of the laboratory. Also the hall narrowed. The way was very dark and there was an odd heaviness in the air. She might be approaching some very ancient tomb which the living had not troubled for a long time. Then the hall ended abruptly in a flight of stairs that led down into a thicker dark, far beyond any radiance of the Rod or Key to pierce.

So she had chosen wrongly. Her path should have been left rather than right. Could she retrace her steps, or might her escape be already discovered?

Tallahassee was deeply tired, in spite of the energy she drew from the talismans. Her hunger was an additional weakness. To go on down into this dark was folly. Back. . . .

Somehow she inched around, looked back. Now a sound reached her. Footfalls, echoing from sandaled feet, where her own bare ones made no noise. There came a flare of light—though it was very small and far away. Someone had flung wide open the door of the laboratory. She was cut off, with only the dark descent left as a way of escape. Khasti!

Her heart beat faster. What strange weapons he could command she had no way of guessing. That he would pursue her, Tallahassee had no doubt at all. But there was one thing. . . .

Steadying her hands with all the control she could summon, she turned fully to face that distant door, raising Key and Rod. She moved them through the air, drawing invisible lines of force, while she recited under her breath the Words of Power. Let him come then. He would meet with something that might not entangle his body, but would strike at his mind, alien though it might be.

Then, with foreboding, she began the descent. The hall above had felt dry and chill, but as she went carefully from step to step downwards, the chill became damp. The air about her, in spite of that odd dead quality, held a touch of moisture.

New Napata was on a river. Did this warren run down close to those sites where the river had been long ago covered over and hidden? She listened, both for an outcry from behind, and for any sound below. What she had done to seal this way in her own defense had drawn from the store of energy in the Rod and Key. Now their radiance was faded, did little more than light a single step ahead. Smells assaulted her nostrils—of wet, or rot, of nauseous things she could not set name to. Still the steps descended into the heart of a dead-black pit. Who had wrought this way and what use it had been in the past she could not imagine. At least it had been unknown to Ashake before.

On the steps led, down and down. Tallahassee was so tired she trembled from head to foot. Only her will kept her mind clear. Clear enough to—

She halted, her feet together on a step slimed with moisture, and raised her head high.

"Akini?" There was a presence here again. No, more than one! They were pressing in against her, as wayfarers in a desolate land might press inward to warm their hands by a camp fire. And what drew them were the talismans!

She was right, one of those was Akini. But who were the others? If she could only communicate, discover what they wanted, for their emotion touched her mind, grew in her thoughts. They were avid. As her own bodily hunger gnawed at her, so did some greater hunger tear at them—a hunger that was centered in what she bore. They did not even seem to be aware of her, only of what she carried.

"Akini!" Again she tried to reach that one presence she could put name to.

"Give—us—the—life. . . ."

Only a flutter of thought, so faint and far away that she could barely pick it up.

The life? Did the Rod and Key mean life to these wisps of identity?

"Life!" The word was no stronger this time, but more imperative.

Ashake took firmer hold on the talismans. It seemed to her that the presences were trying to clutch at what she held, drag them from her grasp. But they were too weak to achieve that.

She took a deep breath and then made her answer: "Guide me hence, if you can—and I, who use the

Power, will also try to give you life!" Could she bargain with these lost things? And if she did strike such a bargain, then how might she fulfill her part of it? She did not know. But there were Zyhlarz, Jayta—the others of the Upper Way—surely among them all they could give these wraiths either life or eternal peace.

That weak plucking at the talismans quieted. But they were not gone. She took heart from that. Perhaps they had understood. If they were creatures of this darkness, they surely knew the ways below.

"Akini?" She made a question of that thought.

There was a touch on her wrist. She started and glanced down. A threadlike tendril rested there. And through it came a thought.

"Forward."

She could only trust in this. If it were a true bargain, she had won. But, since there was no turning back, she must accept what came. Down and down she went. The Akini presence was there, the others too, but they had withdrawn a little, trailing behind her.

They reached the foot of the stair and stood in a place of evil smells and air so thick that she gasped as she went. But she did not have to travel far. On the wall to her right that thread, which had touched her wrist, centered on a block of stone that the radiance showed faintly.

Ashake held closer the Key and the Rod. Here was the line of an ancient arch, but it was filled with blocks of stone, wedged in to seal what once opened there. Ashake raised the Rod, willed its power higher. She tapped with its tip against the top stone, and as she did so she muttered the old chant

of the Builders. This she had never done before.
She was not even sure that she knew all the words
that released such power. And in the days when the
Builders had wrought with the Talent, then there had
been a number together wielding their wills into a
single strong force.

But the stone was moving. Slowly Ashake drew
the Rod back toward her, and the stone followed,
to fall at her feet. So much force expended to loose
a single stone! Could she achieve the withdrawal of
another? She was not sure, but once more she lifted
the Rod and whispered the chant. And once more
a stone obeyed the summons of her Talent.

Three more blocks were so dislodged. She could
not do it again! As she stood she wavered on her feet,
her eyes blurred. But there was a hole—large enough
to crawl through? It would have to be!

Her single flimsy garment was torn, there were
bleeding gouges in her skin, grazes on her arms and
legs which burned. But she had won through, to stand
in yet another dark way. But this lacked the dampness of that other, and there was now a current of
air blowing about her, enough to hearten her.

Ashake limped forward on bruised and bleeding
feet, weaving from side to side of that narrow way,
until first one shoulder and then the other scraped
painfully along the stone. But the straight path was
very short. Again she faced steps, very narrow steps,
leading up into the dark.

She pulled herself up from one to the next. All the
world had narrowed for her to that one rough staircase.
And she was not aware, until she came upon it, of a
landing some four steps wide. In the wall to her right, a

little below her eye level so she had to stoop a fraction to gaze through it, was a peephole from which came a wan light. She could see only a small fraction of what lay beyond, but it was enough to both startle and encourage her. For she gazed into the inner courtyard upon which fronted Naldamak's own suite in the Inner Palace!

There was no sign of a door here, and anyway she had no wish to come blindly into the open—not until she knew more about the situation that might face her. Up again . . .

Tallahassee did not count the steps, but here was another landing. No, it was the end of the stair itself. And when she peered through another hole it was into the dark, as if this hole was covered. Taking Key and Rod both into one hand, she felt along the wall before her. Surely there lay some way of opening it!

Her fingers dropped into a hollow in the stone, which was barely perceptible, even when she held the talismans close to it. And it was her sagging weight as she leaned forward that must have released the hidden catch.

Ashake tumbled out through a narrow opening, to become entangled in a hanging which she nearly ripped from its high wall fastenings as she fell. Her head and shoulders lay on the carpet of the room she had entered so secretly, and the smell of delicate perfume, the freshness of good air filled her nostrils, cleansed her lungs of the foulness filling those dark ways below.

She was so spent that she did not even try to move for a space. Khasti himself could have stood before her at this moment and she would not have been able to summon the strength to face him.

It was a frightened cry that brought back her wits. She lifted herself a little, with one arm braced under her, and looked up hazily into a face she knew.

"Sela—"

"Great Lady! But where—"

"Sela," she forced out the name again with her remaining strength. "None—must—find—me. . . ."

Naldamak's old nurse—would she, or could she, understand?

"No—one—Sela. . . . The—Candace is in danger. . . . No—one—must—find—me. . . ."

"Great Lady, none shall." It was an old voice, thin, and weak, but there was the same decision in it Ashake had always heard. "Lady, I cannot carry you; can you walk?"

The words were very far away. Ashake fought to get to her knees.

"Hungry—so hungry. . . . No—one—must—know. . . ."

The Key and the Rod—they lay where she had dropped them on her fall. Now she drew them to her.

"Sela," she said to the woman bending over her. "A cloth—for the precious things. They must be hidden!"

"Yes, Great Lady." There was a soothing in that voice. The age-hunched figure was gone and back again, before Ashake could move, over her arm a long strip of finely embroidered stuff, the cover from a table. She knelt stiffly before Ashake and spread it out, sitting back then on her heels as the girl, making slow work of it, rolled the talisman into a tight bundle.

"Sela—where? . . ."

"Great Lady, trust me—safe they shall be!" Sela had gotten to her feet and into her outstretched hands Ashake thankfully surrendered her trust. If there was one faithful soul in all of New Napata, it was Sela for whom Naldamak was and always had been the whole world.

Ashake did not remember how she came into the bed. But when she awoke it was dark in the room save for a distant lamp. And beside that Sela sat on a stool, nodding.

"Sela." Her own voice was hardly more than a hoarse whisper but it brought the nurse hurrying to her side.

"Lady, Lady," she patted Ashake's shoulder where a dressing of soft ointment was spread to take some of the sting out of the graze that had burned there. "Do you remember now?"

"Remember?"

"You talked so wild, and words I did not know. All the time I fed you the soup and wine—and you did not seem to recognize me. And your poor arms, your legs. Lady, what happened to you?"

"I was a prisoner—for a while." She had spoken words Sela did not know . . . that other part of her memory began to stir. She was Ashake—no, she was someone else. Who? Tallahassee! So that part of her was not forever buried as she feared that it might be.

"The Candace?"

Sela's face wore an expression of worry. "Great Lady—they will tell me nothing! And since you came I have stayed within these walls. There is a maidservant—she is new come since you lived in Napata—but she is of my home village and her

I can trust. It is she who brought us food. And she says that there is talk that the Candace has been—lost! Over the desert when a storm arose. This is whispered widely in the city. But"—she raised her chin defiantly—"I will not believe it. My dear Lady—she is wiser, very wise. And she has good reason to watch even shadows. Also she had with her the Sworn-to-Sword—twelve of them—though they went disguised in the dress of lady-in-waiting or maidservant. Think you such would let her come to harm? I do not think she was lost in any storm, rather that she hopes her enemies will believe that. But you—Great Lady—what happened to you whom we thought were safe at Gizan?"

Tallahassee gave an edited version of what had happened since she had been kidnapped from the villa. Sela drew in her breath with a hiss.

"That there is a secret way now open to this room! That is evil, Great Lady. But you have brought the Precious Things safe out of danger and when the Candace returns—then there will be an accounting!" She nodded her head vigorously enough to send the edge of her sphinx headdress flapping.

"This maid of whom you speak—" Tallahassee sat up in bed. Her sore and bruised body protested every movement so that she felt she, for one, was not in her present state prepared to take on battle with anyone—let alone an enemy as strong as Khasti. "Can she find a way to reach the villa? I do not know whether Jayta and Herihor still live—"

"They do, Great Lady. You slept for two days and three nights—you seemed to drowse even when I brought food and fed you. So you do not know. The

Prince General holds the northern roads, all of them. He summoned his own regiments of command and four others which are loyal and to be trusted. I think he strives to keep open a path for the Candace. And the Daughter-of-Apedemek has come before the walls of Napata and formally demanded entrance—she was seen by many. But the Temple—it is shut by some vile sorcery of this demon from the desert, and none has seen or heard of those who were so locked within.

"The Prince Userkof is said to be suffering from a fever, so his Lady commands in his household. And no man or woman knows where Khasti hides himself or what mischief he plots." Sela sounded out of breath as she finished that rush of words.

"Can a message be sent to the Prince General?"

"Great Lady, there is some strange wizardry set upon the gates. They stand open but no one can pass through. And the people are greatly afraid of this thing. But—Lady—there is something . . ." Sela twisted her robe in both hands. "I saw this for my own self when I went upon the outer balcony watching for the Candace—to see if perhaps her flyer comes."

"What is it?"

"That man cannot pass whatever barrier the vile one has put there at the gates, but animals may. It was a fruit seller's donkey that broke from its master as he argued with the guard. And it passed beyond the gates as if there was nothing there but the empty air we see. But when the master would run after it he could not follow. And the donkey went on down the road."

"An animal can break through." Tallahassee considered the point. "And a bird?"

"Those in the garden fly high," Sela answered. "But how can an animal serve your purpose, Great Lady?"

Pigeons could—if this was her own time, Tallahassee thought, and she had a convenient coop of trained ones. But a wandering donkey, even a horse, who might stray through the gate could not be a reliable messenger. It was a silly and baseless idea, yet her mind clung to it.

Had she been able to reach the Temple, she believed that there would have been no problem. There were a few trained in the Talent who could travel outside their bodies—visit other places. Such a one could reach Jayta and pass a message, for their training was aimed in part toward such encounters. Unless Khasti had foreseen that also and erected some barrier such as the cage he had imprisoned her in until the wraith—

The wraith—Akini!

She turned to Sela. "Sela, you know much of the palace and all those who dwell within it. Have you ever heard the name Akini?"

It was as if she had reached out her fist to thump the attendance gong.

"Akini! Great Lady—what do you know of Akini? Does not his mother come daily to sit in the outer court waiting for him? She has wept until she has no more tears in her, but still she will not believe that he has gone without a word to her. He was fan bearer to the Prince Userkof and between two days he was gone! None know where—only his mother will not believe that he went off with the barbarian—"

"The barbarian? What barbarian?"

"He was as one who came to New Napata with a message for the Candace, but she had already gone north. By our laws, as you know, he could not stay past three sunsets. But the Prince Userkof received him, and it is said that the barbarian took a liking to Akini and offered him good payment to return to the coast, speaking for him with those peoples through whose land he must go. But the mother swears that Akini had no intention of doing such a thing, and she has petitioned that the Candace's officers find what has become of her son."

"This barbarian—what manner of man was he?"

"Great Lady, as you know, the northern barbarians are not like us—they have hair of different colors and their skins are very light. But this man was different yet again. He might have been one of the Old Ones out of Khem, for he looked akin to those ancient stat-ues which are kept in the Palace of Far Memory. He spoke our language badly, and ever he looked about him as if he found all to be strange indeed."

"Did he seek out Khasti?"

"Not so, Great Lady. And as you know he was directly under the eyes of the Sworn Swords while he was in New Napata, for barbarians do not roam our cities freely. No, he wanted the Candace, and when he asked for whoever ruled in her place that one"—Tallahassee knew Sela referred to Idieze—"sent him word that her husband was of the Blood. But whether he knew that he was not dealing with the truth or not, I do not know. They had but one for-mal audience and did not meet again. So, at last the barbarian left . . ."

Another Khasti? They had all they needed with

the one they had, Tallahassee thought ruefully. So Akini—he had been real—a person Sela had knowledge of. But what was Akini now? And how had he been so altered, or entrapped, as to exist only as a wraith, a troubling of air? It was Khasti's doing, of that she was sure. If she could only reach Zyhlarz, for even Ashake memory could not supply the answer to such a riddle as this.

There remained the other question—how might she contact Jayta and Herihor, reassure them that the talismans were out of enemy hands and safe? Animals could go out, but, undirected, what could animals then do? Undirected—she began to consider that. Dogs were noted at running down masters at a distance, nosing out nearly extinguished trails. Cats had been known in her own time and world to cover long distances to be reunited with families who had moved away, or had lost them from cars during trips.

Herihor, as became his rank, had a dwelling in New Napata, but he was seldom there. Certainly not enough to keep a pet animal. But . . . she must think—plan—on a single small and very wild chance.

"Sela, who is at the Prince General's dwelling now? Can you find out?"

"I can find out, though it may take a little time, Great Lady—there are but few I can trust here. However, there is one of the Sworn Swords who had the fever and is now well. Her, I helped to nurse. I can bring her to you, and she will be better able perhaps to discover what occurs in the city. But first, Great Lady, I urge you to eat. You are very weak and your body is so worn that you look as if you have had the fever!"

"Well enough."

Sela apologized that the food she brought was mainly cold but the maid could only smuggle a portion of regular food on the tray supposedly intended for Sela herself, who added dried dates, cheese, small loaves of bread which she could conceal about her person.

Sela had helped Tallahassee into one of the Candace's plainer robes, settling a folded linen headdress over her cropped hair. But looking in the mirror the girl was forced to admit that she did resemble one recovering from an accident. She still felt thirsty and drank deeply of the fruit juice and water Sela brought her. But at least she was ready to face this Amazon guard of Naldamak's, on whom her plan, hazy as it still was, depended so much. When Sela brought the young warrior to her room later that night Tallahassee still wondered if one could do such a thing.

"Great Lady!" The wonder in the newcomer's eyes was clear, but her salute was instant. And Ashake memory recognized her for a girl recruited on one of the northern royal holdings, her family loyal for generations to the throne.

"Greetings, Moniga. These are dark times." She went abruptly into what she would say.

"True, Great Lady. You have some mission for me?" The other girl was intelligent and also came directly to the point.

"Is it possible for you to get into the dwelling of the Prince General Herihor, there locate some object which has been close to his body. A piece of clothing he has worn that has not been washed—though that

may be impossible. If not, something he has handled
and not too long ago?"

"Great Lady, to his place I can go. Whether I can
get what you wish—that is another matter. But be
sure that I shall try."

"There is something else—if you get this thing that
will bear the scent of the Prince General, then do you
also bring to me Assar from the hound kennels."

"Lady, it has been said, so will it be done." The
Amazon saluted and slipped carefully through the
door Sela held open for her.

"Now—" Tallahassee turned to the nurse. "A pen
I need, and ink and paper—these should be in the
Candace's study."

"They are so—but I shall bring them, Great Lady.
Stir not forth from this room. There has been seen in
the upper corridors a maid from the Prince Userkof's
wing. She has no good explanation for why she wandered so."

Involuntarily Tallahassee glanced at the wall where
hung the tapestry covering the secret way. Sela smiled
a little, though her expression was still worried.

"None will come that way, Great Lady, not without
giving good notice of their coming. I have set a certain
alarm, one the Candace herself uses by her other door
on occasion when she wants no disturbance. You may
rest easy for that much."

But could she, Tallahassee wondered? How long
would the protection she had woven in that pit hold
back Khasti if he sought her there? She must be alert
constantly, and her attention swung from the wall
tapestry to the chest in which she had seen Sela lay
the bundled Key and Rod.

-13-

Tallahassee spread the sheet of thick paper on a corner of her "sister's" dressing table, and fingered the pen absently. For a moment she was frightened. She could pen her message in her own words—but that would be unreadable. Ashake memory must provide again, so she opened the door once more for that. Characters slipped so slowly into her memory she had to fold and tear away the paper where she had made too many mistakes in translating the message she hoped, just hoped, could reach Herihor wherever he now might be. It was such a gamble that she dared not build upon success.

With infinite care she wrote out the characters of a running script that had developed from the long ago hieroglyphics of the north.

"Safe—Ashake; also—Precious things. City sealed. Candace—be warned."

She read it over twice to be sure that she had

made no errors in transcription. Then she folded it
into a small square and looked to Sela.

"I would have a piece of cloth about so big"—she
measured it off with her hands—"and it must be
golden in color. Also, there is needed a length of the
stoutest thread you can find, with a needle."

The old woman asked no questions but went
straightway to one of the chests of robes and began
turning out its contents. Among them was a cloak
to which Tallahassee pointed.

"That is the very shade!"

Sela shook out the garment. It was embroidered
heavily along the hem but the upper portion was
bare, and from that she ruthlessly cut the cloth
Tallahassee had asked for. It was a very tough silk
and, as the girl pulled it this way and that to test
it, she saw that it was very tightly woven. Into the
square she folded the note, making a packet that
could have been hidden in the palm of her hand.
Sela had gone out, but swiftly returned with an
ivory spindle round which was wound linen thread
as tough as any cord, with a needle already strung
upon it.

Now it only remained to see if Moniga could
fulfill her part of the task—and how long it would
take to do so. Tallahassee could no longer sit still. In
spite of the pain from her bandaged feet, she paced
up and down the chamber, keeping well away from
the curtained windows along one wall. Even though
those gave only on a garden which was private to
the Candace, and the light within the room was
very limited, she wanted none to guess the suite
was occupied.

"Sela—" She looked to the woman who had gone back to her stool in the corner. "What of the Temple? Has aught changed concerning the Son-of-Apedemek and his priests?"

"No, Great Lady. Only . . ." Sela paused and lowered her eyes.

"Only what, Sela?"

"Great Lady—there are whispers in the city—even those who serve the Daughter of Amun repeat them. They say that the Son-of-Apedemek may already be dead and with him all those who follow the Upper Way—that they were killed because they summoned demons who turned upon them."

"Rumor can cause much trouble, Sela. There is no weapon in the end as difficult to overcome as the tongue of an enemy."

She must get out of here, even if she could not leave the city. At the moment she felt as if she were again caged, if not as tightly as when under Khasti's power, yet nearly as helplessly.

"Sela, this maid of whom you spoke—can you bring her to me?"

"Great Lady, at this hour she is lodged with the maids in the sleeping room where they lie six together. To summon her would cause remarks."

"Can you get for me a garment such as she wears in her daytime service?"

"Great Lady—" Sela started up from her stool and came to stand before Tallahassee. She was a short woman and had plainly once been plump. Now the flesh hung loosely on her arms and her plumpness had centered in her belly. Her face was a network of fine wrinkles so that her kohl-encircled eyes had a strange look, almost as if they were set in a nearly naked skull. But she carried herself with the authority of one of importance in the household, and now a fraction of that authority rang in her voice:

"Great Lady, what is in your mind now to do?"

"I must be free of this room. You cannot continue to hide me here in secret for long, Sela."

"There is no need perhaps to hide, Great Lady. Call forth the Sworn Swords. With them before your door what man can reach you?"

"Khasti—or those of his following can," Tallahassee returned grimly. "Did he not have me out of the villa, with my own guard at the doors? He has more tricks than a camel carries fleas upon its mangy skin. And we do not know what force he controls even now. Zyhlarz, himself, and the others could never lock the gates of New Napata as this stranger from nowhere has done. No, he may believe me here, but perhaps before he can move as openly as he must to reach these rooms I shall be gone."

She crossed to stand before the wide mirror on the dressing table.

"I am tall," she frowned at her reflection, "and that I cannot conceal." Ashake memory reminded her that this height was something that was a part of the inheritance of the Blood. "For the rest, yes, I think it can be managed. Get me such garments, Sela, as a maid wears."

The old nurse hesitated. "Great Lady, I pray you, think of this again. What will you do, where do you go?"

"That I cannot answer, because I do not yet know.

But I will not do anything rashly, so do I swear to you, Sela."

The other shook her head, but she went. Tallahassee sat down on the bench before the dressing table. Her face had none of the cosmetic coating now. She peered a little more closely, advancing her face closer to the surface of the glass. As limited as the light was cut off by the curtains, she could not be mistaken. That stain which they had put upon her body when she had assumed the part of Ashake was beginning to fade a little. Certainly she looked paler now than she had when she had last looked upon herself back at the villa.

But to ask Sela for the use of . . . no! She had no intention of adding to her difficulties by allowing a woman so devoted to the Candace to realize she was not in truth the Queen's sister. Wait—she had seen maids at the villa who were much darker of skin even than Jayta, Herihor, or the two priestesses. She could certainly use that for a basis for her request to the old nurse. Tallahassee was pleased with herself at that bit of reasoning.

She began to open the jars and boxes ranged neatly before the mirror, peering into them. Some held fragrant oils, the perfume of which, concentrated by being lidded, arose headily in the air. There was the familiar eye paint, and two jars of delicately scented creams, a little bottle of red which might be liquid rouge or else lip paint. But most of this would not be worn by any maid.

Her head turned sharply. Unlike the curtains that had veiled the doorways at the villa, the entrance to the Candace's personal suite had a door fitted for

complete privacy. And in the stillness of the night
she had caught a scratching noise.

Tallahassee stole as noiselessly as she might across
the outer room. Then she heard a sound that reassured
her—a whine. Moniga must have succeeded!

But Tallahassee was still cautious as she opened
the door. The Amazon stood there, and, held on a
tight leash, was Assar.

"In!" The girl waved them on, shutting the door
instantly. Assar whined again, head high, sniffing. Of
all the Saluki hounds in the kennel, he was the best
for coursing, the most intelligent of his very ancient
breed. He needed both talents now, and perhaps a
third, to be receptive to orders given in a way even
Ashake had never tried. Those of the Temple had
worked in this fashion with cats, great and small,
since the breed had always been sacred to Apedemek.
But a cat hunted by sight, and only one of the highly
trained palace hounds could course a scent over a
long distance.

"You have it?"

"This, Great Lady." The Amazon produced one
of those broad ceremonial wrist bracelets that had
evolved from the bow guards of the ancient archers.
It was interlined with a padding of leather.

"His Highness sent it to the city a month ago, for
the stone of the setting"—Moniga pointed to a large
carved carnelian—"was loose. There was nothing else
that he had recently worn."

"It must do. You have been both quick and clever,
Moniga."

"The Great One desires, her desire is the law," the
Amazon replied formally, but her face shone.

"Assar—good Assar." Tallahassee rested her hand on the dog's head. His smooth coat was golden, soft and silky. On the ears, legs, and tail, it feathered long and gracefully.

The tail swung at her greeting and he followed her into the bedroom where she reached for the small packet she had made ready. As she sewed it to his collar Assar stood patiently, looking up into her face, now and then whining very softly as if asking what was to be done.

She had chosen the color well, the packet against his throat could hardly be distinguished from his own coloring. Now she took up the arm band Moniga had brought, turning it so that keen nose could sniff at the padding where, if she would have any luck at all in this mad venture, Herihor's scent would linger.

Tallahassee allowed the hound some moments to make sure of the scent, and then she knelt before him, so that they were nearer eye to eye, and put one hand on either side of his high-held head. Now—she willed into her mind a picture of Herihor, then of the way north, again of Herihor. Patiently she kept herself to the task, repeating it a dozen times over. The worst was not being sure whether she was reaching that brain so alien to her own, whether Assar knew what must be done. But she was coming once more to the end of her own power of concentration. She would have to accept, now, either success or failure.

Getting somewhat stiffly to her feet, Tallahassee held out the leash to the Amazon.

"There is the small gate of Nefhor—How late is the hour?"

"It is within two hours of dawn, Great Lady."

"So. This you must do, Moniga, and without being seen if possible. Loose Assar near the gate. If he goes through, then we have a small chance of reaching the Prince General. If I have failed, doubtless he will return with you. But take every precaution you can not to be observed."

"There is the guard of the Prince Userkof at the gate, but they are not alert." The Amazon wrinkled her nose expressively with scorn. "They believe that the barrier is complete."

"Still—go with care."

"That we shall, Great Lady." The Amazon saluted, and Tallahassee let dog and woman out of the door. She sighed and went wearily into the bedroom, to collapse once more on the bed, where she lay staring up at the painted ceiling, her restless thoughts not allowing her any peace.

"Great Lady." Sela had slipped in with her accustomed skill at appearing by the bedside before one was even aware she was there. "You must rest—or the fever will come. I know not what you plan to do, but you cannot attempt it yet."

Her wrinkled hand gently touched Tallahassee's forehead and it seemed to the girl that the coolness of her fingers spread swiftly throughout her tense body, relaxing nerves and muscles.

"Drink, Lady."

Before she could move, a practiced arm slid beneath her head, raising her up until a goblet met her lips. She drank, her weariness overcoming the need for action for the moment.

"Sleep . . ." Sela's hand stroked her forehead, peace

and safety in that gentle and loving gesture. There had been so much—so much . . .

"Sleep . . ."

Tallahassee's eyes closed as if the lids were so weighted she might never hope to raise them again. And if she dreamed, no memory of those dreams carried over into her awakening.

Sunlight edged the window curtains when she roused. And the room held heat—the fans would not be at work with the Candace gone, of course. She felt the moisture in her armpits and gathering along her temples, under her breasts. After blinking for a breath or two, she sat up in bed and reached for the tall glass bottle set on the bedside table, tipping a goodly amount of the water it held into its attendant glass and drinking it down. Sela's stool in the corner was vacant. There was no sound through the hot and airless rooms of the suite.

Piled nearby upon one of the chairs was white clothing. But first of all she wanted to bathe, to rid her body, if only momentarily, of the sheen of sweat and gain what refreshment she could from cool water against her skin.

Bundling the clothing under one arm (it was the servant's dress she had asked Sela for) Tallahassee went into the luxury of the Candace's bathroom where water from one lion-headed pipe fed into a basin in which one could sit nearly awash to the shoulders, and then lapped out an overflow slit in the wall. She dug her hands deep into a sweet-smelling cream that lathered and washed away like soap. But her skin was lighter—several shades lighter.

How good was Sela's eyesight? Had age dimmed

it any? Discovery might depend on that alone now. She rinsed and wiped herself down with one of the towels hanging on a nearby rack. Then she dressed in the narrow white dress which was very close to that of the priestess, save that the bands across the shoulders were not white but red and there was no girdle to confine it at the waist.

"Great Lady—" That was Sela hurrying in.

"Listen." Tallahassee was occupied with her own problem, hoping to so avert Sela's notice of the color change in her skin. "If I am to pass as a maid, Sela, I should be darker of skin. Have you aught to use to make me so?"

Sela's hands were close-clasped together. Now she twisted them as if afraid.

"Lady—they have come." She seemed not to have heard Tallahassee's question.

Herihor? Jayta? Dared she believe that?

"Who have come?" She fought her own rising excitement. Sela's appearance did not suggest that any help had arrived. Instead, there was alarm in the wrinkled old face.

"Four of the greater Nomarchs, Great Lady. They have been summoned to council, yet the Candace is not here. In the Prince's name they have come because they are told that naught has been heard from our Lady for two days, and ill must have come to her from the desert storm! Great Lady, if this be true . . ." She was trembling so that Tallahassee set her arm about the bowed shoulders, led Sela to a chair and pushed her down upon it. Going to her own knees she caught the shaking hands in her own and spoke very gently.

"Dear Sela, if our Lady were dead—would I not know it? I have the Talent and so has she in some measure. Do we not then feel death when it opens the Far Gate for those we love? I swear to you that this has not happened. Be sure that the Prince General is using his forces along the border to find Naldamak, and no men have more knowledge of those lands.

"But tell me, which of the Nomarchs have come to New Napata at such a false summoning?"

Sela's tear-filled eyes held hers.

"It is true, Great Lady—she has not Gone Beyond?"

"Would I not have told you, Sela, you who have loved and served her all her life long—who held her to your breast when she was but an hour old? You have been her mother-in-life. It is to you I would have first spoken had I such ill fortune to know."

"She is my Sun-in-Full, my dearest heart—"

"That I know well, Sela—"

"When she was little I was her guard and her comforter, when she became the Candace she paid me honor, putting me first in her personal service, even though I was old and sometimes forgetful. Never has she spoken a cross word to me, Lady. And now—now they say she is dead!"

"But since she is not, we must prevent any such word spreading before they hold council on it. Which Nomarchs, Sela?"

Sela gave a last small sob. "He—he of the Elephant, and of the River Horse—"

"Both of the south," Ashake memory supplied, "and those that rebelled a hundred years ago."

"And the Leopard, the Ibex—"

"Of the west where the barbarians trade. I see. But the Lion, the Cheeta, the Baboon—they come not? North against south—west against east."

"Great Lady, the Elephant has many mighty warriors. When they arose under Chaka in the old days there was much killing before the Beloved-of-Apedemek—the Pharoah Unie who was then—restored law in the land. And there is talk of new barbarian weapons—"

"Yes. And so we must know of what they plan. Do they dare to meet in the Great Chamber of Council?"

"It is so."

"Well, there are secrets of the Candace that are not known even to as close kin as Userkof." Tallahassee arose. "There will be a listener whom they do not suspect. This, Sela, is what you must do. I will have to go to a certain place and not be marked during the going. Can you get me that with which to darken my skin so that I look like a maid from the south?"

Sela seemed recovered from her first fear. With her head a little to one side she regarded Tallahassee who hoped her own uneasiness did not show. Then the old nurse smiled.

"I think that may be done, Great Lady. The Lady Idieze—you may not know it, but it is true that barbarian blood is hers. She is as pale as the belly of a fish by nature. She allows not even her lord to ever see her so. There is an oil she keeps in secret, only it is not as secret as she thinks. And now that she makes ready to welcome the Nomarchs there will be no one in her inner chamber. It shall be yours to use."

"Do not take any risk, Sela."

"Risk, Great Lady? Has not the Candace given me the power of overseeing all her household? If I check upon the willingness of the maids, and how well their work is done—then I am only about my lawful business." She laughed and Tallahassee echoed her.

"Sela, you are a very wise woman—"

"Great Lady, had I had the tending of you, instead of your being sent to the Temple for the raising, you would know how much one can learn hereabouts by merely listening and saying little."

When the nurse had gone again, Tallahassee sat down and allowed Ashake memory once more to enter her conscious mind. Ashake could recall the day when the last Pharoah had taken Naldamak and her (she being on one of her visits from the Temple school) along a certain corridor and showed them a secret that only Ruler and Heir might know. They had sworn an oath of silence that day. But she would not be breaking it now, for that secret was designed as an aid in just such a situation as this.

This council had been called in Userkof's name. Did the provincial rulers summoned here believe that she, Ashake, was dead also? Or was it they were merely ripe once more for rebellion, a rebellion perhaps financed and armed either by Khasti or by some of the western barbarians who had always resented their treatment by Amun, the refusal of the Empire to treat or ally with their quarrels, for they were a divided number of peoples forever at each other's throats in one political and military struggle or another.

The two southern nomes were at least civilized by the standards of Amun itself. Three Emperors of the past had extended the borders so far to the south that they had garnered in peoples of different races, beliefs, and customs—alien to the Old Knowledge, ever a source of trouble which smoldered into fire now and then. While the western nomes—they contained the trade cities where the barbarians brewed their own kind of poison for the disturbance of peace.

This was the trouble now. She arose and went once more to pacing. It was a fact, as she had assured Sela, that if Naldamak were truly dead she herself would know. The warning from kin to kin was a talent born in those of her family. But the mere fact that the Empress still lived was no assurance of her safety. She could well be in the hands of some secret force raised by Khasti. And what of the stranger who had come out of nowhere, even as Khasti had done, and had asked to see the Candace? What danger did he represent?

That Herihor was in command of the loyal forces in the north where the Candace might be expected to be found—that was the only faint point in their favor. That, and the fact that the talismans were still out of enemy hands. Anyway, she would have her chance to overhear what devil's brew Userkof or Idieze might be boiling here.

If Sela would only hurry! She did not want to miss any of the council hearing. Also—there was something she must not leave here. Tallahassee went to the chest and took out the bundle of the Rod and the Key. She would not feel safe anywhere away from them. There was no place in the chamber that would efficiently conceal the talismans if a strict search was made.

She had not forgotten that passage in the depths. Sela might think it well guarded by the alarm she mentioned, but an alarm would count for little against any attack by Khasti with the unknown forces he could control.

She dropped the bundle on the bed to tighten the fastenings about the roll of cloth. Yes, this she would take with her.

Tallahassee was still holding it, testing those fastenings when there was a click at the door and Sela sidled in, a number of towels clamped to her side by one of her bony elbows, both hands carrying a tall jar with care.

-14-

"Look, great lady, is it not now even as you wished? Who would know the Princess Ashake in such a guise?"

Tallahassee stood once more before the mirror on the Candace's dressing table. Sela was very right. This was not Ashake whom she saw there. Her skin was again dark, even darker than it had been upon the first anointing which the Priestess had given her. Also, careful use of cosmetics had broadened her features, given a fullness that was not normal to her face.

She had folded about her head a sphinx linen cap, and the edges of that fell forward to further shadow and disguise her features. There was only her height which might betray her. But she did not plan to pace any well-used corridor in open sight for long. And she could hope that no one would notice her, any more than any servant was noted when about her normal business.

The bundle she had made of the talismans was

ready to be carried in one of the wide baskets Sela had produced from an inner cupboard, intended for the transport of newly washed bed coverings.

But all this had taken time, very precious time. And the Council could well be in session. She stopped suddenly and set her painted lips to Sela's wrinkled cheek.

"Mother-in-fostering to my sister-kin," she said softly, "I give thanks to the Great Power that you have come to my aid. There is such service in this that not even the Blood could provide. On you be the blessing of That Which Holds Us All."

"Great Lady." Sela raised her hand and in turn touched a finger tip to Tallahassee's painted cheek. "Blessings and good fortune be on what you would do. If our dear Lady comes out of danger, what more can we ask? Wait you now, until I make certain that the corridor is empty. To be seen issuing from here . . ."

She was already on the way to the outer door when there was a scratching at it. Who? . . . Tallahassee hugged the basket tightly and her heart began to beat faster. Sela's head had cocked as she listened to that sound. Then, before Tallahassee could stop her, she swiftly opened the door.

It was Moniga who slipped through. But her neat uniform was gone. Like Tallahassee, the Amazon wore the dress of a servant, and she was breathing fast as she caught the door out of Sela's hold, shut it tight, and stood with her shoulders against it as if to form a barrier of her own body to hinder some pursuit.

"What is it?" Tallahassee demanded and saw the Amazon's look of surprise, her searching stare.

"Great Lady—but you?..." The girl was near to stammering.

"I go in another guise, yes. But what have you to tell us?"

"Great Lady, Assar went through the gate—and he went readily. None saw him in the shadows. It was as if he knew, hound though he is, that he must not be sighted. But—when I returned—Great Lady, in the name of Prince Userkof they had relieved the guard of the palace—"

Tallahassee heard Sela's hiss of breath.

"The Sworn Swords?"

"Great Lady—they were surrounded while I was gone on your order. They are now confined to the barracks. And the Captain—she was disarmed and taken away. They have laid upon the doors of the barracks that same barrier which is on the gates of the city. None can come forth."

"And it is men from the south who stand on guard?"

Moniga nodded. "Even so, Great Lady. I have seen the insignia of the Elephant on their uniforms. By now this palace is theirs. And I think that they are also changing the gate guards. These are barbarian warriors, Great Lady—some even wear the facial scars of the wild tribes."

"You have done very well," Tallahassee said slowly. "Now—stay you here with Sela, and be sure no one knows where you have taken refuge. There may come a time, maybe very soon, when I shall need a Sworn Sword at my back to be sure that no other's knife reaches me."

"Great Lady, what do you do? There are strangers in the Palace, more guards from the south—"

"That I know. But also I must learn more, for the sake of the Candace and perhaps of the Empire itself. Do not worry. This I do is something only I can accomplish, but it must be done."

For a moment, it seemed that Moniga would not stand back from the door. But as Tallahassee eyed her steadily the Amazon gave way.

"Great Lady," she made her plea, "Take me with you! I have this." She reached hand into the bosom of her dress and brought out a hand weapon.

"That we may have need for later. No—this way, I go alone. It is a secret of the Candace that only I also may know—and it will be to our aid. Sela, keep closed this door—do not even open should the maid you mentioned come to it. Khasti has weapons past our knowledge, and some of them are our own people constrained to his will. It was the use of such that brought me into his hands. Do not open this door!"

"The will has spoken, so be it." Sela gave formal answer. Moniga looked as if she would protest once again, but Tallahassee slipped quickly through, and the nurse shut it firmly behind her.

Luckily she did not have far to go. Those who had planned this secret, upon the building of the "new" palace some three hundred years ago, had wished it to be quickly accessible to the ruler. She stood for a moment, listening intently.

There was a series of arched openings to her left, giving to the Candace's private courtyard garden. Through those poured sunlight, and it was the strong western sun of afternoon. She could hear the sounds of birds, the scream of one of those peacocks bred from gifts of an Indian ruler two or three generations

ago. It was a shattering sound, enough at this moment
to make her start.

But the corridor itself was empty. Since the Candace
was known to be gone, there were no guards along it.
Tallahassee sped swiftly along, hugging the right wall,
as far from the arches as she could get.

The garden corridor gave upon a room the rulers had used in the past for more private audiences.
There was a smaller, less impressive throne chair, some
stools-of-honor for visiting members of the Blood, but
for the most part it was bare.

However, beyond the door that led out of it, Tallahassee could hear a murmur of voices. Yes, the council
was gathering! She must be very swift and quiet.

She rounded the wall of the lesser audience chamber to the southern corner where there were panels
of carved wood, oiled and polished with preservative.
Placing the basket at her feet, she raised her hands
to fit them into the spaces she had been drilled to
find so many years ago. She had not forgotten, or
rather Ashake had not. Her fingers went easily into
depressions one could not perceive because of the
depth and high relief of the carving. Now she swung
almost her full weight downward.

There was a scrape of sound, which made her
glance hastily around. Then the stubborn controls,
unused probably for years, worked. Two of the panels opened and she crawled through then stooped
to drag the basket after her before she shut that
cramped door.

It was not dark—light beamed from one side, and
it was there that she crouched to watch and listen—
being well able to see all that was beyond through a

fretwork of carving so intricate that it concealed well its purpose on the other side of the wall.

The Council Chamber might be new to Tallahassee, but Ashake memory found it familiar, though she recognized only two of the six men sitting there—General Itua of the Southern Army, and the Nomarch of the Elephant Nome. There was no sign of Khasti, whom she thought surely would be present, nor was either Userkof nor Idieze here.

However, she had no more seated herself in the restricted crouch her present quarters permitted than the door opened and Idieze swept in, with a fan bearer in her wake.

She dared! Ashake memory gave fuel to anger—that one dares to usurp honors Naldamak never would grant her! She must be very sure that both Candace and Ashake herself were removed or immobilized. Had Khasti not informed her then that his prisoner had escaped?

Khasti believed this woman and her husband were tools to be used and discarded. Idieze herself had come to Ashake to strike a bargain, or pretend to. What then had changed so that now the Princess believed she could call a council and be obeyed?

"This is a time of grave matters," Idieze spoke abruptly, cutting through the murmurs of formal greeting, waving the men back to their seats. "You have been summoned, my Lords, at the call of my husband, the Prince Userkof, who, though he lies stricken with a fever, still knows that the safety of the Empire is above all else, the matter depending upon the strength of such as you—who have been loyal to him."

She paused as she looked swiftly from one face to another, catching the eyes of each in turn and holding that straight stare for a breath or two, as if she so issued some warning or demanded in return another protestation of loyalty. Perhaps she was satisfied by what she saw for now she continued:

"It is now well known that the Candace is lost in the desert storm. And that anyone whose flyer's caught in such fury could survive is not to be believed. And the Princess Ashake—she has of her own will turned aside from the rule, taking instead the final oath of the Temple, tying herself to that service for the rest of her life."

So? Now that was clever, Ashake acknowledged. Her long absences from New Napata on Temple business had left few here who knew her personally. And those who would be her firmest champions to bring her to the throne—Zyhlarz, Jayta, and Herihor—were most conveniently removed from this council. These men would accept the fact that she might do this, mainly because they wished to believe so.

"The Heir must make such statements before the Council, and then at the High Altar before all the representatives of the Guilds and the Masters, as well as the Nomarchs." The man who wore the badge of the Leopard spoke. He used none of the customary honorifics in addressing Idieze.

Ashake did not know him except by name, which was Takarka, for he had only recently come to the heirship of that westernmost land of the Empire, and that upon the death of a distant cousin. But he had dealt much with the white-skinned barbarians of the north and she had automatically judged him to be of the kind that could be suborned by Khasti. To have such a statement out of him was a surprise now.

"Which she shall do at the proper time. Though nothing can be done yet," Idieze covered smoothly, "until the certain death of our Sun-in-Glory be certified as the truth. In the meantime, the Heir has withdrawn to a place of distant meditation and the Empire cannot rule itself."

"Surely, surely," muttered General Itua to second that.

"If the Heir has not yet sworn openly," persisted Takarka, "then she must be summoned . . ."

It was he who now looked from face to face at his companions as if surprised that no voice had been raised to back him.

"It is the Law," he spoke shortly and sharply.

"In times of crisis"—the Nomarch of the Elephant answered that—"law cannot always be relied upon. The tribes beyond the wardship of my own land grow restless. A firm hand is needed to keep them in check. Let them learn that we have no ruler and they will accept that as a sign to invade. It took us two full years to best them before, and that was a hundred years ago. There is good reason to believe that they have been trading with the northern barbarians. There are rumors and more than rumors of their getting weapons to match or even outmatch what we can put in the field against them."

General Itua grunted. "Do not give heed to this constant downcrying of our fitness," he snapped. "Perhaps we also have something now that will surprise them—and others. What, Lady"—he looked directly at Idieze—"of the forces of the north? What part

will they play—for or against your Royal Husband?
It is said that there is an old grievance between him
and the Prince General. And the Prince General is
not only of the Blood, but his betrothal to the Heir
still stands. Think you that he will step tamely aside
if there is such a division in this land?"

Idieze's mouth tightened. "Just as you warn that our
army may have secrets not open to public knowledge,
General, so do I say that there are other secrets.
If Prince Herihor seeks the throne against all cus-
tom, he will never even enter the gates of New
Napata—alive!"

The Nomarch of the Leopard leaned forward a
little on his stool-of-the-presence.

"I have heard that there is a stranger in Napata—one
with new knowledge. Is he the secret of whom you
speak, Lady? If so—why is he not here to let us see
and hear him? We have kept our land because we
have not thrown aside that which was our greatest
gift, in Khem and afterwards. The barbarians depend
upon what they make with their two hands—and look
at the history of their lands. Have they aught to boast
of? The death of kings, some struck down by jealous rivals upon their own seats-of-honor, the killing
of men with only short seasons of uneasy peace in
which they can prepare once more for the flood of
blood across their countries. I have heard them boast
of this—deeming it honorable—for honor is for the
victor, not the crushed. I have heard them convict
themselves with their own boasting.

"How many wars have we of Amun fought?" He
held out one hand, fingers spread, and touched the
fingertip of the other hand to each he named.

"In the far past we expelled the Hyksos who had taken Khem, later we fought with those from the north—three times. We broke finally because we were few and they were many, pouring in new hordes where, when one of our Blood fell, there were none to rise up in his place. Before them we were driven south—to Meroë.

"But our other weapon grew the stronger. Men could fight with mind and spirit—not to conquer the aggressors but to send them back, into their own place. Meroë we held against the men from the east until our faith thinned and we were bereft of our strongest shield. So again we traveled, this time west. And there, under Rameses the Lion, we built this New Napata, and we were not moved again!

"Rather did our fires burn brighter and we learned and grew—so Amun was born. Five wars in all—and one rebellion from the south in near eight thousand years. No northern cluster of barbarian states can match that."

"My Lord." Idieze spoke earnestly. "All you say is the truth. But this is also true—we have come again to a time when the Talent runs thin, fewer are born with the seeds of the Power in them. Even the line of the Blood has dwindled, is that not so? This is becoming again such a time as you cite in the past, when we weaken in that which has defended us. Therefore, that Amun may continue to exist, we shall be driven, in our great need, to other weapons. This is not what we want but it is a fact we must face.

"And one of our greatest defenses is a secure throne. If we have not that, how then can we marshal the nation?"

Clever, clever, clever—Ashake wanted to spit like a battle-inflamed cat. Idieze's logic was unanswerable.

"Can Userkof hold the Power then?" For the first time the Nomarch of the River Horse spoke. He was a man of middle years and, Ashake had heard it said, of more than a little cunning, preferring to get his way by intrigue rather than open action. His obese form must find it uncomfortable, perching on the small stool, and his eyes were always near half-closed as if he were stupid—but he was not.

"He is of the Blood!" Idieze returned sharply.

"And the Power itself?"

"Is safe!" she answered, perhaps too quickly. The Nomarch of the River Horse was the last man Ashake would want to lie to without a wealth of seeming conviction behind her falsehood. But perhaps Idieze, moved by the shortness of time, could do nothing else. What if they demanded that the Rod and the Key be produced here and now?

"Where is Zyhlarz?" It was Takarka again. "And the Nomarchs of the north? This is not a full council, and so we can put forth no decisions."

"The north—" Idieze hesitated. "My lords, this is a grievous thing I must tell you—the northern army has proved traitor. They have declared for Herihor. And think you—who has searched for our Sun-in-Glory—who?"

She made of that question an accusation.

"You have proof?" Takarka faced her.

"Why think you Zyhlarz is not here? The Temple is sealed for mourning. But we cannot prove what we have heard. Only, would the Prince General dare to put on the Lion Helm unless our Lady is safely dead?

If he has found her—he has said nothing, thinking to use the time to argue with the Heir, and so rule in her name as her Royal Husband—"

"We can make no decisions without a full council," Takarka said firmly. "Let Userkof stand before us with the Power, and we shall know the truth: that the Candace is indeed dead and the Heir has put aside her claim. For only he who is the rightful ruler may so appear."

"That is well said, my Lord," the Nomarch of the River Horse agreed.

He of the Elephant was hesitant for only a space and then nodded, also. General Itua's eyes were on the floor before him, as if his mind roved elsewhere, and he did not speak at all, while the other Nomarch, a nervous little man with a twitching eyelid, was quick to nod.

Idieze arose. Her face was a smooth mask, but Ashake could feel her seething anger—and beneath that anger was fear. Had this move been made without the knowledge of Khasti, a desperate attempt to get the support of those nobles she believed would back her even against the reputed resources of the stranger? Ashake began to think so as the Princess swept out of the room, sparing no word of farewell to any of those summoned.

"Userkof." The Nomarch of the Elephant had said only that one word when his fellow southerner opened his eyes wide for the first time and stared for an instant at him.

"Not here—not now, yes," the General said cryptically as he got to his feet awkwardly, nearly as if he had been as heavy and shapeless of body as the man on his left.

They did not leave together, the southerners going first, then the General nearly on their heels, still looking preoccupied, as if he must at once make sure that the troops under him did have the weapons of which he had spoken. The two remaining Nomarchs did not draw together—rather he of the Leopard pushed past the other, and the last man looked after him, wearing an expression Ashake could not read.

She was hot of body in this cubby and hotter yet of mind with frustration. There was no possible way she could spy on them outside this room. They would be housed in the Wing of Noble Visitors with their own guards very much in evidence, since their masters were plainly unsettled in their own minds. There she could not play the part even of a palace maid without fear of being uncovered.

And she had learned so little. Much of that might be guessing. There seemed to be one holdout in the ranks of the enemy—the Nomarch of the Leopard. But she could not order that he be trusted merely on what she had overheard here. However, it was a little comforting to believe that there were doubters and that the councillors were not ready to back Idieze in some sudden action. The more time they were given. . . .

They? Of what did the Royal forces within New Napata now consist? A woman so old she had seen two generations, a single Amazon in disguise, armed with nothing but her hand-weapon, a maid on whom they might or might not be able to depend—and herself, whether she wanted that so or not. In this she was caught and forced to fight Ashake's battle, if not for the sake of Amun, for her own life.

She made the trip back to the Candace's suite, noting that the sun had lost much of its hold on the gallery floor since she had come. The burning sun of the desert—how long could Naldamak survive if it were true her flyer had been lost in a storm? Even if she had lived through its crash, the harsh conditions of that land gave no promise of more than a day or two of further existence.

Yet, she was not dead. For Ashake would have known. Of that somehow Tallahassee was convinced. She had reached the door of the outer chamber and now she scratched her signal on its surface, glancing right and left hurriedly as she did so, the basket containing the talismans balanced precariously on her hip.

They must have been waiting right by the door, for it was speedily flung open. And the Amazon was so moved by her concern, that, thinking nothing of rank, she put out a calloused, hard-fingered hand to draw Tallahassee in as quickly as she could.

"They could not agree," the girl told the two who awaited her. "The Nomarch of the Leopard leads the opposition to Idieze's demands. But she has told them two tales—that the Candace is dead, or possibly prisoner to Herihor—and that he leads a rebellion against the throne!"

"Lies!" Sela hissed.

"So we know. But proof is another thing. Khasti was not there—perhaps she called this council without his knowledge. I believe she fears him—and rightly. If we could only build upon these divisions within their own ranks! If I had but the backing of the Son-of-Apedemek, and even two or three from the Temple, it might be possible to work upon their jealousies and fears—"

"Great Lady!" Sela had come to her side as she stood, the bundle of the Rod and Key in her hands, frustration bitter in her. "You hold," the nurse reminded her, "that which is the heart and soul of Amun—can you not draw upon its Power?"

Tallahassee started. If she were truly Ashake—yes. But those gaps in the Ashake memory were so large. She could summon the two to her as she had in that laboratory, but other uses for them—those were part of the knowledge that had not been imparted by the tapes. But—she might try—the Temple! That could be closed to physical entrance, but was it also shut to the power of thought? If she could contact Zyhlarz, in whose mind lay the deepest layers of the Wisdom in this generation! . . .

She turned upon the other two.

"There is something I may try. You must guard me well, for it may be that what is truly me must quest beyond the realms of the flesh that holds me."

"Be sure, Great Lady," the Amazon answered first, "that we shall do what we can. Though where—?"

"With any fortune perhaps to Zyhlarz." If they knew the truth, they might be more zealous. "Now let me prepare."

-15-

She floated in space which did not exist in any world she knew. Before her was a tall, dark wall, holding her back from what she sought. Zyhlarz, the others of the Upper Way, were behind that. But this path was closed—at least to one who had not all of what Ashake had once known.

Baffled, Tallahassee tried again and again to pierce that wall, haunted by the thought that the fault lay in herself, in the imperfect memory she had been given. She lacked the deepest secrets of their schooling. And whether this wall was of the enemy's devising, or born of the need for defense against some psychic attack, that she did not know either.

Though Khasti might not have raised such a barrier in this between-the-worlds place, there were those from the far south (the medicine men of the wild tribes) who held perverted and dark powers—who would fear above all else the Light of the Temple. And they might well have been harnessed by the rebel forces.

The wall held; she was wearied and defeated by it. In this place her half-knowledge could not hold her safely for too long. Yet she still clung to a fragment of hope.

Then . . .

Before the wall there flashed a column of pure flame as golden as the mask Jayta wore. Out of that flame arose that mask itself to face the disembodied Ashake.

Daughter-of-Apedemek?—There was no speech in this place which could be shaped by lips and tongue, for only a sense of identity existed.

I come. The mask image answered her.

There is great need . . .

There is greater that you win to us, Sister-in-the-Light. . . .

How may I do this? demanded the Ashake-self.

Seek once more the lower ways. There are secrets there that can lead you. You have done very well, and fortune has favored you. There will be those—

But a cry rent the air and at that sound the shadow world fragmented and was gone. Ashake—Tallahassee—was whipped by a force greater than any wind, driven away from the wall, from the light that was Jayta. She could not escape that overwhelming pressure. Then came a sense of anchorage, or return. The girl opened her eyes dazedly.

Two lamps threw odd shadows on the ceiling above. And nearby she heard a faint moaning. Somehow, in spite of the vast weariness that burdened her, she managed to turn her head.

Someone crouched there, hands across her face. And, as Tallahassee groggily pulled herself up, she saw that another body lay upon the floor. That small crumpled form—Sela! And that other, shaking with terror—the Amazon Moniga. But what had struck here? Some attack launched by Khasti?

She put feet to the floor, sat up, though she wavered in her slow movements.

"Be still!" Her voice was low, but she put into it all the sharp authority she could now summon.

The Amazon did not raise her head, her moans were growing louder. Somehow Tallahassee stood up and took two steps to the side of the women. She leaned over, in spite of the peril to her own balance, and struck Moniga across the cheek. For the Amazon had lifted her head to show a face near witless with what could only be sheer terror. And knowing of the Spartan training that had shaped her, Tallahassee could readily believe that whatever had sent her into this state must have been well beyond any normal experience.

"Be still!" she said fiercely. Then those staring eyes focused upon her and a little of the blank panic faded from the other's face.

Tallahassee fell to her knees, her hands going out to the still form of Sela. At first she thought that the old woman was dead, then her searching fingers found the faintest of pulse beats.

"Help me!" She gave a second order.

The Amazon moved stiffly, as one who answered orders without understanding them. Together they managed to get Sela up on the bed Tallahassee had just quitted. Her small, wizened face was very pale, almost greenish, and her mouth opened slackly, a thin thread of moisture running from one corner.

"Wine," Tallahassee ordered. "Bring wine." Under

her hands Sela's body felt very cold. The old woman was in shock. The girl drew up the covers about her; and when Moniga, her hands still shaking so that the wine nearly spilled, brought her a goblet, Tallahassee raised the nurse's head to her own shoulder, supporting her so that she might dribble into that mouth a little of the liquid.

Sela choked, gasped, and swallowed. Her pulse was growing stronger. Tallahassee settled her back on the bed, turned to the Amazon.

"Tell me, Moniga, what happened?"

Luckily the girl appeared to have recovered something of both her courage and her wits. Now when Tallahassee looked at her she flushed as if ashamed.

"Great Lady—it—there were things . . ." she half stuttered. "I fought with the Sworn Swords at Menkani when the desert men broke into the Fort and we went to retake it. I have seen much, Great Lady, that was full of horror. But this—this was not of our world!"

"In what way?" Tallahassee asked quietly, knowing that she must use patience.

"When you were asleep, they came. They were like shadows—or a kind of troubling in the air. How can I find the words to describe what I have never seen before? But they were—they were angry in some manner and their hate—it could be felt!"

The wraiths again.

"I myself have seen these things, Moniga. They do exist. And I believe I know what they may be seeking. Only I have not the power to give it to them."

"Great Lady—they gathered about you as you lay. And when we tried to protect you—they . . ." Moniga's hands went to her head. "Somehow they got into our minds—with terrible thoughts. They would have me kill . . . but I held out against that, Great Lady—I did!

"Then they brought pain and the Lady Sela cried out. I thought she was dead. And when they turned on me—Great Lady, I was not sure how long I could hold against them! I think I screamed—"

"You could do no else, Sworn Sword. These things are not to be met by any weapon one can hold in hand. That you resisted their strength is a battle of honor for you," Tallahassee reassured her.

She had gained at least a part of Jayta's message. But to seek again the lower passages, where the wraiths had hung before, when she did not believe that this time she could expect anything but hostility from them, was perilous indeed. She sat on the edge of the bed and tried to think. Sela seemed to be sleeping naturally. Her face had lost the stamp of intolerable fear. And Moniga was herself again.

"Listen well now." Tallahassee knew that there was no escape for her. Jayta's message had been very clear. She would have to win free from New Napata, and there was only one way, that which led through those slimed passages below. "There are things I need—for I have received a message from the Daughter-of-Apedemek through the way of the Talent. Can you find and bring these to me in secret?

"Great Lady, it is ordered, so it is done," Moniga replied with the formal salute of her rank.

"These then—provisions—such as the army takes for maneuvers—enough in a shoulder sack for several days. Also a night torch with a newly fitted unit. Bring these as speedily as possible. And with them bread, meat, what I may eat at once."

"These I can get, Great Lady." Moniga was already moving to the door.

When that had closed behind the Amazon, Tallahassee set to work. Her strength had returned a little, and she must not allow herself to imagine ahead, as to what it might be like to be caught somewhere in that thick darkness below by the wraiths. No, think rather of what she must do right now.

She went through the chest of Naldamak's clothing to find what she needed—the uniform the Empress wore when reviewing her troops on formal occasions. Using scissors from the dressing table, she cut away all the insignia of rank, leaving a one-piece garment, not unlike what her own world called a jump suit.

It was a little tight for her across the chest, but she was able to fasten the buckles, and luckily the boots fit, though they cramped her feet after the looseness of the sandals. Sela still slept—dreamlessly, Tallahassee hoped.

The talismans she would have to carry bare. But, lest she might drop them, she looped cords about each to fasten around her wrist. She covered her head with a scarf knotted under her chin. She was finishing that when she heard the signal and let Moniga in.

A sack, well-filled, hung from the Amazon's shoulder, and she balanced a tray on which was the food Tallahassee had asked for. As the girl sat to eat and drink she gave her last orders.

"I leave here, Sworn Sword, by a hidden way. Do you hold guard and see that the Lady Sela wants for no attention. Keep secret that I have been here if you are discovered. And watch well the way I go so that none can come upon you secretly."

"Great Lady, I would go with you." Moniga had changed into her uniform and her weapon swung at her belt.

"Not so. This is a path where only the Rod can lead me. You will offer greater service by guarding this door. It may be that when I return I shall come again by this way, perhaps bringing help with me. We must be sure, should that be our plan, that we do not walk into an ambush."

"Great Lady—be sure that I shall keep such guard!"

Tallahassee shouldered the bag of provisions. She looped the cords of Key and Rod about her left wrist, picked up the torch with the other. At her order Moniga held aside the wall hanging and she entered the secret way. There was a jingle and she remembered Sela's setting an alarm. To the Amazon she explained that signal before she set off down into the dark.

This time the hand torch gave her far more light than the radiance by which she had earlier come, its ray cutting clearly to light step and wall. And it was not long before she reached the ancient walled door and crawled through the break into that place of bad smells and suggestion of lurking danger.

Orientating herself by the palace above, Tallahassee turned left into the unknown way. The stair was one of those secrets of another age, probably constructed first as an escape for the Royal Family should disaster strike as it had at Meroë. Therefore, there must be some exit outside the city. And that, she hoped, would not be guarded by the barriers Khasti had set.

The moisture and fetid smells were both stronger.
She had to pick a careful path as the footing was slimy
enough so now and then her boots slipped. The beam
of her torch caught for an instant the raised head of
a creature—either a large lizard or a snake. But it
flicked out of sight as if light were a threat. She had
expected an assault from the wraiths (after all this
might well be their lurking place) and was constantly
waiting for it, not daring to allow herself to relax even
when time passed and that did not develop.

Moisture gathered here in viscid, evil-smelling pools
which she skirted as best she could. Then the corridor ended in a sullen flood from which arose such
a stench as she did not believe could be breathed for
long. She tucked her torch for the moment into her
belt and drew down the kerchief that covered her
head to enfold her mouth and nose in a vain attempt
to filter out some of the nastiness.

The flood was fast flowing, and she was sure this
was one of the main sewers of the city. How deep
that offal-filled stream was she had no idea. She
hesitated. The way stopped here. Which meant that
whoever followed it had to take to the sewer at this
point. But to venture out into that with no idea of
depth, when she could be swept from her feet and
rolled under the filth to drown? No, she must find
some other way.

Bracing one shoulder against the wall, Tallahassee
leaned forward as far as she dared, to flash the beam
of the torch along the wall toward her right, for the
passage had met with the sewer at a sharp angle.
There did exist a footpath—if one could call it that,
for it was hardly wider than her two feet put side to

side. Though the flood lapped only a little below its edge, yet it was thickly encrusted with foul deposits that higher waves must have left.

To take that way was to risk her footing at every step, yet there was no alternative. And how long could she breathe this polluted air without succumbing? There was no use in lingering—if this was the road, then it was the one she must take.

She squeezed around the corner where passage and sewer met to step gingerly out on that befouled ledge. Her guess had been very right. Here the slime of the inner corridor became a thicker morass that sucked at her feet every time she raised one for another step. She had to move so slowly that the foul air grew more and more of a threat to consciousness.

Tallahassee lost all track of time. Her head ached, and she felt nauseated, dizzy. Once a scaled head arose from the flood and jaws opened, to close with a snap when she flashed the light directly into small, vicious eyes. A crocodile—luckily not large enough to be a true menace, and it seemed to hate the light. But where there was one there might well be more.

She came suddenly to a niche in the wall that contained a sealed door and flashed her light within. There had been an arch farther back, but like the one she had broken through in the other passage, this also had been filled in. She edged herself within this larger space and tried to think more clearly.

If her calculations were correct, this sealed door was in the wrong direction to go beyond the walls. And in her present state she was not sure she could even use the power of the Rod enough to tumble a single of the locking stones. Better to go on—the sewer did have a place to emerge, that she could be sure of.

She longed to rest in the small place she had found, save that the air here was no better than in the sewer channel. So, reluctantly, she groped her way on. She couldn't be sure, but hadn't the height of the water pouring along beside her begun to drop? The ledge was level and had not climbed. Also—almost she could believe that now the air was less foul. She braced herself again and flashed the torch overhead. There the light caught on the edge of a well-like opening which she was seeing from the reverse, from its bottom. Also, there showed a series of hoops large enough to hold with a hand, rest a boot upon, extending upwards into the well. Outside the wall of the city, or in? She was afraid this still was in. There would be no reason to set such an opening without the walls. And if she were to expend her strength to climb it, and then find she was still a prisoner . . . She did not believe that she would be able then to make herself descend again into this place of stench.

Yet an unknown opening within the city. Something stirred far back in her mind; she could not yet clarify it.

Step by uncertain step she moved on along the ledge. Now there was no mistaking that the water had dropped. So, the stone she trod was less befouled, patches of the rock from which it had been hewn showed clear here and there. Also, the air cleared somewhat.

She—

At that moment they struck; when she had been

lulled into forgetting them. The wraiths made their attack upon her mind, not her body. She staggered, but she did not fall. Nor did she drop the torch. Rather she put her shoulders to the wall, as if she could so protect her back, and swung her light back and forth across the water.

There was movement there. Not of the wraiths but perhaps of some creature they summoned to pull her down.

"If I die here," she said between set teeth to the empty air—empty to her sight, yet alive with a company she could sense—"then do your hopes fail. I have not in me the power to help you. But there are others greater and stronger than I, and those I seek. Do you wish in me now the death of your chance, as well as that of my body?"

The thing in the water was coming closer. Still she could detect no waver in the air.

"Akini." She called the only name she knew. "I have told you the full truth!"

Still they hung there in menace, and she could not distinguish among them that one stronger identity to which she had given name. There was a swirl of water as a hideous, armored head broke the surface of the sewer, its jaws agape enough to show stained teeth. This crocodile was not the small one she had earlier sighted. It must be old, so long a swimmer in this place of rottenness that it carried in it all the evil years could accumulate.

Tallahassee grasped the Rod tightly. Against this thing out of the foulness of ages she had only that. As she had raised the Rod by her will to lift the protective cage Khasti had set over it, so now did she swing its point toward the thing that was hitching its scaled body higher. Massive, clawed forepaws reached for the ledge on which she stood.

Power—

The light she trained on that cruel head had no effect. It had been urged to attack by the influences of those who now watched avidly from out of the darkness.

Power!

Tallahassee schooled herself not to scream. The sewer dweller embodied all that was of nightmare.

Power, she demanded of Ashake memory—give me that which you know and have used. Give me—or I—we die!

From the point of the Rod there shot a line of fire more fiercely brilliant by far than the torch. It struck between the small eyes of the crocodile. The creature gave a bellow which echoed so harshly through the narrow tunnel, the sound continued to ring in her ears even as, kicking, it fell back and the flood covered it once more. The girl watched it disappear, hardly believing that Ashake memory had so answered her.

Did that memory have an identity? It could not, it was a thing that had been taped, forced into her own mind by the technology of these people. Ashake was dead. Yet more and more did Ashake sustain her—could a memory mold another?

They were still there—the wraiths. But they would not try that again. There was a hesitancy about them that she could sense. They were drawn by what she carried, but there was a fear underlying their need.

She waited for a long moment for some further

attack, some blow from the unseen. When that did not come she spoke again.

"I have made a bargain with you, Akini. But I cannot fulfill it unless you give me a chance to draw together those who know where you are and what holds you. I do not forget—nor shall I."

They were there still, but no answer came. She could wait no longer. Resolutely Tallahassee started on, but she knew the wraiths followed after. Let them—if they wished.

There came a curve in the water tunnel. And a breath of clean air puffed into her face. Somewhere, not too far ahead, must lie the exit from this waterway. She switched off the torch, standing still for a moment or two until her eyes adjusted and she could see by the radiance of the Rod and Key. Then step by very cautious step she advanced.

There was an opening, one crossed by bars. Through a lower exit spilt the wash of the sewer, but this was higher, near the ledge. She hurried toward it for the path here was relatively free of slime. Then she jerked off the covering about her nose and mouth, sucking avidly at the sweet air.

She thrust the torch inside her uniform for safekeeping and began to trace the bars of the grill with her hands. Outside it was night, and there seemed to be a stiff wind blowing. Grit and dust sifted through the grill, making her cough.

Though she found where the bars were embedded in a frame, she had not yet discovered any fastening on this side. And it was secure, yielding not an inch under her pull. The Rod—must she cut her way through—

From the outside came a sound, freezing her hands on the metal grill, making her alert and tense. There was a soft whine—a shadow pushed against the bars.

She smelled the scent of dog.

Assar? Had the hound just gone beyond the gates and then roamed around the city? Her hope had been so slender that she did not realize how much she had built on it until this moment.

"Assar?" She whispered the name.

There was an excited bark and she realized her folly. That sound was enough to alert any human ears in the vicinity. And it could well be that Khasti or the southern Nomarchs had their men outside the locked wall.

"Ashake?"

A whisper in return—one she had not expected to hear. "Who? . . ."

"Ashake—Jayta had said you would come—in this way. You are here?"

"Herihor?" She had almost called "Jason."

"Yes, my lady. And you shall be out speedily—stand back a little."

She withdrew along the ledge a pace or two. There was another shadow before the grill, and she heard the grate of metal against metal. Then something gave—the grate fell outward, and she heard a grunt as if Herihor had not expected it to be so easy.

Seconds later she heard him call.

"Come, Lady, the way is open."

He was reaching forward to draw her into the clean air of the night.

-16-

The group in the tent was mixed. In this war council they held nearly equal rank. Jayta sat next to Tallahassee, and beyond her was Herihor, to the right, the Candace Naldamak. To her left were two northern generals and the Colonel of the Sworn Swords.

Tallahassee's mouth and throat felt dry. She had been talking steadily ever since Herihor had brought her here, going over the details of the laboratory where Khasti wrought his mysteries, the passage she had found. On a piece of paper Herihor himself had sketched out the underground ways as she remembered them. And by Naldamak's hand lay the Key and the Rod.

The Candace was spare and thin, her face, fine-boned under the dark skin, was older than Ashake memory had painted it for Tallahassee. But there was no mistaking the quick light of intelligence in her dark eyes, the way she caught pertinent facts in Tallahassee's recital and asked for a report in detail.

"Khasti!" the Candace said as Tallahassee finished. "Always Khasti." She turned her head to speak to the general on her left.

"Nastasen, what have your scouts discovered in the desert lands?"

"Sun-in-Glory, the report of the desert rovers is that years ago this stranger was found by a dead camel and brought by them to one of our patrols, since he superficially resembles a man of Amun. They believed then that he was an outlaw fleeing our justice. But there is another story, newer, that a second man has recently come out of the same quarter of desert and this one is like unto Khasti. However, he asked not for his fellow, but rather for your Glory. And he was sent on to New Napata to await your pleasure—even as the Heir has reported his coming. This man's camel bags were searched, in secret, and found to contain a very small amount of rations as if he had come from only a short distance.

"Therefore, after he passed, the Captain of a Hundred at that fort sent out another patrol to trace him. They came to a valley among the rocks and, though no wall could be seen there, yet there was a barrier through which no man could force his way."

"And this was the man who came to New Napata?"

"He was seen to walk from out the gates, those sealed gates. Glory, and then he disappeared."

"So what is a barrier to us is not to these strangers," cut in Herihor.

But the Candace spoke again: "As you know, I and my people were found by a desert patrol. But we would not have lived had not two strangers come out of nowhere earlier, given us food and water, and pointed us the direction to follow. I am beginning to think that Khasti may have his enemies among his own kind, whatever or wherever they may be. But the core of his strength lies in New Napata and there he must be faced. Sister"—she smiled at Tallahassee—"very well have you wrought within the city, and outside it, too. We owe you the return of these," she gestured toward the talismans, "and now a chance to attack Khasti in his own lair. Userkof and his play at treason—that does not matter at the moment. It is this stranger who furnishes such rebels with their strength.

"You have marshalled your advance force." She looked to Herihor. "Can they be fed through this noxious tunnel, so to strike not only in the palace, but in the city, and, most of all, at the nest of Khasti?"

"Glory, give but the command," he replied swiftly. "If they know you live, most of the city will rise at your war cry."

"Then let it be done!" ordered the Candace. "Only strike not at the nest, merely guard it until we come." She nodded to Jayta and Tallahassee. "For with the Temple immobilized, we three may be the only ones with the Greater Knowledge to be used against whatever devilishness this Khasti devises—"

Jayta suddenly raised her head, not to look to Naldamak but back over her shoulder. Their conference tent was well guarded. Sworn Swords and picked men of Herihor's own guard formed its defense. And they had spoken in low voices that could not be overheard. But now the priestess's hand swept up in a commanding gesture which silenced even the Candace, who watched her with narrowed eyes.

"There is one coming." Jayta's voice was hardly above a whisper. "A stranger—"

Naldamak made a small sign and the priestess arose from her stool, looped back a fraction of the hanging door curtain, and peered out. A moment later she nodded to the Candace.

"It is not Khasti. But one of his breed."

Herihor's expression was that of rising anger. "How did such come through the outer guard?" he demanded fiercely, perhaps not of them but of those guards.

"It appears," Naldamak said thoughtfully, "that such as he can do this. For those who came to us in the desert we did not see before they stood there before us. Bring him to me."

"Glory—" One of the generals began a protest. But Naldamak shook her head at him.

"If I owe my life and those of my people to such a man, I do not believe he intends to harm me now. Bring him in, Daughter-of-Apedemek!"

The priestess bowed her head in assent and slipped out of the door. But Herihor and the two generals ostentatiously drew their hand weapons and kept them at ready. Tallahassee moved a little on her folding stool so that she could better see whoever entered.

For a second or two as he stooped his head to come under the hanging Jayta pulled aside for him, for he was a tall man, she was sure that by some trick Khasti himself had won into the heart of their camp. And she half arose to call out a warning. Then she saw that even if they were of the same race there was a difference between the newcomer and him who held New Napata to his will.

This one wore the robes of a desert raider, yet she could sense they were not his natural dress. And he was older, though he had an air of inborn authority such as one of the Blood might show. As he faced Naldamak he raised one hand, palm out, in a salute they did not understand but realized was one of dignity meeting dignity, of peer facing peer.

"You are the Candace Naldamak." That was half-question, half-statement.

"That is the truth." Herihor leaned forward a little, his suspicion plain to read on his open face. "And who are you, outlander?"

"It does not matter who I am," the man replied with the same authority as was in his manner of walking, of being. "Your Empress owes her life to us. Now we ask something in return."

"I know you . . ." Naldamak said slowly. "You were the third man in the desert, the one who stood aside and did not approach us. Yes, I owe you life and the lives of those who are my most faithful servants. What do you want of us in return?"

"There is one in the city, of our own blood and kind. He has offended against our custom and laws by coming here. Even as we offend in seeking him. But this we must do, no matter what price we will pay later. He has taken your city, he wishes to rule here. Do not count him as an unimportant enemy, Candace Naldamak, for when he fled from whence we all come, he brought with him devices beyond the comprehension of your world. Those must be destroyed, the man taken. But we are bound by oath not to loose upon him our own weapons. . . ."

Jayta had returned quietly to the group, but she

did not reseat herself. Instead she stood staring at the stranger. Tallahassee caught puzzlement and then a dawning wonder which was half awe in her expression. Suddenly the priestess's hand rose in the air and with a finger she traced some pattern strange even to Ashake memory.

The man fronting Naldamak turned his head, met Jayta's stare, to return that with something near to menace in his look.

"What do you?" he demanded.

Deliberately, for the second time, Jayta traced that symbol.

"You can't know—" For the first time his outer self-confidence cracked somewhat, and then quickly he added:

"That such knowledge remains—"

"After all these centuries?" Jayta completed his sentence. "I am the Daughter-of-Apedemek, in the direct spiritual line, oh, far traveler, from those who—"

"No!" His gesture was forbidding. "That you know at all is contrary to all we believed. But if you do, then you also recognize what this Khasti is and that he has no place here. It is a great and final sin that he has come."

Naldamak looked from the stranger to Jayta and then back again. Then she spoke decisively.

"We do not gather here to argue about what part of this world Khasti came from, but how we may handle him. You say, man out of the desert, that he has devices beyond our control. Yet you will not yourself go up against him. How then do you think we may handle him?" And she made of that question a challenge.

"Only get him out of his own place, or the place he has made his own, and he will be ours to take."

Herihor laughed without mirth. "A small deed and one easily accomplished, would you say? Why not net your own fish, stranger? We have learned there are inner ways to his hole, and we shall be only too ready to show them to you."

"I can take no part in your battles, Prince General. Even as your own priests, I have certain restraints laid upon me which I cannot break. But this I warn you—if you come by secret into this place of his, destroy it utterly. There are devices there which, used by the unwary, could not only turn New Napata into dust to pollute the earth, but would also loose death on all your world. He came well prepared for what he would do."

"Retake perhaps an ancient heritage?" Tallahassee did not know where those words came from, or why she said them aloud. It was as if she repeated something that was born of neither of the memories that were hers.

Now that searching, near-menacing stare was turned on her. She felt an odd sensation, a probing at her thoughts. Instinctively she tightened the guard that Ashake knew, fortifying it in part with the strength that had always been her own.

"You!" He took a single step toward her, the menace in his face growing. Then it gave way to puzzlement. "You are not—" he began and then checked himself. "No matter what you are—you do not serve him. But it may be that, of all this company, you can best stand against him. There is that in you which is a natural barrier to the forces at our command. I would suggest, Candace Naldamak, that this one"—he pointed deliberately to Tallahassee—"is best suited of all your people to front Khasti."

Herihor was on his feet. "Who commands here, stranger? Who are you to tell us whom to risk? You speak to us as a general speaks to a first recruit, and we are not for your ordering—"

"Your manner," interrupted the Candace, "does not impress itself well upon my officers. I will accept your warnings as the truth, but our battle plans remain ours—"

He was gone!

"What!—" Herihor's weapon came up, but all he faced was empty air.

"Where did he go?" One of the generals appealed to Jayta, as if she alone might have some answer to the riddle. "You knew him, or his like, Daughter-of-Apedemek. What is he then, and that other devil, making his mischief within Napata itself? Or is this some secret too great for our minds?"

"It is an old secret, Nastasen, and one I have no right to share. But this much I say—his kind were known to the first men who were of Khem. And for some generations there was intercourse between our ancestors and such. Then they were gone, but they left us that knowledge upon which all our long history and learning is built. As for how he went—he may not have been here in flesh at all. They were able, legend tells us, to project images of themselves for long distances—"

"The wraiths?" asked Tallahassee.

Jayta frowned. "No, those wraiths which both aided and beset you are born out of the wickedness of

Khasti. They are—or were—once people of our own kind, sent into a non-world for purposes of Khasti—a world into which they are imperfectly sealed, so that their thoughts and longing can reach through, if they can build up energy to do so by drawing it from us. Whether with the going of Khasti they can be restored—that even I do not know."

"If Khasti can also wink out after this manner," observed General Shabeke, "it would seem that our task is that much the greater. Perhaps the sooner we start upon it, the better."

"It has been near a day since Ashake came out of New Napata. We cannot be sure if Khasti knows where she is now. It would seem that, in spite of his boasted power, he could not search the palace, or he would have hunted you down there, Sister. So there may be a few limits yet on the power he would seize. I think that the Nomarchs Idieze summoned have not yet proclaimed Userkof Emperor either. Thus it is better that we move as soon as possible. My lords,"—Naldamak spoke to the generals—"marshal the forces you have selected. I trust you have picked men who cannot be troubled too much by these 'wraiths.' Make sure to tell them what Ashake believes, that these lurkers in the invisible have good reason to hate Khasti; that one, at least, served the Princess in her great need. Ashake . . . Jayta . . ."

Naldamak paused. "I do not send others where I do not go. We shall head directly for the inner palace. I and half my guard shall ascend the secret stair into my own chambers. There I shall show myself. And—"

"I shall go to the laboratory." Though again

Tallahassee had no intention of saying that, the words came from her lips. "Yes," she waved aside the protest in Herihor's face. "This stranger has said that I can stand best against Khasti. So be it—"

Naldamak's hand hovered over the Key and the Rod. "Take this then, Sister." She pushed the Key in Ashake's direction. "It is the symbol of all your learning. Thus it may profit you in this hour."

"I go with her." Jayta raised the lion mask from where it had rested beside her stool. "As Daughter-of-Apedemek I have certain powers of my own, as Khasti shall discover."

"So be it." The Candace nodded. "Let darkness be well advanced and we go."

Tallahassee had never thought to be returning through the noisome ways of the sewer, yet here she came, and at the head of no small company, with Naldamak herself between some of her guards not far behind, and Jayta at her very shoulder.

They had an abundance of light now, and though the girl watched carefully for any seeming curdling of the air to announce the presence of the wraiths, it would seem they no longer hunted.

They passed beneath the well which led upwards, and there they shed a full half of their force, the generals leading their men in that climb that should bring them out well within the walls of Napata. If they could force an exit through whatever topped off that well, excellent. If not they were to descend again and take the palace way. But their planned strategy was for simultaneous attacks from without the palace and within.

"This is a strange road." Jayta's voice sounded

ollowly from within her mask. Ashake-Tallahassee
wondered whether the mask filtered out some of the
horrible stench. They went slowly, being careful of
their footing. But the added light and the company
lightened the passage for her.

Finally they reached the foot of the stair that led to
the Candace's suite and here two of the guards went
to work, prying out the stones to open the way fully.
Naldamak's hand fell on Tallahassee's arm.

"Good fortune be with you, Sister. This is a harsh
gamble we take, not only with our own lives, but with
Amun as well. Should we fail, Amun falls. Use the
Key as you must, so will I use the Rod."

"And good fortune go with it," Tallahassee had
wit enough to answer. Even Ashake memory could
not give her a feeling of closeness to this resolute
woman. From early childhood their lives had been
lived apart. But that she could trust Naldamak, of
that Tallahassee was very sure. In time she must
trust her with the last secret of all—that there was
no longer an Ashake.

With Jayta, three of the Amazon guard, and two
men Herihor had insisted she take, Tallahassee sought
Khasti's own stronghold. It was on the way there that
she met the wraiths.

She heard a small gasp from Jayta, who raised
her hand, her fingers crossed, in a certain way. Tallahassee swung up the Key, its natural radiance lost
in the torch light. But it felt warm within her hand
as if it now broadcast energy of a sort she could not
understand, even with Ashake's knowledge.

There was no movement, only that feeling of being
hemmed in, as if invisible fingers plucked at their

clothing, pulled at their hair, tried in every way to draw their attention. Ashake spoke without turning her head.

"These are those of which you were told," she said softly. "They can do you no harm. Perhaps they may be persuaded to aid us in some manner."

There were no answers from those who followed her, but she could sense their uneasiness at such company. And she gave their courage high rating as they moved on, their boots ringing faintly on the ancient stone, with a firmness suggesting it would take more than what the wraiths manifested now to deter them from their purpose.

Unfortunately, something more just might lie ahead. What safeguards Khasti was able to throw about the center of his activity, the girl did not know, but he might have armed himself since her own escape.

Catching sight of the stairs, she passed the order to extinguish their torches. Climbing those stairs, they paused to listen for any sound from ahead. The wraiths were part of their company. Still they gave no sign of wishing to communicate. Perhaps they, too, waited to be sure Khasti had prepared no ambush.

Step after very cautious step the two women went up and on, the men following them. Without the torches, the Key shone with its own particular force as Ashake came into the hall, Jayta one pace behind. She had expected to see some light perhaps from the door of the laboratory, but if it were occupied the door must be firmly closed.

Whispering that what they sought lay now just a little ahead, Tallahassee edged close to the wall so that her shoulder brushed its surface as she went. It could not be much farther. No—there in the light of the Key she saw its smooth panels. But there was no sign of any opening latch. It might as well have been sealed like the stones that had earlier choked the other way.

Tallahassee slipped the palm of one hand along the surface, up and down to the length of her arm in both directions. There was nothing she could catch hold of. And when she pushed, first gently, and then with much more force, it remained immobile.

There remained the Key. She had not put it to any such test. She had used only the Rod before. But if it were a key, then what better way might she employ it? Concentrating on what she held, she raised the cross, clutching it by the loop at the top, and advanced its foot to the surface of the door as if she were in truth fitting a key to a lock. At the same time she felt Jayta's hand close about the arm that held the Key and from that touch poured a force to match her own, so that their united wills fed the ankh.

There followed a burst of sparks—though not such a great flare as the Rod had brought from the cage in which Khasti had earlier pent her. Then—the defensive barrier that had held the door was gone in an instant. Under her touch it swung open, so she was able to send it spinning back against the inner wall, two of the guard crowding up to shield both her and the Priestess from any waiting attack, with their own bodies if need be.

But there was no one inside. Tallahassee could see the cage still standing, the burnt-out hole in its side. And there were all the rest of the many things that crowded the tables, lined the walls. Yet something was missing. Tallahassee tried to remember what.

In a moment she understood. This was a deserted workplace, nothing bubbled, seethed, nor clicked. The activity she had seen before had ceased. Did that mean that Khasti had fled, having had some notice of their coming? Tallahassee did not believe that, rather that he had transferred his activities elsewhere. What remained here might now be valueless but they certainly would render all of it unusable.

"Be careful, my Princess," Jayta said as if she had read the girl's thoughts. "There may still be much that is harmful. We must move with caution since we do not understand."

Tallahassee accepted the prudence of that warning. But how could they understand? Or beware of harmful things they had never seen before? In her own time and world she had only the slightest knowledge of chemistry or physics. What she could draw upon as a warning was very limited.

"The Key will tell us." Again Jayta prompted her.

Ashake-Tallahassee advanced to the nearest table, her hand bearing the Key outstretched. Twice during her slow progress, while the guards kept watch at the doorway, the Key moved in her grasp, against her will, pointing down like a diviner's rod. Once it was above a small box of metal and again above a beaker of turgid yellow liquid. Each time Jayta took what was so indicated and carried it to the broken cage, setting her spoil within. Two more boxes and a rod, not as long as the talisman but rather like it in some ways, save that it lacked the lion mask, were added to those others before they were done.

Then Tallahassee called two of the guard to her while the others kept watch.

"Destroy," she ordered and pointed to the tables.

They smashed and splintered all into bits, moving rapidly along. There was a case like a file against the wall and from this Tallahassee herself tore the contents, sheets of tough paper covered with figures and diagrams foreign to her. These she hurled into the cage until they were heaped high about the objects the Key had marked as dangerous. For she knew now how to put an end to those and maybe the whole of this devilish chamber.

"Out—all of you! Back toward the Candace's stair and do not linger!"

"What are you doing?" Jayta asked, as the well-trained troops did as they were bid.

"I would see if Khasti's place of torment can still be used! Get you also to the door, Daughter-of-Apedemek. For what I may loose here might be a grave danger. And take you this." She pushed the Key into the priestess's hands.

Jayta backed away, she was at the door now. Tallahassee's hands went to those four buttons on the front of the box that had controlled the cage. It might be in breaking out of that prison that she had also broken this. But she could try.

Her fingertips spread and punched—hard.

There was a glow on the wires of the cage at the back where they were still intact. She leaped back, pushing Jayta before her, to reach the outer wall.

"The stairway—let us make the stairway!" she cried out, catching the priestess's hand in a hard grip and hurrying her along.

-17-

They were well down on the stairs leading to the lower level, hearing the clatter of the guards' boots on the stone before them and seeing the beams of their torches, when the answer to Tallahassee's reckless gesture came. There was a roar of sound and a fierce burst of light from behind. The thick walls about them shook.

Both women took the last few stairs in leaps they would not have attempted earlier. The sound had deafened them, but Tallahassee waved the guard on and they plunged ahead to the second stairway leading to the Candace's chambers. Here they had to climb in single file and she came last, panting and dizzy from the shock of the explosion.

At the top they found Naldamak and Moniga. Sela was at the outer chamber door, listening. Tallahassee saw Naldamak's lips move as if she asked some question, and she had to shake her head.

"The noise—I am deaf," she said. "But we have

destroyed, I believe, much that Khasti could have used against us."

She dropped, gasping for breath, on the end of the Candace's bed. Sela brought her a goblet of water and she drank thirstily.

The curtains had been drawn back from the windows opening onto the private garden so a night wind, scented by flowers, felt soothing against her hot face and arms. It was good to be here, to have another making the decisions.

Slowly her hearing came back.

There was a clamor in the halls—a duller roar from the city. Naldamak stood by one of the garden windows, her head tilted a little as she listened and perhaps so judged what might be happening from the very waves of sound. Tallahassee saw her lips move and this time caught a whisper of what she said.

"The Temple is free—Zyhlarz has spoken to us—"

An Amazon came swiftly through the outer chamber, saluted the Candace. "Sun-in-Glory, the gate barriers have been broken. But those of the Elephant are strong."

"If I show myself," Naldamak's answer came swift, "then they will be in open rebellion, and I do not think that after that they will find they have any cause."

"Glory—" The Amazon tried to step before her. "You are but one. A single blow, sent with ill fortune arming it, can bring you down. We are not enough to protect you—"

"There are those and that which none of these can face," the Candace returned. "We go to the Temple by the inner way."

Jayta's lion mask nodded in support and Tallahassee arose reluctantly. This was Ashake's work, but the memory now swelled in her so she could not resist.

Amazons closed about Naldamak and her two companions. They threaded halls, twice seeing dead lying crumpled against the walls. Their forces had met opposition here even in the heart of Naldamak's palace. Down another flight of stairs—in the distance shouting, the crackling fire of weapons. Then they entered the private way to the Temple, the way that Khasti had closed.

The Candace was running now, and Tallahassee had hard work to keep up with her, tired as she was and still partly dazed by the destruction in the laboratory.

But when they reached the other end of that corridor they found others before them. The Amazons of the guard pushed past Naldamak to form a wall of defense of their own bodies, using their weapons to pick off those who wheeled in shocked surprise to meet them. It would seem that, Khasti's invisible barrier having failed, he had sent men of the deep south, those who had never owned the belief of Amun, to hold in the priests.

Beyond those fighters Tallahassee saw one body wrapped in temple white—a white now dappled with scarlet. But the Amazons were finding targets, too. And Tallahassee, moved by Ashake's horror at what might happen, threw herself at the Candace, bearing her to the floor of the passage even as a flash of light passed over their heads, the discharge of a weapon new to her.

The Amazons plunged on, their battle screams

rising above the sound of the weapons. It was the very fury of the women, whose fabled ferocity had been a legend for generations, that must have shaken the barbarians, battle-thirsty as they were. They went down in a struggling, heaving mass beneath the sheer weight of the maddened women.

The skirmish was over before it had scarcely begun. But three of the Amazons lay among the dead as the Candace and Tallahassee struggled to their feet.

"Blood in the Temple!" cried Jayta. "What blasphemy have they wrought here?"

"Evil," replied Naldamak. She looked to the Amazons. "Sworn Swords, what have I to say to you who have served me with life and death. Sisters in battle are you."

"Glory," their captain, nursing an arm from which blood flowed, replied, "it is our right to make smooth your path. There is no honor in doing one's duty. But it would seem"—she nodded toward the dead priest beyond—"that those of evil have already made an entrance here. I beg of you, go with care—"

"That I not undo all you have wrought? Yes. A life that has been bought by the blood of friends must not be thrown away. But within lies that which can end this slaughter."

They went on into the lower floor of the Temple warily, the Amazons scouting ahead. Naldamak spoke to Tallahassee and Jayta.

"There is no welcome. Do you not feel it? There is silence where there should be the force about us."

Ashake memory provided fear. Yes, to those of the Blood, of the Talent, there should have been an instant sense of coming home, of companionship,

when they entered. Were—had Khasti brought death
to all here? No rebel, not even a southern barbarian,
would have dared such a thing. They had their own
gods and sorcerers, but many feared with a healthy
fear the Power of the Temple, alien though it might
be to them.

Jayta held up her hand. "Do not seek!" she commanded. "Such a thought call could be a warning.
We must go ahead in body only, keeping our minds
closed."

They had come to the foot of the steps that led
to the great central chamber, the very heart of the
Temple. Tallahassee saw now, that, in Naldamak's
hold, the Rod had become a staff of shining glory,
producing a bright fire. And the Key Jayta held blazed
high in answer.

The Candace turned at the foot of the stairs to
face the Amazons.

"Sisters, here we part, for none but those of the
Power may enter the inner way—not because of any
need for secrecy, but because you, yourselves, would
be burned by the fire that dwells herein and that only
initiates can stand."

"Glory," protested the captain, "if the barbarians
have come this way before you—"

"Then they are already dead or mindless," returned
Naldamak. "This is of the Power. I forbid you on your
Oaths to follow."

The captain looked as if she would raise a second
protest, but Naldamak was already ascending the stair
and Tallahassee fell in on her left, a step behind,
Jayta on her right.

On the three climbed, alone, and all the while they

listened, with their minds and their bodies rather than their ears. It could well be that they were ascending into a place of death. For what the Candace had said in warning was the truth, no one not prepared to stand the emanations of this place could live within the strength of the force that generations upon generations of calling upon the Talent had built here. Like the Rod and the Key, it was a reservoir, but a much greater one, of all the Power they had drawn upon.

They stepped out into the vast chamber. The very walls here were alight with ripples of energy. And by that light they saw those whom they had come to seek. A dozen men and women, white robed, mostly old. And to their fore, Zyhlarz himself, his dark face thinner, sharpened, and yet masterful.

Facing him—Khasti!

And at that moment Tallahassee sensed what was going on. They were engaged in a silent duel. The stranger out of nowhere had shielded his mind by some secret of his own, and between his hands was a circle of brilliant shining metal, the focus of what he sought to use to batter down the defenses of the Temple company.

They were matched so evenly, power thrust against power, that they seemed nearly dead to any mental probing. Nor did any face in that silent company of priests or priestesses change as Naldamak and the others came swiftly up behind Khasti's back.

The Candace held the burning rod now as a hunter might hold a lance, bringing it near shoulder high. And she was edging to the right of the immobile Khasti as if she would come even with him before she attacked.

She stopped and her two followers drew level with her. Jayta, holding up, heart high, the blazing Key, reached out her other hand and touched Naldamak's shoulder, giving good room to the Rod. Ashake's memory moved Tallahassee to do the same on the Candace's left.

It was like thrusting one's hands into a fire. There was heat in the flesh she touched, enough to nearly make Tallahassee jerk back her fingers. Now followed a drain from her own body, into Naldamak's.

At the same moment Khasti turned his head, though they had come noiselessly across the pavement. His eyes widened but he did not move.

Naldamak cast the Rod. It was a clean, well-aimed throw, passing through the ring of metal that Khasti held.

He threw back his head and laughed. "Not so easily do you win. Mistress of Magic."

"Stranger—your time here is finished. Choose death or go—"

"What death, Candace? Look to your Rod—it dies."

It was true. The Rod on the floor of the Temple had faded in brilliance as the coals of a fire will subside into grey and powdered ash. But there was no horror or fear on Naldamak's face.

"The Soul of Amun dies not, stranger." She held out her hand and the Rod arose from the floor, returned to her. Once in her grasp it flowered again with the same brilliance, yet Tallahassee felt the drain of her energy into the Queen's increase even as that brilliance grew.

"With this"—Khasti held the ring a fraction higher

s if so to draw all their attention—"I can drain your
soul' again and again and yet not be harmed."

"Daughter-of-Apedemek"—it was Zyhlarz's
esonant voice that cut across Khasti's arrogant
words—"whom have you brought with you into
his place?"

He pointed into the air between Khasti and the
Candace. Tallahassee could see the curling of the
ir, even though she had not yet felt the presence
f the wraiths.

"Ask of them who and what they are, Son-of-
Apedemek," Jayta replied. "They sought us in darkness,
ut they seek another more eagerly."

Again Khasti laughed. "They are my discarded tools,
riest. To such can I reduce men. They served me,
ot too well. Now they would come to beg life once
gain. In their weakness they cannot harm me."

"Opener of Forbidden Gates," Zyhlarz answered
im, "perhaps you have opened one too many."

There were three writhings in the air. They moved
o box Khasti in on three sides. But he shrugged and
miled.

"I am not one to be driven from my goal by ghosts—
or by such 'Knowledge' as you cling to, old man.
he Talent has run very thin, has it not? And my
nachines can best it in the end."

Tallahassee raised her own voice then:

"Akini!" she called. "I name your name, I give you
vhat I have to offer . . ."

She held out the hand that had hung by her side,
ut she did not break contact with the Candace and
hrough her with Jayta. One of the troublings in the
ir, the one behind Khasti, swooped closer.

"She has named a name!" Zyhlarz's voice swelle
through the lofty hall. "Let hers be the Power!"

Just as energy had drained from her as Nald;
mak had wrought with the Rod—seemingly to n
purpose—now it came flooding into her.

Her flesh tingled along the length of her slend
body. She could feel a stirring on her scalp as if h
clipped hair moved, each strand rising to discharg
some force.

Something touched her outheld palm—so cold th;
it was like a thrust of pain following on the strok
of a knife. But Tallahassee held steady. And fro
that touch, even as had happened in the cage,
substance arose, milked out of her, absorbed by th
thing in the air.

She saw Khasti half wheel, turn his circuit in h
direction, but between him and her those two oth
disturbances of the air slid into place, so that his figur
wavered before her eyes. But she did not drop h
hand and the thing that fed on her strength continue
to draw nourishment.

What was forming in the air bore no resemblanc
to a manlike form though that had been what sh
expected to see. Rather it was a serpent, ever thic
ening, ever pulling on her strength, draining n
only herself but her companions also. Now, diml
she could hear a rising chant from Jayta, saw fro
the corner of her eyes to the right that the Pries
ess was using the flashing Key to draw lines in th
air, lines that glowed dimly and hung even after th
key withdrew.

Tallahassee thought, with a stab of fear, that h
strength was being sapped past the point of no retur

et that thing she had allowed to fasten on her did
ot abate its sucking. Had she condemned them all
· failure?

"Akini!" That was Zyhlarz's call. "The door has been
ade ready—do you come through!"

The snake-thing loosed its hold from the girl's
alm and her hand dropped weakly of its own voli-
on to her side. She could see, even without turning
er head, that there was indeed a doorway sketched
pon the air.

But Khasti, his lips flattened against his teeth,
is eyes showing a trace of madness, was raising his
rclet, not aimed any longer at the priests and priest-
sses he had held so long at bay, but rather as if he
ould focus whatever force he controlled through it
1 the door in the air.

"Akini!" After Zyhlarz's call, her own voice sounded
ry weak and thin as if it came not from her lips
1d throat but from a far distance.

The serpent coiled in the air, looping as if it rejoiced
· own even this much of a form. But neither it nor
1e whirling wraiths made any attempt to go through
1at opening Jayta had provided for them. A door to
2re from there, wherever there might be. Yet they
d not come.

Instead the whorls kept guard between Khasti and
1e three he menaced. And the serpent thing—it
1unched at him as might a rope sent flying on Tallahas-
·e's own world to ensnare a wild steer. It lifted itself
ove the level of his hands and the circlet, making
·r his head. He tried to dodge, dropped the thing
2 held, raising his arms to beat off the serpent.

But it was not to be denied. Wreathing itself around

his head, it blotted out his features, covered his fac
instantly. He tore at it with no effect, staggering fo
ward. Now the whorls ranged themselves on either sid
so that when he stumbled and wavered, he seeme
to bounce from one to the other, they keeping hi
upright and urging him on. It was he whom they hu
ried, blinded, perhaps suffocating under the serper
folds, into the door Jayta had opened.

He took one step and then another—and—wa
gone! The door vanished even as he passed throug!
leaving an eerie feeling of emptiness in the chambe
as if something had been closed, drawing with it a pa
of their lives in a way Tallahassee could not describ
even to herself.

"But—I thought they wanted to come through t
us," she said blankly. The Temple people were hurryin
forward. "Why did they not come through?"

"Perhaps they could not. They had been so lon
exiled to that existence. What they wanted more," Jayt
said slowly, "was him who had sent them there."

"Then—he will be a wraith . . ." Tallahassee coul
see the peril of that. She had felt the danger fron
those others, and they had been weaklings in strengt
of purpose when compared to the stranger out of th
desert. What if he returned so to haunt them?

"They closed the door, Daughter." Zyhlarz wa
beside her. "You had the courage to treat with the
after a fashion, and they have now removed him wh
alone had the power to destroy everything we ar
and have done."

"He was—" Jayta said, but Zyhlarz held up hi
hand in warning.

"Let it not be spoken aloud as to what he was. Suc

nowledge lies buried in the past and well buried. It
s enough he was not of our flesh or of our world."

"There are those who have come seeking him,"
Naldamak said then.

"They will have their own way of knowing that he
s gone. And on such a journey as even they are not
eady to face. Time and space may be conquered by
man—there remain other dimensions we dare not
venture into if we would remain human."

Tallahassee sat in the Candace's garden. The city
which had been in turmoil was now patrolled by loyal
guards. Also the Temple was open so that there flowed
out of it a peace that could soothe inflamed minds
and quiet restless spirits.

Restless spirits! Since the vanishing of Khasti she had
found herself at intervals watching the air, listening,
sending out that inner sense of which Ashake made so
much to test for alien thought, an alien wraith. Was
it true that when Khasti had been swept away, by the
"tools" he had despised, he had indeed been sealed
from this world? He had been summarily thrown into
another space-time even as she had been in the ruins
of ancient Meroë?

Another space-time . . .

She was Tallahassee tonight as she sat here alone
in the dusk. Though her begrimed uniform had been
changed for the silken robes of her borrowed personality, a wig of ceremony covered her head, she was
not Ashake!

She thought of what Jayta had hinted in the last
council they had held a few hours ago—that Khasti
had not come out of time but out of space. That the

fabric of Khem itself in the earliest days had been born of the experiments made by intelligences not of this world, and that their blood and gifts had lingered on in certain descendants, to become part of another path of knowledge, turning inward. Thus, those whose far-off forefathers had known the stars now chose rather to know themselves, perhaps better than any of their species had done before.

They had seen no more of that second stranger. Perhaps they could believe it was true he and those he represented had known of their quarry's fate and gone their own ways thereafter.

But there remained Tallahassee Mitford, who was not of Amun and who should now go her way, too. She had seen Jayta open a door through which Khasti had vanished. But she did not want to be caught in the non-life of a wraith. If there was a door possible between her world and this it must be real—

"You think strange thought, Royal Lady."

Tallahassee raised her eyes from the shadowed path at her feet. Jayta and Naldamak, and with them Herihor, one arm in a sling to bear witness that he was not Prince General to order and not lead his men into battle, and lastly, Zyhlarz, stood there. Now to these four she must speak the truth, no matter what would come of it.

"I am not your Royal Lady. You"—she spoke directly to Jayta—"know who and what I am. Now I ask you, since I have served your purpose, to let me go."

Jayta must have shared her knowledge with the others. Even in this dim light Tallahassee could see that none showed surprise.

"My daughter—" Zyhlarz began, when she interrupted.

"Lord Priest, I am not your daughter, nor one of your kind!"

"No, you are less and more—"

"Less and more? How can one be both?"

"Because we are each shaped from our birth, not only by the blood and inheritance that lies behind us, but also by those we love and by whom we are loved in turn, by the knowledge given to our thirsty minds, to the learning of ourselves. You are not Ashake—though Ashake, in part, has become you—nor can you indeed ever tear her out of your memory and thought. But you are also yourself and so have different qualities—which are yours alone."

"Can you send me back?" She asked that bluntly.

"No." Jayta did not wear her lioness mask now and in the dusk her face looked very tired and drawn.

"Why?" She had seen the priests do things she would have believed impossible. "You have the Key and Naldamak has the Rod—and you," she spoke now to Zyhlarz, "have all the learning of the Upper Way wholly yours."

"There must be an anchor to draw one," Jayta said. "When Akini was sent through, and those others—the nameless ones—they were anchored upon the power of the Rod—first to remove and conceal it. Then the Rod was taken into a place where such like it had once been. When the Key was stolen, it could be borne there also because the Rod was there to draw it.

"But when Ashake went to search, in turn, her hand upon the Rod and Key, her right to hold and call upon them, was such that it drew you also. For you were—in your world—the one whom she would have been had she lived in your time and place—you were equal within you. Do you think otherwise the memories of Ashake could have been given you? Now there is no anchor existing beyond. When Akini and those others were not drawn back in time—you saw what they became. For in your world, it would seem, they had no counterparts—so they were lost between. Perhaps Khasti has so been lost. It is our hope that his like does not exist elsewhere.

"Ashake died because she could not draw her other existing self through without giving the full energy of her body. There is no door left for you because nothing lies there to fasten upon."

"You are Ashake and you are more . . ." Herihor spoke for the first time.

Naldamak held out both her hands. "The Prince General speaks the truth, Sister. Was this other world of yours so beloved to you that you cannot live without it? If there was a dear love existing there, perhaps that could pull you. But if that were true the Son-of-Apedemek would have known. Thus I say to you, Sister—you are not less than Ashake in our eyes. Look upon us now and read the truth!"

Tallahassee's searching glance went from face to face of those who shared her secret. Ashake—all Ashake, more or maybe less—but never a wraith out of time. Here she was real, welcomed. She took the hands Naldamak offered her and accepted all else that was in their faces and hearts as they looked upon her.

Andre Norton ✺

> "The sky's no limit to Andre Norton'
> imagination . . . a superb storyteller
> —*The New York Time*

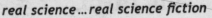